The Treasure of Islay

A New England Seashore Novel

Sara Wade

Wild Mouse Press

Copyright © 2022 by Sara Wade

All rights reserved.

No portion of this book may be reproduced in any form without written permission from the author, except for the use of a brief quotation in a book review and as permitted by U.S. copyright law.

This is a work of fiction. Names, characters, places, and incidents either are the product of the author's imagination or are used fictitiously. Any resemblance to actual persons, living or dead, events, or locales is entirely coincidental.

Book cover design by Consuelo Parra, Digital Artist, Designer, Book Covers

www.facebook.com/ConsueloParra.DigitalArt   www.facebook.com/C.PBookCoverdesigns

To my sister, Ginny

Contents

Chapter 1	1
Chapter 2	7
Chapter 3	18
Chapter 4	22
Chapter 5	29
Chapter 6	37
Chapter 7	48
Chapter 8	64
Chapter 9	77
Chapter 10	81
Chapter 11	95
Chapter 12	107
Chapter 13	118
Chapter 14	127
Chapter 15	143
Chapter 16	163

Chapter 17	170
Chapter 18	180
Chapter 19	189
Chapter 20	197
Chapter 21	209
Chapter 22	225
Chapter 23	240
Chapter 24	251
Chapter 25	270
Chapter 26	276
Chapter 27	287
What's next?	297
Acknowledgments	300

Chapter 1

June 27, 1954

Maura fiddled with the knob on the gleaming Philco until she found a station playing popular music. Rosemary Clooney sang *This Ole House,* a rendition that had just released and was rapidly rising in the charts. Feeling this was an appropriate title for someone about to spend the summer in an old sea captain's house, Maura adjusted the volume and returned to packing a few desk items that she would take to the island tomorrow. She smiled and hummed along; freedom from the women's institute, of which Maura was a director, was exactly thirteen hours away.

Wailing could now be heard coming down the corridor, accompanied by a woman's scolding voice. Maura considered hiding in the closet, but she knew from experience that they would just wait for her. When sharp rapping commenced on her office door, she reluctantly opened it and found a small group congregated outside.

The wailing, coming from a boy shaped like a watermelon, had changed to aggrieved blubbering. He was clearly having difficulty keeping it up and watched his mother for a clue that he could stop. The mother's righteous anger was directed at a skinny four-year-old girl with a long, red braid and a scowl, whose arm she held firmly. Maura calmly pried the woman's fingers off Lizzie and pulled her daughter to her side.

"What's going on?" she asked cheerfully. She had found that few people could sustain an emotional outburst with someone who wouldn't play along. The mother faltered for a moment, then gave a dramatic account of Lizzie's attack on her son.

Mary Ann Broek, Maura's co-director of the institute and one of the few people she couldn't stomach, drifted up to enjoy the spectacle of Maura's daughter in trouble.

"She shoved Arthur, for no reason!" The boy's mother pointed a finger at Lizzie. "And his head banged against the wall!"

"What happened, Lizzie Lou?" Maura asked.

"He looked under my dress so I pushed him away!"

"Is that true, Arthur?" The watermelon-shaped boy wiped his nose on his hand and nodded. Maura looked him in the eye.

"If you ever look up another girl's dress, Arthur, we'll make you wear one. Got it?" He nodded again.

Mary Ann, ignoring Arthur's confession, crouched down in front of Lizzie.

"I'm sorry to hear of such unladylike behavior, Elizabeth. Little girls must never, ever push other little children!" The boy's mother nodded vigorously. Mary Ann was in a perfect position for Maura to shove her sprawling on the floor and she had her knee up when a voice said,

"There was a boy where I'm from... he lifted girls skirts up and wound up being a pig farmer. No lady would go to the dance with him because he smelled like pigs. You wouldn't want that to happen to you, would you?" Arthur's mouth dropped open and he shook his head no.

In the doorway stood one of the tallest women Maura had ever met. She wore a shapeless dress over enormous breasts and her colorless hair was skinned back in a tight bun. A baby slept in a hammock contraption slung around her neck. It was clear she hadn't missed anything in this scene, from Arthur's snivels to his mother's outraged face to Maura's foot ready to flip Mary

Ann over like a beetle. From her grin it was obvious she was enjoying the drama.

Maura later described Paulette Baker's arrival in a phone conversation with her friend Rebecca. They would be meeting at the ferry in the morning to go to the island of Islay together. Rebecca would only stay for the day to see Maura and Lizzie settled and would take the ferry back again that afternoon, followed by a long drive home to Maine.

"I don't know how you found her, Bec. She'll be a wonderful replacement for me. She had us all behaving in minutes." Rebecca had founded the institute four years earlier and gotten it up and running with help from Maura and Mary Ann.

"She's fantastic, isn't she?" agreed Rebecca. "I loved her on sight. What did she do?"

"She said, 'Hello! I'm Paulette Baker, sent by Mrs. Savard.' She held her hand out to Mary Ann, who mechanically took it. Paulette pulled her to her feet and shook her hand, accomplishing three things at once: She got on Mary Ann's good side by treating her like she's in charge, she rescued Lizzie from the lecture, and she got Mary Ann out of range of my foot."

"Clever!"

"Yes. She called Mary Ann 'Mrs. Broek', from which I deduced you didn't let on that Mary Ann is an unwed mother."

"Yes, I did. I told her everything."

"Well, Mary Ann left to check something and Paulette asked Arthur and his mother to go to the kitchen and make her a cup of cocoa. She was obviously clearing the field. The mother started to object to being treated like a servant, but suddenly Paulette looked her in the eye and said, without a trace of the folksy voice she had used up to this point, 'I'll schedule an appointment with you to discuss expected behavior from resident children. Disrespect for the girls will not be tolerated.' The mother scuttled out of my office and headed for the kitchen, brat in tow. Paulette gave me a wink and a big smile. I have no doubt that she'll have this place under her control in no time."

"What did Lizzie make of all this?"

"When they had all left, I sat down and pulled her onto my lap. She was trying not to cry. I told her that she should never push or hit anyone without a good reason. A boy lifting up her dress, I said, was a good reason."

"Indeed!"

Rebecca Savard had been Maura's best friend since grade school. Having inherited a fortune from her first husband after only three minutes of marriage, she felt compelled to share it. The institute was one of her more ambitious projects, but she was always happy to help her neighbors in the little town of Rushing River, where she was currently the mayor, with an expensive medical bill or a missed mortgage payment.

"People feel funny about taking her money," Rebecca's second husband once confided to Maura, "so she's always looking for sneaky ways to foist it on the ones who won't cooperate. A few people in Rushing River have gotten small inheritances from relatives they never heard of. A teenager received a full scholarship from a college she didn't apply to. They all pretend they don't know the money came from her and everybody's happy."

Maura knew that Rebecca would have been very glad to support her when her marriage fell apart, but she was determined to be self-sufficient and raise Lizzie by her own means. Rebecca seized the chance to do her friend a service, however, when their old schoolmate, Will Howe, happened to mention that his aunt's summer home was standing empty while he came out on weekends to check on the progress of renovation work. Rebecca instantly proposed that Maura be installed as caretaker for the summer, to let the contractors in during the week and to make sure the house was secured at night. By that same evening, Will's aunt had consented to Maura and her daughter living in the house rent-free for the summer.

Islay, pronounced EYE-la, was several hours off the coast of Massachusetts by ferry. Lizzie had been wild to take her first boat ride and for a while insisted on being held up so she could see over the side. A very early start followed by a plateful of pancakes she ate in a diner before they boarded the ferry made her sleepy, and before long Maura found herself on a bench with a sleeping Lizzie straddling her lap, her face in Maura's neck.

"How was your last night at the institute?" Rebecca asked softly. She sat down next to Maura and handed her a steaming cup of coffee that she had purchased inside. The early morning sun sparkled on spray thrown up by the little ferry as it pushed through choppy waves. The faint smell of diesel fuel, combined with the scents of coffee and fishy seawater was a heady mix that added to Maura's sense of adventure.

"I sat up too late with Paulette," she said, "going over last-minute details. At least we started with that, but then we stayed up with a bottle of wine, talking. Do you know her story?"

"Not really. Just that her husband died and she's been in dire straits financially."

"Mary Ann tried to get it out of her but when Paulette said, 'you first!' she remembered something urgent she had to do. We know that Mary Ann would die before admitting she's an unwed mother. Which is pretty silly; we're all at the institute because we're unwed mothers or married to men who beat us or, as in my case, ran away with their eighteen-year-old students. And it's 1954, not the middle-ages.

"Anyway, Paulette's story is awful. She and her husband owned a gas station and kept a few cows. She went out to the barn one night when she was expecting her baby and found that he had shot himself in the head. She really loved him, Bec. But instead of feeling like he had abandoned her and their unborn child, she just said that no one really knows what hell people are living inside their heads and no doubt the decision made sense to him. I had had a couple of glasses of wine by that point, which may have been a factor in my bursting into tears. It took her a while to calm me down, which is ridiculous. Bec, you know this is the real reason I couldn't stay at the institute, right? You saved me after David left and I would do anything to help you, but when I hear what these women have been through it tears me up. All the residents have come to me at some point with their stories, and they all need something desperately. I feel helpless to do anything for them except to make sure they and their children are warm and fed. You and Mary Ann, drat her, are the ones who are making a difference in their lives by helping them get back on their feet, get training and find jobs. Paulette is a stronger person than I am and will be much better at this."

Rebecca squeezed Maura's arm.

"You're much stronger than you think, but I always knew it wasn't the right job for you. You and Mary Ann did wonders getting the institute off the ground and I'll be eternally grateful for that. But I know you rarely had a chance to have Lizzie all to yourself at the Institute. Somewhere you got the notion that it's your responsibility to fix everyone else's problems and the mothers took advantage of that. They demanded too much of your energy and attention. You spent so much time helping the residents that there wasn't much left for your own little family."

Maura checked to see if her daughter was still sleeping.

"I want so badly for Lizzie to have a normal upbringing," she whispered. "My own was awful, as you well know. Because I was never really off duty at the institute she was spending as much time with the women we pay to watch the working mothers' kids as she was with me. The other women and their children eventually move on, but we would have been there year after year. It would never have been just Lizzie and me as a family."

"And now you have a whole summer of adventures ahead of you, just you and Lizzie, before you start your new job."

Maura smiled and gently tapped her coffee cup against Rebecca's.

"To Islay!"

"To Islay."

Chapter 2

The house crouched on the edge of the village green like a fat brown toad at a garden party. To its left and right and all around the green, houses of different vintages intermingled in a jumble of architectural styles. Flowers in riotous colors, neat white fences around tiny emerald lawns, weathered gray shingle and flagged walkways were the order of the day, whether modest Quaker cottage or Greek Revival. The dirty clapboard and stone exterior of the toad house, its dark windows partially hidden by overgrown shrubbery and its randomly placed turrets and chimneys were ridiculously out of place on this lovely little island. A massive front door under an arch and two large windows with rounded tops positioned over it gave the appearance of an alarmed face. The absurdity of the house was underscored by its contrast to the beauty of that morning in June, the azure sky and the scent of fresh cut grass mingling with the salty tang of the sea. There was no mistaking the house: it was the only one that had a Sutton Real Estate sign in front, just as Will had described.

"If this isn't typical," Maura remarked as she and Rebecca inspected the decaying mansion through the bars of a wrought iron gate. "You got millions and millions of dollars, a great husband and a few exciting murders. I get a haunted house."

They had just taken the only island taxi from the ferry to the house where Maura and Lizzie would spend the summer. Lizzie sat on the sidewalk, carefully removing all the items from Maura's purse in search of a pack of gum.

Rebecca laughed.

"Cheer up! I'm sure you'll have your murders too. There's no way you can avoid them if you're going to live in that thing."

Rebecca could have reminded Maura that she only became a multi-millionaire when her first husband died on the way out of church on their wedding day, or that she herself came within a hairsbreadth of being murdered.* Rebecca never pointed out the obvious, however. She always knew what Maura meant despite what she said, which explained why they had been best friends since fifth grade.

"What style do you suppose it is?" Rebecca wondered, still grinning.

"American Ghastly Gothic." There must have been at least twenty houses around the green, each one more charming than the last, Maura thought. This one *would* have to be hers. Well, hers for the summer, if she could bring herself to live there.

"It reminds me of your Uncle Irvin," observed Rebecca. "I don't think I ever told you this, but when I was eleven, he tried to get me to sit on his lap."

"What? That's disgusting!"

They agreed that the house looked like it would ask young girls to sit on its lap.

"I was thinking it looked like a toad at a garden party, but then so did Uncle Irvin." Maura stared at the house through the gate's wrought iron bars. "It's definitely haunted."

"I don't know if it's haunted, but a witch lives there!" The women turned to find a boy on a Roy Rogers bicycle that was too big for him. He was about nine years old and wore a Boston Red Sox cap. Long, skinny legs and knobby knees showed beneath swimming trunks. He unwrapped a package of baseball cards, frowned at them, then stuffed the square of bubble gum in his mouth.

"I thought the lady moved out last year." Maura wondered how Will would feel about grubby little boys referring to his Aunt May as a witch.

CHAPTER 2

"Nope! Still there." It was hard for him to talk around the enormous wad of gum. He wiped a little spit from the corner of his mouth then wobbled off on the bike.

Maura and Rebecca had turned their gazes back to the Uncle Irvin house when Will finally coasted up on a rented bike. It was expensive to bring a car to the island, so most people didn't bother.

Will took in the women's position in front of the Gothic house and their hands gripping the bars of the gate. His eyes lowered to the real estate sign leaning against the brick wall that the gate was set into and a slow smile spread over his face.

"So, what do you think of the house?"

"I think you stink at descriptions," Maura said with narrowed eyes. "You told us your aunt's house needed some repair but that it had lots of charm." She gestured at the hulking pile and raised her eyebrows.

"This is a house of bed-wetting nightmares," Rebecca concurred.

Will's smile got even bigger.

"Hold on while I move this," he said, getting off his bike.

He picked up the real estate sign and carried it to the yard of the house to the left, found the hole the wooden stake had previously occupied and pushed it in.

"The kid who cut the grass this morning must have leaned it against the other house's wall to get it out of the way." He laughed to see the women's blank stares.

"*This* is my aunt's house. Come on, I'll give you a tour."

Maura's relief in finding that her summer home was not the Uncle Irvin monstrosity was enormous. She later wondered if it was responsible for her immediate infatuation with Aunt May's house.

"It was built around 1826 for a retired sea captain named Josiah Watts," said Will. The house sat close to the street, like many homes of that period, positioned for the convenience of the owners, callers and tradesmen. Considering that there were few automobiles on the island, Maura didn't expect to be bothered by the proximity to the street.

"He was something like thirty-eight when he moved here with his wife, Mary, and a half dozen kids," Will continued. "He was on the young side to retire but he had done well in shipping and his wife had had enough of him being away for long stretches. It's one of the first houses built here on Islay, not counting the original colony of shipwreck survivors."

They had paused just inside the fence that separated the tiny yard from the brick sidewalk that ran around the green. From where they stood, the house appeared small but sturdy enough to survive the storms and winters of the last one hundred and thirty years. Unpainted cedar shakes covered the exterior, weathered to a soft gray. The door was positioned to the right of center as one faced the house, with two windows to its left and one to the right. Wide trim in need of paint framed the door and three steps led up to it. Windows on the upper story lined up with the door and windows on the first floor. Inexpensive shutters that hadn't aged well and a door that didn't fit the period were only minor detractions from the simplicity and grace of the Watts house.

"How did two adults and six children live in this little house?" wondered Rebecca. "I suppose they might have had some domestic help too; if he retired at thirty-eight, he must have been well-to-do."

Will led them up the steps and pulled a key from his pocket.

"Eight kids, actually. Two were born after they moved here, but then they lost at least two to illness. The oldest of the surviving children was my great-something grandfather. The attic is partially finished; I suppose they threw some kids or the maid up there."

Maura and Rebecca knew that the house had been in Will's family for generations but were surprised to hear he was descended from the original owner.

"There's always at least one poor kid stuck with Watts in every generation," he grinned. "I'm William Watts Howe, and my cousin Clare had Watts too until she married and dumped her middle name. She named her dog Watts so the family wouldn't expect her to saddle her children with it. You can't name your kids after the dog."

Will's Uncle Charlie and Aunt May kept the island house as a summer home. Will had described magical summer vacations on the island, riding waves or fishing off the pier by day and sleeping in a big bedroom at night with his three cousins and his brother, James. Several years after Charlie died, May moved to a retirement home and gave up her summers on the island. None of her children lived close enough to want to take the house on, and as it needed more repairs and updating than anyone wanted to pay for, May and her children reluctantly decided to sell the house. A real estate agent was engaged and the house duly put up for sale. As time passed and it became clear that the house wasn't generating interest, they enlisted Will. He had joined a firm of architects in Boston several years earlier and was thus the closest member of the family to the island, which was straight out to sea from Gloucester. He agreed to arrange workmen to do basic repairs and updating, and to check on progress when he was able.

They stepped from bright sunshine into a parlor which must have been the main living space for generations of Will's family. Lizzie spotted the suitcases and boxes Maura had sent on ahead stacked neatly in a corner and settled herself on the floor with her box of toys and stuffed animals. Opposite the door, a steep narrow staircase, its treads worn from over a century of use, led to the upper story. To the right of the front door was a wall with another door, low enough that a man above average height would have to stoop. Maura pushed the door open and found a tiny room with odds and ends of discarded furniture. A large wooden desk sat under the front window with a comfortable chair pushed underneath. No pictures hung on the white plaster walls.

"Uncle Charlie used the room as an office, and as a place to escape from the family," Will called from the parlor where he was opening windows. He came to the doorway and stooped to peer in. "I've been collecting broken or cheap furniture from around the house and piling it here. I meant to get rid of it last weekend but couldn't get out here. Somebody's coming this afternoon to haul it away."

Maura, who hoped to do some writing this summer, stood for a happy moment while she mentally transformed the space into a writing room. From its position at the front corner of the house, sunlight streamed in through two windows. The only detraction was the view of the wall surrounding the Uncle Irvin house, the trees and tangled shrubbery that overhung it and the house itself, with its blank, dirty windows, rising above.

"You can put some sheer curtains over that window that will block the view but allow light to come in," said Rebecca, seeming to read Maura's mind. "A big carpet would be nice for Lizzie to play on while you're writing, but I don't think you'll want to totally cover these beautiful floorboards."

Maura smiled at Rebecca's enthusiasm. Although her friend was mayor of a small town and oversaw the businesses she had inherited from her first husband, one of her happiest experiences was renovating her old cottage on the edge of a cliff overlooking the sea.

A fresh ocean breeze now stirred the curtains in the parlor window, replacing the close air of the old house. That closeness hadn't bothered Maura. The hints of long-ago fires that seemed to linger in the hearths mingled with the lemon polish Aunt May used. They spoke of generations of families coming and going, making meals, dealing with day-to-day joys and upsets. Mismatched yet comfortable-looking furniture intermingled with pieces from earlier generations of the family, giving a sense of timeless tranquility. A large sofa with wide seats took up more than its fair share of space but looked very inviting. If this old house is haunted, thought Maura, it's by contented ghosts. Lizzie and I can share.

A doorway led from the parlor to a kitchen that ran across the back of the house. A large fireplace, blackened with age and use, included a built-in brick oven and a tinderbox. A more practical wood-burning stove sat squarely in the middle of the fireplace. An aging range and a serviceable refrigerator shared the back wall with a small wooden counter and pitted sink. An oak table, large enough to accommodate Uncle Charlie and Aunt May's family and guests, was positioned in the center of the kitchen. It was apparently used both for dining and as a work surface. On the far end of the kitchen, close enough to the big fireplace to be warmed by it but not so close as to be roasted, a sofa and three comfortable chairs surrounding a low coffee table made a cozy nook for reading or playing games with the family.

"It doesn't look too bad," said Rebecca approvingly. "The appliances need updating, of course, and the linoleum is in pretty bad shape. This is a wonderfully large kitchen, though." Maura caught her friend's calculating look. She knew Rebecca must have a list of recommendations she was dying to make but was restraining herself.

"There are some plumbing and wiring issues that have to be taken care of before we can sell the house," Will replied, "then we'll see how much of our budget is left over for cosmetic updates. It's those big items that have been keeping the house from selling. We'll repaint, naturally, and tear down the worst of the wallpaper." He put his hands on his hips and gazed around the kitchen, as though assessing the minimal work needed to make the house attractive to a buyer. He looked at Maura with a wry grin.

"Are you getting cold feet? There will be workmen coming and going all summer and sometimes it will feel like you're camping. There may be times when they have to shut off the water or electricity. If you want to change your mind no one would blame you."

Lizzie had followed them into the kitchen. Maura looked at her happy smile as she hopped around the room inspecting first the enormous fireplace then shelves stacked with old board games. Long summer days stretched before them, early mornings gathering shells on beaches where sand was swept clear of footprints during the night; catching crabs off a dock in the harbor where she had seen boys crabbing with chicken legs tied to strings. They would explore the island and come home tired and happy. She would make Lizzie's favorite suppers and they would eat with all the windows in the kitchen open to the cool evening air. The noise and bustle of Boston would be left far behind, replaced by the night breeze rustling the leaves of the roses that climbed the sides of the house, and the chirping of crickets. She cleared her throat.

"No, I'm not changing my mind."

"Come on, let's see what's out back." Rebecca opened a door in the rear wall of the kitchen.

They stepped onto a brick patio with a rusting metal table and chairs. Grass and weeds grew where chunks of brick were missing. On the patio was a shiny new cycling contraption with one wheel in the front and two in the back. A wooden cart, just the right size to carry Lizzie and a few bags of groceries, was suspended over the rear wheels. A red satin bow was tied to the handlebars.

Lizzie shrieked when she saw the bike and skipped around it, clapping her hands and demanding to be taken for a ride.

"Don't be mad, Mo," Rebecca smiled, using her friend's nickname from grammar school. "I know you don't like me giving you things but if you don't have a way to get around, you're not going to have much fun. It makes me happy to think of the two of you exploring the island with it." There was no doubt the bicycle and cart would come in very handy, so Maura thanked her friend with good grace.

The yard wasn't the velvety, uniform lawn that many of the neighbors carefully maintained. Upon close inspection, it was a mix of grass and local island plants, mowed that morning into a thick, natural carpet. The area was much larger than Maura had expected. The houses around the green were built on narrow lots, but now she could see that the property stretched back quite a way. The lawn was level until it rose in the back and ended in a stand of trees.

"Am I going to have to mow this?" asked Maura. "Because I've never worked a lawn mower." She had never actually had a yard before; her earliest years were spent in a rundown city apartment building. After her father left them, Maura's mother moved the family to Barlow Ridge where they lived in a converted garage on a parking lot. It was The Great Depression, but her mother found work cleaning houses and serving food in the school cafeteria. Maura was just twenty when she married her ex-husband David and he convinced her to drop out of college to keep house for him. They lived in a series of apartments, each smaller and more dreary than the last.

Will reassured her. "No, I've arranged for the teenager who cut the grass this morning to come all summer."

To their left, a line of fat rose bushes separated the yard from that of a graceful Greek Revival. Together with the roses that climbed over both houses, they created a spectacular display.

Will turned to the six-foot wall that separated the yard from the Uncle Irvin property. "There wasn't much my aunt and uncle could do about that. One of the first things Aunt May would do when they arrived each summer was plant flowers all along our side. It's been a few years since she could manage it. These shrubs close to the house are blueberries. My aunt said to tell you that if you water them really well, you'll get mounds of berries starting around mid-July. There's a hose on the side of the house but watch the water pressure – it's so strong, it will blow the berries off the bushes."

"Who lives there?" Maura whispered, aware of the possibility of open windows. "A scruffy little kid informed us that it's occupied by a witch."

Will laughed and answered in a lowered voice.

"I think my aunt mentioned that a woman moved in about ten or twelve years ago and keeps to herself. I never met her since I haven't spent much time here after I left for college." Maura stared at the house for a few moments, wondering why anyone would want to live in such an atrocious pile all alone.

"How do you get to the beach?"

He pointed to the rear of the property.

"To the left of the tire swing, there's a path through the trees. When you get to a fork you can bear left and go downhill to the beach. If you bear right, you'll come to a terrace of bungalows at the top of a cliff and from there it's a short walk down to the beach. The path is quicker if you're walking, but if you and Lizzie are going to take the bike there's a street that leads from the east end of the green down to the water. Just remember that it's all uphill coming back. This neighborhood was built on one of the higher points of the island because the land right along the shoreline has a habit of flooding in big storms."

After spending a few happy minutes sitting in the bicycle cart where she had been placed by Rebecca, Lizzie wandered over. She stared at Will while he spoke, then turning to her mother, whispered "Mommy...is Mr. Howe a giant?" To a four-year-old, Mr. Howe might indeed appear to have gigantic proportions. He was well over six feet tall, and while he may have been slim and all angles in high school, at thirty-five he had filled out remarkably well. In May, when he, Maura and Rebecca had had their reunion lunch, he mentioned that he and several friends often went sculling on the Charles River. Maura, casting him a furtive look, attributed the well-developed muscles along his shoulders and back to the rowing. She felt her cheeks turn pink at the unexpected thought.

A look of ludicrous outrage overtook Will's face. Lizzie giggled nervously. He chased her down the yard bellowing 'fee-fi-fo-fum" while she screamed with laughter. Maura and Rebecca followed behind, smiling.

Will caught up Lizzie and deposited her in the tire swing that he had hung a few weeks ago in anticipation of the arrival of a four-year-old. He gave her a few spins, then he and the women wandered over to a structure about midway between the house and the woods at the back of the property.

"We think it was originally built to house a horse and buggy, so we grandiosely call it the carriage house," said Will. "My family never brought a car here, and they just used it for storage. It was full of junk that I had to sort out. Once it was empty, I thought it might have potential as a guest cottage, so I've been working on it when I come out to check on things."

After completing the house inspection, they went to Wally's Lunch-o-Rama for coffee and sandwiches. Maura later discovered islanders merely referred to it as 'the coffee shop'. Rebecca and Will then took the afternoon ferry to return to their respective homes.

The next day, Maura discovered a body.

* *The Three Minute Bride*

Chapter 3

Maura took a few steps onto the pier and looked out over the water. She loved this time of day, just after sunrise when the sky was soft and clear, still gently tinted with pink. A little flurry of pleasant anticipation surprised her.

Lizzie squatted in the parking lot behind her, petting a well-fed cat and inviting him home with them. They had risen early, unable to sleep any longer on this first full day of their first ever vacation and had ridden to the harbor to see the fishermen set out. Most had already left by the time they arrived, so after watching the bustle on the remaining fishing boats for a time, they wandered over to this quieter spot. Here the small craft belonging to island residents were either tied up to the pier where Maura stood or moored nearby. The boats bobbed gently in the ripples made by the last of the fishing boats chugging their way out of the harbor.

"...and Mommy will make you pancakes," Lizzie was promising the cat.

Maura smiled and had just turned toward Lizzie when her attention was caught by a flash of bright pink in the water. With the sun at a different angle than when she had first stepped onto the pier, she now saw what hadn't been visible before: a woman in a bright pink suit lay in the water next to the pier. A white handbag was looped over her arm and floated above her but didn't quite reach the surface. The tide eddied a swirl of water over her then subsided, revealing a black circle in the middle of her forehead.

Maura stared into the water incredulously, her blood pounding in her ears. Help - she had to get help. Did the island have its own police station? How was she going to report this with Lizzie in tow?

The cat had had enough attention and wandered off in search of better entertainment.

"Mommy, I'm cold." With the departure of the cat, Lizzie was ready to leave. Maura quickly joined her in the parking lot to prevent her from coming onto the pier.

"Here. You can wear my sweater and now you have two." Maura admired her own calm voice.

After buttoning the sweater up to Lizzie's chin, she lifted her and put her into the bicycle cart.

By now there were signs of activity in many of the old houses in the crescent surrounding the little harbor. These homes were unpretentious, built for the most part at the end of the last century to accommodate working residents and to rent to families with modest incomes. Maura was pedaling toward a duplex with a collection of old buoys on one side of the yard when she noticed a faded 'Harbormaster' sign tacked to the mailbox post of the second house.

A small man with a round belly opened the door on Maura's third knock. His nose was red and veined, whether from years in the sun or from liquor or both, but his expression was affable.

"Don't you go anywhere!" A woman's voice called from somewhere behind him. "Breakfast is almost ready." The homey scents of coffee and bacon frying wafted out into the morning air.

"Mommy, I'm hungry." Lizzie's whisper was loud enough for the man to easily hear. He grinned.

"What can I do for you, ma'am?"

"There seems to have been...an accident." Maura's eyes went from the harbormaster to Lizzie and back again, trying to convey a message. To her relief he seemed to understand.

"Ruth!" he called over his shoulder. "We have a hungry visitor here."

A woman who was even smaller than her husband pushed him aside and stood in the doorway. When she saw a little girl with wildly curly red hair looking at her hopefully and took in the mother's white face and shocked expression, she smiled.

"How about you come in and help me stir the eggs? Would you like to have a little breakfast with Ruthie?" Lizzie looked at her mother, who nodded.

"Thank you!" Maura said gratefully.

The harbormaster came outside and closed the door behind him.

"So, what's the trouble?" his voice had become more businesslike.

Maura quickly explained how she had found the body.

The harbormaster stared at her for a moment.

"Hold on, let me get a few things."

He returned, smiling, a well-used rope coiled over his shoulder and a folded tarp under his arm.

"Your little girl is working her way through a plate of eggs, bacon and toast. She's got a big appetite for a skinny little thing!"

Maura laughed a little shakily.

"I'll have you know this is her second breakfast today!"

It took the harbormaster, who introduced himself as Clay Grady, only a moment to spot the body. He stood up and stared at Maura, shaken. His Adam's apple bobbed as he gulped a few times.

"It's Violet Wilson!" Since he didn't follow this with an explanation, Maura asked,

"Who is Violet Wilson?"

"What?" He pulled his gaze from the water. "Oh, she's a year-round resident. Into every club and committee there is. Kind of a busybody but nobody minds her. Look," he said, running his hand through his hair, "I know dead and that's dead. Can you ask my wife to call Vic and Krol – that's the island police – to get here on the double? Tell her we have a body."

As Maura hurried back to the harbormaster's house, she thought of the round black hole in the center of Violet Wilson's forehead and remembered Rebecca's words as they inspected the Uncle Irvin house: "Cheer up! I'm sure you'll have your murders too."

Chapter 4

Maura awoke the next morning to find Lizzie curled up next to her, cocooned in Aunt May's quilt against the cool morning air coming through the open window. Lizzie's flaming curls fanned out across her pillow and tickled Maura's cheek. A threadbare stuffed panda, which no amount of washing would ever make white again, lay across her daughter's neck. Lizzie had spent almost her entire life at the women and children's institute where she shared a room with Maura. While she loved her sunny new room with its rose-covered wallpaper and pink carpet, she was accustomed to a house full of people, the noises of a city and the comforting sound of her mother's even breathing. She had crept into Maura's room the last two nights.

Careful not to wake Lizzie, Maura put on her robe and went downstairs to make coffee. She took her steaming cup outside to the picnic table and gazed morosely over the backyard. Fat bumblebees meandered around the shrubs that separated Aunt May's property from that of the Greek Revival, and the heavy scent of roses mixed with the intoxicating aroma of the morning's first cup of coffee. The sun warmed Maura's outstretched legs and, as she took a sip, she found a sense of well-being steal over her despite herself.

As the shock of finding a dead body yesterday began to wear off, it was quickly replaced with worry. Ever since Will's family had agreed to her staying here, Maura had been looking forward to having special time with Lizzie for a whole summer. When she tried to convince herself that Violet Wilson had died from accident or natural causes, an image of the black spot in the woman's forehead sprang to her mind's eye. She had never seen the hole a bullet left in a human being before, but at the time it seemed clear that that was what she was looking at. That meant murder, not an accidental death or suicide. If the woman had wanted to kill herself it would have been unnecessarily awkward to point the gun at her own forehead when her temple would have been much more convenient. She remembered the coordinated suit, blouse and shoes that Violet Wilson was wearing when they pulled her out of the water, and the fuchsia lipstick that made the whitish-gray skin starker in contrast. Appearance was clearly important to her, and Maura found it hard to believe that she would purposely put a disfiguring bullet hole in her face. Then there was the handbag, still looped over the crook of the dead woman's elbow. Maura tried to imagine Violet stepping onto the pier. She raises the gun to her forehead with the purse dangling from her arm, likely knocking against her chest. She was right-handed, according to her acquaintances, and the handbag was looped over her right elbow. Violet either fires the gun from her right hand in this awkward way, or even more awkwardly, fires with her left. She then pitches into the water, handbag and all. No, it would have been more believable if Violet had set her handbag down on the dock then maybe waded into the water so there was no chance of the fall from the pier hiking her skirt up around her waist or something equally undignified. And why shoot yourself on a pier anyway? So that in case a gunshot to the head doesn't finish you off, drowning will? And, of course, where was the gun? If it was indeed a bullet hole in the middle of Violet Wilson's forehead, then Maura was sure that murder was committed.

How could Maura keep Lizzie here if there was a murderer at large? The contemplated loss of this promising summer made her angry and dispirited. She remembered her feeling of anticipation as Will unlocked the door on their first day. *If Lizzie and I follow him inside, what's in store for us?* It seemed momentous somehow, as though by entering the house their lives would be changed in some way; that they would become part of its history. Lizzie was, of course, happily unaware that her mother had found a dead body. How could Maura tell her they had to pack up and go...where? Paulette had taken her job at the institute. The little apartment they were to move to in the fall wouldn't be available until the first of September. She knew Rebecca and her husband would take them in for the rest of the summer, but that would be the end of her special time with Lizzie.

"Hellooooo!" a voice called. Maura looked up to see a cheerful, round face peering through a gap in the tall rose bushes. She self-consciously pulled the belt on her robe tighter and walked over to the row of bushes that divided her yard from that of the lovely Greek Revival.

"I'm your neighbor, Lillian Noonan." Maura needn't have worried about her robe. Lillian was dressed in a flowered housecoat and pink slippers that were soaked with dew. Her silver-white hair was a perfect sculpture that looked as though it would make a metallic echo if someone knocked on it. Maura wondered whether Lillian slept sitting up.

"We've been away for a few days" said Lillian, "which is why I didn't stop by to say hello earlier. My husband, Howard, owns car dealerships in Reading and Andover. I only tell you that in case you're the kind that's impressed by that stuff, but I can see by your smile that I could have saved myself the trouble."

Maura's smile became wider.

"Hello, Mrs. Noonan. I'm Maura Gertz. My husband didn't do anything to brag about."

Lillian laughed, her round cheeks pushing her eyes into slits.

"Honey, if all wives were honest, we'd say the same thing. Call me Lillian." She looked over her shoulder then inched as close as she could get to the gap in the bushes. With her grandmotherly look and apple red cheeks, clutching a cup of coffee and surrounded by roses, Maura thought she looked like an advertisement for baking powder.

CHAPTER 5

Maura's interest in the occupant of the Uncle Irvin house was piqued on their first night. After too much excitement that day, it had taken Lizzie several extra bedtime stories to fall asleep. Maura wandered across the hall to take a closer look at what she thought of as the boys' dormitory. It had four twin beds in a row, their headboards on the wall closest to the Uncle Irvin house. Each bed was covered in a matching blue bedspread, and the closets contained fishing tackle and sports equipment. Aunt May and Uncle Charlie had had two boys and a girl, she knew. When Will and his older brother, James, joined them this room would have been full. If Will's parents or more cousins or friends came, the boys moved to the room in the attic. It must have been a full and lively place in those days, before children grew up and moved away. Will told Maura and Rebecca that James and one of their cousins had been killed in the war.

On impulse, Maura turned off the light and sat on one of the beds, peering out the window at the hulking monstrosity next door. At this height she could see over the fence and noticed that the backyard was dimly lit as though light was cast from a rear window. The rest of the house was dark.

Suddenly, a wavering light appeared in one of the windows on the bottom floor. It slowly moved to the front of the house and then disappeared for a moment. It reappeared on the second story, then the third. It moved slowly and wobbled, evidently carried by hand. Although there was nothing sinister in this mysterious light, Maura felt the hair on her arms prickle. The house had electricity; why this stealthy progress through the house by flashlight or lantern? The light disappeared once again – Maura supposed the bearer was going up a flight of stairs – and was seen briefly in an attic window before it was extinguished. Maura was fascinated and leaned close to the window, waiting to see what happened next. After fifteen minutes she had begun to wonder if the resident of the Uncle Irvin house had set up her bedroom in the attic and had retired for the night, when the light came on again. It slowly descended through the house, just as it had gone up. Maura watched it move to the back of the house where she lost it.

This procession was repeated nightly. Maura made sure to be in the boys' room at nine o'clock the first few evenings. She entertained herself during her vigils by making up stories that would account for this odd phenomenon. She typed up several versions, realizing she had a taste for the sensational.

When neighbors dropped in for coffee, Maura would ask a casual question or two about the owner of the Uncle Irvin house. She didn't learn a great deal. The woman's name was Opal Hansen; she had been there about a dozen years and kept to herself; neighbors would occasionally encounter her in the market where she would politely greet them then scuttle away. They deplored her house in general; it was bad enough when it stood empty for years – at least the children of the last owner paid for some sort of upkeep until they found a buyer. Mrs. Hansen had let the place go, however. The yard and shrubbery were grossly overgrown, the windows were dirty and the paint peeling. No one could describe her personality or hazard a guess as to her background. Most of the houses around the green were summer homes, but Opal Hansen hunkered down in her enormous, decaying house every winter, never varying her routine, never receiving visitors that anyone was aware of.

Maura met Opal the Thursday after their arrival on Islay. She had been planting daylilies along the Uncle Irvin house's wall when she suddenly heard Lizzie talking to someone toward the front of the house. She dropped her trowel and stripping off

"Did you hear about the dead body?" Lillian asked breathlessly.

"Yes! I found her." Maura wasn't above indulging in some speculation with her enthralled neighbor.

"And here's the weird thing," Maura added, after recounting her discovery of the body. "When I saw the harbormaster at the coffee shop later in the day, I mentioned the bullet hole in Mrs. Wilson's forehead. He stared at me for a minute then looked out the window. 'What bullet hole?' he said. I couldn't believe my ears. 'The round black hole right in the center of her forehead!' I reminded him. He didn't say anything for a minute then waved to the waitress for more coffee. 'It was probably seaweed or something. I don't remember seeing it.'"

"I hadn't heard that! Why would anyone shoot Violet? I mean, she's annoying and a little officious – joins every club and committee and always has to be in charge – but she has a good heart. Had, I should say."

Maura began to have misgivings about starting a murder rumor if Violet's death was indeed an accident and some sea flotsam had just stuck to her face. The shock of finding a body may have affected her observation. Maura would have loved Violet Wilson's death to be an accident, but she still had strong doubts.

"Lillian, I may be wrong so please don't mention what I said to anyone. It's OK to tell people what I said about finding the body, but maybe skip the part about the bullet hole. I don't want to cause trouble."

"Honey, don't worry. I may look like the world's biggest gossip but I'm not. If you don't want me to say anything I won't."

Maura believed her.

"I guess I'm upset because I brought my daughter here for the summer and I'm afraid to keep her here if there's a murderer on the loose."

"What? You wouldn't leave the island because of something like that? In all the years, OK five, that we have been coming here there has never been any crime worse than a few wallets taken from beach bags last summer. That's because we don't get day people coming through; we're too far out. If by some chance Violet was murdered it would have something to do with her, not a little girl and her mother who have come for the summer. Speaking of which... Will Howe was here with his fiancé last weekend. His Aunt May and I were friendly. Will mentioned that he's fixing up the old carriage house on your property and would be staying there from time to time since he'll be working on the house. He didn't want me to think there was anything fishy going on, what with you in the main house and him staying out back. He told me you're old friends, and with his fiancé standing there smiling I knew there would be nothing going on. Not that it would be any of my business anyway. We mostly live on the bottom floor of our house and I would have to stick my face in this hole to see what was going on over here." She winked.

Maura laughed and confirmed there was nothing fishy going on. She wondered how Junie would feel about Will staying on the island with another woman on the weekends. Well, staying out back in the carriage house. When they met in May, Will had told them that he was getting married in November. Junie, his fiancé, was the sister of another architect in the firm. He said she wasn't happy about the amount of time he was spending on Islay but put up with it because his family would give him a small percentage of the profit when they sold the house. They were planning to put it toward a down payment on their own home.

"My husband's going to be looking for his breakfast," said Lillian, "so I better skidoodle. It's been wonderful meeting you, Maura honey. Stop by with your little girl soon and I'll stuff her full of cinnamon cookies."

Maura wandered back to the house in a somewhat better frame of mind. If Lillian wasn't worried about murderers running around Islay, maybe she shouldn't be either. She stepped into the kitchen just as Lizzie wandered in from the parlor asking for pancakes.

CHAPTER 4

Over the course of the next few days, speculation about Violet Wilson's death was the main topic of conversation among island residents. Having been given permission to tell people that Maura was the one who found the body, Lillian lost no time in sharing the details with her friends. True to her word, she didn't mention the bullet hole so there wasn't a great deal to talk about.

If there was speculation about the absence of Maura's husband, no one was rude enough to ask her outright. The wedding ring Maura still wore led most to assume that she was either a war widow – judging from the little girl's age, it would have been Korea – or her husband had stayed in town for work while his wife and daughter enjoyed a summer on the island. Maura was aware that some people assumed she was a widow and wasn't sure what she should do about it. Even though it was 1954, divorces were still uncommon and considered tawdry in many circles. She didn't want to mislead people, but she had no inclination to explain that her middle-aged husband had run away with a high school student. They were only there for the summer, so she would let people think what they liked.

When Maura imagined her summer with Lizzie, she hadn't figured in the distractions from neighbors and the workmen. These were chipping away at her precious time with her daughter. So accustomed was Lizzie to interruptions from the residents of the institute that when the doorbell rang at the Watts house, she wandered away from whatever activity they were engaged in without complaint. Maura found this more distressing than she would a show of temper, and she began planning outings that would take them away from the house.

A benign curiosity about the new summer residents in the Watts house rippled through the community. Several neighbors on the green stopped by with pies or cookies and were urged to stay for a cup of coffee. Maura groaned inwardly whenever she heard the gate squeak out front, but visitors detected nothing but a cordial welcome from their hostess. She was genuinely interested in her neighbors because, in part, she was creating character studies and vignettes of island life as practice exercises. When they left, she often ran to her typewriter and tapped out a few quick notes.

Uncle Charlie's office had been cleared and converted to a writing room. One of the first things that Maura had unpacked that first day was her typewriter. It sat squarely in the middle of the desk, a tray of typing paper to the left and an empty tray to the right where she would place each typed sheet. She would begin her new job teaching second grade in the fall; her dream was to be able to augment her salary by writing articles for newspapers or magazines. Creating the little character studies of her neighbors was entertaining, but she felt an urge to try her hand at something more ambitious this summer, maybe a novel. It would be slow going, as she only planned to write when Lizzie was in bed. Maura's mind became blank when she tried to come up with a storyline, though. Maybe Islay would offer an adventure or two that she could use.

her gardening gloves, hurried to the street. Lizzie was nowhere in sight and Maura soon realized the voices were coming from inside the gate of the Gothic house.

"How come you don't get up?" asked Lizzie

"Wuh!" This was more of a grunt.

"Do you have a cat?"

"Go get your mother or father," a voice wheezed.

"If I had a cat, I would name him Jelly Bean."

Maura pushed through the open wrought iron gate. She saw a very large woman on the ground, struggling to get up.

"Here, let me help." Maura grasped the woman's hands and pulled. This had no effect. She suggested the woman roll over onto her knees and push herself up. When she tried this, she let out a cry.

"It's my knee! I tripped over a root and landed on it."

After attempting and discarding various ways to get the woman on her feet, Maura suggested she get help from neighbors.

"No! I can do it." The woman finally managed a slow scoot backwards until she reached the steps of her house, where with Maura's help she was able to pull herself up using the railing. Lizzie trailed behind, offering helpful suggestions.

"My friend is a giant. He could pick you up and carry you inside. How come you're so fat?"

"Lizzie!" Maura was aghast.

"Because I ate all the cats in the neighborhood!"

Tears welled up in Lizzie's eyes and her lower lip trembled.

"I'm just kidding! Don't cry. You can't call somebody fat and expect to get away with it."

"Honey, nobody eats cats," Maura quickly reassured her. "The lady was just being funny. Don't ever, ever call someone fat."

Lizzie gave the woman a resentful look and stayed behind Maura, just in case the woman ate young children too.

They were finally inside, the woman leaning heavily on Maura for support.

"If you can help me to the kitchen in the back, I'll be all right."

Maura gazed around with lively curiosity. The heavy front door had a beautiful panel of stained glass, quite filthy with spider webs and grime. The rooms they made their way through were shadowy, the dirt on the generously proportioned windows only allowing dim light through. She got a glimpse of satin-paneled walls coated in a film of dust, an ornate fireplace and old, worn carpets strewn on parquet floors. The house seemed even bigger from the inside than it had appeared as it skulked over the top of the wall. If Aunt May's house had gentle, contented ghosts, those that lived here were undoubtedly floating from room to room, running their fingers over dusty marble mantels and muttering in disgust. Maura wondered what had happened to make the woman cloister herself in this rambling mausoleum.

In contrast to the other rooms, the kitchen was well-lit and clean. A narrow bed and an old-fashioned wardrobe against one wall suggested this might be the one inhabited room in the house.

Maura helped the woman to a sturdy armchair where she plopped with a *woof!*

"Thank you, dear. I don't know how long I would have lain in the yard if you hadn't come along." She shot a look at Lizzie, who frowned back.

"Are you Mrs. Hansen? I'm Maura Gertz."

"Is that German?" It wasn't the first time Maura had gotten that question. Nine years after the war, Maura still received some suspicious stares when people learned her name. With her divorce, Maura had wanted to revert to her maiden name of Sullivan but was faced with either having a different surname than Lizzie, or risking David's involvement if she tried to have Lizzie's name changed. In the end she did nothing.

"Yes, but my husband's family came over during the Revolution. I was a Sullivan."

CHAPTER 5

Opal Hansen's mind having been relieved of the possibility of Nazi sympathizers living next door, she asked Maura if she would put a kettle on and have a cup of tea with her.

"Do you have a phone? I think I should call the doctor first." Opal, as she requested Maura call her, pointed to a heavy black telephone on the end of a counter next to a pile of books. On the wall above the telephone was tacked a card with neatly printed phone numbers. Maura had learned that island phones only connected to the local Islay phone service. There was talk of running a cable to the island to connect it to the Bell Telephone system, but it would be an expensive proposition given the distance to the mainland. Off-island communication was mostly done via ham radio. The police station had one and a few of the island residents had sets.

After the doctor's receptionist promised that he would stop by shortly, Maura put the teakettle on to boil. Lizzie stayed close to her and never took her eyes off their hostess. Opal became uncomfortable under the unwavering stare.

"Little girl, why don't you bring me that round tin next to the stove?"

Lizzie looked as though she would refuse so Maura gave her a nudge. "Do as you're asked, Lizzie."

"Lizzie. That's a pretty name." Opal was clearly trying to make amends. Lizzie approached her with dragging feet. Opal took the tin from her and pried up the lid. Inside were butterscotch brownies. "Have one!"

Still not convinced that the woman didn't eat cats, Lizzie started to back away. Maura hurried over and took a brownie from the tin.

"Mmmm! Definitely no cats." Lizzie reached out a tentative hand. Her expression changed as she experienced her first butterscotch brownie. She sat on the floor near Opal with the tin in her lap.

"And that answers your question about why I'm so fat. I love to bake and there's no one to eat the stuff except me!"

Maura poured three cups of tea, liberally adding milk to Lizzie's. They chatted in the comfortable kitchen, waiting for the doctor to arrive. Opal told Maura that she had moved to the island in 1942. A friend already lived on the island and she thought it would be nice to be close by. There were few houses for sale on Islay, but this house was on the market at an exceptionally low price. Although it had stood empty for years, it seemed to be in fairly good condition. The ridiculous style and extensive proportions appealed to her sense of humor. When the friendship failed and her investments lost money, she found herself isolated on an island that no longer held any charm for her.

Suddenly a pile of clothes on a small sofa began to move. A sleepy orange face emerged and stared at them.

"A cat! You do have a cat!"

Opal laughed.

"Meet Molasses. As in 'slow as'." Lizzie ran to the couch to make friends.

"So, where's your husband?" Maura was taken aback at the sudden question. Opal was not as circumspect as her other neighbors. She decided to be honest; it wasn't likely that Opal would engage in gossip with the rest of the neighborhood, and Lizzie wasn't paying attention.

"Somewhere in South Carolina, I think. He ran away with his eighteen-year-old student after my daughter was born. The student's father and brother caught up with them in New York and beat him enough to put him in the hospital. Or so my in-laws told me. My mother-in-law blamed me for the whole business. My father-in-law refuses to let him ever set foot in their house again.

Opal blinked. At that point there was a knock on the door.

"That will be the doctor," she said. "Sometime, when I know you better, I may tell you my real story. Or maybe not. It's worse than yours." The last sentence was said under her breath.

After a quick inspection, Dr. Weinstein announced that it was a mild knee sprain and if Mrs. Hansen kept off it for a day or two, she would recover quickly.

"And eat more salad," he winked. "You're quite a bit heavier than when you first moved here. Take some walks!"

"I might be more inclined to if the kids around here didn't point at me and call me a witch!"

The doctor looked at her, nonplussed.

"Has anyone else called you a witch? Any adults?"

He seemed a little relieved when Opal shook her head.

"Not to my face, anyway."

"Just keep your house locked up for a bit, will you? There are a couple of fellas from one of the fishing boats who were in the tavern the other night, giving their opinion that the island witch was responsible for Violet Wilson's death. I don't expect that anyone is stupid enough to believe them or to try to make trouble but coming on top of what happened to Bob Welch some people are a little nervous." He turned to Maura.

"Bob was a retiree who lived in one of the bungalows. He disappeared last fall and hasn't been seen since."

Maura felt her unease over Violet's death return.

"And what the heck is the 'island witch'?" she asked.

The doctor rubbed is chin and looked at Opal.

"The first settlers on the island were from a shipwreck off the east coast of the island. They weren't far from shore and some of the passengers and crew survived by holding onto bits of the ship and cargo and letting the surf wash them in." Most of the passengers were from a weird religious sect, he continued, heading ultimately for Pennsylvania where they were tolerant of that kind of thing. One of the survivors was the wife of the pastor, and she made herself unpopular. They built a house for her away from the settlement - here in fact, or so the legend went. She was reported to have cursed her land to keep the settlers away. Some years later a passing ship took shelter from a storm in a cove on the north side of the island. They found the settlement clearing strewn with human bones.

"Legend has it that the preacher's wife, also known as the island witch, killed the lot of them."

"And my house is supposedly built on the site of the island witch's house," Opal grinned. "Making me the resident witch!"

"It's all nonsense," said the doctor gruffly. "Anyway, take care of yourself, Opal. If your knee still bothers you in a couple of day, give me a call."

As she closed the door behind her, Maura realized she was no closer to solving the mystery of the flashlight in the dark.

—·—

Chapter 6

It was Friday, and the plumbers had arrived for their third day of banging and clanging. They warned her that the water would be turned off until they left that evening, so after filling several pots with water from the tap and putting them in the refrigerator, she and Lizzie headed down the path to the beach.

At nine o'clock, it was early enough that the beach was mostly empty. At the water's edge a young woman in a yellow cotton dress accompanied four children who were picking up shells and putting them in buckets. Lizzie stood for a moment watching them. A filmy scarf was tied over the woman's hair and she wore sunglasses in the latest style. She seemed preoccupied but as soon as one of the children flicked sand at another, or took a step too far into the water, she snapped a word or two and brought the miscreant back in line.

Lizzie loved the playground, particularly the metal slide. By noon it would be too hot for her bare legs, but at this time of the morning, wearing a pair of pedal-pushers over her bathing suit, she could fly down the steep slide and land sprawling in the sand with perfect enjoyment. Maura knew that the slide would entertain her daughter for some time, so she wandered over to the swing set. The narrow canvas sling seat was uncomfortable for her hips so she thought she would try the approach she used in third grade. Facing away from the ocean, she slid the seat up her back until it came to her armpits. She took several steps backwards and swung her legs up in the air, hooking her ankles around the chains. She was now swinging upside down, watching the water approach and recede as the swing went back and forth. Lizzie saw her and laughed delightedly. A feeling of contentment spread over Maura.

A yellow dress and tanned feet in expensive sandals moved into her field of vision.

"Want a push?" Maura reluctantly unhooked her ankles from the swing chains and dropped her feet to the sand. She stood up, aware that her face must be red from blood rushing to it, and that her wavy, auburn hair was probably in a tumble from the wind off the ocean and from hanging upside down.

The young woman was smiling a little and there was a distinct twinkle in her eye.

"I'm Gracie Fletcher." She thrust out her hand, which Maura shook after a brief pause. The handshake made it seem more of a business meeting than two mothers meeting casually on a beach. The woman was beautifully made up, with perfectly penciled eyebrows and lips wearing Persian Melon. The yellow and orange chiffon scarf set off her dark hair.

"Maura Gertz. That's my daughter, Lizzie, on the slide. You have four kids?" She had the impression that Gracie Fletcher wasn't paying any attention to her children, who were now playing on a large, spinning disc that had bars around the outside for kids to hold onto. The oldest boy was holding onto one of the bars and running around the disc as fast as he could, making it spin faster and faster, while the other children tried to hold on. Maura was about to step forward in some alarm when Gracie's hand shot out and pulled the boy away from the disc. With her other arm she caught a little girl who was losing her grip on the bar.

"Oh, these aren't my kids. Well, they are every weekday morning from eight-thirty to twelve. I run a day camp out of one of the bungalows. Camp Boogie-Woogie. The original name was Little Fishies Day Camp but no self-respecting kid over age four wanted to go. We play on the beach, do art projects, go for nature walks and bake stuff. Hey, Midge!"

A little girl wandered over.

"How do you like camp?"

Midge grinned.

"We get to eat cookies and color and you read us stories. It's not boring like back at my house."

"Have I ever smacked any of you?"

"No," the girl smiled.

"Have any of the kids gotten hurt?"

"Nope!"

"OK, go say hi to that girl who's hogging the slide. Her name is Lizzie."

Midge happily ran to the slide and climbed up the ladder.

"So...you want to sign her up?"

It had been a business meeting after all.

"Well... I don't know," Maura said cautiously. "I've been looking forward to spending more time with Lizzie."

"Don't you have anything you want to get done for a few hours every day? We're only talking weekdays. I don't expect you to decide for sure without references. Two of the kids live on the green and you can talk to their parents. Since I know you're not in the bungalows I'm guessing that's where you're staying."

Maura was about to decline Gracie's offer but remembered Lizzie's wistful look when she saw the campers playing on the beach. Accustomed to spending her time around other children, Lizzie was a gregarious child. She and Midge even now had their heads together, giggling over something. While Maura wanted to spend more time with Lizzie this summer, she realized that her ultimate goal of giving her daughter a normal upbringing would not be achieved by sequestering her.

"She'll be fine," Gracie said gently, an understanding smile curving her lips.

A few hours a day would give Lizzie the chance to play with other children, and Maura could certainly find productive uses for that time. She could get a real start on her writing. She asked how much. The cost was reasonable, and she had managed to save much of the generous salary Rebecca had paid her to run the institute.

"Hey, Lizzie honey," she called. "Want to go to camp with Midge and the other kids in the mornings?"

Lizzie answered with a big grin.

Almost a week had gone by since Maura found Violet Wilson's body. There had been plenty of speculation as to why she died and what she was doing alone on the pier. If she had a companion, he or she would have pulled her out of the water. A few mentioned Violet's fondness for gin and tonics, but no one could remember her drinking more than would make her flirt with all the husbands at a party. Only Maura and Lillian had any reason to suppose that Violet might not have been alone. They frequently discussed this through the portal of roses, holding coffee cups or wine glasses depending on the time of day. It wasn't until Violet's island friends and neighbors were planning a little memorial service that they realized they didn't know much about her at all. They didn't know where her family lived or how to get in touch with them. The police had relayed the phone number found on an emergency contact card in Violet's bungalow to the Gloucester police via radio, and they had apparently been able to reach her family. By Sunday night the body had been whisked away from Islay.

Maura, riding through town one morning with Lizzie in the cart, saw an official-looking sign with the words 'Islay Police' pointing down the side of an old colonial that had been converted to a hardware store. On impulse, she got off the bike and wheeled it down the path to an extension that had been built onto the house in more recent years.

The door opened into a plain room with two wooden desks and an empty holding cell. A uniformed man in his fifties sat at one of the desks talking on a big black telephone. An ashtray was half full of cigarette butts. The nameplate proclaimed that he was Sgt. Leonard Krol. The empty desk belonged to Capt. Victor Stokes.

Krol had been haranguing someone when she opened the door but switched his side of the conversation to yes, no and grunts when he saw her.

"I'll call you back." The officer leaned back. "What can I do for you ladies?" His smile took over the lower part of his face in a startling way; the ends tipped up toward his eyes revealing a missing tooth in the back and heavy tobacco stains. Maura blinked and Lizzie hid behind her.

He wasn't the officer who had taken her statement at the dock when she found the body. She wondered how she was going to have this conversation with her four-year-old daughter behind her.

"Hello. My name is Maura Gertz." He waited, still smiling. "I, uh... I'm the one who found Mrs. Wilson."

Sergeant Krol turned his smile off.

"That must have been shocking for you."

"Yes. I wanted to ask about the..." She glanced down at Lizzie. "The ... oh drat. Do you have a pen and paper?" Krol raised his eyebrows but pulled a lined pad out of a drawer and handed her his pen.

Maura wrote and handed the pad back to Krol.

The bullet hole in Violet Wilson's forehead.

He stared at it long enough to have read the sentence five times over.

"What bullet hole?"

She gave him an annoyed look and surreptitiously pointed to Lizzie. He wrote and handed the pad back to her.

What bullet hole?

She mentally rolled her eyes and scribbled on the pad.

The black hole in the middle of her forehead which I clearly saw.

Must have been some seaweed or something stuck there. He handed the pad back to her with a smirk. He was clearly ready to play this game all day.

"Mommy, can we go?"

"Yes." She wished Sergeant Krol good day.

Maura was washing supper dishes that evening when the doorbell rang. Lizzie, scribbling in a coloring book at the kitchen table, didn't look up. She had lost interest in the coming and going of workmen and neighbors unless they came bearing something good to eat.

Maura recognized the man standing on the doorstep as Victor Stokes, the police captain who had taken her statement at the dock.

"I understand you stopped by the station today and that Len wasn't very helpful. He thought the notebook thing was funny. Sorry, he can be an ass." Stokes' voice was well-modulated but he spoke in an undertone, as though everything he imparted was confidential. Maura found herself leaning forward to catch what he was saying.

She invited him to come back to the kitchen and Lizzie wandered off.

Stokes was in his early forties, had a stocky build and was no taller than she was. His dark hair was neatly oiled in the current men's fashion and his uniform crisply pressed.

"Coffee?"

"Tea if you have it, thanks."

Maura put the kettle on and joined him at the table. She got right to the point.

"So, Captain Stokes, was there a bullet hole or wasn't there?"

Stokes smiled a little.

"In a way I wish there was." His lips moved but little sound escaped. "No, I don't mean that. Violet Wilson was harmless and she didn't deserve a bullet or whatever happened to her. I just meant that this island is very peaceful and there's not much for Len and me to do except break up the occasional fight at the tavern. Sometimes I think about moving to a city so I can see some action, but I love it here and stay put. And call me Vic; we're not formal around here."

"Then what did she die from?" Maura realized she had barked the question in a subconscious effort to pull Vic's conversation onto a more audible level.

He shrugged and smiled again.

"Good question. We're not equipped to do autopsies here, naturally, so we radioed to the mainland. They must not have had anything better to do because they were over here like a flash and took her away."

"What did they say was the cause of death?"

"We haven't heard back yet. They only came for her three days ago, so may not have done the autopsy yet."

Maura felt like she had gotten all the information she was going to get, and now they had to make conversation until he had had his tea. She picked out one of Aunt May's pretty but diminutive teacups and dropped a teabag in it. After adding boiling water, she gingerly placed the cup and saucer in front of her guest. It shouldn't take him long to finish such a dainty cup of tea. He carefully removed the cup from the saucer and turned over the latter to inspect the backstamp.

"Rockingham – very nice! These are antiques."

"They belong to the family that owns the house. They're descendants of the original owner and the contents of the house seem to be passed down along with the house through the generations."

"Interesting. I buy and sell antiques in a small way, more as a hobby. I saw the For Sale sign that was up before you moved in. Are they still planning to sell?"

"Yes. It will go back on the market at the end of the summer."

"A shame. I wonder if the owners would let me look through the house and make an offer if I find anything in my line. I suppose they'll have an appraiser in if they're not planning to keep everything in the family?"

"I don't know. I'll mention it if you would like." She didn't actually plan to mention it since she felt she had spent sufficient time with the island constabulary. He finished his tea and left.

Maura had noticed that Vic Stoke's voice took on animation and volume when discussing antiques that weren't present when he assured Maura there was no bullet hole in Violet's forehead. Then his voice had been smooth and plausible, with that confidential undertone. Why did he feel it necessary to pay her a visit, just to tell her what the sergeant had already said – that there was no bullet hole? Was it purely from courtesy because he knew Krol had been rude, or did Vic think he could do a better job of convincing her so she wouldn't cause trouble? If it was a murder, the police were clearly not going to say so.

At ten-thirty Saturday morning, Will rode up on a rented bicycle. Maura was washing the old linoleum floor in the kitchen and Lizzie was out back on the tire swing. "It doesn't look a whole lot different," Will observed on his way to the kitchen, "but it feels different. It's nice to have a family here again. What's been going on since I was here last Saturday?"

With no phone service to the mainland, he was unaware of Violet Wilson's death.

"Sit down and I'll make us some coffee."

As she put a kettle on to boil and scooped coffee into the filter, she told him about riding out to the pier on Sunday morning and finding Violet Wilson in the water. Will listened in wide-eyed silence, not fooled by her matter-of-fact tone.

"What a way to start your summer vacation. It must have been a pretty bad moment for you."

Maura nodded. She opened her mouth to say something then shut it again.

"What? Tell me."

"OK, this is going to sound weird. When I first saw the body under the water, there was a very black hole in the middle of her forehead. Like...a bullet hole."

Will was startled.

"She was shot? Or she shot herself?"

"Maybe neither. I just don't know. I didn't notice a gun, but I was too shocked to think to look for one. I was still there when they pulled her body out of the water and I saw the hole again plainly. But when I asked the harbor master about it later, he said there wasn't a bullet hole. He suggested I might have seen a piece of seaweed."

"Do you think it could have been seaweed?"

"Only if seaweed comes in almost perfectly round black discs." She blew out her breath. "I stopped at the police station a few days ago and they said the same thing – no bullet hole, probably seaweed. I don't know, maybe I'm wrong."

Will rubbed his jaw.

"I wouldn't have said you were a person to let her imagination get the best of her. Just to be on the safe side, maybe you shouldn't mention it to anyone else."

Just then Lizzie burst through the door and came to a surprised halt when she saw Will.

"Hi Mr. Giant! Did you come to play with me?"

"Lizzie –" Maura began.

"Yes, I definitely came to play with you, but first I have to get some boring work done." He fished in his jacket pocket. "Can you go plant these in the dirt next to that brick wall? Just make a little hole for each one, poke in a bean and push some dirt back over it."

Round-eyed, Lizzie nodded and ran off.

Maura grinned. "Let me guess. Magic beans?"

Will's deep laugh rumbled.

"What kind of giant would I be without a beanstalk?" He leaned forward, his coffee cup between both hands.

"OK, on to business. There's been a change in plans with the house."

Maura felt a stab of alarm. She wondered if they had already found a buyer for the house, or if Aunt May and her family decided not to sell after all. She couldn't bear the thought of leaving before the summer was over, despite Violet Wilson's death.

"Rebecca called me on Sunday. She thinks this house has a lot of potential, and if it was fixed up right Aunt May could make a pretty decent profit. The deal she proposed is that she would supply the funds to fix up the house properly – top quality materials, workmanship, no corners cut. When the house is sold, any profits made in excess of what my aunt is hoping to get for the house would first go to reimburse Rebecca. After that, she gets a percentage of the remaining profit."

Maura sat for a moment taking it in.

"I could tell she fell in love with the house and was holding herself back from making recommendations. Her first husband used to buy real estate, fix it up and sell it at a profit as a hobby. That's how she got her cliff house, and lately she's been buying run-down houses in desirable areas and sending crews in to renovate them. I think she's making good money on the resale and she really enjoys bringing old houses back to life. I guess I'm not surprised that she wanted to get involved with this one, but I wouldn't think she'd make much because she's sharing the profit."

"Rebecca admitted as much, but said that once having seen the house, she couldn't resist bringing it back to its original glory. She's going to be sending you some details about the renovation, by the way. Did you register at the post office?"

"No. I don't even know where it is but I'll look for it this week."

Will inspected the work the plumbers had done so far, and while he wasn't a plumbing expert, he thought they were doing a good job.

"One of the changes Rebecca wants to make is to have a powder room installed downstairs. The room between the kitchen and the writing room is actually a dining room, although my family always ate in the kitchen and used the dining room for storage. A small space on the kitchen end of the dining room will become a pantry and the rest will be the powder room with a little hallway. So unfortunately, that means more plumbing work for you to deal with."

Maura shrugged. If that was the price for her summer on Islay it was well worth the inconvenience.

Will spent the rest of the afternoon working in the carriage house with Lizzie handing him tools. He had to take the late afternoon ferry back because Junie was expecting him to accompany her to a party that evening.

"I'm planning to come back next weekend, though, to meet with Rebecca's contactor and plan the rest of the updates. Would you mind if I stay in the carriage house some weekends? I can't get a lot done when I'm sandwiched between the morning and afternoon ferries."

"No, of course not. I suspect you'll have a little shadow trying to keep you from getting your work done but I'll do my best to keep her distracted."

Will laughed.

"No, don't do that! She's good company and fetches things for me. She spent about an hour this afternoon talking about the adventures she and her cat Jelly Bean would have if she had a cat named Jelly Bean."

"I think I'm going to have to get her one, if only to preserve my sanity."

Will offered to do a little scouting for a Jelly Bean during the week. Before he left for the ferry, he warned Maura that a storm was forecasted for the next day.

"Being out in the middle of the ocean like this, storms can get pretty wild. The house hasn't blown over yet, so don't let it worry you!"

CHAPTER 7

Rain was pelting the windows when Maura awoke the following morning. Unable to guess the time from the dim light, she reached for her wind-up alarm clock. Ten minutes after seven. A gust of wind shook the house and subsided. It was the fourth of July. Maura didn't know how Islay normally celebrated Independence Day, but she suspected any festivities would have been canceled.

The kitchen had a cold, dank feel. She turned on the lights and put water on to boil. Shivering a little in the cold drafts that seeped in around the old window panes, Maura eyed the wood stove. She resolved to scrounge up firewood to keep ready for any other storms that might come their way this summer.

When Lizzie came downstairs an hour later, the kitchen was warm from the oven and full of the scent of cinnamon apple cake. They spent the day playing games, drawing pictures and baking bread. While Lizzie napped on the hearth rug, Maura brought her notebook into the kitchen and wrote character descriptions of Opal and Gracie for practice.

The next morning, a sharp knock on the front door let Maura know that Opal's groceries had been delivered. Made more nervous by the doctor's warning than she liked to admit, Opal wasn't leaving her gate unlocked for the delivery boy. Maura took the groceries next door, adding one of the loaves of bread she and Lizzie had made. She used the spare key Opal had given her to get through the gate. The older woman's knee was much improved, and she had spent the day of the storm baking as well.

CHAPTER 7

Grateful for the dinners Maura had been bringing over since her fall, Opal presented Lizzie with a tin of cookies and brownies.

The damp grass glittered in the morning sunlight and the flowers in the little yards of the houses around the green glowed with vibrant color. Maura took a deep breath of the intoxicating sea air and decided that this would be a perfect day to explore the island. It was Monday, and Lizzie was starting camp tomorrow.

Both the plumber and the electrician were expected today. The electrician arrived first, and he promised to let the plumber in. Maura loaded a beach blanket, towels, a lunch basket and a canteen of lemonade into the bike cart and lifted Lizzie into it. They took the road from the east end of the green down the steep hill to their little beach, Maura nervously applying the brakes the whole way. At the bottom of the hill they joined the perimeter road. This ran the full circuit of the island and would allow them to reach the nature preserve on the east end. The only structures on the other side of the island were an active lighthouse and a small inn. Maura hoped to reach these today and leave the rest of the island to be explored another day.

The perimeter road was quite easy to navigate for several miles, as it ran at sea level. The island was relatively flat here, which accounted for the fact that no one had built vacation homes out this way. There was ample evidence that the surf from yesterday's storm had washed up over the road and it still hadn't fully receded. Maura pedaled them along the road at a spanking clip while they sang silly songs. Seagulls wheeled and called overhead and spray off the waves sparkled in the sunlight.

When the road began to curve north, following the shoreline, it also started to rise. The lighthouse, which was their destination, had been visible for some time and was now quite close. Before long, Maura had to lift Lizzie from the cart and push the bike up the hill. When they reached the summit, they found that they were at the top of a cliff that was guarded by a metal railing. Holding the bars tightly, Maura peered down and saw that while the sand was wet from the storm right up to the base of the cliff, the water had mostly receded. An occasional shallow ripple would advance half-way up the little beach and swirl around jagged boulders.

A bronze plaque bore an inscription:
Landing Point
Island of Islay, Massachusetts
In the year 1732, the merchant ship Temperance foundered in the treacherous waters that have claimed more than a dozen ships. Survivors washed ashore at the base of this cliff and founded the first colony on the island. Islay Light was constructed in 1912 to warn ships away from underwater rocks and dangerous currents.

The lighthouse wasn't as tall as some Maura had seen, but that was likely because it sat at the top of a cliff and extra height wasn't required. There was no one around and the door was locked, so after circling around it and staring upwards, they unpacked their lunch and spread it on the beach blanket. As they ate ham sandwiches and pears, Lizzie speculated as to whether the family that lived in the lighthouse had a cat.

The remains of the lunch having been packed up and put in the cart, they took one last look around. On the other side of the lighthouse, they found steps that led down to the beach. Each holding the railing and the hand of the other, they made their way to the bottom. Maura looked around, imagining washing into shore on a piece of broken ship, calling for loved ones who might not have survived. The only way off the beach would have been a steep climb on either side of the cliff. The women's long gowns would have been sodden and heavy, restricting their ability to walk let alone scrabble up such an incline. She could almost hear voices wailing in fear, pleading for help and calling the names of their spouses and children.

Lizzie had spotted a small, dark shape lying up against the cliff, partially covered in seaweed and other debris. On closer inspection it appeared to be an oilskin sack in poor condition. Maura gingerly opened it and found roughly carved ivory pieces. Lizzie pounced on one that seemed to be shaped like a horse.

"Can we keep these?"

CHAPTER 7

Maura wasn't sure what she was going to do with a waterlogged set of chess pieces, at least she assumed that's what they were, but agreed.

The day had become hot, and after climbing the steep steps back to the lighthouse Maura had to decide whether to retrace their route home or continue on. They had finished the lemonade and Lizzie was complaining that she was thirsty. Looking at the simple island map she had picked up at the market, she saw that the Bayberry Inn shouldn't be too far ahead.

The perimeter road ran gently downhill as it continued north, away from the lighthouse. The person who drew the map was evidently an amateur, as the inn was much farther away from the lighthouse than was represented.

When they finally arrived at the inn, they were tired and quite thirsty. There were two cars in the parking lot and a small rowboat tied up to a pier. The inn had been built in a little protected inlet, flanked by stunted pines. It was rather squat, made of stone and with a steeply pitched roof. Maura guessed it was built late in the last century.

They stepped through the doorway into a dim reception area. The sound of glasses clinking and a male voice or two could be heard in the lounge to the left. As Maura's eyes were adjusting to the change from sunlight, she saw a woman in her forties approaching. She was slim and athletic looking, her hair cut rather short and her face devoid of makeup.

"What can we do for you?" she asked with a friendly smile.

Maura explained that she and her daughter had explored a little further afield than intended and hoped they could get something cold to drink.

"Of course! Come into the dining room. It's mostly empty." The only other occupant was a man sitting against the far wall with a newspaper spread over the table. He had a cup of coffee and the remains of a sandwich pushed to the side and was intent on an article.

The woman settled them at a table and brought them glasses of water with ice cubes.

"Do you have a cat?" asked Lizzie.

The woman smiled.

"No, I wish I did. I do have a nice lemon chiffon cake, though. Would you like a slice?" Lizzie nodded vigorously.

"Yes, please!"

When the slices of cake were set down, Maura took a bite of hers and closed her eyes.

"This has to be the best cake I've ever eaten. Well, it's tied with a coconut cake I had at the coffee shop last week."

The woman laughed.

"That's because it was baked by the same hand. The coffee shop supplies us with a lot of our baked goods. Wally's baker is a genius. Why he's on this island I can't imagine, when he could do much better back on the mainland. I'm Sally Fortier, by the way. My husband Jim and I run the inn. Is this your first visit to the island?"

Maura explained that they had just arrived and would be staying for the summer.

"In the bungalows?"

"No, in a house on the green."

Sally remarked that that was quite a way from where they were, and when Maura said they had come by bicycle she suggested they return by a little used route through the center of the island. "It's more of a track, but Jim sometimes takes his old motorcycle that way when he goes into town so it's passable. Your bike should be OK and it's definitely a shorter route."

When Sally left the room, Lizzie extracted the carved knight from her pocket and set it on the table. Maura knew the man with the map had been listening to her conversation with Sally while ostensibly looking at his paper. Seeing the chess piece, he gave up the pretense. Lizzie jumped when he suddenly appeared next to them.

"What do you have there?" He pulled a chair over from another table, turned it backwards and straddled it.

Maura was taken aback by this intrusion. She stared at the man, her eyebrows raised in surprise. Her annoyance wasn't lost on the interloper, who grinned at her. He was about her age, with a triangular-shaped face, very white teeth and startling blue eyes. Her impression was of someone who spent a great deal of time in the sun; his face was deeply tanned and his short brown curls tipped with gold.

He picked up the chess piece and turned it over in his hands. Lizzie shot her mother an outraged look. Maura grimaced back.

"I'd say last century. Hand carved by a bored sailor, no doubt. Where did you find it?"

"At the bottom of the cliff by the lighthouse."

"All kinds of things wash up there, especially after storms. There have been a lot of wrecks in this area." He held his right hand out to Maura.

"Patrick Dunn, salvor. Not Pat. Patrick."

Maura gave a reluctant smile and shook his hand.

"What's a salvor?"

"We salvage cargo from sunken ships."

"Are you telling me there are gold doubloons out there?"

He shrugged.

"Who knows? My first mate, Steve, and I have found some crazy stuff."

"If Steve is your first mate, how many other people work on your boat? Are you the captain?"

He looked her in the eye and said in a mock-serious voice, ""Yes, I'm the captain and there are the two of us. It's my boat so I can call him whatever I want!"

Maura's eyes crinkled with amusement. Patrick Dunn looked at her with apparent interest.

"I told you my name, but you didn't tell me yours."

Her smile widened, but she didn't say anything. Patrick's eyes narrowed a little and his expression became intent.

Just then Sally came back to check on her customers.

"Hey, Sal. Look what this little girl found."

Sally picked up the knight and turned it over in her hand.

"Nice! Too bad you don't have the set. You need to keep it wet; ivory will be ruined if it dries out without professional treatment."

"Sally and Jim are also salvors, but they do it as a hobby. I do it for a living."

Sally snorted.

"We're treasure hunters. It's a mess if you actually find anything worth salvaging... there's the government – governments, I should say, if the ship was from another country. And the dreaded marine archeologists. But it's fun to hunt for wrecks."

"We do have the full set of chess pieces, actually." Maura turned to Lizzie. "Would you like to show the other pieces to Mrs. Fortier and Mr. Dunn?" Lizzie nodded and went out to the bicycle cart to fetch them.

Sally and Patrick looked it over carefully.

"A nice set, but probably not valuable. There wasn't a lot of skill there." Sally put the chess pieces back in the wet oilskin bag. "One of the maritime museums might be interested in it though. My suggestion is to let Patrick take it around; he's always got bits of stuff he finds so they all know him. Unless you want to keep the set." She looked at Lizzie.

"No...they're kind of icky."

Sally went to the kitchen and came back with a sopping wet dishcloth. She wrapped the ivory pieces in it then put them back in the bag.

Maura asked for the check but Sally waved her hand and said it was her welcome-to-Islay treat.

"Ready to go, Patrick?" A man with sun-bleached hair was standing in the doorway. He gave Maura a quick, surprised look.

"Steve, the first mate?" inquired Maura with a grin.

The man rolled his eyes and grimaced at Patrick.

"Really?"

Patrick laughed and got up.

"We would give you and the kid a lift back, but we've got a small rowboat and that doesn't do you any good." As he left the inn's dining room, he shot Maura a look that was oddly assessing.

Sally suggested they wait until Jim came back with his truck, but it was only four o'clock and Maura said she thought they would just head out now. Lizzie looked like she might sleep in the cart and she was assured that the route was faster over the middle of the island.

Maura spread the beach blanket in the bottom of the cart and Lizzie curled up and closed her eyes. Sally pointed out the path through the nature preserve that would lead them to the town.

"You'll pass the settlement where there are remains of the original colony, then you'll come to a crossroads. Just keep going straight and you'll find yourself in town. Since you've been to the coffee shop, you'll know your green is right beyond that. Come back and visit us!"

The track was packed hard and although bumpy, not difficult to make headway. This end of the island was set up as a nature preserve because of the variety of seabirds that made their nests on the cliff and inland every year. The trees here were stunted from the sea wind, and masses of wildflowers and grasses carpeted the landscape. It was lonely but beautiful, and wisps of romantic stories began to weave themselves in Maura's mind. The further they went inland, the taller and thicker the trees grew. The track went down into a hollow and here the tree branches met overhead, filtering out the sunlight.

A little farther on, they came to a small plaque on the side of the path that marked the site of the original colony. Maura looked at Lizzie and saw that she was fast asleep. She parked the bike under a stand of trees and moved cautiously past the plaque, remembering the stories she had heard. What might have happened that would cause the shipwreck survivors to all die suddenly? A plague? Murder? Food poisoning?

It was very quiet in the clearing where she stood. The National Park Service maintained the area, although Maura doubted many visitors made their way to this lonely spot with no paved access road. Around the clearing were several stone foundations.

Two had chimneys and one had a partial timber wall. A bird cawing interrupted the stillness as it flew across the clearing, startling her. How sad, she thought, that the crew and passengers of The Temperance had survived the shipwreck and made themselves a home here, only to die mysteriously. The loneliness of this abandoned place began to steal over her and just as she was about to turn to leave a sound behind her made her spin with a gasp. Lizzie stood behind her, her hair tousled and her eyes wide.

"Mommy, I don't like it here," she whispered. "Can we go?"

The fact that Lizzie felt it too sent a chill down Maura's spine. They quickly returned to the bike and cart and were on their way. A hundred yards beyond the sad clearing with its ruined houses was a small graveyard. Maura didn't stop to inspect it, but she briefly saw leaning stones, streaked with moss. She wondered whether headstones had been erected for the bones found in the clearing.

Maura was glad when the bumpy track turned to pavement. They passed a small cluster of residences huddled at the edge of the nature preserve. She pedaled through town without stopping and they were soon home.

Lizzie wasn't herself that evening and wouldn't let Maura out of her sight. A warm bubble bath improved her spirits a little. Maura used the chicken and rice from last night's dinner to make chicken soup with onion, carrots and celery. She chopped up a little thyme and threw it in. They had thick slices of toast made from the bread they had baked during the storm and spread it with butter and strawberry jam. By eight o'clock Lizzie was sound asleep.

As Maura was coming down the stairs, there was a knock at the door. She was most definitely not in the mood for visitors, so she tiptoed into the writing room and peeked out the window.

Gracie Fletcher, the woman from the beach who ran the day camp, was standing on the doorstep holding a bottle of wine and staring back at her with a mischievous smile.

"Yes, I see you. I watched you come down the stairs and sneak into that room. You need to get some curtains. Come on, open up."

Maura unlocked the door and held it open, smiling a little sheepishly.

"Sorry. We were out all day on a long bike ride and I was going to read until it was time for bed. All my muscles ache."

"Oh. Well, do you want me to go? I guess I was feeling a little sick of my own company and thought I'd officially welcome you." She waved the bottle of wine. "I think you're the only other woman my age spending the summer on the island without a husband. At least, that's what your neighbor, Mrs. White, said. She's Buster's mother."

Maura laughed.

"No, of course I don't want you to go! Come in and I'll see if I have a snack to go with the wine."

Gracie's dress rustled slightly as they walked through the parlor into the brightly lit kitchen. Maura turned to inspect her outfit with interest. Her visitor was rather petite, and the form-fitting bodice, wide skirt and petticoat of her crisp summer dress showed off her figure nicely. The tangerine and cream stripes, the thin-strapped sandals and perfect makeup would have been appropriate for a luncheon date with friends or shopping on Boston's Newbury Street.

Maura noticed the amused, carefully-shaped eyebrow raised at her.

"Why don't I look like you, Gracie?" She fished around in a drawer for the corkscrew.

"You know all that time that you spend playing with your Lizzie? Making her meals and giving her baths and everything? Well, I spend all that time making my own clothes and playing with make-up and hairstyles. It's how I entertain myself, but I would trade it in a second for what you have."

Maura had been teaching Lizzie to play *Sorry!* and the board and game pieces were still on the coffee table in the little family nook near the big fireplace. She pushed them to one side and set down two wine glasses. Gracie filled them while Maura sliced up a block of cheddar cheese and put it on a plate with some crackers. Her guest's voice held a familiar note as she cheerfully complained about the lack of anything interesting to do on the island.

"Do I detect New Jersey roots?" Maura smiled, sitting down and picking up her wine glass. "That's where I'm from, but I haven't lived there since college." She didn't mention that when she married David, her irascible mother refused to let her back in the house for a year. Mrs. Sullivan was a staunch Catholic and David a non-practicing Protestant. They had been married by a justice of the peace.

Gracie stared at her for a moment.

"Close. New York. Where did you and little Lizzie go today?"

Maura told her about their ride out to see the lighthouse and finding the bag of chess pieces.

"And we met a real-life treasure hunter and his first mate!"

"Let me guess: Patrick-not-Pat, and the droolable Steve?"

Maura laughed. "I didn't get a close enough look at Steve to confirm his drool-worthiness but, yes, it was them! How did you meet them?"

"I was in the coffee shop for breakfast when they came in one day. They were in town getting supplies. Patrick picked a stool at the counter and immediately swung around and started chatting. He's not at all shy, which you probably noticed. I have to say he is really good-looking in a dashing movie star pirate way, but Steve is more my type. He kept looking at me with a little smile but let Patrick do all the talking. I thought one of them might ask me out, but they paid their bill and left. Maybe because I was wearing my wedding ring."

While she was talking, Gracie had been setting up the Sorry! board. "I used to play with my little brothers and sister, but it's been years. You're blue, I'm yellow. You go first." Maura drew a card.

"One! I get to move a piece out." She placed a pawn on the first space.

"Nuts. I got a four."

The play continued.

"So, what are you and Lizzie doing, spending the summer out in the middle of the ocean by yourselves? Yes, I'm just as nosey as everybody else but the difference is, I won't pass it on. It's OK to tell me to mind my own business."

Maura stared at the *Sorry!* board in silence for a minute.

"OK, here it is." She repeated the story she had told Opal about David leaving her. She surprised herself by adding that it hadn't been his first affair, and that he emptied out their meager savings account when he left. "His note said he had given me every opportunity to improve, but his love just couldn't survive, and he owed it to himself to find a better life. Oh, and he told me to go to his parents if the baby or I needed anything. Which was hilarious, because he took all our money and I couldn't even buy food or diapers, let alone pay the rent." She swirled the wine in her glass. "His mother blamed me for her son being a total jerk, but his father was so mad he told his wife she was never allowed to let him in the house again or mention his name. It was quite a scene. Anyway," she was starting to feel embarrassed at sharing this miserable story, "my wealthy friend, Rebecca, came running to the rescue and gave me a job. The family of yet another school friend let me stay in this house for the summer while they fix it up to sell in the fall. Lizzie and I move to an apartment in Marblehead in September where I'll start teaching second grade. Now you know absolutely everything about me, which tells me I should stay away from wine. What is a fashion plate such as yourself doing on Islay? Are you just here for the summer?"

Gracie had listened intently to Maura's story, frowning and turning a *Sorry!* pawn over in her hands. She ignored Maura's question.

"Isn't there a way we can get back at him? People like that shouldn't be allowed to get away with treating women like mud."

Maura was a little touched by the earnestness in her voice. The few people who knew about David commiserated, but this stalwart partisanship from a new acquaintance and the call for revenge were heartening.

"Are you sure you're not from Jersey?" she grinned. Gracie shook her head. "OK, so you haven't told me your story. You don't have to, but if you don't, I'll feel even more embarrassed."

Gracie refilled their wine glasses.

"That's fair. My story isn't very interesting. I was married to my husband, Ernest, for twelve years. He was an accountant and did OK. We wanted children, but it didn't happen. He tried to find ways to make it up to me and when he saw an advertisement for inexpensive, new bungalows that were being built on a pretty little island off the coast of Massachusetts, he bought one as a surprise. He knew how much I love the beach and I'm sure he pictured us having lots of romantic getaways. When he was killed in an accident two years ago, I found that most of our savings had gone to the bungalow. I guess he thought he could easily replenish our account with just the two of us and his decent salary. I already knew he didn't have a life insurance policy; he was superstitious and said it was inviting death. He'd get one when he was older. So," she blew out her breath, "I live here all year round because the bungalow is paid for and I can't afford to live anywhere else. I get a little money from the government, but otherwise I live on what I make from Camp Boogie-Woogie. That dries up over the winter, of course, so I have to put whatever I can away while the families are here." She shot Maura a sidelong look. "How's that?"

"Gosh, Gracie. I'm so sorry." There was more to the story; Maura was sure of it.

Gracie shrugged.

"He was a good man, but he didn't always make the best decisions." She leaned forward and picked a card.

"Fourteen!" She began moving one of her pawns.

"Wait! There is no fourteen. They only go up to twelve! Are you actually cheating?"

Gracie gave her an aggressive glare.

Maura narrowed her eyes and picked a card. Five. If she had a six she would have landed on a square that one of Gracie's pawns occupied, which would have sent Gracie's back to Start.

"I got a six."

"I don't believe you. Let me see it!" Maura sat on the card then moved her pawn six spaces. When she landed next to Gracie's she knocked it so hard it landed in the fireplace.

Gracie let out a shriek of laughter then covered her mouth with both hands and looked at the ceiling. When Lizzie didn't appear after a few moments, they resumed the game.

"You can't slide if it's your own color."

"Go jump in a lake."

They added the red and green sets of pawns. The game became impossibly complicated, with each finding creative ways to cheat. Through a mutual fit of giggles they heard the clock on the parlor mantel chime.

"Holy mackerel, Maura! Is it eleven o'clock?" She stood.

"Did you walk here? It's awfully dark out to be walking home and there was the... you know...Violet Wilson."

"Why did you say it like that?" Gracie was suddenly serious. "Like it wasn't an accident."

Maura hesitated.

"Tell me!"

Maura told her about seeing what appeared to be a bullet hole in the middle of Violet's forehead.

"But the police and the harbormaster said there wasn't one, so I must have been mistaken."

Gracie's eyes were huge and dark. She stared, her mind somewhere else.

"We have a spare room with four beds," said Maura. "I can quickly make one up for you. You should stay."

Gracie shook her head as though to drive away her fear.

"No. Thank you, but I have the kids coming in the morning and I have to be up early to get some stuff ready for them. Lizzie's starting tomorrow, right? Don't worry. I'll be fine!"

Maura stepped outside with Gracie. An old-fashioned women's bicycle with a white basket and a big metal headlight was leaning against the fence.

Gracie switched on the headlight and it lit up the darkness on the road ahead.

"See you in the morning!" She began to push off from the curb.

"Wait! Do you have a phone? Call me when you get home." She repeated her number several times.

"Maura, you're kind of giving me the heebie-jeebies!" But she recited Maura's number back to her, then pedaled off with a wave.

Returning to the house, Maura stayed in the kitchen straightening up and waiting for the phone to ring. She looked at the shambles of their ridiculous board game, and at the pawn still lying in the fireplace. As she washed the wine glasses, she smiled, wondering when she had had such a light-hearted silly time with a friend. It must have been high school. Everything put away, she glanced at the clock. 11:42 p.m. Gracie should have been home by now. To reach the bungalows, she would have ridden downhill to the beach then taken a right on the road that ran steeply uphill a short way to the double strip of bungalows. Gracie had told her that hers was the third one in. In daytime it might have been a ten or fifteen-minute ride. Had she just forgotten Maura's phone number, or forgotten to call altogether? What would Maura do if Gracie never called? If she had fallen off her bike and was lying hurt somewhere? She couldn't leave Lizzie and get on her own bike to go look for her. Call the police station?

When she got to that point the phone rang.

"Hello! Gracie?"

For a moment there was only quick breathing on the other end.

"Maura!"

"Gracie, is everything OK?"

"There was somebody…a man… at the corner of your street and the one that you take down to the beach. He was behind a tree. I saw him step out just as I passed him. I went wide around him then pedaled too fast downhill. I hit a curb and wound up in someone's yard. I got grass stains on my dress!" Annoyance was added to fear in this last sentence.

"Sorry it took me so long to call, but I've gone around my house about three times making sure the doors and windows are locked and nobody's hiding under the bed or in a closet. You should do the same. Why would a man be standing behind a bush on your street this late at night?"

Maura agreed to make sure everything was locked tight and told Gracie to call her if she wanted to during the night. After hanging up, her nerves were a little on edge. There could be a perfectly logical explanation for a man being out at this late hour. Maybe he was a neighbor out for a midnight stroll and cigarette. Did he really step out to accost Gracie? She remembered her guest saying that Maura was giving her the heebie-jeebies and felt badly that she had sent her off in a nervous state of mind. Nonetheless, she carefully went around the bottom floor, checking all the windows and doors. Leaving a parlor table lamp on, she went upstairs. It had been an odd day. She remembered the eerie stillness of the clearing in the old settlement, the stone foundations and the chimneys around which people had once huddled for warmth and cooked their food, then something evil had overtaken them. Maura paused as she was brushing her teeth. The wisps of stories that began to weave themselves in her mind earlier that day were becoming more solid.

Chapter 8

On Tuesday morning they set out on the path through the woods at the back of the property. Where the path split, the left fork being the route they normally took to the beach, they went to the right. This brought them to the backyard of the house next to Gracie's, in the rear row of bungalows. This row looked across the street to the first row which sat atop a small cliff overlooking the beach below, giving those homes a spectacular ocean view.

Lizzie stood shyly behind Maura when Gracie opened the door. The other children were already there, sitting at two little tables placed on a big bedsheet. The reason for the sheet was soon apparent, as bits of muffin fell to the floor. Gracie's little house was immaculately neat. Two small white sofas were on either side of a cherry coffee table. Curtain rods lay across the seats, effectively blocking anyone from climbing on them. Silvery-gray carpeting covered the floor and a few modern framed prints hung on the walls. It was not at all the sort of room you would expect a day camp to be run from, thought Maura.

"Lizzie! You're just in time. *Challenge of the Yukon* is on." Gracie, in a white piqué sundress, red lipstick and sandals in the same shade waved in her new charge.

"Is it about a cat?"

"No, it's about a guy called a Mountie and his dog." The other children, ranging in age from four to seven, listened intently to the radio although Maura guessed that only the oldest had any idea what the story was about.

"Here, kid." Gracie put a paper plate with a blueberry muffin on it at the place next to Midge. Lizzie's eyes lit up, whether from the muffin or her new friend wasn't clear.

"Here, Maura. Don't go yet." She pulled her into the tiny kitchen where she set two more muffins on a plate. Maura looked around with envy. Like the rest of the bungalow, and its owner, the kitchen was diminutive and neat. The cabinets were painted a glossy aquamarine, very much in style, but when Gracie opened one of them to get napkins Maura saw the insides were cranberry red. There was just room for a table with chrome accents and chrome chairs with padded seats in cranberry. The floor, covered in a fashionable gray-speckled linoleum, looked like it was just waxed and buffed.

"This place is adorable," Maura said sadly. It was the kind of cozy home that she had always envisioned for herself and Lizzie. After the summer they would be living in the upstairs apartment of an old house in Marblehead. The landlord and her husband seemed nice, but it wasn't the same as having their own place.

"Oh, stop it." Gracie waved away Maura's envy. "Listen, sorry if I scared you last night. I'm not used to drinking more than a glass of wine. The man behind the bush really scared me. He might have had a reason for standing there, but it was very weird. So, anyway... I had fun last night. Don't think I'm crazy."

Maura laughed and told her about her visit to the clearing in the abandoned settlement.

"I'm not kidding when I say the hair on my arms stood on end. And then Lizzie creeps up behind me and whispers in a spooky voice that she wants to leave because she didn't like it there."

Gracie shuddered.

"You wouldn't get me out there. Patrick-not-Pat said a lot of people think it's haunted, and that's why nobody goes there."

"Miss Gracie!" called the oldest boy. "The show's over."

Maura gave Lizzie a hug and promised to bring her home for lunch. She felt a little pang when Lizzie merely smiled and turned back to Midge, unconcerned that her mother was leaving. She was, after all, so accustomed to being left in the care of others at the institute while Maura worked.

The power was off at the house when she got back. The electrician assured her that he and his assistant would be done in an hour and the food in the refrigerator should be fine. Maura, with her first morning to herself since Lizzie was born, went to the writing room and put a sheet of paper in her typewriter. The story that had started to take shape during their island ramble yesterday needed to be put on paper. Her plan was to just tap out the story bits that were popping into her head with increasing frequency, each new bit, she hoped, encouraging more.

She typed:

The Island Witch

With her hands paused over the keyboard, she stared at the three words. If anyone saw them on a book cover, they might assume it was about some place in the Caribbean and would possibly expect voodoo. She pulled out the sheet of paper and crumpled it into a ball.

The Witch of Islay

She liked this better but scribbled a list of other potential titles on a sheet of typing paper. Realizing she had wasted twenty minutes on the name of the book, Maura decided to make a story outline. It was at this point it occurred to her that she knew almost nothing about the island lore. She wanted to write this story from the witch's point of view, but she would have to do some research first.

Maura wondered what Lizzie was doing and if she was having a good time. The house seemed unnaturally empty without her. Feeling a little lonely, she put a notebook and pen in her bicycle's basket and rode to the coffee shop. There was an open booth near the kitchen; she sat down with her back to it and breathed in the lovely scents of yeast bread and cinnamon baking.

When the middle-aged waitress took her order and brought a cup of coffee, Maura asked her where she might find out more about the island's history. The waitress tapped her cheek with her pencil.

"Well...there's a historical society of sorts. But it was run by a woman who died last week. I'm not sure when it will reopen." From what she had learned about Violet Wilson, Maura wasn't surprised that she ran the historical society. She seemed to have been in the middle of anything of interest on the island.

"Wally lives here year-round; maybe he can answer your questions. He owns this place. I'll ask him to stop over here when he's got a minute."

Maura put her notebook and pen on the table, feeling slightly ridiculous, and took a sip of her fragrant coffee. A few minutes later, a large piece of warm coffee cake was set in front of her. She looked up to see a man in his late sixties with thinning gray hair and a mustache.

"Shirl said you had a question?" His smile was engaging and the eyes that looked at her from under bushy brows showed friendly interest.

"Oh. Yes! I'm..." She started to say that she was writing a book, but her face turned red and she couldn't get the words out. She felt like a fraud; throwing some ideas out on paper was not writing a book. "I'm doing some research on the island." Please don't ask me what for, she thought.

"Is that right? What do you want to know?" He slid onto the bench on the other side of her booth. "Shirl! Can you bring me a coffee and warm up this young lady's?" He leaned his arms on the table. "OK, shoot!"

'OK, well... what do you know about the original colony?"

"The guys who were shipwrecked? Well, I think they lived here for about five or ten years, then something happened. Much later, a ship stopped at the island for repairs and they found a bunch of skeletons and one crazy old guy."

This was pretty much what Maura already knew. She took a bite of coffee cake. It was buttery and moist, with a thin layer of peaches topped with streusel.

"Oh! This is as good as the coconut cake and the lemon chiffon!" She took another bite.

Wally grinned.

"I know! The guy is a genius. He throws some stuff in a bowl and magical things happen. It's why I put up with him. He's quite a weirdo."

"I heard that!" a voice called from the kitchen. From Wally's smile and the cordial tone of the voice in the kitchen, Maura assumed this was a long-standing gag. She grinned.

"Listen," said Wally, "I don't really know much about this stuff. There are pamphlets in the Islay Historical Society office, which is a locked room in the back of the library. Violet Wilson had the key and you might have heard she's, er, no longer with us. I don't think they were much better than tourist brochures though."

Just then the door to the coffee shop opened.

"Here's a guy who might be able to help you. Hey, Patrick!"

Maura stifled a feeling of annoyance as the treasure hunter made his way over to their booth. She wasn't sure what she thought about Patrick Dunn. She and Lizzie had been hot, thirsty and a little out of sorts when he sat down at their table uninvited the other day. She hadn't been particularly impressed with his engaging smile or his seeming interest. Both were at odds with what she felt was a rather intense scrutiny.

"What's your favorite dessert?" Wally stood and pointed his finger at her.

"Oh... chocolate layer cake with a scoop of ice cream!"

"You got it," called the voice in the kitchen. "Come Friday for lunch."

"Thank you!" she called back, with a laugh.

Wally briefly explained that Maura was doing some island research and he thought maybe Patrick could help.

Patrick, who had been staring over her shoulder with a slight frown, shifted his attention and said that he would be happy to assist if he could. He continued to stand after Wally left to ring up a couple at the cash register.

"I don't want to delay you if you need to be somewhere." Maura was slightly embarrassed.

"Not at all. It's my week to buy food and supplies for the boat. I was just heading over to the market." He continued to stand.

"Won't you sit down?"

He lowered himself, rather gracefully thought Maura, onto the bench and looked at her expectantly. He seemed different today, a little more reserved, although not unfriendly. She liked this Patrick better. He was rather good-looking, she observed. Although his clothes and bronzed skin were consistent with someone who spent a great deal of time on the open water, the quality and style of the clothes and his neat haircut were very much 1954.

'What would you like to know?" he asked. "I'll see if I can answer. Thanks, Shirl!" The waitress had set a cup of coffee in front of him. Apparently he was a regular here, Maura thought, and no wonder. The coffee and dessert alone were enough to make her keep coming back.

She began asking general questions about the island, when the next wave of inhabitants arrived after the bodies of the original colonists were discovered, whether many people lived on the island year-round. While Patrick didn't seem to have much information about present day Islay, he was surprisingly well-informed about its history.

He laughed when she mentioned this.

"Don't forget, I search shipwrecks for historical artifacts. History has always been a passion with me. My parents got tired of taking me to museums when I was a kid. When I reached my teens I began scuba diving around wrecks just to look at them, then started finding bits of things lying around. I would bring them to museums and actually made a couple of good sales before I got in trouble for disregarding laws for marine salvage. I was young so got off with a stern lecture. By then I was thoroughly hooked on exploring wrecks, both for the history and the possibility of making good money. When I heard about all the shipwrecks in this area I did a some research at the Boston Public Library, grabbed my friend, Steve –"

"Your first mate, Steve," Maura murmured with a mischievous smile.

"My first mate, Steve," Patrick grinned, "and we set up shop. I spent some time with Violet Wilson who ran the island's historical society. They have a few interesting artifacts; if they open again, I'll give you a tour."

"Did your research turn up anything about how the colonists died? I have to say, the clearing in the settlement gave me the creeps!"

"You stopped there?" Patrick raised his eyebrows in surprise. "It's got a reputation that keeps most people away."

"It was fascinating, in a way. Sad, and so still. Then a black bird suddenly streaked across the clearing, cawing right over my head. I couldn't get out of there fast enough!"

Patrick leaned forward with an arrested look.

"Odd," he murmured. "The same thing happened to me there."

Maura felt a tiny shiver run up her spine and gave an uncertain laugh. Patrick stared at her but she didn't think he saw her. He shook his head suddenly and smiled a little.

"Sorry. One of the hazards of being a history buff is that it takes hold of your imagination and won't let go." He grinned suddenly. "Want to hear why the island is named Islay?"

"I just assumed some of the crew or passengers were homesick and named it for wherever they were from."

"Scotland. Islay is an island off the west coast, famous for its whiskey. When Steve and I first came to the island last year, we spent a day at the settlement exploring the ruins. We were careful not to disturb anything, but we did find an empty whiskey bottle inside the flue of a chimney. We looked around and found the remains of empty casks here and there. Quarter casks, to be more exact. They were made to hang on either side of a saddle. Where do you think the whiskey was from?"

"Islay!" Maura laughed. "They named the island after their whiskey! Which is particularly fascinating when you consider that the passengers were part of a strict religious sect."

"And that their ship was named the *Temperance*! The whiskey must have floated in with them from the shipwreck. People may have grabbed onto the small casks to keep from drowning."

They both sat for a moment, picturing this scene.

"So, where are you from?" Patrick asked, startling Maura a little by the sudden change of topic. "Are you just here for the summer?"

"Yes, until September," she said shortly. She wasn't sure why she hesitated in giving Patrick any information about herself when she had been open with Gracie and Opal.

"You couldn't have picked a more beautiful vacation spot. Where are you from?" he asked again. "I think I'm picking up a slight Jersey accent."

She smiled a little reluctantly. "New Jersey originally, Boston most recently."

"Whereabouts in Jersey? I have friends there." He seemed to be settling in for a lets-get-to-know-each-other conversation. Maura, suddenly noticing the time, thanked him for his information on the island and said she had to run to pick up her daughter.

"Would you like to meet for a drink some evening? Dinner?"

"Oh," she said awkwardly. "I can't. I have Lizzie. But thank you!" She put money on the table and hurried outside to her bicycle.

"I still don't know your name!" he called, following her out the door. She smiled and waved as she pedaled off.

The next morning, Maura stopped at the post office to check for mail. There were several people in line ahead of her, held up by an elderly woman who was trying to send a package that was improperly wrapped.

The woman in front of Maura leaned forward and said, "Well, hello Mrs. Weinstein!"

Mrs. Weinstein turned around and smiled politely. "Oh, hello Mrs. McCarthy."

"Did Dr. Weinstein figure out why Violet drowned? Had she been drinking?" Mrs. McCarthy whispered the second question.

Maura listened intently. She recalled that the doctor who had examined Opal's knee was named Weinstein. His wife was tall and slim, her blue linen dress and short curls conservatively fashionable. She hesitated, apparently reluctant to engage in gossip.

"No," said Mrs. Weinstein reluctantly. "My husband didn't examine her. She was taken away quite quickly. I suppose the authorities on the mainland took care of it." She had a slightly troubled frown.

"There's something evil afoot on this island!" The rough voice behind Maura made her jump. She turned to see an older man in work clothes, his face a network of lines and his bulbous nose sporting odd growths.

"First Bob Welch, then the Wilson woman. And we know who's behind it!" He thrust out his chin.

Mrs. McCarthy stared with bright-eyed interest. The doctor's wife regarded him with thinly-`veiled disgust.

"You should make an appointment with my husband to have him look at your nose."

She turned to face front, murmuring "Absurd!"

Maura made a mental note to ask her neighbor, Lillian, about Bob Welch.

When she finally reached the front counter, she handed the clerk the form she had filled out for mail delivery for the summer. In exchange she was given a letter and a package, both from Rebecca.

She waited to open the package until she had retrieved Lizzie from day camp. It contained several little sun dresses and a four-year-old-sized bathing suit. These were ruthlessly tossed aside when a Betsy McCall doll was found underneath. Lizzie was in raptures. Maura looked at the doll's neat hair, red like Lizzie's but without the little girl's wild curls and thought that it would never look like that again. There were five packaged outfits for the doll and a tiny, exquisitely handmade ballgown. It was in ice blue satin, with layers of petticoats, ribbons and lace. Rebecca had included a note with the package:

I know that in the hands of a four-year-old the doll will be unrecognizable within a week. I hope that she puts your lipstick on it, combs the hair into a rat's nest and loses its shoes. Presents from Auntie Bec are meant to be thoroughly enjoyed and not put on a shelf.

Do you remember Lucia from the gallery? Before she was married, she made a living as a seamstress. She now has three boys, and when she knew I was sending the doll she dropped everything to create that lovely ballgown. She said to tell you that she had a wonderful time making it and not to worry if it's destroyed. She'll make more.

Maura opened the letter next. Rebecca had sent it the day after coming to the agreement with Will's family to become a partner in the renovation.

This will probably make things harder for you because there will be even more workmen coming and going, but I just couldn't let them fix a wire or two, slap some paint on the walls and sell the house to someone who won't love it as much as it deserves. It was like a stray kitten calling out to me. I'm sending my renovation team to Islay soon. You'll like Leo and can trust his judgement. He'll be contracting out a lot of the work, but he'll stop in every few weeks to check on things. Will promised to finish converting the carriage house to a guest cottage and to do some of the other jobs. He'll be there most weekends and will call Leo if any of the work doesn't meet his approval.

At six o'clock Maura poured herself a glass of chablis and nonchalantly wandered over to the opening in the shrubbery between the Watts house and the Greek Revival. She held pruning sheers and snipped a leaf here and there until Lillian spotted her and came out with a glass of sherry.

"Finally," grinned Maura. "It's hard to prune roses with a wine glass in one hand."

Lillian smiled. The late afternoon sun glinted on her silvery-white hair. She looked rather elegant in a cream-colored blouse with ruffles running around a deep V neckline. A large amethyst pendant lay against her tanned skin.

"You could just come knock on my door or scream my name if you want to chat. Or here's this, we have a phone."

"What fun would that be? Hey, Lillian. Who was Bob Welch?"

Her neighbor looked startled.

"Bob! What made you ask about him?"

Maura checked to make sure Lizzie was still at the picnic table, a basin of warm water and dishwashing liquid soap bubbles in front of her. She was washing all the new doll clothes, except the ballgown which Maura rescued in time. Her stuffed panda lay on the table in a soapy, sodden lump. Maura lowered her voice.

"I was in the post office today. An old man with bumps on his nose said that evil things are happening on the island and he knows who's responsible. First Bob Welch, now Violet Wilson."

"Basker Beeks. Howard hired him to do our yard once and he muttered to himself the whole time."

"Lillian, what happened to Bob Welch?"

"Well... he and Howard were kind of friends. Now and then Bob would come here to play cards with Howard, and sometimes Howard would walk down to his bungalow. Other than that, and an occasional bike ride to the bar down by the harbor, Bob pretty much kept to himself. Then one day we noticed we hadn't seen him in a while. All his stuff was still at the bungalow – he was renting and the owner let the police in – but no sign of Bob. This was about the end of October, right before we closed up the house for the winter. When we came back this spring, we found out that Bob hadn't been seen since, and his stuff is still here."

Maura looked back at Lizzie. The doll clothes, still full of soapy water, were laid out on the picnic table to dry. The doll was about to be plunged headfirst into the water for a bath.

"Sweetie, don't get the doll's hair wet!" Maura grimaced.

She turned back to her neighbor.

"Lillian, how well do you know Opal Hansen?" She kept her voice low.

"Opal? Not well. She was here when we bought the house. Back then she would sometimes walk to town and do her shopping and we would exchange a greeting. She's never been unfriendly, but she's not particularly friendly either. She's really let herself go since I first met her, and that house! It's an eyesore."

Maura relayed Dr. Weinstein's account of overhearing a few members of the crew from a fishing boat blaming Violet Wilson's death on the island witch, and that he seemed to think they might have been referring to Opal.

Lillian was startled.

"Why would he think it was Opal?"

"You know the story of a pile of skeletons found in the settlement clearing? Legend has it that a witch and a curse were involved, and her house was somewhere on Opal's property. It's long gone."

"That's pretty far-fetched." Lillian snorted. "Opal's been here about a dozen years. What, they think the witch's spirit is suddenly taking over Opal and making her kill boring old men and over-sexed middle-aged women?"

"Violet was over-sexed?" Maura grinned.

Lillian leaned in.

"Well, I'd say she was about fifty but she had this, well, this very rounded hiney. Like a pumpkin. When she walked, she would sway it slowly from side to side. Especially if there were men in the room. She wore tight pencil skirts so you could get the full effect. The funny thing was that she wasn't pretty, by a long shot. She had a face like a frog. Huge mouth and pale blue buggy eyes. Her hair was mousy brown, but she went to the hairdresser regularly to keep up her Deborah Kerr hairdo. At parties she would say something arch, if you know what I mean, to one of the gentlemen over her shoulder. She'd slowly close and open her eyes with a coy smile, then walk away with that hiney wiggle. It was like she practiced at home. The women rolled their eyes but didn't take her seriously. She was so homely, and she dished it out to all the men no matter how old they were. I think the husbands didn't know what to make of her act. She embarrassed the hell out of Howard one evening. But that was her party self; she was much more businesslike on her committees. And she was pretty smart and fun to talk to when it was just the girls."

"Do you think one of the husbands might have taken Violet up on an offer and the wife got mad?"

"If you mean me, it wouldn't have been worth the effort. If another woman makes Howard happy, it takes the pressure off me."

The thought of Lillian shooting Violet Wilson in the head while holding a sherry glass in the other hand made her smile.

"Seriously, though. Do you think there could be an irate wife?"

"I think it's more likely that she'd put somebody's nose out of joint on a committee. She could be a little bossy."

"Lil! I'm hungry!"

Lillian looked over her shoulder and made a face.

"It's feeding time. Let me know if you hear anything else about Violet and I'll do the same. Tell Opal to watch out for herself. And to trim those bushes!"

CHAPTER 9

Workmen appeared at the door every morning that week and spent the days banging, yelling to each other and knocking into furniture. Maura kept a pitcher of iced tea in the refrigerator for them and made sure the cookie jar was filled. She was trying to build out the story line for *The Witch of Islay* but the racket made it impossible to focus. She finally made her way to the attic. It was stuffy and had only the barest furnishings, but after opening the small windows at either end of the room, a fresh cross-breeze swept away the mustiness. She placed her typewriter on a small table under the window and closed the door at the bottom of the attic stairs.

Although the sounds of a powder room under construction could still be faintly heard, the soft summer breeze and the drone of a bumble bee drained the tension from her. She wrote a little vignette about neighbors who gossiped through a portal of roses, then, feeling brave, made a start on the island witch's ill-fated sea voyage to Islay.

After becoming lost in her story, Maura arrived late for after-camp pick-up. Lizzie, wearing a cherry-red satin gown and matching lipstick that clashed with her fiery curls, greeted her with a huge smile.

"Don't worry about it," Gracie waved away her apologies. "We've had fun dressing up. My little sister is much younger than me and I miss those days."

"Is today Chocolate Cake Day, Mommy?" asked Lizzie, reminding Maura that the baker at the coffee shop had promised to have her favorite dessert if she came for lunch today. Gracie accepted her invitation to join them, and they took the path through the woods to the Watts house. Lizzie and Gracie climbed into the cart behind the bicycle and Maura pedaled the short distance into town.

They settled in a booth and Gracie looked around brightly.

"Don't look," she whispered, "but Patrick-not-Pat and Droolable Steve are at a table by the kitchen."

"You really need a better name than Droolable Steve."

Shirl came by to take their orders.

"A couple of boys over there sure perked up when you three came in. They've been here for an hour and a half, watching the door. The blonde one, Steve, he must've drunk a whole pot of coffee by himself. The other one's been chain smoking. As soon as you girls walked in they sat up straight and tried to look like they weren't interested." She half turned to take a look at them and smirked. "Oh well, what a surprise! They're finally done with lunch and heading this way."

A few moments later the men strolled by their table on their way to the cash register.

"Hello, ladies!" Patrick said casually, then did a double-take when he saw the little kid wearing red lipstick.

Steve murmured a greeting and smiled generally at the table. Up close, Maura could see that he wasn't as young as she first supposed. His features were boyish but there were lines at the corners of his eyes. When Gracie flashed him a smile, he turned red. Interesting, thought Maura.

"How's the treasure business?" she asked.

"It's a little slow at the moment, but we had one success this week." Smiling, Patrick reached into his pocket and pulled out a wad of dollar bills. These he placed in front of a startled Lizzie.

"A small museum in Rockport bought your chess pieces. Twelve dollars!"

In single bills, twelve dollars looks like quite a bit of money to a four-year-old. It was more than Maura would have expected for the lumpish bits of ivory. Lizzie had never had money of her own and now appeared to be regarding the treasure hunter in a new light. Patrick, quick to follow up his advantage, suggested that the three of them join Steve and himself for an afternoon on their boat this weekend.

"Would you like that?" he asked Lizzie directly. She smiled and nodded.

"What do you think, Maura?" Gracie hadn't noticed her frown. "It wouldn't hurt to get away from your workmen for a few hours!"

"Aha! Maura!" Patrick laughed. "Your secret is out."

Maura, who still hadn't told him her name, capitulated.

"Maura Gertz. Pleased to meet you."

Steve cleared his throat.

"Your husbands are welcome, of course." He blushed after speaking, probably realizing that this was an obvious attempt to discover where there were husbands in the picture. Maura noticed that his voice had a pleasant timbre.

"My husband passed away a few years ago," Gracie said quietly.

"I suppose Lizzie and I can join you," Maura said, answering the original question. "We have company coming for the weekend; maybe one day next week?" The company was only Will, but she thought she should stick around while he was working in case he needed anything.

They settled on Tuesday after camp and the men left.

"Do we have dates?" Gracie asked with a grin.

Maura rolled her eyes. The nature of Steve's interest in Gracie was made clear by his blush and admiring gaze. Why Patrick invited Maura and Lizzie on the outing was less clear. She didn't fool herself into thinking that her looks were superior to those of several younger women whose eyes followed him out of the coffee shop. He didn't seem at all the type that would want to spend an afternoon with a young child. And yet Maura clearly sensed Patrick's interest in her...she just didn't know what it was all about.

The promised chocolate layer cake was still warm, and the melting rivulets of vanilla ice cream made swirling puddles on the plate. The icing was thick and fudgy. As they were leaving, Maura called into the kitchen.

"Thank you for the cake. It was fabulous!"

"You're welcome!"

Chapter 10

Will arrived in the island taxi Saturday morning, accompanied by a pleasant looking man in his late forties. The reason for the taxi was apparent when the driver opened the trunk and extracted several boxes and stacked them on the sidewalk. Will held another box in his arms, this one with holes punched in it. An outraged wail was coming from it.

Lizzie stood in the doorway with Maura, her eyes fixed on Will's box. Maura grimaced as she remembered Will's promise to keep an eye out for a cat. He carried the animated box in first and set it on the rug in the parlor. His companion followed him inside carrying the other boxes, and after putting them down, offered Maura his hand.

"Mrs. Gertz? I'm Leo Conti, Mrs. Savard's contractor." His handshake was firm and his smile friendly. Maura knew that Rebecca had a high opinion of him.

Lizzie continued to stare at the box from which high-pitched meows emanated.

"What's in the box, Mr. Giant?" she whispered when Will set the last carton down.

"Well," he responded as he lowered himself to the floor next to her. He pulled a pen knife from his pocket and began to cut the packaging tape that sealed the box. "I was walking through a field yesterday when I met a princess. An ogre was trying to steal her picnic basket. 'Hey!' I yelled. "You go away!' Well, I was bigger than him because I'm a giant, so he got scared and ran away. The princess was so happy, she said I could have one wish." Will paused in opening the carton so he could finish his tale. "I thought about it for a minute, then I said, 'I would like a cat named Jelly Bean for my friend!' And guess what?"

He dramatically ripped the rest of the tape off the box and opened the flaps. They caught a glimpse of an outraged face with laid-back ears and wild eyes before the cat disappeared into the kitchen in a blur of black and white.

"Jelly Bean!" Lizzie shrieked, chasing after it. Moments later Jelly Bean, unable to find refuge in the kitchen, raced through the parlor and up the stairs. Maura caught Lizzie as she tried to follow and was eventually able to convince her that Jelly Bean needed a little time to get used to his new home. She suggested they all go into the kitchen and try the cinnamon buns she made that morning.

Lizzie stayed behind in the parlor, looking through Will's boxes for the cat supplies he said she would find.

"Jelly Bean was moving too fast for me to get a good look, but it seems to be an Extra Large in the kitty department."

"Yes, he's a big boy. Our secretary says he's part Maine Coon. She had a cocktail party Thursday night and he was lying under the dining table where all the food was spread out, waiting for people to drop canapes. Right now he's suffering the aftereffects of a long ferry ride in a box, but he seemed pretty friendly at the party. As soon as I saw him I knew he would be the perfect Jelly Bean – you'll see why when you get a good look."

"How did you get the secretary to part with him?"

"I could see that her husband loathed him. They were both very relieved when I made them an offer."

Maura stiffened.

"Why? What's wrong with him?"

"Nothing, at least so they said. He's just a big cat for a city apartment. He can't go out so they have to deal with mountains of cat fur, an ever-full litter box and occasional cat vomit. You can just let him out here so he should be easy."

Maura gaped at him.

"Easy! We're only here for the summer! In September we'll be in a little second floor apartment on a busy street. What then?"

Will obviously hadn't thought that far.

"Oh, right. Well, I told Lanie and her husband that you would take him on trial. If it doesn't work out, I'll bring him back."

"They better have room for a four-year-old redhead too. She'll never part with him."

"Have you ever had a cat before?"

"I never had a pet before!" Maura regretted the words when she saw Will's stare. It was true that she had always wanted a pet, but her mother had refused. She said she had a hard enough time feeding her children; she didn't need to be wasting money on a pet.

Leo Conti had been listening to this exchange with interest.

"Things have a way of working out," was his contribution. Maura looked at him with a grimace. He seemed like a person for whom things tended to work out. It wasn't her experience.

While Maura made coffee and put the buns on a plate, Leo filled them in on Rebecca's plans. With the expensive plumbing and electrical winding down, her investment would go to extensive cosmetic upgrades and an updated kitchen.

"This is a beautiful little house," said Leo, "and I think we can restore its youth in the time we have. My team buys items from old houses that are being torn down or updated, so we likely have a door from the right period. We'll get rid of the shutters altogether and paint the frames around the windows white. I'll have a small team start this week."

While Leo went over the house making notes, Will brought his cartons out to the carriage house and Maura went in search of her daughter and the cat. She found them in Lizzie's bedroom where Jelly Bean had retreated under the bed. They set up the litter box in a corner and put down bowls of water and the cat food that Will had brought. They lay down on Lizzie's bed and waited for nature to overcome Jelly Bean's fear, and both soon fell asleep. Maura was awakened by the sound of someone clearing his throat. She opened an eye and saw Will and Leo in the doorway of Lizzie's room.

"Leo has some business to do in town before he catches the ferry," Will whispered. Maura glanced at Lizzie, who was still sound asleep. There was no sign of the cat. Maura stood and yawned.

"Sorry," she smiled. "I was up late last night." She had intended to put some work in on *The Witch of Islay* but she picked up a dog-eared copy of *Jane Eyre* that she found on a shelf and didn't head upstairs until one o'clock in the morning. Unable to sleep, she stood for several minutes in her darkened room, gazing out at a green that was awash in moonlight. All was perfectly still. She drifted to the window that looked out at the Uncle Irvin house and noticed with interest that there was a faint glow at the back of the house which meant Opal had a kitchen light on. A shape suddenly detached itself from the shadow of the wall on Maura's side and moved quickly around the corner of the Watts house, disappearing from her view. She darted to the front window but was unable to see the area directly in front of the house. She dashed down the stairs, taking care not to wake up Lizzie, and peeked around the curtains in the front parlor window. Nothing. Maura felt a frisson of fear. Was the shadowy figure lurking outside her door? She continued to scan the green and the street, until she saw a figure pass in front of a stoop light at the far end of the green. Whether it was heading into town or to the harbor area, she didn't know. It was some time before she was able to fall asleep.

On the way downstairs with Will and Leo, Maura said over her shoulder, "We can't get your cat to come out from under Lizzie's bed."

"He's my cat, is he?" Will grinned. "He was eating when we looked into the room. When he saw us, he froze with his eyes bugging out. A piece of kibble dramatically fell from his mouth, then he high-tailed it back under the bed. I think it must be you, Leo. I fed him lobster patties at the cocktail party where we met and he loves me."

Leo ran through the notes he made during his house inspection. Maura was impressed with his thoroughness; many of his recommendations dealt with replacing hardware, fixtures and other items with versions from the period that the house was built, or with quality reproductions. The patio needed to be pulled up and replaced and the kitchen would get new appliances and flooring. Many of the window screens were missing and the rest needed to be replaced. Will asked a number of well-informed questions regarding the structure. Maura hadn't yet seen the professional side of Will and was a little impressed.

Will and Maura walked Leo outside to await the taxi. The contractor looked up at the decaying pile next door and grinned.

"That's a great house!" he said admiringly.

"What?" Maura and Will said at the same time.

"Sure, it's run down. But think what it could look like. Is it abandoned?"

Maura suppressed a smile.

"No. My neighbor, Mrs. Hansen, lives here year-round."

Leo rubbed his chin and stare at the house appraisingly. "It could make a great inn, if the neighborhood is zoned that way. I mean, sure, it will always look ridiculous but people love that stuff for getaways. I hear there isn't much on the island in the way of vacation rentals. Did Mrs. Savard see it?"

Remembering Rebecca's statement that it was a house of bed-wetting nightmares, Maura couldn't help but laugh.

"Yes, she saw it!"

After the taxi pulled away, Will said he was heading out to the carriage house to do some work. When Maura happened to look out the kitchen window, she saw him squatting next to the little garden that ran along the wall between the Watts house and Opal's. He held two paper cups that he must have brought with him from Boston, and he was now digging a hole for the young plants the cups contained.

She crept up behind him and said, "New beanstalks?"

He jumped at the sound of her voice and gave her an answering grin.

"I brought them in case there weren't any surviving sprouts from the seeds." he whispered. "And if there were, I was going to replace them so they would be magically bigger!"

Maura was surprised to feel a stinging in her eyes. The thoughtfulness shown by his bringing Lizzie a cat and magic bean plants reminded her what a sweet boy Will had been in school.

"They started to come up," she told him, "but Lizzie watered them with the hose and they went flying about halfway down the yard. You were right about the water pressure."

Lizzie chose that moment to open the screen door. Will hastily threw the paper cups over the wall into Opal's yard.

"Jelly Bean won't come out!" she pouted as she wandered over. "He's still under my bed." When she caught sight of the new plants her eyes grew round.

"My beanstalks! They came back!"

The giant suggested that the beanstalks might like to be watered from a watering can from now on. They couldn't find one, so Lizzie got some of her money from the chess set and she and Maura set off with the bicycle and cart for the Island 5 & 10. When they arrived back at the house, Will had assembled four simple walls from the planks that had been piled on the patio and they now lay flat on the grass. While Maura put the groceries away and made lunch, Will hammered together a rough platform for an outdoor shower. She came outside and held walls in place while he hammered and installed brackets.

They took a break for lunch and had sandwiches and lemonade in the cool kitchen. Lizzie disappeared upstairs with scraps of turkey to entice Jelly Bean out from under her bed.

"What's the rush on the shower?" Maura asked.

"Well, the plumbing isn't hooked up in the carriage house yet. If I'm going to stay here on weekends, I'll need a place to clean up. The outdoor shower is all ready to go – it just needs the enclosure and a drainage trench."

Maura stared.

"This is your family's house! Why don't you use the shower upstairs? You're already using the new powder room." Maura and Will had arranged that he would use his key to let himself in to use the bathroom as the need arose, knocking on the door and yelling "hello!"

"No, no. This is your home for the summer. Yours and Lizzie's. Anyway," he said, changing the subject, "I should be able to get part of the drainage system in tonight and finish in the morning. We're going to send it through a pipe to the end of the garden. You'll like having an outdoor shower when you come back from the beach. You and Cat Girl can wash all the sand off before going in the house. Aunt May always wanted one but for some reason they never put one in. She was always cleaning sand out of the bathtub."

"It will be wonderful to have an outdoor shower. I'm making meatloaf for dinner. You're eating with us, right?"

"Well... I figured I'd head down to the tavern by the dock and get something to eat there."

"Oh! I just assumed you would eat with us while you were here – we always have too much left over – but I'm sure the tavern is more fun." She suddenly felt embarrassed, wondering if he wanted to avoid any implication of intimacy. He was engaged to be married after all, and here she was treating him as though he was on a personal visit. The truth was that he was sliding comfortably into Maura and Lizzie's summer on Islay; their old friendship, Will's easy, good nature and his pending marriage removed any of the awkwardness she might have felt with another man staying on the premises.

"It isn't much fun, actually," Will responded. "I've eaten there most of the nights I've stayed here since my aunt started this project and there's usually at least one fight every night."

Having settled that Will would have dinner with Maura and Lizzie, he went back outside to work on his project. Maura did some household chores then headed to the writing room to get a little work done on her first chapter of the island witch book. She had typed a paragraph when a long paper-wrapped rolled carpet was delivered along with a little table for Lizzie and two chairs. Lizzie came hopping down the stairs as Maura was unrolling the rug in the writing room. It was just the right size, filling most of the room but leaving a glimpse of the old floorboards around the perimeter.

Lizzie cried out with excitement when she saw the little table and chairs.

"Look what Auntie Bec sent us!" Maura felt like her list of things she was obliged to Auntie Bec for was becoming alarmingly long. The note accompanying the delivery read, "Don't get mad - the rug isn't for you. It's to impress prospective buyers in the fall. But you might as well enjoy it!" There was no explanation in the note for sending Lizzie the table and chairs. While Rebecca was usually careful to respect Maura's ban on gifts and money from her friend, Auntie Bec didn't consider that her beloved Lizzie was part of that restriction.

Over the next few hours, Maura wrote and rewrote a few pages of the island witch story. She finally gave it up in disgust and settled happily in her desk chair with *Jane Eyre*. Lizzie, who had retrieved crayons and paper from her room, spent the time alternately coloring on her new table, running up upstairs to check on Jelly Bean and lying on the new carpet, pretending to make snow angels. When they went into the kitchen to start dinner her hair was zapping with static electricity.

Maura had just laid a platter of meatloaf and bowls of mashed potatoes and green beans on the table when Will came in the back door with a bottle of red wine. He sniffed the air appreciatively.

"It smells incredible in here! I ran into town a little while ago to get this bottle of red wine since you said we were having meatloaf." As he applied the corkscrew, he eyed Lizzie's halo of static hair waving in the warmth of the kitchen. She gave him a sunny smile, which made him laugh.

"Snow angels on a new rug from Bec," Maura explained.

Lizzie took up most of Will's attention during dinner with demands for Lizzie and the Giant stories. The ease with which he rolled off these silly tales with no apparent forethought made Maura the Writer a little jealous.

"And since they didn't have a Christmas tree, Lizzie wrapped Christmas lights around the giant and plugged him in. She hung candy canes from his ears and put a big ball of tinsel on his head."

It was still light when they finished eating. Will dried the dishes that Maura washed then headed out back to put away his tools. As she put the last dish in the cabinet, there was a knock on the door. When she peered out from behind her new curtains in the writing room, she saw Gracie staring at her with a smile.

"I can still see you!"

Maura opened the door and ushered her in.

"Not worried about going home after dark?"

"Nah. I just came for a quick visit and will get home before the sun goes down. I've been sewing all day and needed a break."

"Come meet Will. His family owns this house."

Will was hanging his towel on the clothesline he had strung behind the carriage house but walked over when he saw Gracie. Introductions were made and all formality quickly dropped among three people who had no desire to impress each other. Gracie wanted a quick tour of the house to see the improvements that had been made and approved of the outdoor shower.

The long summer days were slow to fade into evening. Sunlight filtered through the trees and dappled the houses as the sun moved gradually toward the horizon.

"Anybody want to go on a walk?" Maura asked impulsively.

"Have pity!" Gracie objected. "I just walked up here and have to walk home again."

After a moment Will jumped up.

"Everybody in the cart! I've been wanting to try this thing!"

Lizzie squealed with excitement. Will wheeled the bicycle out to the street and the women climbed into the cart. It was a tight squeeze; Maura and Gracie sat crammed together and Will deposited Lizzie on their laps. He pushed off, leisurely pedaling with his knees akimbo. Maura wondered whether the bicycle would stand the strain of Will's large frame and the weight it was pulling, but they made steady progress around the green. Will began singing a song that was wildly popular that year and the women joined in. Around the green, windows were open and people were taking advantage of the beautiful early evening to work on their gardens. Will nodded to neighbors as they passed and the girls waved. An elderly man recognized Will and stopped their progress for several minutes while he asked about his Aunt May. Will introduce Maura, Gracie and Lizzie. When the man's wife understood it was May Harding's nephew Will she dropped her hedge clippers and insisted they wait while she ran inside. A few moments later she came out with a box of ice cream cones and a tub of peach ice cream. Her husband loaded scoops on the cones as his wife held them. Lizzie's promptly fell into her lap but Maura deftly flipped it back into the cone.

They continued around the green, receiving smiles, waves and a few laughs.

"You drunk?" called a wizened old woman.

"You know me better than that, Mrs. Wallace!" When she realized this well-grown man was the beanpole nephew of her dear friend May, he good-naturedly repeated his family updates.

Long violet shadows were now stretching along the ground. Gracie looked at the sky uneasily; the sun had dipped below the horizon although the sky was still translucent blue.

"I think I better head back."

They left the bicycle at the house and all set off for Gracie's bungalow. On the way, Will entertained her with stories of Maura from high school.

"You will now hear the tale of the prunes."

Maura stared for a moment then laughed.

"What prunes?" Gracie looked from one to the other with a smile of anticipation.

"Maura had a lot of friends in high school," Will began. "She had a way of making you feel like you were in on some joke with her. Heaven help you if you crossed her, though."

"This is getting interesting - yikes!" squeaked Gracie. "Was that a bat that just flew overhead?"

"It's that time of night. Anyway," Will continued, "there was a kid named Bernard Flick whose father made a bundle on defense manufacturing at the end of the depression."

"I remember him well," said Maura darkly. "He had pale blonde hair and a personality like a poison ivy rash."

"Yes, that's him." Will turned back to Gracie with a smile. "For some reason I got to the band room a little early one day and caught Maura slipping an empty bowl from the cafeteria under her chair. People started coming in and setting up their instruments. Bernard had gotten his French horn out and was across the room annoying some girl. When it was time to warm up, he put his hand in the bell the way French horn players do. He immediately pulled it out and it was covered with goo, which dripped onto his trousers. It turns out someone had stuffed prunes into his instrument. Quite a few, syrup and all."

Gracie and Maura burst out laughing.

"Of course I knew you had done it, because I saw you with the bowl and he teased you a lot. He deserved every prune, and I was humbled to be in your presence."

"And I remember that you turned to me and shook my hand! Mr. Fleming thought both of us had done it so we got detention. He wouldn't believe me when I told him you had nothing to do with it."

"I didn't want him to! I got a little unearned glory from that. I was surprised we got off with a couple of days detention though." Maura was quiet for a moment then changed the subject. Before they reached the bottom of the hill where the street ended at the beach or turned left onto the perimeter road, they turned right on the steep hill that led up to the bungalows. Lizzie, who had been skipping on ahead of them, now faltered. Will picked her up and set her on his shoulders. Dusk had settled and the lights from the bungalows made warm patches on the pavement. While Gracie fished for her house key, Will wandered to the other side of the street to look out over the ocean with a sleepy Lizzie.

"Come in with me and help me look for vampires in my closets." Gracie grabbed Maura's arm and pulled her inside. The bungalow was tiny and it took no time to assure themselves there were no vampires or other uninvited guests.

Maura wished Gracie goodnight and said she'd see her Monday morning when she dropped Lizzie off. Gracie put her hand on her arm and held her back.

"Maura, I really like him."

Maura was a little taken aback. Was Gracie interested in Will?

"Well, he's nice... but he's getting married this fall." She tried to keep an irrational prick of jealousy out of her voice.

Gracie quirked an eyebrow and searched her face.

"Maura, sometimes you are such a dope."

Maura blinked.

Gravel crunched under Will's feet as he came up the driveway. He had a big grin and was holding firmly onto Lizzie, who still perched on his shoulders but had flopped forward, her cheek resting on Will's head.

"Oh no! Shall I carry her?" Maura reached out for the sleeping Lizzie. Will said he was fine and after a few parting remarks to Gracie they set off for the green.

M aura woke early Sunday morning and took a leisurely bath, enjoying the way the steam mixed with the cool air that came in through the open window. Sounds of other early risers drifted in with it: birdcalls, the soft whoosh of bicycle tires on pavement, a man calling to his dog. The sense of well-being that was becoming more frequent stole over her. A small bird perched momentarily on the windowsill then flitted off. Maura hoped that the new screens would come in that week; they definitely needed one in this bathroom.

She got out of the tub when the water cooled and after toweling off, wrapped herself in her summer bathrobe. Maura heard the carriage house door open and shut, telling her that Will was up. She was combing her wet curls in front of the mirror when she heard the water in the outdoor shower running, immediately below the bathroom. She assumed Will was testing it and without thinking leaned her head out the window and looked down. There, in full view, was a large and well-formed man soaping his hair, completely naked. She pulled her head in so fast she hit it on the open sash and stood in the bathroom with her cheeks flaming. She scurried back to her room and pulled on her clothes, quickly checked on Lizzie who still slept soundly and raced down the stairs to the kitchen. By the time Will tapped on the back door, fully dressed and shaved, she had made a pot of coffee and was mixing up pancake batter. The effect she was hoping to present was someone who had been downstairs for some time, not looking out bathroom windows.

"I was hoping to get a cup of coffee," Will smiled hopefully.

"On the stove - help yourself." Maura had her back to him, pouring batter onto a hot griddle. "I'm making a ton of pancakes and you have to eat some before Lizzie comes down or you won't get any."

Will sat at the table with his steaming mug and talked a little about what he hoped to accomplish before he caught the ferry at the end of the day.

Maura lifted the first stack of pancakes off the griddle and put them on a plate which she laid in front of Will. When she returned with butter and maple syrup she said in what she thought was a nonchalant voice,

"What do you think about putting a little roof over the shower?"

"A roof? Well, I could put one on but it's great to be able to look up and see the sky. It really makes you feel like you're – " He froze, suddenly noticing Maura's over-casual tone, the pink in her cheeks and the still-damp curls. His face turned scarlet.

"Tell me you didn't look out the window!"

"I thought you still had to put the drainage in and were just testing it! I was going to say good morning."

His put his head down on the table and covered it with his arms.

"I couldn't sleep last night so I put the drain in – it was easy." His voice was muffled. "I'm leaving this island right now and never coming back!" When she realized Will was laughing, she relaxed and grinned.

"It wasn't anything I hadn't seen before and I only caught a quick glimpse." Which wasn't quite true, but he seemed to accept it. "Eat your pancakes before they get cold."

Lizzie drifted into the kitchen when the next batch was ready. Jelly Bean followed her as far as the doorway and sat staring at them. His eyes were round and his expression ludicrous, as though someone had just sneaked up behind him and screeched. When Will had brought Jelly Bean to the island he said they would see why his name was a good fit. The first time he came out from under Lizzie's bed and Maura got a good look at him, she laughed. Jelly Bean was white with large, almost perfectly round black spots all over. A black mask came just below his pale-yellow eyes.

"When you met Jelly Bean, did he look like someone had set off a firecracker behind him?"

"Oh yes," said Will. "That's his normal expression."

Maura overrode Lizzie's suggestion that the cat would like a pancake and emptied a can of cat food on a plate. She put it on the floor a few yards away from him where he regarded it without interest. It was a start, though. Jelly Bean couldn't live in Lizzie's room.

Nothing more was said about the shower before Will left but one of the first shipments delivered that week was a small pile of planks.

Chapter 11

Quite a lot was done on the outside of the house that week. The ugly front door was replaced with a beautifully simple antique door from the right period, painted a cloudy, grayish blue. The shutters were gone and all the woodwork and the little fence out front were scraped and painted snowy white. A landscaper came and judiciously pruned the wild masses of roses, retaining their tumbling, joyous essence. Bare patches in the lawn were seeded and bushes were planted along Opal's wall that would sport red foliage in the fall.

The boat ride with Patrick and Steve, originally planned for Tuesday, had to be postponed. Patrick called from a phone at the tavern to say that he and Steve had to leave unexpectedly to take care of some business. Steve wouldn't return until the following week but Patrick was planning to be back on Friday. Would she and her daughter like to go out on the boat with him on Saturday?

Maura hesitated. Lizzie had been invited to Midge's birthday party on Saturday and Maura had the entire afternoon free. Did she want to spend it with Patrick? And why was he so interested in spending time with her anyway? Her mind blanked and she couldn't think of an excuse not to go, so she accepted the invitation. It was a point in his favor that there was no hint of relief in his voice when he discovered it would just be Maura. She smiled a little as she hung up; Patrick may not be comfortable around children, but he was interesting and a little dashing. She thought that when she and Lizzie moved into their cramped apartment in Marblehead and she started teaching, it might be nice to look back on a summer that included a date with a treasure hunter.

Two men came on Wednesday to put in the new patio. The heavyset man in a uniform with a logo on his pocket was the professional, hired by Leo Conti. He was all business and worked in silence, except to direct his companion. The second man was tall and rail thin, with a hooked nose and prominent chin. His sandy hair was too long and hung over his eyes as he worked. Maura and Lizzie knew him, as he was a local handyman who was brought in by several other contractors renovating the Watts house.

It took them a good part of the day to break up the old surface, haul the chunks of brick away and prepare the ground. Maura was dusting the parlor when she heard Lizzie's voice out back and went to investigate.

"Lizzie! Stop pestering Randy."

He looked up and grinned. He was about Maura's age, but there were telltale signs of a heavy drinker that made him appear older. His skin was dry and crisscrossed with fine lines, but the eyes that looked at her through puffy lids were friendly and humorous.

"No! Don't take her away. This guy won't say two words to me except to order me around and I've been bored stiff." The man in the uniform ignored him, but his mouth tightened into a thin line. Maura knew that Randy worked hard and followed directions, and guessed the contractor was willing to put up with a certain amount of lip. "Madam Lizzie was telling me that she has her very own giant and a cat named Jelly Bean."

"Both are true!" Maura laughed. She went inside and made a platter of sandwiches and lemonade and brought them out. The men were glad to take a break. The contractor went out to his truck to read a newspaper while he ate, and Randy sat at the picnic table with Maura and Lizzie. He had grown up on the island and was happy to answer Maura's questions about what it was like off-season.

"Well, I'm happy when all the summer people are here because I get enough work. And the place is more lively. But I guess I love the island the most in late fall and winter when it's deserted and there's a kind of...desolate beauty." He laughed a little self-consciously. "My wife hates the winters here."

Maura found the thought of an Islay in the shrouded mists of winter, abandoned by its summer residents, appealing. It occurred to her that when she and Lizzie left the island it didn't have to be forever. Maybe she should talk to Sally Fortier about renting a room at the Bayberry Inn in November or December, if they stayed open all year. Gracie and Opal lived here year-round and might be glad of company.

By the end of the day Thursday the patio was finished. Two neat flower beds had been dug on either side, which Maura planted with a variety of bright flowers.

Lizzie was delirious at the prospect of going to her friend Midge's birthday party on Saturday. Entertainment plans included running through the sprinkler and playing games like Red Light, Green Light. After a supper of hamburgers, corn on the cob and ice cream there would be a game of Barley Bright. The boys would then go home and the girls would stay for a slumber party. This was a new addition to the agenda and Maura had some misgivings. Lizzie was only four and had never been away from her for a single night since she was born.

When Maura brought Lizzie to the party, which was at the far end of the green, shouting and squealing could be heard from the back of the house. They followed a brick sidewalk around back and were greeted by a cheerful woman who was filling paper cups with pink lemonade.

"You're a better man than I am, Dottie," Maura said raising her voice to be heard. "I couldn't do it!"

Midge's mother smiled and waved her hand.

"This is my fifth kid. I've got it all figured out. And if things get out of hand, I'll spray them with the hose. The water pressure on this island is fierce."

Maura laughed. "So I've discovered. Whose idea was Barley Bright? That's kind of a creepy game. You know the girls are going to wind up sleeping in your bedroom with the lights on, right?"

Dottie rolled her eyes.

"Midge was wild to play after her older sister had it at her party last fall. Wendy wouldn't let Midge play so my husband said she could have it at her own party just to get some peace. He thought she'd forget about it. Lizzie's younger than the rest of the kids so I'll ask her if she wants to come in and help me fill the party cups with candy. They'll each take one home with them."

Maura wished her good luck and kissed Lizzie goodbye.

"This is your first time going to a slumber party," she told her. "If you want to come home just ask Midge's mommy to call me or Miss Gracie, OK?" Leaning in, she whispered, "And you don't have to play Barley Bright if you don't want to. It's a little scary!"

Maura hurried home and put a pair of shorts and a cotton blouse on over her bathing suit. She rubbed suntan lotion into her skin and fished out her wide-brimmed hat. Despite the light tan she had developed since her arrival, Irish skin was Irish skin, and she was spending the afternoon on a boat. Will hadn't arrived so she assumed something had prevented him from coming to the island this weekend.

Patrick was waiting on the pier when she coasted in on her bicycle. He was wearing a loose pair of cotton trousers, an open necked shirt and a cap. He reminded her of Humphrey Bogart in *The African Queen*, only better looking. She wondered if it was a conscious attempt. He saw her wide smile and answered it in kind.

"Ready to look for treasure?" A craft the size of a small fishing boat was tied up at the end of the dock. A cold prickle ran up

Maura's arms as they walked past the spot where she had seen Violet under the rippling tide, and she couldn't help but peer into the water as they passed. No bodies today.

Patrick's boat was compact but well organized. The small cabin had compartments for maps, tools and personal belongings. A shelf was crammed tightly with paperbacks and aged hardcovers. From a quick inspection of their spines, they appeared to be a mixture of classics, history and adventure books. Two sleeping bags were neatly rolled and stowed away. The deck was just large enough to hold a couple of wooden chests that were bolted down. One contained diving gear and snorkels. Another held smaller storage crates, trays with lids, clean cloths and a box containing small bottles of chemicals, brushes and tools.

"This chest has a lot of our salvage equipment in case we find something worth keeping. If we find bigger or fragile items, we usually have to make special arrangements for extraction and transport." Maura inspected the salvage chest with interest while Patrick steered them out of the harbor toward the north end of the island.

As the busy harbor area disappeared from view, Maura watched the shoreline. There were boulders here, with scrubby trees and no signs of habitation. An oystercatcher perched on a rock and watched their progress suspiciously.

Maura returned to the cabin.

"Who was Lorelei?" She asked, referring to the name painted on the bow. "An old girlfriend?" Patrick shot her a quick glance, then looked away with a little smile.

"German folklore. Lorelei was a woman who was betrayed by her lover. She fell to her death on a rock and became a siren, then made a career of luring sailors to their death with her singing." He saw her look and grinned. "I did name her after an old girlfriend and didn't find out about the legend until after she left me. It's better than the *Pammy Bee*. The guy I bought it from second hand had named it after his wife. I drove the boat for a month then I couldn't take it anymore."

"A good move. *Lorelei* beats *Pammy Bee* hands down."

"Yes, but..." Patrick lips folded in grim line and his thoughts seemed to go elsewhere.

"But what?"

After a moment's consideration, he began.

"I met Steve scuba diving some years ago. His parents are part owners of a marina in Connecticut, so I asked him if he'd let me know if the right kind of boat for a small salvage operation came up for sale at a good price. He was really interested in the whole salvage thing and asked a lot of questions about what I'd found so far. Did you know he's a professor at the University of Rhode Island? Something to do with marine science. Anyway, we lost touch after a while but then two years ago he called me to say that a guy was trying to sell his boat quickly because he needed the money. It was the middle of the semester, so Steve wasn't there when I drove to the marina to look it over. He had his father inspect it for me and he said it was a good deal, so I bought it. I hated the name *Pammy Bee* from the start, but I hoped I'd get used to it. It was such a relief to change it. I even bought new life preservers with *Lorelei* printed on them and had it stitched on the pocket of a jacket, which my girlfriend got a big kick out of. That's when the boat felt like it was really mine."

"But I can tell that wasn't the end of it."

"No." He looked her in the eye and whispered, "you never rename a boat."

For the second time that morning, Maura's skin prickled.

"Why?"

"As I found out too late, there's not a boat owner anywhere that would change the name, at least not without going through the ceremony first. Even though I'd been on a lot of boats, I had never heard about the danger of changing the name. Last summer I wasn't far from Steve's family's marina, so I stopped in to see if he was there. Even before he came onboard, he noticed the fresh new *Lorelei* painted on the side." Patrick eased up on the throttle as he was talking and the boat slowed.

"He just stood on the dock and gave me a funny look. He said, 'You renamed her?' 'You bet,' I answered. 'I can't have a boat named the *Pammy Bee.*' He asked me if I went through the purging and renaming ceremonies. When I laughed and shook my head, he said 'Oh boy' with a weird smile.

"That's when I found out that nobody ever renames a boat, not unless they want bad luck to follow them for the rest of their lives. It can be done, but you have to follow a strict set of rules."

Maura blinked. Bad luck? She could tell Patrick was serious.

"What are the rules?"

He searched her face to see if she was laughing at him, but she was carefully keeping her expression neutral.

"It's complicated. The first thing is to purge the old name. You have to get rid of every single thing onboard that has the old name. I mean *everything*, even old maintenance logs. A lot of people burn the items to make sure the old name is completely obliterated. You can't bring anything on the boat with the new name or even say it out loud until the entire renaming process is done.

"After you get rid of anything with the old name it's time for the purging ceremony. You write the old name on a metal tag with something that will come off in the water. You and your friends stand at the bow of the ship with a bottle of champagne. You recite some specific lines to Poseidon, explaining that you want the old name expunged from his records. You throw the metal tag with the old name into the water so he knows the one that's being changed. Then you pour half the bottle of champagne in the water, starting in the east and going to the west. After that, you can start the renaming ceremony."

To Maura, this sounded like an excuse for a group of friends to have a party, but Patrick appeared to take it seriously.

"Poseidon?" she asked cautiously.

He seemed to recollect himself and laughed self-consciously.

"According to tradition, Poseidon has the name of every vessel that ever launched recorded in the Book of the Deep. If you rename your boat without taking the proper steps, Poseidon will think you're trying to pull a fast one on him and bad luck will follow you forever. Steve said he doesn't believe that stuff and I didn't have to worry, but to be on the safe side I went through the whole purging and renaming process."

"So you're OK now, right?" She felt a little sorry for him. This business had obviously taken the fun out of owning his first boat.

Patrick opened the throttle and the *Lorelei* gathered speed. When he didn't answer she said,

"Oh. You bought life preservers with *Lorelei* on them and had it stitched on your pocket. You broke the rule that said nothing could be brought onboard with the new name."

Patrick nodded grimly.

"I thought about giving her a different name but I spoke with someone who knows about this stuff and he said to save my money – the damage was done."

"It doesn't seem to bother Steve," Maura pointed out, "and his family owns a marina. He spends a lot of time on this boat, right?"

"Just during the summer when he's not at URI." He seemed to relax a little at the reminder that Steve, who had spent his life on boats, had no concerns about Patrick or the *Lorelei* being cursed.

They were now motoring along the north end of the island. Maura left the cabin to watch the shoreline slip by. It was less rocky here, but there were no sandy beaches that would attract the public. Now and then she caught sight of a roof or the chimney of a cabin poking up through the thick trees. They passed an elderly couple in a rowboat, the woman deeply tanned and wearing a yellow bathing suit. Maura called a greeting and they smiled and returned her wave.

Eventually they came to a break in the trees that revealed the entrance to an inlet. Patrick slowed and turned into it. They came around a bend and Maura saw they were in a sheltered cove whose wild beauty made her exclaim. Patrick idled the *Lorelei* and came to the rail where she stood.

"Nice, isn't it? I thought we could anchor here later and walk to the Bayberry Inn for an early dinner."

"I'd like that." Maura gazed around with delight. "What a lovely little spot!"

Like most of this side of the island, trees crowded close to the water. Dead limbs from storms were scattered on the pebbly shore. Vegetation grew thickly and the whir of insects increased as the sun emerged from a passing cloud. The calling of gulls and the wash of the tide on the tiny beach added to the sounds, but Maura had a sense of utter peace and stillness.

"I'm surprised no one has built a house here," she said. "I know it's far from town and the harbor, but to wake up to this every morning…"

"Thankfully, this is part of the nature preserve and no one can build on it. I drop anchor here every night and sleep on the deck. Steve too when he's here." Maura remembered the two sleeping bags neatly stowed in the cabin. "If it's raining, we can squeeze into the cabin but it's not comfortable. If the weather is really bad and Sally and Jim have room, we stay at the Bayberry. See that break in the trees? There's a path that leads into the middle of the preserve. When you reach the fork, the left branch will take you to the inn. The right branch goes to the old colony."

Maura had a momentary urge to go exploring, remembering the eeriness of the clearing where the shipwreck survivors settled. She wondered if it would feel the same on this sunny afternoon, with Patrick at her side.

"We don't normally take the path to the inn," Patrick continued. When Steve is here we have a small rowboat. He sometimes uses it to get to the *Lorelei* when he comes back after being onshore – leaves it tied up in the harbor when he's away like today. The water is too shallow at the inn to dock this boat, but the rowboat is fine." Maura remembered the little boat tied up to the pier in front of the inn when she and Lizzie first met Patrick.

He opened the throttle again and they left the cove. They picked up speed as they headed east, leaving the island behind.

Maura felt a little thrill as she stood at the bow and waves smacked against the hull and sprayed her.

"Want to drive?" Patrick called.

She smiled happily and joined him at the wheel.

"OK, there's nothing to worry about out here. You're not going to run into a ferry or dock or anything. Maybe a whale." He laughed at her look.

Patrick gave clear directions, standing closer behind her than he needed to. Maura didn't mind… it was the first adventure she had had in so many years she couldn't count, and she was with a good-looking man who seemed to find her attractive. She hadn't thought of herself that way since about two months after she married David.

At Gracie's urging, Maura had left her friend's phone number in case there were any problems at the birthday party before she got home. The afternoon stretched in front of her with no responsibilities.

As they plowed through the water, Patrick occasionally consulted a map pinned to the wall and a gyroscopic compass he had bought second hand.

Maura asked what they were going to be looking for today.

"A long shot!" Patrick grinned. "I only go hunting for it when Steve isn't with me because he says I'm wasting his time."

"I'm intrigued!"

"OK, here's the story." After a glance at the compass, Patrick lit a cigarette and took over the wheel for a moment, adjusting their course slightly.

He was trying to locate the wreck of a ship belonging to a highly successful English privateer by the name of Simon Herridge. Captain Herridge operated legally during the War of Spanish Succession in the early part of the eighteenth century, making extensive use of his letter of marque to attack and capture enemy ships. As a privateer, he had earned local fame in his native Dorset for outsmarting captains with larger ships and crews. He sometimes set out in a captured ship and let his Spanish prey get close enough to identify Herridge's vessel as one of their own. They pretended to be a ship in distress and on more than one occasion had young prostitutes, posing as virtuous young ladies, wave at the Spanish seamen and call for help. When the enemy belatedly discovered the ship in distress was a fully functioning warship, the fight was more-or-less over. Herridge deposited his prisoners in the dark of night on some rocky shore and let them find their way home. Some of the girls went with the released prisoners and advanced their positions in life to upstanding wives.

The Treaty of Utrecht was signed in 1713, at which point all privateers were ordered to cease and desist. Captain Herridge had no taste for peace and enthusiastically carried on as he had before the treaty. As a privateer, men had drunk toasts to his exploits. As a pirate his popularity was seriously diminished, especially since he wasn't picky about the nationality of the ships he captured. England became too hot for him after he attacked a heavily laden merchant ship returning from the East Indies. Herridge was known to the merchant captain, who cursed him and swore he would get even as he was abandoned on a remote shore. By the time news had gotten back to London, Captain Herridge had swapped the merchant ship for a smaller vessel called the *Starling*, sold off a small portion of his spoils and set off across the Atlantic.

"The last that was known of Herridge was that he had landed in Newfoundland where two of his brothers had emigrated. After a few months of repairs and restocking, the *Starling* headed south for parts unknown. They had taken on a load of salted cod, probably to make them look legitimate. Nothing was ever heard of Captain Herridge or the *Starling* again, except a British merchant ship was attacked just north of here around that time. It escaped, and one of the seamen swore he recognized Simon Herridge."

"Why do you want to find an old ship that was carrying cod?"

Patrick let off the throttle, glanced at the map then went to the rail to throw his cigarette butt off the side.

"Herridge was a pretty famous character in Dorset, for being a successful pirate but also for the enterprising way he went about it. He's become kind of a legend. There's been a fair amount of research on him in recent years on both sides of the Atlantic, and speculation about what happened to him. Well, I want to be the one to find him."

"How would you even know it was the same ship? You've said the area around the island is a ship graveyard. What makes you think the *Starling* is here?" She was pretty sure there was something he was holding back.

Patrick gazed over the water.

"This is about where I wanted to look today." He avoided Maura's eyes, but she was still awaiting her answer. He finally laughed and turned to her. After searching her face for a moment, he sighed.

"OK... Steve is the only other person I've mentioned this to. You have to swear not to mention it to anyone, including your pretty friend."

"I solemnly swear!"

"There's a painting of Herridge in Dorset that shows him holding a cane with a gold head. According to the book I found that in, it was inscribed with the Latin words '*Exitus Acta Probat*' - 'The result justifies the deed.'" He went to the stern and, after shifting a pile of tackle items, pried up a rectangular square in the deck. His body blocked the cavity and after a moment he put the square back in place. He was holding a package that was wrapped up in several layers of waterproof material and cloth. After laying it down gently on the deck, he proceeded to unwrap the object. She wasn't really surprised when he held up a wizened piece of wood that looked like it might have been part of a cane. On one end was a gold ball with a faint inscription. She could make out '*Ex*' and '*oba*'.

"Where did you find that?" Maura breathed.

"On Islay, in the old settlement. Wrapped up and buried." His eyes were bright, looking into hers.

"Simon Herridge, or at least his cane, was on Islay."

Chapter 12

Caught up in an enjoyable sense of adventure, Maura had a happy afternoon searching fruitlessly for shipwrecks with Patrick. He and Steve limited their operations to shallow waters, not having the equipment to search and salvage deeper. Steve and several of his students had made underwater viewers from lightweight pipes, eight inches in diameter. The concept was simple: glass was cut to fit across the end that went in the water and tightly sealed. This would allow the viewer to peer in from a comfortably dry vantage point. For many, New England waters were barely tolerable at the beaches. Away from land the water temperature dropped enough to make a wetsuit desirable for anyone who was going to spend much time in the water.

"We go to a spot and each hang over the side with a viewer. We'll spend a few hours to a day in an area, depending on whether we have any reason to think we'll find something. We'll look around then move the boat a little way. If we see anything worth checking out, we'll put on the wetsuits and take a closer look. Sometimes we use snorkels but more often we need the scuba gear. Lucky for us, most of the wrecks occurred where the water was shallower than the crew was expecting and they hit rocks. It gives us a chance to find something."

Maura wasn't sure how she felt about jumping into the water wearing Steve's wetsuit and using his snorkel, if she was offered the chance, so was content looking through her viewer at the sunlight playing on the ocean floor and schools of fish swimming by.

"We're lucky," Patrick called from the other side of the boat. "Visibility is pretty bad, generally, especially in the summer. Sometimes you can only see down about ten feet. Today we can see twenty or thirty feet – enough for our purposes since it's pretty shallow here."

Maura watched a school of fish dart by under her viewer, sunlight filtering through the water and touching their scales with glitter. Suddenly an enormous shape moved under her viewer, followed by a second. She yelped and jumped back.

"I see them too!" Patrick laughed, following the monsters with his viewer. "Blue sharks, after the fish. I don't see them very often out here. Don't worry, they don't eat people."

They moved the boat several times but didn't see anything more interesting than an outboard motor.

"How did they get home without their motor? And how do you lose one of those in the first place?"

"I sometimes lie awake at night wondering about some of the crazy stuff we find."

By late afternoon Maura was feeling like she had had enough sun. They went back to the cove and anchored the *Lorelei*. Although the shore was a short distance away they would have to swim; they stripped down to their bathing suits and rolled their clothes and shoes up in towels. They paddled through the water holding their towel rolls over their heads and after reaching the pebbly sand of the little beach dried off as well as they could. Clothed and shod, they set off on the path to the Bayberry Inn.

Patrick had made an early dinner reservation, knowing that Maura had to get home in case Lizzie didn't want to stay for the slumber party. As they moved away from the inlet the breeze died, and cicadas called loudly in the still air. Fern fronds brushed Maura's legs as she followed Patrick along the trail. She felt far from civilization.

Within a few minutes they came to a broader trail that Maura recognized as the one she and Lizzie had taken when they left the inn that day. They turned left to go to the inn; to the right lay the way to the clearing in the old settlement.

"Nice to see you again!" Sally Fortier smiled at Maura as she handed her a menu. "You two look like you spent the day on the *Lorelei*, which knowing Patrick, means he took you treasure hunting. Find anything?"

"An outboard motor and two blue sharks the size of city buses," Maura informed her.

"They were about ten feet long," Patrick grinned.

"You don't need to worry about those." Sally waved her hand. "It's the white sharks that are trouble. So, what will you have? Jim and his friends caught some bluefish this morning." Patrick enthusiastically ordered it for both of them, then caught her expression.

"You don't like bluefish? You haven't had Sally's." Maura said she was perfectly willing to try Sally's bluefish.

They shared a bottle of chilled wine while they waited for their food. Their table was at an open window that looked out onto the pier and the little bay. The sky had a translucent clarity and the breeze that drifted through the window was gentle and faintly fishy. A thought popped up in Maura's mind and was guiltily squashed: *What a lovely evening this would be if I was here with someone I really cared about.* She was enjoying Patrick's company and he was unquestionably attractive, but she wasn't sure she wanted anyone who believed he needed to placate Poseidon around Lizzie.

"Tell me what brought you to Islay." Patrick refilled her glass. "I've told you about me."

Maura took a deep breath and blew it out. This was her day of freedom and adventure, and she didn't want to talk about her past. Patrick was looking at her with an expectant smile, so she told him the bare bones of her story.

"I've been working at an institute for single mothers and their children for the last few years. I ran into an old friend whose family owns the house Lizzie and I are staying at. The family offered it rent free for the summer in exchange for my keeping an eye on the renovation work being done."

"Nice opportunity! And that's it?"

"The rest is even more boring."

Sally deposited two casserole dishes on the table. One contained the bluefish, cooked in oil, garlic and onions. Fresh tomatoes had been chopped and tossed with oil and basil then sprinkled over the fish. The other casserole was filled with sliced potatoes, baked with butter, cream and pepper. Maura was surprised by how much she enjoyed the bluefish.

"The other day you told me you were originally from New Jersey," Patrick said, refilling their wine glasses. "Is your husband from there too?" Maura flushed a little. He was assuming that a husband was still in the picture, but it hadn't stopped him from inviting her on a day trip or taking her to the inn for a cozy dinner. It suddenly made their outing feel a little tawdry.

"My ex-husband," she said quietly. "We were divorced several years ago. No, he's from Boston originally but I met him at college in Pennsylvania."

"Ah, you're a college girl."

"Well, I went for three years but quit when I got married. I picked it up again recently and just finished this spring. I start teaching in the fall."

"I know New Jersey fairly well. What part are you from?"

"First Trenton, then Barlow Ridge." Maura never liked talking about herself and her responses began to drag. Patrick seemed to sense this because he smoothly moved the conversation to books. Maura remembered the shelf crammed with books in the *Lorelei's* cabin, and since she was an avid reader herself, the remainder of dinner was taken up with a lively conversation about the books they had read.

"I'm writing one myself," she blurted out, then laughed. "Sorry, it's hard to say that with a straight face." When she told Patrick that her book was about the witch of Islay he was immediately intrigued. He was fascinated with the colony of shipwreck survivors, and of course any association with Captain Herridge.

"Maybe I can help you a little when we have more time," Patrick offered. "I might have some information you can use."

Maura noticed that pink was faintly tinging the sky over the bay and said she thought they better get back.

When they started up the path behind the inn, long shadows were casting themselves on the ground. Under the canopy of trees dusk was creeping, violet shadows filling the gaps in the brush on either side of the path. Whip-poor-wills called to each other, flitting among the trees in search of moths and beetles.

They came to the path to the cove and Patrick quickly turned right toward the *Lorelei*. When Maura called "Wait!" he looked back with a frown.

"Can we just take a quick look at the clearing with the ruins? The first time I was there it felt spooky. This is my adventure day... I'd love to see it as twilight is falling."

Patrick looked as though he was going to refuse, but when he saw her hopeful smile, he gave in.

"Well, just for a minute."

He followed her down the path, away from the boat, away from the inn into the breathless stillness. When they reached the clearing, he stared at the crumbled foundations and whispered, as though to himself,

"It always feels like something is waiting, and that you don't want to speak too loudly and wake it up."

Maura walked a few steps into the clearing. Patrick was reaching for her hand to pull her away when she said softly,

"This is the perfect place to play Barley Bright."

He was startled.

"What? What's Barley Bright?" he whispered.

"It's an old game that's been played for hundreds of years. I don't actually know the official way to play, but when we were kids we had our own version. We always played in a boy's backyard that backed up to deep woods. The game couldn't start until the sun had fully left the sky and it was pitch black. One kid was appointed the witch. She would hide in the edge of the woods somewhere along a path we had picked out. After the rest of the kids counted to a hundred, we would start along the path, chanting. At some point along the way the 'witch' would jump out and start chasing us. If she caught one of us before we reached home base that person would be the next witch. Even scarier than not knowing when the witch would jump out at you was actually being the witch and having to hide alone in the woods."

Maura's voice suddenly took on a whispering sing-song quality.

"How many miles to Barley Bright?
Eight, eight and another eight!
Can we get there by candlelight?
Yes, if your horse be strong and light.
Will we get there and back tonight?
Look out! The witches will get you!"

Just then a black bird flew silently over their heads and through the clearing. Patrick grabbed Maura's arm and dragged her away. She didn't need any urging. The eeriness of that spot was tenfold what it had been on her first visit. They ran along the path and overshot the turn-off to the cove. Patrick had been that way enough times to realize their mistake before they had gone far. As they retraced their steps, Maura had an absurd feeling that there was something running silently behind her. Even as her heart pounded she realized it was her own telling of Barley Bright that had spooked her, and by the time they burst into the clearing around the cove she was laughing a little. Patrick jumped into the water wearing his clothes and began to swim for the boat, but Maura stopped to remove her shorts and blouse and roll them up in the towel with her shoes. Patrick turned mid-way to the boat and looked back.

"What are you doing?" he shouted furiously. "Come on!"

She waded into the water then pushed off. Out of the woods the sky still held enough light to see clearly. Her heart rate slowed as the cool water swirled around her. She swam with one arm holding her clothes over her head, but easily reached the boat where Patrick stood at the top of the ladder and grabbed her roll of clothing from her. She could see he was making an effort to get his anger under control.

"That's exactly the same reaction I had to Barley Bright when I was a kid!" She laughed apologetically as she pulled herself up the ladder.

If she was seeing humor in their mad flight from the clearing, Patrick wasn't.

"What possessed you to chant that?"

Maura looked at him questioningly as she stepped onto the deck. "Lizzie is at a birthday party where Barley Bright is on the entertainment schedule. It was in my head!" She stood at the rail, rubbing her towel on her wet skin. Patrick took a quick step toward her and her eyes widened.

"There are some things you don't ever fool with!" His voice was low and fierce. She stared at him in surprise. After a moment he turned and went to the anchor to pull it up. The *Lorelei* was soon chugging its way through the inlet. Maura dressed then leaned against the railing, watching Patrick's back through the cabin windows. He stood rigidly, keeping his eyes straight ahead. She sighed, thinking how much fun it would have been if he had been able to share her appreciation of their absurd adventure. She gave him time to regain his composure then went into the cabin.

"I'm sorry," she said, putting a hand on his arm. "I tend to find things funny when normal people don't." She felt him relax and he turned to her with a wry grin.

"No, I'm sorry. I've been standing here for the last five minutes feeling like a jerk and not knowing what to do about it. I guess..." He broke off and turned to face the bow again, opening up the throttle a little. "I guess you'd say I'm a little superstitious. If you had read some of the things I've read and talked to the people I've met, you might acknowledge that there are things in the world that stay hidden. Dark things that..." Maura shivered, not so much at his words but by the way his voice dropped on the last sentence and trailed off.

She changed the subject and asked when Steve was coming back. That led to lighter conversation topics and before long they were back at the harbor. Patrick tied up the boat and helped

Maura alight. As she tossed her belongings in the cart behind her bicycle, he looked a little uncertain.

"Are you sure you aren't afraid to ride home by yourself?" The last of the sun had disappeared over the horizon and all that was left of the day were a few violet streaks in the sky. Clouds were moving in but it didn't feel like rain. The raucous calling of gulls had quieted and despite the laughter and music coming from the tavern on the other side of the harbor it was a lovely, peaceful evening. Maura assured him she was fine and would enjoy the ride. She was anxious to get home in case Lizzie had had enough of her party. He stepped up to her and put his hands on her shoulders.

"Have I scared you off? Would you go on another date with a guy who doesn't like to play Barley Bright?" Maura had been thinking that she wouldn't, but she was a little charmed by his uncertainty. When she had first met Patrick, everything about him had told her he was a playboy without any particular depth. She was still revising her opinion and wasn't sure where it would land, but for now, she was willing to give him a second chance. She told him so and didn't avoid his kiss when he leaned in and put his mouth on hers. Her reservations about Patrick aside, it wasn't unpleasant for a thirty-four-year-old divorcee to be kissed by a handsome hunter of pirate ships.

Maura switched on her bicycle's headlight as she rode away from the lighted harbor area. To reach the green and the Watts house, she followed a series of narrow lanes. Most of the automobiles on the island were used by workmen, which meant the streets were mostly deserted at night. She passed a couple on bicycles who she guessed were headed for the tavern, but after that she was alone. Her headlamp made a pool of golden light on the road ahead and faintly lit the bushes and tree branches on either side. A light wind rattled the leaves and a cacophony of night insects drowned out the sound of her tires. The sky had clouded over and with no moon or stars the night was quite dark beyond the beam of her light. Maura was not an especially nervous person and spent so little time alone that the first part of the ride was pleasantly exhilarating. Her mind drifted over the events of the day and inevitably came to her suggestion that they visit the clearing. She was aware at the time that Patrick didn't want to go, and now she felt badly that she had subjected him to what was clearly a fright. It was a fright for her too, but one that quickly turned to amusement. For her it was an adventure, but Patrick seemed convinced they had woken something there, something he wanted to avoid at all costs. The recollection of Patrick's terror, more than her memory of their adventure in the clearing, raised goosebumps on her arms.

The thought drifted into her mind that if there was another bicyclist behind her, or if someone stepped out from behind the trees as she passed, she wouldn't hear them with all the raucous insects. Her heart began to beat a little harder and she pumped the pedals faster, laughing a little despite herself. She felt a sense of relief when she reached the little town with its streetlights and sidewalks. The coffee shop, which was on the corner closest to the green, appeared to be closed but someone was emptying garbage into a can as she passed. Maura turned into the quiet street that ran around the green and felt a comforting sense of coming home. Windows around the square were open to the cool night air, light spilling out into little front gardens and sidewalks. As she passed a window, a radio was playing *Arthur Godfrey's Talent Scouts*.

Maura pulled up in front of the Watts house and saw that someone had turned the front light on. Will, of course. She found him in the back, washing paint brushes in a bucket. He looked up and smiled, and as he inspected her his smile widened.

"What have you been up to?" Will asked. "Your hair is all wild and tangled and you have a nice swath of sunburn and freckles across your cheeks!"

"Treasure hunting. Hold on while I call Gracie. Lizzie's at a slumber party and Gracie offered to go get her if she didn't want to stay."

"No need! Gracie called to say that she checked with the mother to see how things were going and all was well. The boys had left and nobody wanted to play Barley Bright except the birthday girl who threw a fit. The mother was reading them bedtime stories and Lizzie was sound asleep."

Maura told him the choice bits from her day, faithfully omitting any mention of the pirate Herridge. The passage of two blue sharks immediately under her viewer got a chuckle, but her account of the episode in the clearing brought out his booming laugh.

"Only you would trot out Barley Bright when the poor guy was already quaking in terror! Is that the last of the treasure hunter?"

"Maybe not! He forgave me by the time we got back."

She noticed the new roof over the outdoor shower but didn't mention it. They sat at the picnic table and talked for a while, then moved inside to escape the mosquitos. She poured two glasses of sherry and made toasted cheese sandwiches. They sat at the kitchen table while they ate, playing Rummy and talking about their old classmates from Barlow Ridge.

"Rebecca has done well for herself, hasn't she?" said Will, drawing a card. "I would have guessed she would marry someone from the Barlow Ridge Country Club and settle down near her family. And now here she is, mayor of a town and owner of a publishing empire."

"She takes her job as mayor very seriously, but she's got some hand-picked people running her businesses. Besides MacKenzie Publishing, she owns a lot of real estate and some smaller businesses."

"Sounds exhausting. How did she find time to pick up a new husband?"

Maura laid four kings on the table and held her hands up to show she was out of cards.

"You stink," Will said cordially, and began to shuffle the cards.

"Rebecca got involved with an artist collective, which is funny because she couldn't draw a pumpkin in Mrs. Sander's art class. All of them were mixed up with a murder before Lizzie was born and they've been a tight group ever since. Her husband

Dan is a vet, not an artist, but he somehow got dragged into all of it. I spent some time in Rushing River before Rebecca and Dan's wedding, when Lizzie was a baby. They're a fun and crazy bunch. She showed me pictures from a Halloween contest they were in where they went as the murdered passengers from a ship that had been taken over by a real pirate in the nineteenth century. They looked a little gruesome, which is what you would expect when a group of artists are determined to win the big prize. Rebecca had a big black musket hole in her chest and seaweed in her teeth. They dabbed their costumes with phosphorescent paint so they glowed in the dark." Will laughed and drew a card. "I wish I had been there to see it."

Maura sighed.

"Bec has had all the adventures. Nuts!" she exclaimed as Will laid a set down with his remaining cards and claimed victory. She threw her cards down.

It was 2:30 in the morning when Maura glanced at the clock. They had given up on cards and had sat talking for the last hour. She yawned and reluctantly told Will she needed to get some sleep before she was expected to pick up Lizzie. As she headed up to bed, she reflected on the fact that she had had only one true friend since she married David, who was of course Rebecca. And suddenly she had Gracie, Will, Opal and Lillian. Maybe Patrick. How she and Lizzie would miss Islay when summer ended.

Chapter 13

The next morning, Will went to the ferry landing to meet his fiancé and her sister, who were coming to see the progress made on the house repairs and to go to the beach. Maura was in the writing room when the island taxi pulled up and she saw Will help two women alight. One was young and slim, with pale blonde hair rolled under at her shoulders. From the laughing look she gave Will, Maura correctly assumed this was Junie. Junie's sister was somewhat older and more solidly built, but there was a strong family resemblance.

"Come in!" Maura smiled and held the door wide. "The house is extra chaotic right now because they're redoing the kitchen." Will introduced his guests as Junie and her sister Marge.

"We're so sorry to intrude, but Will insisted you wouldn't mind." Junie appeared to be in her mid-twenties, with rounded cheeks and flawless skin. Her look was direct and her smile genuine. Maura detected a slightly affected manner of speech which made her smile in return. She wondered, not unkindly, which movie star her young guest was imagining herself to resemble. During Maura's stint at the women's institute, she had encountered enough star-struck residents to recognize the signs. She immediately felt the difference in age between herself and Will's future wife.

"They wanted to see how the house was coming along," Will explained. "We'll go to the coffee shop for lunch and head down to the beach for the afternoon, so we won't be in your way."

"Well, you own the house after all," Marge said in an annoyed voice. She had Junie's full cheeks and extra weight was distributed on a shorter frame. Like Junie's, her clothes were stylish and clearly expensive. Both women were subtly made up, with carefully shaped brows and just the right amount of color applied to lips and cheeks. Marge's brown hair was short and permed. Maura thought she would be attractive without the frowning look. She wasn't sure if Marge disapproved of the house or herself and wondered how either could have triggered animosity so quickly. Her curiosity and sense of humor were piqued.

"It's not my house," Will responded evenly. "Maura is my aunt's tenant for the summer, so the house is hers at the moment." Marge flushed and Junie frowned at her sister.

"Oh no!" laughed Maura, taking them past the awkward moment, "you can't make me responsible for this hellhole! Try as I might to keep up with it, the house is always covered in dust. There are constantly workmen underfoot, tearing down walls, prying up old floors and drilling holes. I've been tripping over piles of wood and plumbing fixtures since I arrived. Lizzie and I are squatting here, nothing more. My job is to make sure the workmen don't walk off with Aunt May's salt and pepper shakers."

Will smiled at her gratefully and Junie laughed.

Marge was already heading toward the writing room and reaching for the doorknob. Maura felt an unreasonable urge to divert her from her favorite room in the house.

"Come see what they're doing to the kitchen," she said quickly. They all wandered to the kitchen doorway and peered in. "They're hacking it to pieces and you would get dusty if you go in there, but you can see where it's going. They're about a third of the way through laying the black and white tile squares, which is a huge improvement over the ancient linoleum. They had to take out the stove and the refrigerator so they could lay the tile down. The stove was hauled off but the refrigerator is plugged in in the new pantry, which we can get to through the writing room. We can't cook but we can keep milk and luncheon meat. The new cabinets and countertops are already installed along the back wall there, and you can see the big new sink lying over there in the corner."

Will whistled.

"There's been a lot of progress since I was here last weekend!"

"I thought you were going to keep the renovations true to the period," objected Marge. "The floor and cabinets are very 1954."

"Our investor, Maura's friend Rebecca, thought the kitchen and bathrooms should be up to date."

"I think it's going to be wonderful!" Junie enthused. "It already looks so much better than when I was here the first time."

The only interest in the writing room that the visitors expressed was in the big black typewriter that sat on the desk, the stacks of writing paper and the bin that contained the meager pages from *The Witch of Islay*.

"What's this?" Marge reached for the bin. Maura reacted without thinking and dove in front of her. She picked up the bin and held it. The others stared at her in surprise, Marge with her hand still outstretched.

"Well, really!"

"Sorry," Maura smiled, attempting to take the offense out of her action. "These are top secret!" She didn't want to tell them she was writing a book and open the door to questions she didn't want to answer.

"Maura's a writer!" Will said proudly. She shot him a look.

"Well, playing at it anyway!" she forced a laugh. "Now this door takes us into a little hallway with the new powder room and pantry." She succeeded in moving them along, but she caught Marge giving her glances of dislike.

Lizzie came bouncing down the stairs as they came back to the parlor.

"Mr. Giant! Mr. Giant!"

"Princess Lizzie!" Will laughed. "Say hello to Miss Margie and Miss Junie. They're friends of mine."

Lizzie stared at the women curiously. Miss Margie and Miss Junie stared back. The four-year-old seemed to find them uninteresting and wandered off, but the sisters' eyes followed her.

Junie and Marge waited on the front stoop while Will went to get his wallet for their lunch. Maura, in her bedroom changing into her bathing suit, was an unwilling audience to their whispered conversation.

"You're a fool, Junie," said Marge. "You said she was a middle-aged caretaker, but she's young and attractive!"

"Will said they went to school together, and he's thirty-five! She must be close to his age."

"So am I! Do you think I'm middle-aged?"

Silence from Junie.

"And you know what?" Marge's voice sounded nettled. "That kid is crazy about him. He must be spending a lot of his weekend time with them. You should never have thrown George Ashton over for him. He could have given you everything you wanted. If Will doesn't marry you, George will never take you back!"

"I know that!" Junie's whisper was petulant. "And Georgie is engaged now anyway. Will isn't going to... shh! Here he comes."

Maura quickly finished changing, her cheeks blazing. Marge had done her best to instill suspicion in her sister's mind where none was warranted. How awkward would it make future weekend visits for Will if Junie or Marge started questioning his motives? Would he stop coming?

After Will and the two sisters set off for lunch at the coffee shop, Maura packed sandwiches for a picnic on the beach with Gracie. She wished she hadn't overheard the sisters' conversation, and hoped they took their time over lunch.

Maura, Gracie and Lizzie ate their picnic lunch then began a search along the water's edge for tiny shells and bits of driftwood that could be used for a day camp craft. The visitors appeared for their afternoon swim when a nice pile had been amassed and Lizzie was filling her pail with sand at the water's edge.

"Hi, Gracie!" called Will. Gracie waved, and she and Maura walked over to the beach blanket where the sisters were settling themselves. Introductions were made and Will asked who wanted to go for a swim.

"Not me! I just went to the hairdresser yesterday." Gracie checked herself in a compact mirror. The sisters had been staring at her, taking in her fashionable two-piece bathing suit, the picture hat that dipped over one eye and the very stylish sunglasses. Gracie's toenails and fingernails were painted the same red as her lips. "You're not going to budge Miss Lizzie either," said Gracie. "She's making a sand castle."

"We have to put on suntan lotion," said Junie to Will, "but then we'll come out. You go ahead!"

"OK. Come on, Maura!" The two ran across the sand and straight into the ocean. A wave came rolling in but they plowed through it and dove under the water.

Gracie watched them, then noticed that Junie had paused while removing her beach robe. She had on a silvery-green one-piece suit with a skirt.

"They're from Jersey," Gracie explained, not sure how to interpret Junie's expression. "That's the best way to get into the ocean without getting knocked over. The waves are bigger there." She made herself comfortable on their beach blanket and while they applied lotion, asked them for news about the latest movies. This topic was of high interest to Junie, so she was able to oblige with details of all the latest films. Marge was silent, her eyebrows drawn in a frown as she watched Will and Maura laughing and bobbing in the waves.

Will came out of the water and halfway up the beach. He beckoned to the women on the towel.

"Come on! It's a little cold at first but you get used to it eventually."

Junie stood.

Gracie, who was looking at Will over the top of her sunglasses, turned to the young woman with an appreciative smile. "He's a big one, is our friend Will. But so nicely assembled. I congratulate you, Junie!"

Junie's face turned scarlet. Marge made a disgusted sound and grabbed her sister's hand.

"Come on, June."

They didn't stay long at the beach, as the three visitors had to catch the late afternoon ferry. After returning to the house Maura, Will and Lizzie took turns using the outdoor shower to wash away the sand and salt. Junie and her sister preferred to use the bathroom upstairs.

Gracie had stopped at her bungalow to change and was coming up the lawn from the path in the woods when Junie moved impulsively to Will's side and put her arm through his.

"Will, this house will be beautiful when it's finished. Couldn't you ask your aunt to sell it to us at a good price? I can just imagine our children playing in this nice yard every summer and going to the beach!"

Maura knew that Junie's suggestion wasn't possible given the arrangement they had with Rebecca, but she felt an irrational stab of resentment. For the summer, this was her territory and she didn't like Junie's proprietary attitude.

Will was surprised.

"Honey, you know I can't ask Aunt May to sell the house to us at a reduced price. We have an investor involved, and my aunt needs the money." He patted her hand. "Besides, I can't afford a summer home! Not if we're going to build that year-round house you want."

"My father would—"

"No, Junie." Will's voice was quiet but firm. She flushed.

"This is OUR house!" Lizzie had been sitting in the grass nearby with a pot of warm soapy water, giving her doll and its clothes yet another washing. She stared belligerently at Junie.

"It's not *your* house," Marge said with a sour look.

Lizzie's ferocious stare was now directed equally at Junie and her sister.

"What a weird kid," muttered Marge.

"You know it's just our home for the summer, Lizzie Lou. Then we'll have a new home when I start my job." Maura's voice was mild but the look she directed at Marge gave the woman a slight shock.

Gracie plopped down in the grass next to Lizzie and put her arms around her. "And I hope you and Mommy will come back and stay at my house for vacations. Won't that be fun?"

"OK, ladies. Time to leave to catch the ferry. The taxi should be here any minute." Will's voice was even, but there was an angry glint in his eye and his mouth was set in a firm line. As the women climbed into the taxi, he turned to Maura and said softly, "I'm sorry."

Some of her indignation melted and she smiled. "I like Junie." Will gave her arm a quick squeeze and nodded gratefully.

Maura waved as the taxi pulled away, wondering what made men pick the women they would spend the rest of their lives with.

"What do you have against virgins?" Maura later asked, in response to her friend's comment that they were overrated. She took a plate from Gracie and wiped it with her dish towel.

"All I did was congratulate Junie for catching a guy who looks as good as Will did at the beach. Her face turned as red as my lipstick and her sister acted like I was corrupting little Junie. Or maybe she thought I had designs on Will."

Maura inspected the plate she had just dried.

"Do you?"

Maura hoped her question sounded casual but she realized she very much wanted to hear Gracie's answer. She hadn't reached the age of thirty-four without developing a fair amount of self-perception. There was no possibility of a future for herself with Will, even if their relationship was more than friendship. If Junie stepped out of the picture for some reason, Maura would never try to move in to take her place. She knew that she was too emotionally damaged to ever be happy in a marriage. What might start out as a lovely partnership would be doomed by her own expectations of failure.

When Maura was a teenager, she would often ride her battered bicycle around the well-to-do neighborhoods of Barlow Ridge at dinnertime. She loved that time of day, when mothers called to their children to come inside and wash their hands before supper. The scents of onions and potatoes roasting, and maybe a chicken for those lucky enough to afford such a thing in the Depression, flavored the evening air. She coasted by lit windows and saw the families inside. Their lives would never include her but for those brief moments as she passed she could imagine herself sitting down at the table, surrounded by cheerful faces and people that loved her... so different from their cold and cheerless apartment and her mother's habitually stony expression. Maura realized that she was regarding her summer on Islay and Will's presence in the same light. His welcome arrival at the house on weekends, the obvious affection he and Lizzie had for each other, the comfortable conversations over a glass of wine in the darkened rose-scented back yard all felt like a play that showed her how life could have been. How it would be for Will and Junie. How it could be for anyone who wasn't Maura. She knew it was all make-believe, but this time she was an actor in this brief summer production rather than a dim figure on a bicycle rolling past and looking on enviously. Junie's desire to own the Watts house and even Gracie's admiration for Will made it harder to believe in her little delusion.

Gracie stared at her. "Do I have designs on Will? Of course I don't." She turned off the faucets and gave Maura a sideways look. "I don't waste my time on men who are already taken. Now Delectable Steve is another story!"

"I like 'Delectable' better than 'Droolable'. Did you know he's a professor at URI?"

"Really? No! We have barely exchanged three sentences. All of our dates have been in my head." She washed and rinsed a glass. "What were you looking for when you married your ex?"

"David? Well, I was twenty when we got married. My mother was a lunatic and my father left us during the Depression. My family lived in ratty apartments and barely scraped by. I wasn't in love with David, although I thought I was at the time. I was in love with the idea of having a peaceful, secure life and a pretty little house in a college town. I managed that well, didn't I? What made you marry Ernest?"

"He was my first boyfriend. I never doubted he was the right one; Ernest was a good man. Maura, people shouldn't settle."

"I think you're right. And now we need to figure out how to entrap the shy but delectable Steve into going on a real date with you."

They spent the next half hour scheming, then Gracie left before the sun went down.

CHAPTER 14

After dropping Lizzie at day camp Tuesday morning, Maura let herself through Opal's gate and knocked on her door.

"Got anything good to eat?"

"What is this, Halloween?" Opal opened the door and waved Maura in. "Of course, I have something good to eat - look at me. I was just about to make a fresh pot of coffee."

In a few minutes, Opal had pushed aside stacks of bills and set delicate china cups and saucers on the table.

"Part of my wedding set. I figure why not use them; it's not like I need to preserve them for my descendants. I didn't get much else out of my divorce."

Maura stirred a little cream into her coffee.

"So when are you going to tell me your dark history that's worse than mine?"

"Eh?" Opal's look was evasive.

"When we first met you said you would tell me your story sometime, and said it was worse than my tawdry past."

Opal sighed.

"You'll think I'm a terrible person."

"So? I'll still come over and beg for coffee and dessert." She took a forkful of iced angel food cake and looked at Opal expectantly.

"OK... I was married when I was in my early twenties. Things weren't bad for the first fifteen years or so. Ronald was your average husband. He had a decent job, worked a little too much and made enough money to support me and our four kids. I'd put on a lot of weight, especially after my youngest, Clara, was born. He was a little fastidious, and not thrilled about coming home to a messy house with all the craziness you have with four kids. As time went on, I could tell he wasn't interested in me as a woman anymore, if you get my drift, but he was always polite and would help out if I asked.

"Well, he started working later and later, and going into the office on weekends. Or so he said. I didn't have any family left and we lived on kind of a busy road, not a neighborhood, so I got lonely. I started walking to town while the kids were in school, going into the shops just for company. There was a small grocery store that had great meats and produce. I went in there a lot. The owner was friendly and whenever he saw me walk in, he came over to say hello. He'd stand there as long as I wanted to talk, while customers went around us. We started with polite chatting, the way you do with strangers, but almost right away I knew we were...I don't even know how to describe it. We were the same underneath. As corny as it sounds, it was like a jigsaw puzzle where two pieces fit together perfectly. He was really funny and had me laughing all the time. I made him laugh too... I never thought of myself as a funny person before, but he brought it out in me. Part of me felt guilty for looking forward to seeing another man but I told myself he was just a good friend. Men and women can be friends, right?

"One day he told me it was his time for a break, and did I want to come back to his office for a bottle of cream soda. Sure, why not? My feet hurt and I'd just stay for a few minutes.

"We sat down and right away he leaned forward so his knees were touching mine. 'Opal, are you happy? Every time you come in here you look kind of forlorn.' He said it in a real gentle, kind voice and I started crying. I was pretty sure Ronald was seeing someone on the side and my kids were old enough by then to have no interest in family things. All this came tumbling out of my mouth before I could stop it, and the grocer put his arms around me and held me until I calmed down. I knew at that point that there would never be anyone I would feel the same way about. We liked the same things, we loved each other's company and he appreciated the way I looked. He wanted me to leave my husband and promised he would take care of me no matter what. You may be wondering if the fact that I was a mother of four slipped my mind. Well, it didn't. If it wasn't for the kids I would have left my husband like a shot. Pretty soon I had clear evidence that he was seeing another woman. Well, who was I to say anything? We weren't actually having affair but I was in love with another man.

"Ronald's floozy must have dumped him because he started coming home for dinner every night and hardly ever went into the office on the weekends. He seemed to notice me a little again. I didn't love him anymore but we kind of felt like a family. I wanted to break it off with the grocer but every time I saw him, I couldn't imagine cutting him out of my life.

"I don't know what made my husband suspect something was going on. One day he supposedly left for work but parked his car on another street and followed me into town. He saw me walk hand-in-hand with the grocer to his little house a few streets over from the store and disappear inside. We just played cards and listened to the radio but Ronald imagined the worst. That night he had it out with me, sitting in the car so the kids couldn't hear. I said I would break it off with the grocer and cried hysterically. He slapped me hard – I don't know whether to stop the crying or because he was in a rage - but my head hit the passenger window with a bang and I was dazed for a few minutes. He told me to never set foot back in the house or on the property, and the kids were off limits. I was wailing and telling him I was sorry but he left me in the car and went into the house. When I tried to get in the door was locked. A few minutes later he threw my purse out the upstairs window and a small suitcase with a few things in it. As I mentioned we lived on a busy street, so I must have been quite the spectacle, a crazy woman screaming and crying."

"The jerk! And he had been having an affair."

"Right, but I'm not excusing myself. Well, to wrap up this depressing story, the grocer expected that we would be together now. He said if I was worried about the scandal, he would open another store somewhere else. He had been thinking about it anyway. Once my divorce was final we could get married. He couldn't believe it when I said no. My husband was working to get full custody of the kids and wouldn't let me see them. I didn't want him to have the ammunition of me still seeing my boyfriend for the divorce case. I had inherited some money from my mother a while back that I hadn't touched, so had enough to live on in a small apartment. I kept trying to see the kids, would wait outside the school but when they saw me they got these ugly looks on their faces and walked past me. It was horrible. They were teenagers by that point and you know how insufferable they are even under good circumstances.

"The next thing I know the divorce is final and he's got full custody of the kids. I had a cheap lawyer who didn't manage to get anywhere with my husband's affair. I walked past the house one night, hoping to catch a glimpse of any of them in their windows. Instead, I found a Sold sign out front and the house was dark. Ronald had gotten a position in the Chicago branch of his company and moved out there with the kids. I've never seen them since. I got his address from one of his old colleagues and sent the kids a lot of letters, but they were never answered."

"Oh Opal," Maura whispered. "How awful. If I was separated from Lizzie it would kill me. How did you wind up here?"

Opal blew her nose.

"After a year or two the grocer asked me to marry him again. I was still shell-shocked by the whole thing and hated myself for causing my marriage to fall apart. I thought if I lived the life of a nun, I could atone a little and maybe I would see my kids again. I admit I was a little crazy then. When I once more refused the grocer, he sold his store and moved away. A few years later one of his employees told me he had moved to Islay. I loved him just as much as I ever had and by then I had accepted the fact that my kids didn't want me in their lives. I wrote him a letter asking if I could come see him. He wrote back a few weeks later and said that I had broken his heart and he didn't want anything more to do with me. Moving here was the craziest thing I've ever done. I had to live somewhere and didn't want to spend my whole inheritance paying rent until it ran out. I should buy a little house and live on a budget. So I visited a real estate agent to see if there were any houses for sale on Islay. I guess I thought if I was here on the spot, some day we would run into each other and make it up. Well, the bungalows hadn't been built yet and all there was for sale was this crazy house and one side of a duplex down by the harbor. This place appealed to my sense of humor; the last owners had done a lot of repairs so most of the problems are cosmetic. I loved the green and the pretty houses around it. The place was going for cheap because it's hideous."

"What happened with the grocer?" The owner of Islay's main grocery store was in his eighties, a good twenty years older than Opal. Could he be her ex-lover? Or maybe he was running one of the smaller shops down by the harbor.

"Right after I moved in, I strolled past his place until we ran into each other. He looked at me with unbelievable fury and just kept walking. And that was that."

"No chance of reconciling?"

Opal shook her head sadly and Maura patted her hand.

"You were right. Your story is worse."

Patrick rang the next morning and suggested she meet him for breakfast at the coffee shop. He had some information he thought might help her with her book. Maura had planned to spend the morning at her typewriter but agreed to meet him. She had gotten the *Temperance* near Islay, about to be wrecked, but now what? She hoped Patrick had some useful information.

Only a few of the tables were occupied when Maura arrived at the coffee shop. The treasure hunter had gotten there first and was putting sugar in a cup of coffee. He smiled when she sat down and signaled the waitress.

"Now I know how to lure you out of your house."

"Don't get too smug until I see what you have for me today."

Maura had already had a bowl of cereal for breakfast but ordered a plate of scrambled eggs and toast. She would skip lunch. Patrick ordered cherry blintzes.

After the waitress left, Patrick put a brochure of mimeographed sheets on the table. The cover showed an inexpertly drawn shipwreck, a man and a woman dressed like Thanksgiving pilgrims and a border of cabbage-like roses.

"Violet Wilson thought of herself as an artist," he said.

The brochure title read "Islay's Romantic Beginnings". Maura picked it up and turned to the first page.

"She wrote a history of the island?"

"She plagiarized the journal of one of the original settlers, the *Temperance's* first mate, and added her own embellishments. In her defense, the journal was a mix of mind-numbing supply inventories, melodrama that even Violet couldn't aspire to and self-loathing at his spiritual failings. She thought that if she pulled out the choice parts and added in her own commentary it might be more appealing."

"Where is the actual journal? I'd love to read it."

"Unfortunately, it's disappeared. Violet kept it in the Islay Historical Society office, which is now open since the library got Violet's key back from the police. She might have taken it home for some reason; maybe they'll find it in her house. She managed to get the basic history in the pamphlet so it's worth reading. Fortunately, I read the journal itself. Would you like my version?"

The waitress set their breakfasts in front of them and warmed up their coffee.

"Absolutely! Fire away."

"OK, some of this is right out of the journal and some I've pieced together. You know that history is my obsession, so you won't be surprised that I did some research." He took a sip of his coffee and began.

"Most of the *Temperance* passengers, as I mentioned before, were part of an intolerant religious sect. It was headed by an ignorant preacher and his young wife. Somewhere along the voyage his flock discovered that he was in cahoots with the ship's captain to indenture the passengers upon arrival, splitting the spoils."

Both captain and preacher drowned in the shipwreck, Patrick went on, but the preacher's wife made it to shore. The surviving passengers felt that they had been saved from more than a drowning death and finding the island able to support a small colony, decided to remain for a while. Under the influence of new freedom from their sect's intolerant laws, and of the casks of whiskey that floated ashore from the breaking up ship, they set up a very lax style of government and began to intermarry, or at least cohabitate, with the ship's crew. The preacher's wife railed against those fallen from grace, to the point where some wanted to put her quietly out of the way. A few kinder souls prevailed on the others to build her a small house along the southwest coastline, where she would be sufficiently distant from the colony which had set itself up in a sheltered hollow in the center of the island. They gave her an allotment of seeds and gardening implements that had been salvaged from the wreck and occasionally brought her fish or a squirrel. In exchange, she was not allowed near the settlement. The preacher's wife began to collect plant specimens from around the island and add them to her garden, mixing health remedies as her mother had taught her back in Wales. According to the first mate's journal, the colonists eventually referred to her as the island healer or witch, depending on their frame of reference. There was a truce of sorts where the settlers gave her basic supplies in exchange for her remedies.

Many years after the colony was founded, a passing ship looking for shelter from a storm found the inlet on the north side of the island where Patrick and Steve anchored the *Lorelei*. Venturing onto shore, they soon came to the settlement clearing and found it strewn with bones and partially intact skeletons. They were lying on the open ground or under rough-made tables. The only life they found on the island was an old man and his daughter, or so they thought her. When he saw the ship's company approaching, he kissed the girl on her forehead and walked out to meet them. He silently handed one of them a notebook and walked off. A few days later, after they had dug graves for the assortment of bones in the settlement, they found the body of the old man at the base of the cliff where the shipwreck victims had been washed in.

"Since he had a notebook," said Maura, "I'm guessing the old man was the first mate. Who was the girl?"

"There weren't many young women who survived the shipwreck and there were no children. There were a surprising number of stillbirths in the years after they set up the colony – well, maybe not so surprising considering the time and the fact that there was no doctor. One baby was born alive and was found by the first mate and the preacher's wife when the rest of the settlers died."

"How did the first mate and preacher's wife survive? How did everyone else die? Were they a couple? What happened to her? Drat! I have to go pick up Lizzie. Come by after dinner for a drink."

Patrick hesitated.

"I can't."

"Oh...OK. Some other time." Maura felt her face turn pink.

"No, I mean, if I step foot onto your property I might die. The witch put a curse on her land."

As it turned out, Maura didn't have to wait long to hear the rest of the shipwreck survivors' story.

She and Lizzie did some errands in town then spent the afternoon playing with Jelly Bean in the backyard. It had taken some coaxing to get him out the door, but Maura was tired of cleaning the litter box every few hours and was determined. They finally enticed him outside by Lizzie running around the backyard trailing a long string. Jelly Bean, who had been sitting in the doorway looking around nervously, launched himself after her. By the time he realized he had been tricked, the door was closed and he couldn't get back in. For the next hour he hunkered under the picnic table, his expression that of the heroine in a horror film who just realized she's not alone in the house.

They were in the writing room after dinner, drawing pictures on Lizzie's new table, when Maura chanced to look out the window. There was Patrick, across the narrow street, spreading a blanket on the green. He took a bag out of his bicycle's basket and put it next to the blanket. Maura was torn between wanting to hear the rest of the story of the settlers and her doubts regarding the advisability of spending time with someone who thinks he'll be struck dead in your yard. He was looking at her house, clearly trying to figure out how to get her attention without getting close enough to ring the doorbell, so she took pity on him.

Patrick looked relieved when she opened the door and stepped out.

"How do you know the green wasn't part of the witch's property?" she called from the step.

He grinned.

"Because I toured the whole island my first few months here, before I read the diary. I didn't know there was a curse. Steve and I got coffee and took a walk around the green. I survived, so I'm guessing the road and green are safe, or there's no curse. Can you come over here so I don't have to shout and let the whole neighborhood know I'm crazy?"

Patrick's bag contained three bottles of root beer and a plastic jar of bubbles. Lizzie didn't like the fizz of the root beer in her nose but happily took the bubbles and ran around the green, her hand holding the bubble wand outstretched. The early evening sun glinted on the trail of little bubbles and sparked colors.

"Kids are easy to entertain, aren't they?" Patrick watched Lizzie run.

"Sure. For about two and a half minutes. Why would the witch put a curse on her own land?"

"There weren't enough young women on the island. The male settlers were getting in the habit of finding excuses to bring things to the witch and were getting too familiar. They didn't like her and were a little afraid of her, but she was young and pretty. One night the settlers were celebrating something and broke out the whiskey. A handful of drunks headed to the witch's side of the island meaning business. The first mate had been paying a lot of visits to the witch himself but with purer motives, or so he told himself. He was spending hours there most days, doing odd jobs around the house and garden. He followed the drunks that night and managed to help the witch fend them off. She stood in front of the house and chanted with her arms raised, putting a curse on any man who stepped foot on her land with an impure heart. According to the first mate, who wrote in a revolting, flowery style, all the dark powers of the sea and earth seemed to swirl around her and speak from her lips. It was enough to scare them off that night. One of the men died within the week, and another several weeks later. It was a while before any of them tried to get at the witch again, but this time she and the first mate were ready for them. There was a wedding, with the usual whiskey, and sometime during the night a group paid the witch a visit. She held a lit torch in each hand and waved them around, speaking in tongues."

"I like her ingenuity. That must have been a creepy effect."

"My mother spoke in tongues," Patrick said a little stiffly. "It can be very impressive."

"Oh." Maura didn't know what else to say.

Lizzie wandered over, complaining that she was bored. Maura suggested she get her pad of paper and crayons and bring them out.

"Anyway," Patrick resumed, frowning at the interruption, "only one of the men was drunk enough to get any closer after that and she ran at him hissing. He fled after his friends and died a month or two later from some cause not mentioned. No one came around again, except the first mate, who seems to have eventually moved in with her. How he reconciled that with his prudish little conscience, I don't know."

Maura considered this.

"They could have died of anything back then – sepsis from a wound, a burst appendix, a brawl... it doesn't seem much for the legend to live on. Or for a modern-day treasure hunter to worry about! Why are you worried, anyway? Do you have an impure heart?"

His smile answered hers.

"I'm a man, and let's just say I have a colorful past. The witch was narrow-minded and I doubt she would have approved of me."

"If the land is cursed, why haven't there been more deaths over the centuries? I'm sure there have been lots of men living here, and there must have been some corkers here and there."

Patrick leaned forward.

"I did some checking and there have been a fair number of unexpected deaths. The last owner of that dump", he nodded at Opal's house, "died of a heart attack after being investigated for embezzlement. The original owner was killed in a sailing accident right after they moved here. One of the electricians who put the first wiring in the house you're staying in dropped dead on the spot."

Maura thought that any old house would have its share of deaths, but she didn't argue that this was hardly proof of a curse. Patrick wasn't taking chances, and she didn't think she wanted the complication of him hanging around her house anyway. Lizzie was yawning and giving Patrick annoyed stares that he was having a hard time ignoring, so she wished him goodnight.

The settlers of Islay invaded Maura's dreams that night. She woke up a little after midnight, her heart pounding from a partially-remembered dream where the Watts house was being surrounded by shadowy figures, low chanting coming nearer and nearer. Maura had closed all the windows in the house when a rain shower started before she went to bed, and now her room was hot and airless. She pushed the sashes of her bedroom windows up and cool, rain-rinsed air filled the room. She tiptoed into Lizzie's room and did the same. Jelly Bean didn't open his eyes but he stretched luxuriously and let out a gusty, contented sigh. With remnants of her dream still clinging, Maura lay awake for an hour. She imagined how terrifying it must have been for the young preacher's wife to be visited by drunken gangs with only her own ingenuity to save her.

When she woke the next morning, Maura's head ached a little and she felt listless. Gracie commented on her lack of joie de vivre and invited her to stay for lunch when she came back for Lizzie.

The path home through the woods was uphill most of the way. She sometimes had company when another parent from the green had dropped their child off at the same time, but today she was alone. Maura was usually a little out of breath by the time she reached the house with her leg muscles aching, but today she welcomed the exercise. It seemed to clear her head and she let her thoughts flow freely. The trees were stunted on this end of the island but grew thickly. There was no sign of human occupation here, and Maura thought it must have looked the same in the island witch's day. What was her name? She wasn't a witch and Maura didn't like calling her that. She was a young woman, cast out by her community, trying to survive. She would ask Patrick if he knew her name.

Maura's thoughts turned to Junie and Marge's recent visit. She had been prepared to like them because they would soon be Will's family, and because she generally liked people until she had a reason not to. She remembered her irritation at the assessing way they looked over the Watts house, how they fingered the fabrics and commented on the changes that she, Will and Rebecca had made. Their lack of interest in anything that wasn't decorative was palpable. They asked Will how much money he thought the house could get, then Junie made that absurd suggestion that they get Aunt May to sell them the house. Will was patient and gentle with his fiancé but clearly wasn't thrilled with her sister. To what extent would Marge disrupt Will's peace in the coming years? It was clear she and Junie were close, and that Marge influenced her sister. Much of the women's conversation that afternoon had centered around their friends and acquaintances from the country club and the anticipation of upcoming grand events, leading Maura to suppose that their family was established in Boston high society. Junie seemed to expect to continue this lifestyle after her marriage. Will had made it clear that he wouldn't accept financial help from his future father-in-law. Would Junie be happy living in the kind of house Will could afford and on a budget?

As soon as she returned home, Maura made a fresh pot of coffee and headed to the writing room. She put a piece of paper in her typewriter with the intention of outlining a general vignette about the disruption to island life that outsiders inflicted on the residents. She sat for a moment to consider her first words. The sun had disappeared behind gathering clouds with purple-gray bottoms. Storms blew up quickly on the island and often passed just as fast, but they could be fierce this far out to sea. She hoped any storm would blow over by the time she had to get Lizzie. What would the island witch have felt when a storm approached? It seemed she lived on occasional handouts from the colony and anything she could grow or scavenge. Would her precious belongings survive the storm? Her roof had been laid by men who had no affection for her and only wanted to assuage their consciences for expelling her from their settlement. Did she worry that it would hold in high winds? How did she manage the severe New England winters?

Maura stared unseeingly for several minutes then began to type.

Prudence stood at the deck rail, wondering which would be the greater sin: to throw herself overboard or to remain the wife of a man who had abominated himself before God? She had been rigidly raised by a traveling preacher, indoctrinated in the most intolerant of creeds. Her father, tired of supporting her, gave her to a fellow preacher when she was fifteen. He was some twenty years her senior. She fervently believed the tenets of their sect and wholeheartedly supported their congregation's dangerous voyage to America where they could practice their faith without reprisal.

Last night, her husband Abdiel had come to her drunk. He had been with the ship's crew and she could smell whiskey on his breath. She knew that odor well, since her father drank whenever they had made enough money at a prayer meeting. He would then beat her mother, and sometimes he beat his daughter. The next day he would make it clear that the fault was theirs. Tonight, Abdiel was barely concealing his glee about something. Closely surrounded as they were by their congregation, he tried to plant wet kisses on her mouth. Her duty was to submit to him in all things, but his intentions had her covered in shame. Sensing her reluctance, he put his mouth against her ear, and whispered:

"We will soon be rich, Prudence! You'll have pretty gowns and a carriage."

"Rich! How? We disdain the trappings of wealth! A rich man cannot enter heaven." (Maura rolled her eyes at her own character.)

He squeezed her arm painfully.

"You say that because you have never had wealth."

She frowned. "Abdiel, what are you about?" (Would that have been the equivalent of "What shenanigans are you up to?")

Then he told her. He had made a bargain with the captain that they would force the congregation to indenture themselves to pay for their passage. They had already sold everything they owned to pay for the voyage for themselves and their families, but the captain would say that the money had been stolen and he must be paid. Abdiel would instruct his followers to agree to the five years of servitude after which they would congregate together as originally planned.

Prudence pulled away in horror. Families would be separated and forced into labor because of the treachery of their leader. In the dim light of the lantern in their communal area, he saw the disgust in her face and began to shake her. Their nearest neighbors had caught some of his drunken whisperings and soon voices were heard exclaiming in outrage as the news spread throughout the hold.

She ran up the ladder to the deck. Abdiel stumbled after her and caught up with her when she tripped over a coiled rope. He dragged her to her feet then slapped her. When she cried out, he slapped her again. In all their years of marriage she had given him only loyalty and obedience. Her disgust now enraged and frightened him.

"Here! Stop that!" A strong arm spun Abdiel away from her. The preacher took a wild swing at the first mate who had interceded on Prudence's behalf but was easily deflected.

"This is a matter between my wife and me and doesn't concern you!"

John Kellow, the first mate, was the younger of two sons in a family that had done well in textiles. The elder would eventually take over the family business and John hoped to have his own ship one day. Both sons had been well-educated and having been raised by kind parents with strong principles, were generally liked and respected. John was revolted to think that this aging drunkard was married to the young woman who now regarded her husband with such loathing. She –

She what? Prudence needed to get to the ship rail without her husband, and without the first mate trailing after her, to contemplate suicide. The ship would hit the rocks at any moment, taking the decision out of her hands. Was there a storm going on, or were there survivors because the seas were relatively calm? Maura had followed an impulse to write Islay's story from the witch's viewpoint but was now realizing how much of the tale had to be fabricated around the few known facts. It probably didn't matter because it wasn't likely she would ever be able to publish it, but the thought of giving the young woman a voice was satisfying. It felt good to give her a name, even if apocryphal. Why 'Prudence'? Given the time and her religious beginnings, Maura supposed her name would be biblical or depressing – something along the lines of Patience or Silence. Remembering the woman's smart thinking when she chased away the marauding colonists, Maura picked Prudence. If Patrick knew the woman's real name, she could always change it.

It was almost time to pick up Lizzie, so Maura put the typewritten sheets in a drawer. She suspected her writing time would be better spent crafting more of the little vignettes of island life, but the story of Prudence and the other shipwreck survivors had grabbed her imagination and wouldn't let go.

Midge's mother, Dottie, was talking animatedly to a white-faced Gracie and another mother when Maura reached the bungalows. When she saw Maura, Gracie turned to her and said,

"The baker has disappeared."

Chapter 15

Dottie and her friend had gone to the coffee shop for an early breakfast that morning and found it closed. The two island policemen were inside talking to Wally. A sign on the door read 'Closed Until Further Notice'. Nothing was known except that the baker had taken the garbage out after the restaurant closed the previous evening and he hadn't been seen since. The mainland had been radioed but so far no real action had been taken.

Maura shared her concerns with Lillian through the rose portal.

"Coming after Bob Welch and Violet Wilson, you have to wonder if something's going on. The coffee shop is right around the corner, Lillian. The weirdness is getting a little too close!"

Her neighbor only shrugged.

"The man is such a hermit, hardly anybody knows what he looks like. He leaves the island. What does it have to do with us?"

Many of the other island residents didn't share Lillian's lack of concern. Neighbors stopped each other in stores to exchange theories and any bits of news. By the time Will arrived mid-afternoon on Saturday, a few men from the mainland sheriff's office had questioned the business owners and ferry crew and had done perfunctory searches of the lesser traveled lanes and walking paths. It was clear that they thought the baker had left of his own accord due to lack of any evidence that said otherwise. Gracie's jitters continued to fuel a little knot of worry in Maura's mind, though, and she wondered again whether Islay was safe for Lizzie.

Will hadn't taken the Saturday morning ferry. He and Junie had gone to her cousin's wedding, which was followed by a formal breakfast. When he eventually arrived, Maura knew at once that he was out of sorts. He seemed to be trying his best to hide it and accompanied Lizzie to her 'bean patch' to admire the progress of her magic beans. Maura had made a tall trellis for them, which Will informed her was optimistic. He accepted a cup of coffee but took it to the carriage house, stating his intention of finishing the interior this weekend. They didn't see him until dinner, and then he devoted himself to telling Lizzie stories about the giant and Jelly Bean. The hint of formality in Will's conversation with her, and his faintly remote air puzzled her. They had parted on their usual good terms last weekend and she had had little conversation with him since he arrived today, so she assumed something had occurred during the week to bother him. She was sorry for it; she and Lizzie had both come to look forward to his weekend visits and it appeared they wouldn't see much of him this time. She remembered the conversation she had overheard between Junie and her sister and had a niggling worry that her presence on Islay might have caused an argument.

Will was absently drying dishes after dinner when he noticed the look Maura gave him as she handed him a dripping plate. He answered her questioning smile and raised eyebrow with a reluctant laugh.

"Sorry. I know I'm not good company tonight."

"You don't need to be. Lizzie, Jelly Bean doesn't eat grapes." She shook water out of a wine glass and handed it to Will. "And actually, it's a good thing that you spent the entire dinner telling Lizzie stories and ignoring me. I type them up, you know, and Lizzie draws pictures to go with them. We're making a book of Lizzie and the Giant and Jelly Bean stories."

He grinned. "Is that right! Can I see it?"

"When it's finished. We'll mention you in the acknowledgements."

Hours later, Maura sat at her desk in the writing room, trying to puzzle out a painfully complicated paragraph of dialogue in *The Witch of Islay*. Lizzie had been asleep for hours. Maura yawned and took a sip of cooled tea, wondering how her characters could stand each other. Earlier she had typed up the stories Will told at dinner, as best she could remember them. She added them to the growing pages in her Lizzie and the Giant and Jelly Bean folder.

There was suddenly a shout outside her window. Maura quickly turned off the lamp on her desk and looked out. A small crowd had assembled on the street in front of Opal's gates. She could clearly see the individuals in the crowd because some were, unbelievably, carrying lit torches. More had flashlights, and the glow of cigarettes dotted the crowd like lightening bugs. Maura recognized one or two people from the harbor crescent, including the man from the post office with growths on his nose. The rest were unfamiliar, but she guessed that some were men who worked on the fishing boats and a few of their wives and girlfriends. They appeared to have started their evening at the tavern; more than a few carried beer bottles and there was a lot of laughter and boisterous bravado. Small groups of neighbors had started congregating on the green in their bathrobes, asking querulously what the racket was about. A large man moved and Maura was shocked to see her handyman, Randy, and his wife.

The man whose shout had first gotten Maura's attention raised his voice again.

"Come out! We know you're in there." This was directed generally at the Uncle Irvin house, and was followed by mumbled suggestions from those standing closest to the speaker.

"We won't hurt you," he added. "We just want to talk." Laughter rippled through the crowd, making Maura's scalp prickle. A teenage boy grabbed the bars of the gate and shook them.

Opal's wavery voice called out, "What do you want with me? Go away! I'll call the police!" Maura thought she must be in a second story window.

"What did you do with the baker?" a different voice called from the crowd. "Let him go or we're coming in after him."

Maura flew to the phone in the parlor and tried to call the police station, but no one picked up. Thankful that Lizzie was a heavy sleeper, she let herself out the back door and ran to the faucet at the rear corner of the house. Wally, the owner of the coffee shop, ran past her with his plaid bathrobe flapping over his pajamas. She saw him dart down the length of the wall and disappear around the back of Opal's house.

Maura turned the faucet handle as far as it would go and ran up the side of the Watts house toward the street, dragging the hose. She heard the carriage house door slam and Will call out to her, but she didn't pause. No one in the crowd saw her coming because it was dark in the shadow of Opal's wall. When she burst into the torchlight and began spraying them with the hose they were completely taken by surprise. The torches were extinguished by Islay's infamous water pressure. Cigarettes were knocked out of mouths and eyeglasses flew into the street. Maura did her best to spray every person in the crowd while they yelled and jostled each other to get away from her. When she stopped, they all stared at her with their mouths hanging open, hair plastered to their heads and clothes dripping. Her eyes caught Randy's, his full of disoriented dismay, hers with outrage.

"What's the matter with you, scaring a harmless old woman?" Maura yelled at the crowd, adrenaline shooting through her. "You should be ashamed of yourselves!" She strode up to a man who appeared to be the spokesman for the crowd and grabbed the front of his shirt. He was six inches taller than her and a hundred pounds heavier, yet he took a step back.

"Do you have something you would like to say to me?" Maura closed the gap between them again. He only gaped at her, so she sprayed him under the chin. He yelped and fell into the street. She turned and began spraying the crowd again. They shouted and stumbled over each other in their hurry to get to their bicycles and cars. The last of the mob passed a lone cyclist who stopped and watched their retreat. There was a smattering of applause from the group of neighbors on the green as well as a few surprised stares. The mob having disbursed, the neighbors began to return to their homes and Maura started for her unlocked back door to check on Lizzie. Will stood in the shadows, staring at her in disbelief. He grabbed her shoulders as she passed him and gave her a little shake.

"You could have been..." he checked, seeing Maura's look of triumph and exhilaration. Her curls were wild and damp where the night breeze had blown spray from the hose; her cheeks were flushed and her eyes bright. He tried to speak again but laughter, born of the fear for Maura's safety that he had been experiencing moments ago and the absurdity of the situation, burst out and choked his words.

Maura's adrenaline was still running high. Boosted by an intoxicating sense of power, she joined Will's laughter.

"That's the Maura I remember!" he gasped.

With the departure of the torches, only the glow from a streetlight several houses away made its way to where they were standing. Will had been reading in bed when he heard the commotion and had only paused to pull on his trousers and shirt. His hands now tightened on Maura's arms and all at once she became aware of his unbuttoned shirt and the fine, dark hair on the inches of bare chest visible in the light from the street. In a moment, Will seemed to slide from a comfortable compartment in her mind to dangerous and unfamiliar ground. She stared at him in confusion and his eyes widened.

"Maura!"

Patrick Dunn looked from her to the handsome giant in the unbuttoned shirt who clutched her in the shadows. She quickly recovered herself and Will released her.

"Patrick! Were you part of the mob or were you coming to save Opal?" Maura smiled a little but she wanted an answer. Patrick frowned.

"Of course I wasn't part of the mob," he said, annoyed. "I was in the tavern when I heard the fatheads planning to come here, so I rode out looking for the police. Neither of them were home and it cost me precious time. I got here just as everyone was leaving." He eyed Will, who was looking at him curiously. Maura didn't miss the hint of humor in Will's expression, and judging by Patrick's thinned lips and narrowed eyes, he hadn't missed it either. She thought that the good-looking treasure hunter wasn't accustomed to that sort of response from other men.

"Patrick," she said hastily, "this is Will Howe. His family owns this house, and he comes on weekends to help fix it up so they can sell it this fall. There's a guest house out back. Will, this is Patrick Dunn, the treasure hunter I mentioned."

"I had no idea there was treasure on Islay!" Will smiled as the two men shook hands.

"My treasure is more in the way of historical artifacts," Patrick said coolly, "and scattered on the ocean floor rather than the island. So what happened here?"

"Maura doused the mob's torches and drove them off with the garden hose!"

She laughed at Patrick's surprise.

"I have to make sure Lizzie didn't wake up, although I'm quite sure if she heard anything she would have been out here in the thick of it. Will, can you check on Opal and make sure everything's locked up tight? Just wait a minute while I call her so she'll let you in. I'll ask her to come stay with me."

Will nodded.

"Dunn, want to help me scout the property and make sure everything's secure?"

Patrick held up a hand. "I think I better try again to locate the island police, if you can check on the old woman, Howe. They should patrol the street for the next few nights."

They watched as he rode off on his bicycle.

"He's an interesting character," Will remarked. "Where did you find such a rakish specimen? He almost jumped when I suggested he help me check things out." He paused. "Maura, are you seeing him?"

She didn't know how to answer the second question. Did one outing and meeting for breakfast to discuss her book mean she was seeing Patrick? Instead she said,

"He won't leave the sidewalk. According to something he read, the island witch put a curse on any man with an impure heart who steps onto her land. He's not sure whether her house was built on Opal's land or your family's, but he doesn't want to take a chance. He's fascinatingly superstitious." Will laughed but Maura noticed his slight frown as he watched Patrick's retreating form disappear into the night.

Maura's call was picked up on the fourth ring. When she recognized the voice of Wally from the coffee shop, she remembered that he had run past her to the back of the property. Opal must have let him in. He told Maura that Opal was all right, and he would open the gate for Will.

Lizzie, thankfully, was still sleeping soundly. Jelly Bean sprawled on his back, spread-eagled, taking up the center of the bed. He narrowed his eyes at Maura but didn't move.

"You look ridiculous," Maura whispered. She wasn't sure how she felt about having a cat, but since Jelly Bean came Lizzie slept through the night in her own room. Maura enjoyed the luxury of a bed to herself.

She quickly dressed then prepared for her houseguest, putting lavender-scented sheets on one of the beds in the boys' dormitory and laying out towels.

Maura had just put the kettle on when there was a tapping at the back door and she heard Will's voice say her name. She opened the door and was surprised to see the dark shapes of three people behind Will. They filed into the kitchen and Will immediately went to each window and drew the curtains closed. The normally undemonstrative Opal put her arms around her.

"Thank you, honey. You were inspiring. Who would have thought you had it in you? Except you didn't have to call me an old woman. I'm not that ancient. I was sixty-eight last month."

"You were a Valkyrie." This statement came from the man who entered behind Wally and was directed to Maura. She gaped; the voice belonged to the missing baker. He smiled slightly at her surprise and held out his hand.

"I don't think we have officially met. Joe Fabiola. It's not my real name," he added as they shook hands.

"Maura Gertz. I hate my name."

The tea kettle began to whistle, and Maura mechanically turned off the burner and began to pour water into the coffee filter. She set mugs on Aunt May's big kitchen table and put out a pitcher of milk and the sugar bowl. The coffee dripped into the pot and began to fill the kitchen with its homey aroma. Her guests sat at the table and thanked her quietly as she filled their cups then took her seat.

"Lizzie slept through it?" Will asked.

"Yes, as expected. She'll sleep through anything. So, what's going on?"

"Go ahead, Joe," Wally urged after a moment of silence. "It's your story."

The baker's long face stretched into a grimace. He folded his arms on the table and began.

"OK," he told Maura. "Bear with me while I give you a little background. It doesn't make me look good but it's true." He took a sip of coffee. "I'm from Jersey. I was a punk when I was a kid and got into trouble – nothing terrible, just a lot of low-level stuff. I was sent to a reform school where I got into a trade program. They taught me to bake and I found I had a knack for it. If I had kept my nose clean when I got out I could have gotten a decent job, but my pal and I stole a car and I went to prison this time. Nobody wanted to hire me when I got out and I was pretty desperate until my cousin Gerald got me a place in a bakery in Newark. It didn't take me long to figure out it was a front for the mob. They ran their operation from a room behind the kitchen and I heard all kinds of stuff when they didn't know I was within earshot. They didn't worry about me too much... Gerald was in it up to his neck and I was his cousin. Not only that but I had done time in prison, so they must have thought I wasn't much of a risk. To be on the safe side they paid me very well for a junior baker and made a few vague threats. After a while I ran an occasional job for them – mostly delivery or guard services. I learned a lot from the head baker and when he died, I took over the baking operation. We were doing real well and they stopped pulling me out for jobs unless they couldn't find somebody else. I got married and we had a daughter, who's living in Brazil with her husband now. His firm has an office there."

The baker stared at the table.

"I stayed as far away from the crap in the back room as I could and focused on baking. They had been fairly small-time as organizations go, but about ten years ago they were taken over and things became more serious. I wanted to get out – start my own bakery in New York or Connecticut but they wouldn't let me because I knew too much. Thanks to Gerald, I knew a lot. The dope used to sit on the counter while I was baking and brag about the worst stuff he and the rest of the knuckleheads were into. I think he wanted to impress me because I'd been in prison, and he wanted to show he was a tough guy too.

"The state came to me one day with the news that the boss had been arrested on murder and racketeering charges. They gave me the option of going to prison along with my cousin and the rest of them or testifying against the boss. I didn't want to go back to prison; my wife had cancer and wasn't expected to live the year out. If I went to jail she would die before I could see her again. Plus, my daughter didn't know anything about my past and I wanted to keep it that way. What worried me was that the rest of the mob organization would get me if I testified against their buddies. The DA made a deal with me: if I testified, they would move me and my wife to a safe place, far away, and give me a little money to live on for a few years until things died down. I'd have to get a job to supplement the payments but they'd give me a fake driver's license and references to help with that. If my family wanted to get ahold of me they could send letters to a connection of the DA's in the Midwest, who would then put them in new envelopes and send them on to me. My kid was already married and in South America at that point, so I agreed."

"And the DA picked the island of Islay," guessed Maura. "Too far off the coast for casual day trippers to come across you. But what happened? Where have you been this last week?"

"I'm coming to that. Well, my wife died before the trial was over. I've been here about six years. They put me in one of the bungalows first, but when Wally here hired me as his baker, he offered to rent me a room in his apartment over the coffee shop. I have to start baking before the sun comes up and it's easy to just run down the stairs. I've mostly kept to myself in the restaurant kitchen and nobody's bothered me.

"Then not long ago – maybe seven or eight months – Bob Welch disappeared. I recognized him from the papers when I saw him in the coffee shop one day. I've had the Newark paper delivered to me through the mid-west connection since I came out here. He had been an accessory in a high-profile murder case and had turned state's witness. His name wasn't Bob Welch then. Right after the trial he disappeared and it was assumed that he was the victim of a revenge killing, but here he was, hiding on Islay like me. Soon after he disappeared from here, he was found in Jersey trussed up with his throat slit. It made headlines because he'd been a witness in that notorious case."

Maura was shocked.

"Nobody here knows what happened to him."

"Right. People here don't read Jersey papers and the name was different anyways."

The relocation to Islay of witnesses from two cases which the DA was directly involved with seemed too much of a coincidence. When Violet Wilson was found dead, the baker became alarmed. There wasn't enough information about Violet to know whether there was any connection to an earlier crime, but Joe was suspicious. Unsure what danger lurked on the island, he confided his situation to Wally, who had become a close friend over the years. They talked about going to the police but figured there was a good chance the DA had set up the arrangement with the help of the local police. If that was the case, maybe the police were tipping off the mob.

"Wally usually takes the garbage out last thing before closing up, but sometimes if I want a cigarette I do it. The cans are right behind the coffee shop. Wally waited inside that night, turning out lights and stuff. Well, I had just put the garbage in the can and was lighting up when somebody puts a bag over my head, then tries to whack my skull in with a heavy stick. I yelled and held my arms over my head." He pulled up his shirt sleeves and showed them angry, purple-black bruises. "Thankfully I fell into the garbage cans because Wally heard the commotion and came running out with his old revolver that he keeps in a drawer in the kitchen. It didn't have any bullets in it, but the guy didn't know that and went running off."

Wally picked up the story.

"I thought about chasing him but," he grinned, "I was scared I'd catch him. And no, I didn't get a good look at him. He had a stocking cap pulled low, and a scarf tied around the lower part of his face. Definitely a guy, and not very old by the way he ran. Could have been any one of a dozen guys from the docks. Heck, it could be anybody. Except you," he amended, eyeing Will. "You're about twice the size of any fella on the island."

"Just for the record," said Will amiably, "I'm six foot four. I am not twelve feet tall."

Their first thought was to get Joe off Islay, but that would have meant taking a public ferry ride or hiring a boat. Unable to trust anyone, they didn't want to take a chance that someone would follow the baker. They decided to stage his disappearance rather than wait for another attack. They hoped that his assailant would assume that Joe had somehow left the island, and they would eventually find a way to sneak him off. Where he would go after that, they didn't know.

"Opal here is an old friend and agreed to hide him for a while. She has lots of extra room and was getting nervous about the rumors somebody was spreading that she was a witch. You were glad to have a man in the house at night, weren't you Opal?"

"Sure, but I'm on constant KP duty. Wally was now out a baker so we worked it out that Joe would bake in my kitchen and a boy would pick up the stuff twice a day and take it over to the coffee shop. Wally told his customers he hired somebody else to bake out of her kitchen until Joe came back. Joe's been doing the baking, but he has to follow my recipes. People would have known it was him if he made all his usual stuff. The deal is that he bakes and I do the pots and pans."

"Wally, how did you know something was going on here tonight?" Maura asked.

He stared at her a moment, then shrugged.

"I can see some of the houses on the green from my bedroom window. I've been taking a look to make sure everything's OK before I turn in at night."

And Opal had been going up to her attic every night when Maura arrived on the island... with the hope of catching a glimpse of Wally taking out the garbage?

Everyone sat in silence for a moment, each thinking the same thought – 'What now?'

Maura got up to reheat the coffee. She poured it into a pan and lit a stove burner, then stacked some cookies on a plate.

"I appreciate you telling me all this. But why? Everyone you tell the story to is an added risk."

"We can't figure out what to do next." Wally took a cookie. "Will's family has been here forever. He says you're smart and you and he are old friends. We've got to trust somebody."

"Plus," added Joe with a grin, "we saw what you did with the hose. Opal told us you've been a good friend to her since you came. The witch thing and the witness hunting thing probably aren't related, but it seems like a good idea to have you on our side."

"Maura." Will's voice was quiet. "You've kind of thrown yourself into this witch business. Those idiots in the mob tonight aren't going to forget that you made them look ridiculous." He hesitated a moment. "I don't think it's safe for you and Lizzie to stay here."

Maura, who had already been thinking along the same lines, felt a contrary urge to argue.

"I don't want to give up my summer on Islay because of a bunch of drunks and I'm not a mob witness. Can't we ask the police to patrol for a few nights, as Patrick suggested? Then you'll be back on the weekends, Will, when they're more likely to stay long at the tavern and drink too much. And don't you think some of them are going to be glad I stopped them from going any farther once they sober up?"

"Maybe. I don't know."

"Here's what I think we should do. The only reasons I can think of that they're picking on Opal are because she lives on property that supposedly belonged to the witch, and because she never goes out so is a mysterious figure." She pointed her finger at a startled Opal. "You need to go out more, talk to people, look normal. If you show them you have friends, they'll think you must be OK. We'll go to lunch with our neighbor Lillian and my friend Gracie. We don't have to tell them about the witness thing, just that we want people to stop thinking of you as the Witch of Islay."

After years of living like a hermit, Opal was nervous about going out in public. She reluctantly agreed, however.

With both Wally and Joe spending the night in her house, Opal declined Maura's offer of hospitality. After they left, Will helped her wash the coffee cups. She thought he might offer to spend the night in the house in case anybody came back with revenge in mind, and she was prepared to accept the offer, but he hung up his dish towel and wished her good night.

Maura had only been in bed for a few minutes when she heard the sound of an aluminum beach chair being opened. She put on a bathrobe and peered out the side window. As she expected, Will was sitting in the shadows watching the street. The hose was in his lap.

After a quick check to make sure Lizzie was still sleeping, Maura went out the back door and picked up another beach chair. Will looked up when she put it down next to him but didn't try to talk her into going back into the house.

The night breeze was like an elixir, so fresh that every breath made Maura feel slightly giddy. It carried away the scent of roses, cookouts on charcoal grills and the burned oily cloth of the discarded torches. Instead, it held the essence of the sea, strong and uncompromising, and made her aware that they were a small community, miles out into the ocean.

She took another deep breath and let it out slowly.

"If only I could fill a bottle with the air of Islay and take a breath of it now and then after we leave here."

Will smiled.

"I feel like that every time I come here after a long absence."

They spoke in low voices, given the late hour and the peaceful quiet that had descended on the green. If it wasn't for the debris in the street and on the sidewalk, it would have been hard to believe that just a short time ago there was an angry mob on that spot. Maura got up and gathered the scattered personal belongings she could find, which included a hearing aid and a hair curler, and put them in a little pile on the doorstep. Tomorrow she would put them in a bucket on the sidewalk with a sign that read 'Yours?'

She resumed her seat and Will offered her a brandy snifter he had under his chair. She took a sip and passed it back. They sat in companionable silence, watching for the return of any miscreants. After a few minutes they moved their chairs to the other side of the house where they could still see anyone coming from the direction of town but were within earshot of Lizzie's window in case she called out. They could always dart back to the other side if they needed the hose.

"So...what happened to you, Maura?"

She looked at Will in surprise. He had spoken casually and was regarding her with a friendly smile.

"I mean," he went on, "what happened to you in the years since high school? You were a firecracker back then. Everyone changes as they mature but something seems to have knocked you for a loop. You can tell me it's none of my business."

Maura sighed and held her hand out for the brandy snifter. The fumes made her blink as she took a sip.

"I married one of my professors when I was in college. I was twenty and he was in his thirties." She paused. "You remember what my mother was like?"

"Sure! She was the toughest lunch lady in the school. Most of the kids were afraid of her but they respected her. She had a pretty biting sense of humor and could take down the kids that gave her any lip. She'd say the rudest things in a carrying voice with a big, scary smile. All the other kids would laugh at her victims."

"Yes, that was my mother all right. Imagine living with that."

"I can see that that wouldn't have been easy. Although you seemed to handle it well. I know some kids teased you because you were the lunch lady's daughter, but you would just walk up to them and put your face in theirs – like you did with that idiot tonight – and they'd back down. You and your mother seemed to make a joke out of it. I remember she once asked you when you were going to pick up your dirty clothes in your bedroom in a voice that carried over half the lunchroom. Without missing a beat you said, 'When you pick up your old beer bottles!'"

Maura turned the snifter around in her hands then took another sip.

"What a good memory you have. She was mad because I didn't clean my bedroom when she told me too, so she thought it would be a good idea to humiliate me in front of the school. She laughed at the beer bottle line but I could see I was in for it. When I got home from softball practice that night she was waiting for me and beat me."

Will stared.

"I had no idea."

"You know the prune in the French horn story? Bernard Flick had been teasing me mercilessly since third grade. I forget what pushed me too far that day, but I thought a few prunes were well-deserved."

"Unquestionably."

"You went to detention with me for a couple of days, but my mother had to pay to have the French horn cleaned. It was the end of the Depression and we didn't have any extra money. My mother barely got by with her lunch lady job and cleaning houses. She made me clean the Flicks' house after school every day for two weeks. That creep, Bernard, made sure he was there and followed me from room to room, staring at me and pointing out spots I missed."

Will was appalled. "Bernard Flick was a pervert. He was arrested a few years after high school but his father had a lot of money and hushed it up. I think he teased you because he was attracted to you... I remember he used to watch you. I can't believe your mother put you in that situation."

"She wasn't so bad until my father left us and moved in with another woman across town. After that she was so full of rage and humiliation that she had to find an outlet at home so she wouldn't blow up on her jobs. She was lucky to be working at all since it was the Depression."

"And you were the closest target," Will said, so softly that she almost missed the anger in his voice. She stared up at the stars, remembering, comforted by this belated championship.

"A few years after we moved to Barlow Ridge we got news that my father had died. Even though he had abandoned us, my mother went into a tailspin for a week. She sat up late every night drinking and sobbing. That was the first and last time she ever gave me advice. 'Never fall in love,' she said. 'It will destroy you.'"

Will's dark eyebrows were drawn in a frown.

"I only tell you this," Maura went on with some embarrassment, "so you know why I craved a normal home life, and because I finished your brandy." She passed him the empty glass.

Will took several deep breaths, his jaw clenched. When he finally spoke his voice was mild.

"You're a selfish pig, but I've got the bottle under my chair." He refilled the snifter and took a few sips, then handed it back to her. "You never let any of that show in high school. I think you had your mother's wit and a little of her temper, but you were never spiteful. If I remember right, you had a close group of friends and did pretty well in school. You were on the girls' softball team and weren't you an editor of the school literary magazine?"

"You remember a lot for a kid who was a year older than me and sat next to me in band!"

"Yes, I do. Because I had a crush on you."

Maura turned sideways in her chair and stared at him.

"What?"

His grin answered hers. "Yes, it lasted most of my senior year. I had dated Helen Wayne for a couple of years and we had gotten bored with each other. I screwed up my courage to ask you to my senior prom but as I walked up to you some kid with red hair, I forget his name, came up and put his arm around you. You kissed his cheek and smiled. That was that."

"Red hair... oh! I forget his name too, but I think we dated for about a week."

Will laughed. "If only I had known."

Maura smiled a little, wondering if her life would have been any different if a kind-hearted saxophone player had become her boyfriend back then. She doubted it; he would have gone off to college and she would have had another year of high school before going to a different college. High school relationships didn't usually survive those circumstances.

"So you married your ex-husband to have a peaceful life?"

"Yes. Funny, isn't it? He was my music professor. Did you know I won a scholarship for English and journalism? I never would have gone to college without it. My mother didn't see the point. Anyway, I loved the way David spoke. The subject matter was boring – the History of Renaissance music – but he was genuinely interested in it and his voice was quiet and cultured-sounding. I couldn't imagine him engaging in the kind of fights my parents treated us to. Back then David had all his hair and a lot of the girls had crushes on him. I guess I did too. For some reason he singled me out of the crowd and invited me to dinner.

"He was a good listener, but I didn't realize he was storing up all kinds of information about me – all my dreams, fears and weaknesses - to be used later as ammunition. Our relationship was pleasant and peaceful before we got married and it was enough for me. The only argument I remember us having was after he proposed. He wanted me to quit school and keep house for him. I was only a year away from getting my teaching degree and was determined to finish. He used all the manipulative little tricks I got to know later to make me finally give him his own way. After all, most women didn't work after they got married. Now I know he wanted me to be completely dependent on him and a teaching certificate would give me the power to leave him. Is this story as boring as I think it is?"

"Of course not. Go on."

She swirled the brandy for a moment. It was a little humiliating to admit to choosing to marry someone who was remarkably similar to her mother, but she felt no judgement from Will.

"OK, well, he lost his job when we were married about a year. He said he quit because they didn't appreciate him enough, but our landlord – we were living in a small apartment – worked at the college and told me he was fired for getting involved with one of his students again. I would have left him but I had nowhere to go – my mother was barely speaking to me for marrying a Protestant and I had no money or job skills. When I confronted David about his affair, he was livid – that I talked with our landlord about him, that I had the utter gall to accuse him when he was keeping me fed and clothed, that I thought I was so superior... It was awful. Because he knew me inside and out, he was able to manipulate me into staying. Not just then, but in the years afterwards as we moved around and he got and lost jobs. Everything was somehow my fault; I wasn't supportive enough, clever enough to keep us from spending too much money or pretty enough to impress his coworkers. When he was afraid I was about to leave him he would be very pleasant and charming, like in the days before we were married. I didn't fall for it but it gave me some peace. By the time I was expecting Lizzie, he had done a good job destroying any self-confidence I had. Things have gotten better since our divorce, thanks to Rebecca taking me under her wing, but..." Maura broke off. Her face grew hot with mortification. "Why am I telling you all this? I will never drink brandy again!"

It was a moment before Will spoke.

"If you're embarrassed," he finally said, "I would like to remind you that you saw me naked in the shower. And you only told me what I asked you to. Maura, the people who should have had your best interest at heart have completely failed you. I have to warn you that if your ex-husband comes to visit Lizzie when I'm here, I'll punch him in the head."

Maura laughed a little shakily.

"The family of the young girl he ran off with did the job for you. They put him in the hospital. He hasn't seen Lizzie since he left us when she was two weeks old, thank heaven. The last time I saw him was in divorce court when he wouldn't even look at me."

"You deserve so much better. Now about your friend, Barnacle Bill..."

Maura laughed as she stood and folded her beach chair.

"I'm going to bed. It must be around four a.m. and Lizzie will be waking me up in a few hours."

Will wished her goodnight and said he would turn in shortly. The sun was tinting the sky when she heard him fold up his beach chair.

CHAPTER 16

Maura was thankful that Lizzie slept until eight-thirty the next morning, but after a few meager hours of sleep she was feeling remarkably awake. Her mind was a jumble of sharp memories of the mob outside of Opal's house last night, the late night gathering in her kitchen while the baker told his story and sitting under the stars with Will.

She wasn't surprised that Will hadn't yet made an appearance, given the fact that he was up most of the night. She made a pot of coffee and a platter of French toast, setting Lizzie to the task of mixing the cylinder of frozen orange juice in the big glass pitcher. They carried it all out to the picnic table and Maura knocked gently on the carriage house door. If Will was still sleeping she didn't want to wake him.

He opened the door quickly enough that Maura knew he was already awake. He held a rolled-up towel and his shaving kit under his arm. His eyes were heavy and dark stubble covered his chin but his smile was cheerful enough.

"I was about to head to the shower. I don't suppose you made coffee."

"Extra strong. And there's French toast."

"Ah, bless you." He took her head in his hands and kissed her forehead. Maura blinked in surprise.

Lizzie loved eating at the picnic table and chattered excitedly about a tea party she was going to after camp on Tuesday. Happily for Will, there was no demand for Lizzie and the Giant and Jelly Bean stories.

They all carried the breakfast things to the kitchen and set the dishes in the sink. Maura said she would wash them when Will was out of the shower so the water didn't go hot and cold. She warmed up a cup of coffee and took it back outside. The morning air on Islay was always fresh, its scent depending on which way the breeze blew. This morning the roses dominated. Maura sat in the most comfortable lawn chair and stretched her legs out to let the sun warm them. She was surprised she wasn't more shaken by the events of last night; they had disturbed her sleep but here, in the enclosed backyard of the Watts house with its flowers and stretch of green lawn, the birds calling noisily to each other and mixing with the sound of a distant lawn mower, the peace felt impenetrable. Lizzie ran around the backyard with Jelly Bean scrabbling to grab the string she dragged. She heard Will turn the faucet handles in the outdoor shower and the water hit the floorboards with a sharp spatter. Her eyelids began to close.

"Granny!" Lizzie's delighted shriek brought Maura wide awake. She jerked around to see an older couple standing awkwardly, unsure of their welcome. She stood, her heart sinking.

"Cleve and Norma! What are you doing here?"

Her ex-father-in-law cleared his throat.

"We rang the bell but nobody answered so we came around back. Sorry to barge in on you like this, Maura. We were missing little Lizzie, and you, and thought maybe we would stop by for a quick visit. It wasn't until we bought our ferry tickets that we found out there would only be one ferry back and it's at the end of the day. We would've called but there's no phone service out here. And you didn't give us a way to get ahold of you." He blinked and shifted feet. Maura took a deep breath and attempted to stifle her intense resentment at this intrusion.

"It's fine, Cleve. I'll make a fresh pot of coffee and I've got some apple cinnamon bread."

Norma had avoided taking part in her husband's apology by centering all her attention on Lizzie. She sat in Maura's lawn chair and pulled her granddaughter onto her lap. Lizzie proceeded to give her a long and confusing account of everything that had caught her attention since they arrived on the island. Lizzie's affection for her grandmother was the only lack of taste that Maura had detected in her. She herself despised her ex-mother-in-law; Norma's fatuous and blind devotion to her only child had monstrously inflated his opinion of himself at a young age. As he grew up he began to realize that others were better at sports, or got higher grades or had more friends. He followed his mother's lead in laying blame on the other children – they cheated on exams, or the coach played favorites, or they were jealous of him. She was a stupid woman and believed in her son's perfection absolutely. David was more intuitive than his mother and had greater trouble in reconciling reality with the sense of self-worth she had instilled in him. He cultivated an air of superiority and attracted children, usually younger than himself, who were desperate to improve their social standing. This tactic continued into adulthood and, while it revolted his associates, it allowed him to maintain a bubble of self-esteem that needed constant bolstering from his cultivated pool of admirers – a pool which had once included a young Maura Sullivan.

Maura always had an urge to snap her daughter out of Norma's fond embrace, afraid she would contaminate Lizzie as she had done her son. As time passed, she relaxed a little. A doting grandmother is different than an over-indulgent parent, and when his wife over-praised Lizzie for some mediocre achievement Cleve tempered it with his own more realistic assessment. This Lizzie took with good grace because his comments were kindly given. Cleve was aware of the animosity that existed between his wife and his former daughter-in-law so made the habit of handing Maura a glass of sherry upon arrival for their occasional visits. He would take her aside and engaged her in desultory but intelligent conversation until it was time to leave. Maura had developed a sneaking affection for him despite his failure as David's father, but this in no way extended to his wife. Norma continued to convey her disapproval of Maura and clearly maintained the belief that the blame for David's defection rested squarely on Maura's shoulders.

When Norma heard Maura mention coffee and apple cinnamon bread, she realized there wasn't going to be an unpleasant scene and broke into Lizzie's rambling account of Midge's birthday party.

"This is a nice house," she opined in her flat voice. Maura recognized this as an attempt to be pleasant, since it was accompanied by the rearranging of her small mouth in a tight little smile. As she put the water on for coffee, she wondered what Norma wanted. She rejoined her guests on the patio where Lizzie was introducing her grandparents to a goggle-eyed Jelly Bean.

No one noticed the shower was running until the water was turned off.

"Who–" Norma began.

"Maur," called a deep voice, "you still there? Can you hand me my clean clothes? I left them on the picnic table bench."

Norma raised her penciled eyebrows as far as she could push them and gave Maura an outraged stare. Maura felt her face turn pink but refused to give her an explanation. She unhurriedly picked up Will's clothes roll and handed it to him over the top of the shower wall.

"Will, we have guests."

"Oh? I'll be right out."

No one could think of anything to say until Will emerged, clothed but damp, rubbing his hair with a towel. His eyes traveled from an unknown elderly couple to Maura's tight-lipped expression and back again. To his surprise and amusement, the woman was staring at him with chest-heaving indignation. He held out his hand out to Cleve.

"Will Howe. Pleased to meet you."

"Cleveland Gertz. This is my wife ,Norma. We're, er, Lizzie's grandparents."

"Ah!" Will nodded and smiled at Maura's ex-mother-in-law, blandly ignoring her animosity. She opened her mouth, but her husband said her name sharply, and whatever she had been planning to utter remained unsaid. Maura's suspicions were aroused; the Gertzes wanted something and Cleve wasn't about to let his wife ruin their chances. She shot Will a look of entreaty, which the elderly couple missed. They were surprised when Will pulled up a chair, clearly planning to help entertain them for their visit.

"I'll get the coffee," Maura muttered, and went inside. She watched the group on the patio through the screen door.

Lizzie, no longer the center of Norma's attention, slid off her grandmother's lap and hopped over to Will.

"Mr. Giant! Tell me a story."

"It's not story time yet, Princess Lizzie. Show us how fast you can run down to the tire swing and back." Lizzie set off, long braids flapping. Will watched her, smiling a little, and the Gertzes watched him.

Maura came out with a tray bearing four coffee mugs, a glass of milk and a plate of apple bread slices. She saw that Norma was maintaining her affronted air and rolled her eyes.

"Cleve and Norma, Will's family owns this house. He comes on weekends to work on it so it will be ready to sell in the fall. He lives in the carriage house but likes taking showers outside. So whatever you're thinking, Norma, you can just stop." Her mother-in-law sniffed.

Lizzie, returned from her run, was congratulated by Will and Cleve and flopped down in the grass with a piece of apple bread. They talked about the house renovations, and Cleve and Will quickly became immersed in particulars of the house's plumbing. Lizzie followed Jelly Bean inside, leaving Maura and her ex-mother-in-law to carry on a stilted conversation.

Norma mentioned that they had hired the taxi to take them on a tour of the island and the driver had recommended lunch at the Bayberry Inn.

"We knew you wouldn't want us here all day so we can pass the time until the ferry leaves."

Maura murmured something meaningless and recommended the bluefish.

Eventually the Gertzes exchanged glances.

Here it comes, thought Maura. Now I'll find out why they're here.

"Er, Maura." Cleve rubbed his chin. "Norma and I are planning to take a little cruise up to Nova Scotia the third week in August. We'll do some sight-seeing then we'll go to Montreal and join a tour group there."

No. Maura didn't say it out loud, but she knew what was coming.

"We, er... we would love for Lizzie to come with us. It would only be for eight days." The last sentence came out in a hurry. "We would both keep our eyes on her every minute and won't over-indulge her." Cleve's voice was wistful; Maura could tell he didn't have much hope that she would agree to the scheme.

"Please. We love her so much." Maura was startled by Norma's softened tone and her hopeful look. She felt no pity for them in turning down their request. Eight days taken from her precious summer with Lizzie? Send her daughter off with a couple that had thoroughly botched the upbringing of their own son? Where did they get the gall to take away the one good thing that had come from her association with their family? It took her a moment before she could speak without her voice shaking.

"I'm sorry, but we don't have much time left on the island. I start teaching after Labor Day and Lizzie will be in nursery school. This is our special time together and I can't cut it short."

Norma opened her mouth to object but Cleve held up his hand.

"We understand. Well, our taxi should be here any minute, so I guess we'll say goodbye. Come visit us when you're settled in Marblehead."

Lizzie was distressed to learn her grandparents were already leaving. For her sake, Maura suggested they take her on their tour of Islay and the three happily set off in the taxi. As much as she would like to cut off all connections with David, including his parents, she knew it wouldn't be fair to Lizzie.

When she entered the kitchen after waving them off, Will was washing the coffee cups and plates.

"Thanks, Will. I can do that."

He handed her a dish towel.

"You can dry."

As Maura was putting the cups away, Will remarked,

"Your mother-in-law doesn't like you very much, does she?"

The corners of Maura's mouth turned up.

"Oh, you caught that, did you? Yes, she blames me for her son running off. If I had been a better wife, he wouldn't have had to look for love elsewhere."

"I only overheard parts of your conversation, but I could tell she was a thoroughly stupid woman."

Maura laughed.

"Yes. Although she's right in some respects. I wasn't a particularly good wife. I just couldn't manage it all – the chores, the shopping, keeping to a budget on David's salary. Sometimes I just sat and read a book, surrounded by laundry that needed folding."

"You aren't actually blaming yourself for your husband's infidelity, are you?"

"No, no. Of course not." Will looked at her suspiciously. The truth was that Maura knew she didn't manage the household well, and when she was expecting she didn't feel well enough to keep up with anything. Things were so much easier with just Lizzie. She thought of Will's approaching marriage and felt a little sorry for him. His time would never again be his own; he would always have to weigh his actions and choices according to how they suited someone else's convenience. She had to do that with Lizzie, of course, but that was different. She loved her daughter and would gladly do anything for her.

Maura announced she was going to take advantage of Lizzie's absence and take a nap. Will went up to the attic to make a list of supplies that would be needed to turn it into a real bedroom.

Chapter 17

"Why are you dressed like a hobo?" Gracie frowned at Opal. The young woman's mouth was expertly painted Stormy Pink. A raspberry pink scarf was tied around her neat, dusky curls and matched her pink sandals and the flowers in her flouncy summer dress.

Opal shot her a look of dislike.

"Because I can't afford to deck myself out in trashy clothes made for somebody half my age!"

Gracie put her hands on her hips.

"I made these clothes myself by copying fashions from *Vogue* magazine, and just how old do you think I am?"

"OK, this is starting well", Maura murmured. "Opal, Gracie is going to help us out and I would kill to have her clothes. And you do kind of look like a hobo. That's why she's here. And you," she pointed to Gracie, "can try thinking before you say something."

There was no sign that Joe the baker was living in the house except that most of the clutter was gone. If he was going to bake, he said, he needed clean, empty counters. Maura thought she heard a floor board creak overhead but no one else paid any attention. The group in Maura's kitchen last night had agreed that Joe's whereabouts wouldn't be disclosed to anyone else.

With the exception of a large stack of clothes on one end, Opal's kitchen table had been cleared off so Gracie could use it as a work bench. She was picking up Opal's old dresses and jackets one by one and inspecting them.

"This one's for winter... moths got to this one. This print is hideous..." Opal opened her mouth to retort but Gracie cut her off.

"What's the matter with this one? It's a nice, happy blue for summer and the quality is good. It's a little outdated but we can do something with that."

Opal touched the sleeve.

"It was my favorite dress," she said wistfully. "But I haven't been able to zip it up for years."

Gracie inspected it. "It's got decent seam allowance. Put it on and let's see where we are."

The seam allowance wasn't going to make up for the gap between the two sides of the zipper.

"Don't worry about it." Gracie dug through the clothes heap and found a navy gabardine coat that had been new twenty years earlier. She spent the next thirty minutes with a measuring tape, chalk, pins and scissors. The result of this labor was a pile of oddly shaped gabardine fabric pieces, neatly labeled and stacked. Opal's favorite dress had been opened at the seams and was covered in chalk marks.

"This will be fun! I've never dressed a... anybody beside myself." Maura wondered if she was going to say 'hobo'.

"You think you can get it done in time to go to lunch tomorrow?" Maura knew how to sew but a project like this was beyond her. She watched Gracie put everything into one of the bags she had brought.

"Sure. You forget I'm a lonely widow with nothing to do." She stared at Opal, who began to squirm. "I can do her makeup when I come back with the dress tomorrow, but what about the hair? It's got to be cut. "

"You're not cutting my hair! You'll give me some movie star hairdo that will make me look ridiculous!"

Gracie chewed her lip.

"I guess it's OK if you look like a granny. We're just trying to make you not look like a scary hag. We can give you pink cheeks and you can call people 'dear'.

Ten minutes later Opal's hair had been washed in the kitchen sink. She sat in a chair with a towel around her shoulders while Gracie studied a photo in one of the fashion magazines she had brought.

"You OK with this one? It's a short, curly bob. Thankfully, you don't need a perm."

"You ever cut anybody's hair before?"

"No. Ready?"

When Maura and Lizzie arrived at Opal's house the next day Gracie had almost finished the older woman's makeup.

"What do you think?" Gracie asked Lizzie.

"You look pretty, Mrs. Hansen!"

Opal smiled, gratified.

"OK, now for the dress." Gracie unzipped a garment bag and pulled out the blue dress and a stylish navy jacket with three-quarter sleeves.

"Is that my old coat?"

"Yeah. I cut some pieces out of the bottom of it for the dress, but the top was in good shape. When you have it on it should cover the inserts I had to put into the dress to make it big enough."

When Opal emerged from the bathroom in the dress and jacket, she was smiling. The cheerful blue dress and the makeup brightened her face. The open navy jacket was slimming, as was her short curly hair, brushed and sprayed into an upswept style.

Opal surprised them all by giving Gracie a hug. "Thank you, honey." The younger woman smiled.

Lillian had been recruited for the mission to reintroduce Opal to island society. She and Howard had been away for the weekend so missed the excitement. Maura filled her in the next day, not leaving out her routing of an angry, torch-bearing mob with a hose. Lillian thoroughly enjoyed the story, as Maura knew she would, and signed up for the Opal project without hesitation.

"Some of those fatheads that hang around the tavern are a menace and should stay away from our part of the island. Of course I'll go to lunch with you girls. Can Opal walk that far?"

That was also one of Maura's worries. As it turned out their walk to the coffee shop was leisurely with frequent stops and Opal was able to manage it. The perfect summer day, with its light comfortable breeze, brought many of the neighbors out to take walks or do errands. They were stopped three times on the way to the coffee shop by neighbors wanting to discuss the events of Saturday night. Several women smiled politely at Opal then did a double-take when they realized who she was. Each time they stopped, Opal repeated her rehearsed lines. "I had just gotten ready for bed when I heard shouting. I can't imagine what they wanted from me, or why they would think the baker from the coffee shop was in my house." Since several neighbors were present when that accusation was called out by the mob, Opal's friends thought it best if she mentioned it outright. If she was really hiding the baker, it stood to reason that she wouldn't call attention to him.

They arrived at the coffee shop at the peak of the lunch rush. Most of the tables were occupied by retirees, workmen on their lunch breaks and women with friends or children. Wally had kept a central booth for them by stacking plates and condiments on the table.

"Drat these shoes!" Opal whispered as they sat down. "They weren't made for fat feet." She was about to slip them off when she noticed an old man with growths on his nose standing at the cash register, staring at her. A drab woman with a sour face stood behind him. Opal murmured, "Excuse me a moment." When Maura realized that she planned to confront

Basker Beeks, a member of the mob that had threatened her the other night, it was too late to stop her.

Opal looked her quarry in the eye as she approached. He mechanically took his change from the cashier and shot his wife an uneasy look. Maura guessed that Mrs. Beeks didn't know what he had been up to and Basker was afraid Opal would spill the beans. He tried to usher his wife toward the door, but Opal laid a hand on his arm.

"Don't go. I just wanted to thank you for trying to stop the mob that tried to break into my house Saturday night. I was absolutely terrified!" She allowed a quaver to enter her voice. "I'm so grateful to people like you and my kind neighbors who drove them off. I can't imagine why they thought I had the baker in my house!" Basker blinked, as though trying to work out how his participation in the attack could possibly be construed as coming to her rescue. Since Opal was speaking in a rather carrying voice, many of the diners were following the exchange. His eyes slewed to his wife to see whether she was swallowing this.

Still holding onto Basker's arm, Opal turned to his wife.

"You must be so proud of your husband!" Mrs. Beeks' eyes darted from Opal to her husband and back again. She smiled uncertainly. Basker breathed a sigh of relief and managed to detach his arm from Opal's grip.

"Glad to help, ma'am. Well, have a nice day." He pulled his wife out the door and the other diners turned back to their food. A table of workmen had been watching Basker with frowns. When he left they leaned in for a whispered conversation. Maura recognized at least one from Saturday night.

"Very nice!" Gracie said admiringly.

Opal smirked. "I was understudy for the lead in *Joan of Arc* at St. Agnes."

Wally came out of the kitchen as they were finishing their sandwiches, wiping his hands on a towel.

"I've got to get some help in the back. Joe wasn't just my baker. He did a lot of the cooking and sandwich making too."

He stopped and stared at Opal, a slow smile spreading over his face.

"Well, look at you! Did you take a pill last night that made you ten years younger?"

"Yes, and if I give you one maybe it will put a little hair back on your head."

Wally laughed loudly. If, as Maura suspected, he was the grocer from Opal's past, they seemed to be well on their way to patching things up. Opal's danger must have made him realize how much she still meant to him.

"Dessert is on me today, ladies. I highly recommend the blueberry pie." Since six blueberry pies had been baked in her kitchen early that morning and picked up by the coffee shop's delivery boy, Opal didn't have an urge to eat a slice. Lizzie had a dish of strawberry ice cream while the others sipped their third cups of coffee.

Lunch was considered a success. Two women who were on several island committees stopped by the table to greet Lillian.

"You remember Opal Hansen," she said. "Her health is better and she can get out and about more. She would love to volunteer wherever you need help!" The women smiled and wrote down Opal's phone number then left.

"What's the matter with you? I don't want to serve on committees! I hate committees. And I don't particularly like people either!"

"I thought the idea was to get you out in public again," retorted Lillian. "It's kind of hard to think of somebody as an evil witch when she's wearing a pink hat and selling tickets to a clam bake! Just volunteer now and then and I'll sign up with you."

Steve had been finding frequent excuses to be in town at lunchtime rather than out on the *Lorelei*. From her grin, it was clear Shirl was entertained by his jostling for a seat at the lunch counter that faced the door. His eyes went straight to Gracie today when she entered, a fact which neither she nor Maura missed. Gracie flashed him a smile. He finished his lunch and slowed on his way to the register as though he wanted to stop at their table, but after nervously eyeing Opal and Lillian, changed course to give them a wide berth. Maura secretly commiserated; it would be hard to ask a girl out with three other women and a four-year-old as your audience. Before he could get away, Gracie said his name and beckoned him over. For the benefit of any newcomers to the coffee shop, she lost no time in telling what had happened Saturday night and Opal, who was still perfecting her victim act, added her bit.

When he learned that a mob carrying torches had tried to get into Opal's house, Steve was clearly appalled. He stammered his willingness to help in any way he could, whether guard duty or anything else they could think of. Gracie gave him a warm smile and his voice petered out. The other women were looking so approving that he flushed and hastily bid them good day.

Gracie sighed and made a face.

On Tuesday afternoon Maura was putting the vacuum away when there was a soft knock on the door. Workmen were in the kitchen, hammering the new moldings around the windows. Lizzie had been spraying the wood furniture in the parlor with lemon polish and furiously rubbing it into a shine, a job she dearly loved. When she saw her favorite handyman standing on the doorstep, she gave him a happy smile.

"Randy!"

Maura pulled her away from the door.

"Lizzie, sweetie, go upstairs and polish the furniture in the room with the four beds. It's all dusty."

"But..." She saw her mother's look and stomped up the stairs. Maura waited until she was out of earshot.

"Get out of here and don't ever come back." Her tone hadn't changed but the handyman had no doubt of the rage running beneath it. Her eyes were steely and uncompromising.

"Maura..."

"I said get out. Nobody who would scare a woman half to death for the fun of it comes near me or my child."

He continued to stand, his face miserable. He looked much worse than usual, his eyes more bloodshot and his shoulders hunched.

"I'm not here to apologize," he said quietly. "I'm a weak bastard and what's the good of apologizing? I think there's something you should know though, but I'm not sure you'll want to hear it." His mouth curved into a humorless smile. "But hey, you hate me already so maybe it's a good time."

Maura stared at him for a moment, her mouth in a thin line. "Go around back to the picnic table."

When they were seated and facing each other, Maura said: "OK, what?"

Randy looked at his clasped hands. His hair was greasy and uncombed, and he let off a slightly unpleasant odor. Maura was secretly a little shocked by his appearance, but she kept any concern from showing on her face.

"I'm sure you've figured out that I spend a lot of time at the tavern. Way too much time. The boys that go there are asses but they don't judge, and they like me. Sometimes my wife comes with me, and the two of us were there one night about seven or eight months ago. It was like November or something so there weren't that many people there – just some of the boys from the fishing boats and the regulars who live here year-round. We'd already had a few drinks when in came that treasure guy. The one that goes after all the good-looking women, not the blonde one." He flashed a look at Maura through the stringy hair that had fallen over his forehead.

Maura frowned.

"He comes to Islay a lot when the weather's warm and he can sleep on his boat. He sometimes drops by the tavern for dinner and a beer or two. The boys are a lot rougher than he is, but he's always friendly so they accept him. He likes to talk about the stuff he finds, which pretty much everybody's interested in. Sometimes he starts off on history, which nobody is interested in. I don't know why he was on Islay that time of year, but he's convinced there's some good stuff in all the wrecks around here so was probably following up on a hunch.

"Well, that night, the guys were talking about Bob Welch's disappearance. It had just happened a week or two earlier and there was a lot of talk about where he might be and a bunch of idiot theories.

"The treasure guy joined in suddenly and asked if anyone knew about the island curse. The ones who had grown up here like me and some of the older men had heard stories when we were young about some broad, er, woman, who put a curse on island men in the olden days. Nobody had any details, so it didn't make much of an impression. I think I remember playing a kind of tag when I was a kid where we pretended we were being chased by the witch. So Dunn tells them that one of the original shipwreck survivors had been thrown out of their settlement and forced to live by herself on the other side of the island. There weren't enough women to go around, so some of the men would pay her a visit when they got drunk. To scare them off, she hurled curses at them and a bunch of them died. She put a curse on her land for good measure. He said that by his calculation her land crossed some of the properties on this part of the green. There have been a lot of deaths over the couple of centuries, he said, and it was interesting that Bob Welch lived over this way. Well, in the bungalows, but he probably went for walks around here and maybe visited some of the houses. He mentioned the creepy house next to you and wondered why the old woman wanted to live in a huge mausoleum like that. He never called her a witch but something about the way he said it made the boys say there was something sinister about it."

"What do you think about the witch's curse, Randy?" Maura asked in a hard voice. "Do you think men who aren't pure of heart die mysteriously after setting foot on our properties?"

"Nah. I'm still alive. That proves it's not true."

A fleeting thought went through her mind that Randy might fit the pure of heart category. He was a drunk, had low self-esteem and a host of other problems but despite his presence in Opal's mob she thought he was fundamentally a kind and honest person. She suspected that he and his wife had been quite drunk Saturday night and most likely followed the excitement. Which didn't excuse them in the least.

"Why are you telling me all this about Patrick Dunn, Randy?"

He hesitated but looked her in the eye.

"I saw you with him on the dock last week. He was kissing you."

She felt a stab of embarrassment and knew her cheeks had turned pink.

"I think you're telling me that he started this whole connection between Mrs. Hansen and the recent island tragedies," she said evenly. "I agree he might have done that inadvertently, and maybe it wasn't too smart. Why did you think I should know?"

"Because he brought it up again after Violet died and then again when the baker disappeared."

Chapter 18

That evening, as the sun was starting to sink into the ocean, Gracie's phone rang. It was Maura.

"Get up here quick! A certain delectable university professor has decided to patrol the green. He did say he would. Pack an overnight bag and run! I already have a bed made up for you so you don't have to go home in the dark."

Twenty minutes later Gracie burst through the back door, out of breath.

"Those woods are scary this time of evening! I wouldn't have gone that way but if I came up by the road he would have seen me. Now I'm all sweaty!"

"Relax, he'll likely be here a while. I just wanted you to hurry because I knew once it got dark you wouldn't come." She gave her guest a towel and washcloth, and fifteen minutes later a cool and composed Gracie crossed the street to where Steve had been leaning against a tree. She wore a yellow linen dress that seemed to glow in the gathering dusk, and her dark hair was in a cloud around her shoulders. His mouth dropped open slightly.

"Maura saw you and thought you looked thirsty. She asked me to bring this out to you." She handed him one of the two glasses of lemonade she carried.

He cleared his throat.

"Thanks."

Maura, who was peeking out the window, saw them sit on the curb and start a conversation. Well, Gracie was talking and Steve was listening. It wasn't much of a date, but it was a start.

She and Lizzie were listening to the radio in the kitchen when they heard the front door open and close.

"That was a quick date," Maura said, looking up.

"That was no date. That was me doing a monologue. Maura, he's so boring! I want to cry." She did indeed look close to tears. Maura didn't know what to say. When she had seen Steve once or twice in Patrick's company he had seemed quite different. He didn't say a lot, but Maura was left with the impression that he possessed some intelligence and had a subtle sense of humor. Around Gracie he had as much animation as a tree stump.

"I just wanted someone to take me out now and then and maybe fall a little bit in love with me." A fat tear rolled halfway down her cheek before she wiped it away. "It's so lonely living here all year round," she whispered.

Lizzie didn't understand what was going on but she had seen the tear and started to cry herself.

"Oh, Lizzie honey! I'm just being silly." She wrapped her arms around the little girl and gave her a squeeze. "How about a game of *Sorry!* – I get the red!"

Maura rolled her eyes.

To Maura's surprise, Will rolled up to the house the following morning. He was riding a new bicycle that was built for a man his size.

Maura stood on the stoop while he dismounted and removed leather saddle bags that were strapped over the back fender. A large knapsack on his back appeared to be fully stuffed and long, tight rolls of paper stuck out of an opening at the top.

"I don't know where to start!" commented Maura. "It's not Saturday. Where did you get that gorgeous bike? Do you know it still has a price tag hanging off the seat? What's in all those bags? Why are you here?"

It was a bright day and Will squinted up at her.

"I know it's not Saturday. It's Wednesday. I got the bike at a bike shop. I had to go to a few before I found one that was big enough. I have my architect stuff in the bags plus clothes and other things that I can't remember. I kept dreaming about angry mobs burning down this house before we have a chance to sell it so I'll be staying in the carriage house for a while. Some of the time I'll be working on house things and the rest of the time I'll be working on my part of some plans for a new office building. At night I'll be keeping an eye out for people with torches. I'm kind of hoping I'll get a chance with the hose."

"You'll have to take your turn. Some of the neighbors have been patrolling and the treasure hunter's partner was here last night. One of the policemen has actually been seen riding his bike through here at odd hours."

"That's good news."

'What about your job? Won't they notice that you're gone?"

"Hold on while I roll this fella around back."

She went through the house and met him on the patio.

"So what about your job?"

"I've hardly taken any vacation time since I started working there. They told me as long as I finish the plans I'm working on and bring them in on schedule, I could take the time I need."

"But your honeymoon is in November."

Will pushed the cap he was wearing to the back of his head.

"Maura, do you want me to leave? I know you and Lizzie are used to having the house to yourselves during the week. I promise I'll stay out of your way, but I'll go if you say the word."

"No, of course I don't want you to leave." She felt her cheeks turn a little pink. "We trip over hundreds of workmen all day long so probably wouldn't notice you in the chaos. I just forgot to mind my own business."

Will smiled a little.

"I'll save time for my honeymoon."

He spent the next half hour unpacking and setting up his kitchen table as a work desk, then walked through the woods with Maura to pick up Lizzie at day camp.

Patrick called the next morning, asking her to meet him for breakfast again. Since her talk with Randy, she had wanted him to explain why he seemed to be purposely reviving the witch paranoia after each tragedy. His annoyance at the members of the mob had seemed quite genuine, so she wasn't ready to accuse him of purposely instigating the event. Was it just a matter of trotting out a story that had gotten him attention in the past? She grabbed her purse and the folder with the meager pages from the *Witch of Islay*. In case Will came looking for her, she left a note on the kitchen counter informing him that she had gone to meet a friend for breakfast.

Patrick arrived just as she sat down. Maura wanted to ask him directly about the tavern but Randy had implored her not to say anything to him about it. Everyone knew he did odd jobs at the Watts house, and other houses on the green, and Patrick might make the connection. Randy didn't want trouble.

They ordered coffee and cinnamon rolls. Patrick pointed to her folder.

"What's that?"

"It's the first four chapters of my book. I wondered if you'd take a look at them and let me know where the main story line goes off from what really happened." Despite the reservations she had about Patrick, she felt no embarrassment in handing him her draft pages. Her story followed the events he had related reasonably closely.

"It's based on island history, but it's fiction. I wanted to be free to change or add to the story to make it more interesting Here's a pencil; mark the sections that have problems."

Patrick opened the folder and began reading. His eyes immediately darted from the page to her face.

"How did you know her name was Prudence? I didn't tell you that. I could only remember it started with a 'P' until I read this."

She was a little taken aback by his intense tone.

"I was trying to come up with a name from that period and Prudence just popped into my head. Do you know the first mate's real name?"

He stared at her for a moment.

"He never mentioned his name in the journal and before 1747 records of the crews of merchant ships weren't kept."

"Oh well, this is a fictionalized account. John Kellow he stays."

Patrick continued to read. His coffee grew cold as he picked up one page after another, occasionally murmuring phrases "Yes, it could have been like that" and "No, no...wrong period." He made notes on four pages, which Maura thought wasn't too bad. She had finished eating her cinnamon roll before he put down the last page.

He sat back and looked at Maura consideringly.

"I like it. You tell a good story. You seem to be able to put yourself in the witch's place and tell the story through her eyes. I don't know how accurate it is but most of it could be true." He leaned forward. "Do you ever feel like..." He hesitated.

"Feel like what?"

"Like...she's speaking through you?"

She laughed a little, not sure if he was serious. She couldn't feel flattered by his apparent suspicion that her story was so good it must have been influenced by the actual witch speaking through her; she remembered the sensational paperbacks mixed in with the classics on Patrick's shelf on the *Lorelei* and knew that he wasn't particularly discriminating in his choice of literature.

"No, I don't think so."

"When you write, see if you feel any different. Like, do the words just flow without you thinking about them first. I know you think it's crazy, but you do live near where she did and maybe... Just keep an open mind."

He went back through the manuscript and pointed out the problem spots he had noted. He handed it back to her and she thanked him. The waitress refilled their coffee and put their check on the table. Maura noticed that Patrick stared at it for a moment before reaching for it. She wondered whether he salvaged enough items of value to be able to cover his expenses. She supposed he had a regular job over the winter when he couldn't carry on his operation, but the rest of the year he had no reliable paycheck coming in. She whisked the check out from under Patrick's hand.

"My turn! Don't forget, I'm living rent free this summer." He accepted after a half-hearted demur, and she pulled some bills out of her wallet.

"How do you suppose those people in the mob got the idea that Opal Hansen kidnapped the baker? And that she's a witch?" she asked casually.

Patrick shrugged.

"Because they have the combined IQ of a pumpkin."

And with that, Maura had to drop it. She was no closer to understanding Patrick's role in the affair. When she returned home, a middle-aged couple was looking through the bucket of items Maura had knocked off faces with the hose. She recognized the man as one of the torch bearers. He had just found his eyeglasses when the woman noticed Maura standing there.

"Sam!" she whispered. He turned around and Maura gave them a shark-like smile. They hurried off. She looked in the bucket and saw that about half the items remained. She would leave them out for a few more days then throw the rest away. As she went inside, she reflected on the fact that they had looked like an ordinary couple. The woman had her hair pinned back on either side with little plastic barrettes like the ones Lizzie wore. The man was neatly groomed and as they scurried away, he had a protective hand on his wife's back. Maura wondered what turned people like this into a dangerous mob. And could they be turned again to good advantage?

The doorbell rang as dusk was falling. Will was in the attic, pulling things apart. She could hear Lizzie giving him suggestions. Maura looked out the window and saw Randy on the stoop, holding a baseball bat. She was startled but was unable to feel any alarm at his presence with a potential weapon. She opened the door.

"Randy?"

"Mrs. Gertz." He touched his cap. "Can you call your neighbor and tell her not to worry if she sees me outside with a baseball bat? I'm doing some guard duty tonight. There's a rumor there might be trouble coming." There was a quiet dignity in his voice. He looked like he hadn't slept well in days. Maura stared at him for a moment.

"Wait here." She went inside and used the phone, then called up the attic stairs to say she was stepping next door for a few minutes.

"Come on," she said, closing the front door behind her. She took Randy to the Uncle Irvin house's gate and unlocked it with Opal's spare key. They passed through and he looked around at the overgrown grass and shrubs that badly needed trimming.

"It looks this way because she's afraid to hire anyone."

Randy nodded.

They mounted the steps and rang the bell. When Maura called, Opal, already in her housecoat, had been playing cards with Joe. She opened the door and looked at Randy questioningly.

"Opal, this is Randy Fry. He was one of the jerks in the mob last Saturday."

Opal's eyes widened as she took in Randy's baseball bat.

"Are you here to kill me? Very nice, Maura."

"When he's not drinking, he's an intelligent and likeable person. When he's had too much, he'll follow a mob of torch-bearing idiots to be where the action is."

Randy smiled a little and leaned the bat against the house.

"If I hadn't been drunk I would have done my best to stop them – at least I hope I would have. I know it doesn't make up for anything but I came to guard your house, and Mrs. Gertz's. I haven't had a drink in a few days so I probably won't set fire to anything."

"Randy's a handyman and does nice work. If he doesn't sneak in and murder you tonight you might want to think about hiring him for a few things."

Opal looked at him consideringly.

"Won't you be afraid I'd turn you into a toad or something?"

He laughed. "Nah. Well, I might if I fall off the wagon, but I don't work drunk. How about if I do something with your yard? On me."

Randy seemed to hold himself a little straighter as he took up his position in the shadow of one of the trees on the green. Maura had hoped that if he was able to make amends with Opal it might help him take another step away from self-destruction.

She was on the last chapter of *Jane Eyre* when she heard Randy's voice. It was close to midnight and his voice carried clearly in the stillness.

"Hey Frank. Harmon. What are you boys doing here?"

"Randy! You scared us."

Another voice swore and then laughed.

"I don't know what you have in those bags, but you'll need to turn around and go if you don't want this baseball bat up your nose." Randy's voice was cordial but held a hint of steel.

"Come on, Randy. She's a witch! Why are you here – she put a spell on you?"

"I met her. She's a nice granny and we all scared the bejesus out her. I know *your* granny, Harmon. How about if I tell her what you've been up to?"

Harmon had no answer to that, but Frank wasn't as easily intimidated.

"You listen here, Randy. There's something evil on this island and there she sits..."

"No, you listen," came a deep voice. It was followed by the rush of water from a hose and a hard splat as it hit its targets. Maura had been expecting it since she heard the squeak of the faucet moments earlier. She grinned as she looked out her window into the night. Will was having his turn at the hose.

The men swore as they ran for their bicycles and pedaled away.

Maura took a quick look at Lizzie to make sure she was sleeping then scanned Opal's house from the boys' dormitory. All the windows were dark on this side so she assumed Opal and Joe had slept through the exchange.

She went downstairs and made a pot of coffee. While it was brewing, she made a platter of sandwiches and put a pile of cookies on a plate. Maura knew Will had come back to the island so he could keep an eye on things and was sure he wouldn't go to bed and leave Randy to guard against the possible return of the miscreants. When she stepped onto the green with the loaded tray, they were going through the bags that Frank and Harmon had left when they ran off. Randy looked up when she approached.

"Paint and brushes, some eggs that are probably rotten and a few good-size rocks. Probably to break a window or two. It doesn't look like they meant her harm but are trying to run her off."

Maura felt a little relieved but thought if the witch business kept up someone might try something more deadly.

The men were delighted with the tray. She took half a sandwich and went back to the house, sensing that they were looking forward to being on guard duty. She fell asleep to the murmur of their voices, feeling oddly safe but wondering what was going to happen next.

Chapter 19

It was nearly August and Maura felt a sense of impending loss as the days slipped by. There would never again be a summer like this, with long, glorious days stretching into starlit evenings. Their little world was a jumble of roses, waves washing onto beaches, bike rides around the island and being welcomed home by the lovely old house. She and Lizzie were occasionally invited for lunch or tea with mothers and children from Camp Boogie-Woogie, and once the heaviest of the house renovations were completed Maura returned the invitations.

The kitchen was finished and Maura adored it. With its misty blue cabinets, the speckled countertop in a deeper shade of blue with its chrome border, the new range covered in dials and knobs and the black and white checkerboard floor, it was very modern. Shelves with Aunt May's things and the family's big farmhouse table softened the newness. Rebecca had asked Will whether he would like her to send down a new, modern table but he voted to keep the farmhouse table. He remembered all the meals with his family gathered around it on summer vacations and didn't like the idea of it winding up in a garbage heap when the new owners took possession. He thought he might take it for his new house when he was married.

Maura's highest hope when they arrived on Islay was to strengthen Lizzie's bond with her and to remold themselves into a little family rather than part of a large group of institute residents. She felt that in most respects her hopes were being realized, but the little family seemed to include Will through no one's effort. With him on the island full time now, the stack of Lizzie and the Giant and Jelly Bean stories had grown quite a bit. It became a ritual for Will to spin a tale after dinner, as the sun went down and they sat in lawn chairs. Lizzie would then dance around the backyard in her cotton nightgown and bare feet while Maura and Will talked idly of the little events of the day and sipped coffee or after-dinner drinks. On some level Maura knew this arrangement wasn't good for any of them. Lizzie had become much too attached to Will. She had herself; he was so easy to have around and they could talk about anything or nothing. She was honest enough with herself to admit to an attraction that she had first become aware of the night of the mob visit. How easy it would be to be married to Will, she thought, if he wasn't already engaged. And if she was undamaged. For a moment she imagined life continuing as it was after the summer came to a close, the three of them moving on together but the magic of Islay still wrapped around them. The bitter conviction that she couldn't help but sabotage any such relationship brought the dream up short. She envied Junie but in a way was glad that she was marrying Will. At times she suspected Will had some attraction to herself but his pending marriage would avoid any painful discussions at the end of the summer. Maura was fairly sure he wouldn't enjoy the same easy camaraderie and mutual interests with his young bride and thought this summer's arrangement wasn't good for him either.

Rebecca arrived Friday morning with Leo, her contractor. She was on her way to Boston to meet with the directors of the women's institute and wanted to see the progress on the house. After a tour, both contractor and investor were unable to find fault. Rebecca was enthusiastic about the kitchen and Maura caught herself proudly showing it off. Not only had most of the choices been Rebecca's, but it wasn't Maura's house anyway. It didn't keep her from loving it, though.

Will took them out back to inspect the carriage house conversion. Maura hadn't been inside recently and was interested to see the finished result. They crowded into the tiny living room and admired the gleaming wood floors, the neat moldings around windows and doorways and the immaculate little kitchen. Rebecca and Leo congratulated Will on his workmanship.

"This will be perfect for a couple. The new owners will be able to make a nice little income from it." Rebecca insisted that Will should get a larger share of any profit because of the value a guest cottage added and for all the labor he invested. Will just waved his hand and said that he enjoyed the summer project and if Aunt May got a little more money because of it, he was happy.

"Leo," Will said, changing the subject. "Can you take a look in the crawl space before you go? I dug down next to the foundation to see what it looked like in case there was trouble and found something interesting."

They trooped around to the back of the carriage house and Will pulled a board away from a large hole. It revealed the carriage house's stone foundation, with a small metal door set into it. Leo lay on the grass and lowered his upper body into the hole, shining a flashlight that Will handed him. He inspected the stonework then carefully opened the metal door.

"The door would have been exposed above ground when the structure was built. Over time it's been covered up. Have you been in?"

"I tried," answered Will, "but I don't fit. I did peer in, though. There's nothing interesting until you get to the center of the space."

Leo pulled himself partway into the crawl space and was silent for a few moments.

"Looks like a rubble trench." He pulled himself further in and disappeared inside. It was five minutes before he reappeared, at which point he stuck his head out the door and asked Will and Maura if they had a sack of some sort, at least a foot square. Will retrieved his knapsack and Leo disappeared again.

When he emerged, he was filthy but smiling. He handed Will the knapsack and pulled himself out of the hole.

"As I said, it's a rubble trench. An old-style foundation. Builders would dig a ditch then pack it tight with rocks and pebbles. Because the center area was hollow the weight of the structure would have been on the rocks. It was enough to keep the building from sinking into the ground. Back then foundations weren't built above the ground and any wood siding would have rotted. A lot of times they added a simple drainage system which would have kept some of the dampness at bay, though. There are signs this one had one."

"Why is there a rubble trench foundation inside a regular stone foundation?" Maura asked, already guessing the answer.

"This structure must have been built on the site of an earlier one. They just built the stone foundation around the rubble trench. The original structure was significantly smaller than this one – maybe a single room. Will, do you know when the current one was built?"

Will shrugged.

"I'm pretty sure Josiah Watts put it up when the house was built. That would have been 1826. I don't know what would have been here before that."

I do, thought Maura with a chill creeping over her skin.

Leo held up Will's knapsack and grinned.

"Let's see if this gives us any clues!"

Maura spread newspaper on the picnic table while Leo pulled on a pair of work gloves and gingerly extracted a rotted wooden box from the knapsack. Parts of it fell off as he set it down.

"This was inside the rubble trench. I only found it because I happened to be shining the flashlight in the ditch at that point."

The box was clearly beyond reclamation, but as Leo removed sections he set them carefully aside. Lumps of packing material, long rotted, were pulled away revealing rows of black discs. Will picked one up.

"I think it's a coin."

Maura grinned.

"Buried treasure! Bec, I'm catching up to you in the adventure department. If these are worth anything, do they belong to Will's family?"

No one knew. Rebecca picked up a coin and examined it.

"It looks like badly tarnished silver. Mo, is there any silver polish in the house?"

Maura rooted through Aunt May's cleaning supplies and found the silver polish. Back at the picnic table, she put a small amount on a clean dish towel and looked at Will uncertainly.

"Do you think this could harm the coin? It may belong to your family now."

Will thought Aunt May would want them to polish one coin. Maura gently rubbed and the rag immediately began turning black. After more polish and more rubbing, the coin was relatively clean. She took it inside to wash the polish off then set it on another dish towel so they could all look at it.

The coin was a little irregularly shaped. The letters MASATHVSETS IN encircled a picture of a tree on one side. When they turned it over, they saw the letters DOM NEW ENGLAND · AN · XII and the year 1652. It was all quite legible once the tarnish had been removed, as though the coin hadn't seen much use.

Maura had already come to the conclusion that the rubble trench foundation marked the site of the witch of Islay's house. Josiah Watts was one of the first to build on the island, not counting the shipwreck survivors, so who else would an earlier building have belonged to? The cache of coins had her stumped though. Coins that had been minted in 1652 would have surely shown a lot of wear and tear by Prudence's day seventy or eighty years later. And why would a collection of coins be hidden under her house?

After some discussion, they agreed to keep the polished coin out and hide the rest until Will's family decided what to do about them. Obviously, they would need to find someone who was an expert in old coins. They wrapped the cache in multiple layers of wax paper and cloth, put them in Maura's jewelry box, wrapped the box in one of Will's shirts and put the wad in Will's knapsack. Leo put it back in the crawl space, out of sight from anyone who might stick his head in, and then they re-covered the hole Will had dug.

Leo cleaned up as best he could in the powder room, had a quick lunch then left in the taxi to catch his ride back to the mainland. The others finished their lunches at a more leisurely rate, then Will went back to the carriage house to work on his blueprints for the afternoon. After washing the lunch dishes Maura and Rebecca found Lizzie asleep on the new rug in the writing room, Jelly Bean curled up against her back with one leg in the air, giving himself a bath. He paused and gave the intruders his absurd, goggle-eyed stare.

Rebecca grinned in appreciation. "When did you get a cat," she whispered so as not to wake up Lizzie, "and why does he look like someone stuck his tail in an electrical outlet?"

"Will picked him up at a cocktail party; the hosts were only too glad to get rid of him. He's kind of grown on us and we're immortalizing him." Maura picked up her thick folder of Lizzie and The Giant and Jelly Bean stories and held it out.

"I was going to ask you what you've been writing," Rebecca said, opening the folder. She picked up the first typewritten page and began to read. A slow smile spread over her face, and she lowered herself into Maura's desk chair. The stories were short, and as she finished one, she went on to the next.

"These are wonderful! I was picturing you working on the great American novel. This is much better!"

Maura glanced at the sleeping Lizzie.

"It was a partnership. Let's go back to the kitchen and I'll warm up the coffee."

Rebecca sat at the big table, turning over pages and chuckling, while Maura poured the lunchtime coffee in a pan and turned on the burner.

"Who's your partner for these?"

"Will. He gets most of the credit. Lizzie pesters him mercilessly to tell her stories every night after dinner. It's become a ritual and I think he spends the day working out plots because they've been getting better and better." She poured the heated coffee into cups and set them on the table with a plate of chocolate chip cookies.

"Bec... I'm kind of worried about Lizzie. She's gotten so attached to Will. I guess it was inevitable, his living here on weekends and now full time. He's so patient with her and seems to enjoy her company. After she's in bed, I go straight to the writing room and type up the stories he told before I forget them. I just smooth them out a little." She stared at the cookie on her plate. "I thought if she had a book of his stories, it might help after we leave here."

Rebecca looked at her searchingly.

"Couldn't you invite him for lunch now and then? It's clear you and Will have become good friends too."

Maura laughed a little, avoiding her eye.

"No, he's getting married in November and while Junie was friendly enough, I don't think she would be anxious to visit us. And you haven't seen our apartment... there isn't even a kitchen table. We'll be eating our meals on the coffee table."

"Mo, won't you let me..."

"No, Rebecca Kate. I won't. You know how important it is to me to be self-sufficient. Did I tell you Junie and her sister came to visit?" Maura proceeded to regale Rebecca with an account of the unsuccessful visit of Will's fiancé and her sister. Rebecca laughed in the right places but was then silent for a moment.

"Poor Will."

"Why? She wouldn't be my cup of tea but she's a nice girl and she'll be a good wife."

"Maura... people change their minds."

"If you mean Will might break it off with Junie, you don't know Will. He's too honorable to leave a girl in the lurch like that and he's very fond of her. And you don't know me if you think I could ever bring myself to get married again."

Rebecca's eyes glistened.

"Why?" she asked softly.

Maura arose and carried their coffee cups to the sink. She turned around and leaned against the counter.

"You know my story, Bec. My mother had me thoroughly convinced I was responsible for her problems as long as I can remember. David picked up the baton. The smart part of me says they were wrong but the stupid part of me, which is much bigger, is firmly convinced I'll never be good enough and can't possibly help the people who need me. It's a self-fulfilling prophecy."

"Lizzie needs you and you're a wonderful mother."

"Lizzie isn't asking for much besides pancakes and bedtime stories."

"You've never let me down."

"You've never needed me."

They stared at each other sadly.

CHAPTER 20

"I'm not sure walking into the lion's den is a good idea," said Will with a frown.

Maura looked at him with some exasperation as the taxi approached the Watts house.

"I don't want to spend the rest of the summer wondering when the next attack is going to be. Opal doesn't either." Opal was examining herself in a compact mirror with a little smile of approval. Her hair had been dressed in a style popular thirty years earlier. An ancient hat that she hadn't worn for years before moving to the island was perched on top. Gracie had rubbed pink rouge in circles on Opal's cheeks and applied a matching bright pink lipstick.

"I look like I'm ninety," Opal said with satisfaction.

Maura hid a smile. Her neighbor would be in the most danger tonight but was clearly looking forward to the evening.

"You look like a nice granny. Will, you'll be there and Randy will be inside. It will be fine." They were heading to the tavern for dinner; at least, Maura and Opal were. No more was said of the evening's plans as they climbed into the taxi. Gracie and Lizzie stood on the stoop and waved them off.

It was Saturday night, at a time when the bar could be expected to be full of regulars. Will stationed himself outside as planned, sitting on the curb near an open window so he could hear what was going on inside. He lit his pipe and looked like nothing more than a man who was out to enjoy a fine evening.

The tavern was filled with smoke. All the tables were occupied but as they approached, Randy left his and sauntered up to the bar. Opal settled herself in his vacated chair and looked around, beaming at everyone who looked her way. With her old-fashioned hat, shapeless white dress with blue and pink flowers and her white gloves she looked completely out of place. Maura went to the bar and ordered two glasses of sherry and two steaks.

"Well, isn't this nice!" Opal's voice had an elderly tremble to it, but it carried well.

The waiter who sullenly delivered their sherry stared at Maura. She recognized him as a member of the mob and he clearly recognized her.

"Did you get your hat back?" She smiled cheerfully. "I remember I knocked it about ten feet with the hose." The waiter didn't know what to say to this direct approach and hurried away.

She saw that many of the patrons were looking at her and she recognized a number of them. She stood up and tapped her glass with a spoon to get attention.

"I don't want any trouble!" the bartender called.

"No, no. Of course not." Maura scanned the customers and made eye contact where she could. The room quieted and many with guilty consciences wondered uneasily what was coming next. Others, who hadn't joined the mob, were puzzled.

"I think a lot of you recognize me as the crazy woman with the hose. You may not know this lady, though. This is Mrs. Opal Hansen. She owns the house you were waving torches at."

Maura knew that the mob had only seen Opal at an open window with a light behind her so hadn't seen her features. They now beheld the island witch, except that up close it was almost impossible for them to think she could have anything to do with the recent death and disappearances. The old woman was hunched over and smiling fondly at the young one as though she had no clue that this was the group that wanted to run her off the island. Indeed, she seemed to have no recollection of the event.

"Why are you here?" The belligerent voice belonged to a youth with a deep tan. Probably off one of the fishing boats, Maura guessed.

"We heard this was the best place to get steaks," she replied. "OK, I thought it would be good for you to meet Mrs. Hansen. I know everyone's shaken up by the weird things that have been happening lately. Me too – I have my little girl here this summer. Harassing nice old ladies because you think they're witches is a waste of time and kind of laughable." Here Opal made an O with her mouth and looked around at the people staring at them.

"You mean *me*?" she asked in a tremulous voce. "You think I'm a witch?" Her eyes began to tear up and those close enough to see it looked distinctly uncomfortable. Maura had to bite her lip not to laugh.

"If it's not that," a middle-aged woman called, "why did Violet Wilson die? We don't think it was an accident."

"And where's the baker?" Other voices echoed that: Where's the baker?

"Very good questions! I don't think Violet Wilson's death was an accident either. I'm the one who found her! Why aren't you doing something about it?" She looked from one person to the next but they stared back blankly. "Who are the smart people here?" She raised her hand to indicate that those with a modicum of intelligence should as well. They looked at each other and a few people laughed. Several pointed at one middle-aged man who grinned and raised his hand. The bartender pointed at Randy, who Maura noticed was drinking ginger ale. Randy smiled and raised his hand. A young woman waved her hand while her boyfriend shook his head. Maura's wide grin took them all in and made them suddenly feel like they were part of an adventure.

"OK, smart people. You're in charge. You – Barry? Can you put together search parties to scour the island for the baker? The police looked but they seemed to give up pretty quickly. You'll need a few teams and they should work in shifts. Make a map and mark off everywhere you look. He might be lying out there somewhere, hurt." If Joe the baker had been lying out on the island somewhere instead of reading a paper in Opal's kitchen, he would probably be dead by now. Everyone knew it but they didn't mind searching for a dead body.

"You," she said to Randy. "See if you can find out something about Violet Wilson's past. Try to find out where she was from and then maybe go to the Boston library to check recent newspapers for her obituary. That could tell us who her family is." Randy saluted. She didn't think he was actually going to do any of that but her goal for the evening was to give the crowd some positive action they could take that didn't include attacking Opal. Randy was in on all this. The island search was of course a complete waste of time, but Maura thought they deserved it.

"What's your name?" she asked the young woman who had waved her hand. "Bea. Can you and a friend or two find out which clubs and organizations Violet Wilson belonged to and interview the other members. See if you can find out anything. When was the last time they saw her? Who was she with? Was she seeing anyone?"

Plates with large steaks and baked potatoes were plunked on the table.

"If anyone finds out anything, report back. OK, that's all for now!" She smiled and waved at the other patrons then sat down.

"Nicely done, dearie!" Opal winked at her. Maura looked at her appreciatively. Opal was clearly enjoying herself. The difference between the disillusioned recluse she had met only a month ago and this adventurous Opal with a humorous glint in her eye was astounding. She guessed that her neighbor's decision to stand up to those who threatened her had triggered the transformation and Maura was a little envious.

Although no one had actually told them that the tavern served good steaks, they were beautifully prepared and the baked potatoes had fat pats of butter melting down their sides. They began to eat and conversation gradually resumed around the room. Glances were still shot at their table, and some were surprised to see the blonde treasure hunter make a beeline for Maura upon entering the tavern. She looked up.

"Steve! Have a seat." He looked at Opal and asked her if she minded the interruption before pulling out a chair.

"Fish and chips?" the bartender called. Steve nodded.

"I always have the same thing here. I'm afraid if I try something different I won't love it as much. I've heard the steaks are excellent though." Having exhausted the food topic, Steve seemed to be groping for something else to say.

"Thank you again for guarding our houses the other night. I don't think you've met Mrs. Hansen. She lives in the house that the mob was targeting. Opal, Steve is a professor at the University of Rhode Island, doing some salvaging for the summer."

Aware that there were still eyes on them, Opal kept up her granny act.

"Thank you, honey. That was very nice of you."

Steve flushed and said he was happy to help.

Maura asked him about teaching and as he relaxed, he followed the description of his job with a number of amusing anecdotes about his students. Opal wanted to know more about the salvage work. He soon had them laughing over a story of Patrick excitedly looking into a pewter urn he had just pulled off the ocean floor and, finding an octopus looking back at him, screamed and threw the urn back in the water. "I don't know what he thought he was looking at."

"Poseidon," murmured Maura wickedly.

"Oh, you know about his renaming fiasco?" Steve grinned. "He's an interesting one, is our Patrick."

"How come you can talk to us but you're a big dummy around Gracie?" asked Opal, forgetting her sweet old lady act for a moment.

Steve put his hands over his face and groaned.

Maura's plans to write an entire manuscript over the summer were hampered by the fact that she was writing three things at once. Rebecca helped by taking the folder of Lizzie and the Giant and Jelly Bean stories with her. "I own a publishing company, for heaven's sake. Somebody ought to be able to print it on nice paper and stick a cover on it. I'll give it back to you in a few weeks." This left her small stack of vignettes of island life, which she enjoyed writing because it was a way to capture this lovely summer, and *The Witch of Islay*.

The latter enterprise took up most of her writing time. Prudence seemed to be clamoring to have her story told. Maura had doubts she would ever publish it but it felt like it was something she could let herself go on and gain experience in writing a novel. With the discovery of the coins, the mysteries surrounding Prudence and her probable lover were filling Maura's idle moments. Why did they have the coins? The first mate and a young woman were eventually found on Islay. What happened to Prudence?

After some discussion with Will, they decided she would show the coin to Patrick and see if he recognized it. She would say that she and Lizzie had found it down by the harbor. Because Maura was a terrible liar, she took Lizzie to the harbor that weekend for crabbing off the pier. They spent an hour catching small crabs in a metal cage and letting them go, then left the pier. After checking that no one was nearby, she slipped the polished coin out of her pocket and put it on the pebbles just out of reach of the water. She immediately picked it up again and put it back in her pocket. She felt like she could now tell Patrick she picked up the coin at the harbor.

Maura and Patrick had fallen into a routine where every few days he would call her from a phone booth and they would meet for breakfast at the coffee shop. She would bring the latest pages of her manuscript, which he would read and comment on. She knew the writing wasn't her best, but the story was flowing from her mind to the paper with little effort and she didn't bother to edit as she went. Patrick wasn't a critical audience, and he made no secret of the fact that he looked forward to each installment.

"'John Kellow and Mistress Prudence were keeping watch from behind the wood pile. The woods began to glow, signifying that men with torches were approaching.'" Patrick looked up. "I remembered her last name. It was Payne, which meant 'pagan' back in medieval times. An interesting name for a preacher and his wife." Patrick resumed his reading.

"'Four men straggled to the edge of the clearing surrounding the house and stared silently. This was more frightening to Prudence than drunken bravado would have been. Before any of them could summon the courage to approach the cabin, Prudence thrust the torches they had ready into the small fire they had been tending for the last several hours. The torches caught and Prudence stepped out from behind the woodpile with one in each hand. She held the flames high and advanced toward the men, speaking made-up words in a guttural voice.' How do you know they were made up words? What if she was really speaking in tongues? OK, anyway... 'All the dark powers of the sea and earth seemed to swirl around her and speak from her lips. The men's eyes grew so wide Prudence could see their whites. Their fear empowered her. One was more daring than the others and when he stepped forward, she ran at him, waving her torches and hissing.'"

"I loved the hissing part from the first mate's diary," said Maura. "And the 'all the dark powers' bit. The more I write about Prudence, the more I like her. The first mate must have been hiding while she was doing her act. She was clearly the stronger of the two."

"You might not like her so much if you knew more about her. How come this chapter is short?"

"I don't know where to go with the story after this. Violet Wilson's account has a vague mention of a tragedy striking the colonists and the first mate and Prudence taking the baby from the settlement and raising her. She gets all sentimental about their love for each other and their new daughter. I can't do anything with that."

Patrick was silent for a moment.

"Meet me again on Thursday, but not here. I may have more information for you and I don't want anyone to overhear. I'll tell you where when I call you."

Before they left the coffee shop, Maura reached into her pocket as though she had just thought of something.

"Hey, Patrick. Have you ever seen anything like this?" She put the coin on the table.

His hand was arrested as he was putting his wallet away. After staring at the coin for several seconds he asked in a strange voice, "Where did you get that?"

"Lizzie and I were crabbing in the harbor yesterday and I found it near the edge of the water." She felt her cheeks turn red and was annoyed to know she couldn't lie even after the elaborate preparation.

Patrick picked up the coin and inspected it carefully. He then fixed his eyes on her, seeming to note her discomfiture.

"It's a Pine Tree shilling. Under English rule, the colonies weren't allowed to have their own currency. It was a big problem because there wasn't enough English currency to go around. They had to barter or use Spanish coins. Massachusetts was enterprising enough to mint a series of silver coins but put a fake year on them that predated the no-currency law. One of these is worth quite a bit for its historical value." The whole time Patrick spoke he continued to keep his eyes fixed on her face. "Were there more?"

"No, just the one." Maura found this easier because she was annoyed at the scrutiny. "I have to go pick up Lizzie." She held out her hand for the coin and Patrick returned it after a moment's hesitation.

"See you Thursday," he reminded her.

Since running intruders off with the hose, Will had taken to sleeping in the house. He kept watch in the shadows, sometimes until two o'clock in the morning, then spent the rest of the night in the boys' dormitory. He would be close enough to Opal's house to be alerted if anything transpired, and Maura could reach him quickly if she became aware of trouble on the street. Randy, Steve and the police took additional turns on watch duty, although the last amounted to one bicycle ride around the green before midnight. By tacit agreement Maura and Will didn't mention the new arrangements to anyone, but when Maura picked Lizzie up at day camp Tuesday morning Gracie was grinning broadly. She held onto Maura until the other children had left with their mothers. Midge's mother, Dottie, gave Maura a little smile and quirked an eyebrow. After she left, Gracie said, "Fizzy Lizzie, what did you tell Midge's mommy and me about Will?"

"Mr. Giant sleeps in our house now to make Mommy happy!" Lizzie danced around in a circle.

Maura's face turned bright red. Gracie laughed.

"Lizzie!" Maura stopped, not knowing what else to say. Naturally, no one had told her about the danger to Opal or themselves. Maura had only said that Will was moving into the house for a little while to help with the housework. When Lizzie did her chores without complaining, Maura would say it made her happy.

"It's not what you think, and I see I'll have to drop in on Dottie." The neighbors on the green were all aware of the mob visit to Opal's house and the subsequent patrolling of the neighborhood. A few of the men joined Will on his vigils long enough to drink a bottle of beer and talk about sports or politics. Dottie would understand why Will moved to the house but might be a little disappointed.

Vic Stokes, the island police captain, paid a visit that afternoon. When Maura peeked out the window she was tempted to pretend they weren't home, but Lizzie chose that moment to blow into her new harmonica that she bought at the Island 5 & 10.

Vic removed his hat and smiled when Maura opened the door.

"Hello! I come through here now and then to check on things and thought I would stop by to see if all is well. Do you have a few minutes?"

"Come in," Maura smiled politely. She ushered him into the parlor and offered him a glass of iced tea. Noticing Stokes' interested inspection of the items on the shelves and table tops, she belatedly remembered that she had agreed to ask Will's family if he could look at their antiques. She excused herself and went upstairs to the bottom of the attic staircase to call Will down.

When Will followed Maura into the kitchen, Stokes blinked.

"Vic, this is Will Howe. His aunt owns the house. Will, Vic makes up half of the island police force." The men shook hands. Maura poured more iced tea and they took their glasses into the parlor. She pushed an annoyed Jelly Bean off one of the chairs and took his place.

"How are you getting on here? Have there been any further disturbances?" Stokes asked in the same tone that would be used to ask a pew neighbor for a stick of gum during a sermon.

Will stared at him blankly. "Sorry?"

"Any more disturbances," Maura interpreted. "Yes, some men came by Thursday night. Will ran them off."

Stokes frowned.

"You should have reported it!"

From what she had seen of the island police, Maura doubted that any benefit would have been gained by reporting the incident, but she and Will hadn't even considered it. She murmured untruthfully that she had been planning to go to the police station, and Will supplied particulars of the evening. Stokes wrote these down in a pocket-sized notebook. They sipped their tea in silence as the police captain's eyes scanned the room.

"This is a wonderful place," he said in a confidential whisper.

Will leaned forward, aiming an ear in their guest's direction. "Can you repeat that?"

"This is a wonderful place!" Stoke's voice wasn't any louder this time but he carefully enunciated his words.

"Oh! Yes, it will be hard for the family to let it go, but times change."

"Mrs. Gertz may have mentioned that I have a little hobby where I buy and sell antiques. I wonder if I might take a look around."

Maura hoped that Will would politely fob him off, but his ear was becoming attuned to their sotto voce guest and he cheerfully told Stokes he would give him a tour.

"You won't be interested in the bedrooms," he said after the police captain had turned over every vase and pewter tankard and examined the backs of paintings in the downstairs. There's nothing interesting up there." Stokes looked like he would very much like to look upstairs but smiled and thanked them for their time.

"There are a few nice pieces here," he said under his breath. "You'll want to bring in someone who can value them properly, but I would be interested in some of the china and pewter if your aunt would consider selling those directly to me. I would pay a fair price and she would save the commission on them." He looked around one last time. "Do you have any other silver?"

Maura narrowed her eyes. It was an odd question; why would Will's family have a lot of silver in a vacation home? It seemed to her that Stokes was trying to look casual. Had Patrick mentioned the coin to him? Did they even know each other?

Lizzie came downstairs with her harmonica at that moment and blew in it as hard as she could, over and over. Stokes hastily made for the door. Whatever he said in parting was lost in a blast from the harmonica. Maura and Will nodded and smiled, then shut the door and locked it.

"Nice timing, Lizzie Lou. Can you go up to your room and blow in it? It sounds much better up there." After Lizzie had disappeared with Jelly Bean in her wake, she turned to find Will in front of the side window, giving her an odd look.

"When he was over here looking at the ceramic box, he unlocked the window."

Chapter 21

Will decided to sleep on the couch in the parlor that night.

"How can you be sure he unlocked the window?" Maura deposited a pillow and blanket on the end of the couch.

"Because I've been checking every window and door before I go to bed. Did you unlock this side window but leave it shut?"

"No...I never open that one. Only the windows along the street. I sometimes take naps on the couch, but we don't sit in here much."

They stared at each other for a moment.

"I'll get us some ice cream." She disappeared into the kitchen. Lizzie had been in bed for several hours but Maura wasn't sleepy.

They sat on the couch with bowls of strawberry ice cream. Why Stokes would want to break into the house and whether he was after antiques or the coins was discussed at length. Was there anything of enough value in the house to take such a risk? Should they retrieve the coins from their hiding place under the carriage house and keep them in the house with them? They decided against it; the coins were where they had safely lain for over two hundred years. If Stokes was looking for them, he would be hoping to find them here in the house.

Will asked how her writing was going. She told him she had a short stack of vignettes about island life, but that it was the island witch's story that had captured her imagination.

"She would have been fun to have around, Will. According to the first mate's journal, she drove off attackers by running at them with torches and hissing."

"I guess she didn't have a hose."

Conversation eventually drifted into a comfortable silence. By the time the parlor clock chimed 2:30 a.m., Maura was sound asleep.

Nothing occurred to break the peace that night. Maura awoke as the sun began to streak the sky and stir the birds. She became aware that she wasn't alone on the couch. Will was stretched out alongside her, his back against the cushions. She lay on her back with his head on her shoulder. A large, well-muscled arm lay across her stomach and had likely kept her from rolling off onto the floor. A blanket covered them both. For a moment, before confusion and embarrassment took over, she was conscious of a sweet feeling of comfort and safety. Her breathing began to quicken as panic slid over her. She gingerly lifted Will's arm and laid it along his side. She pushed the blanket aside then slid off the couch, taking care that his head didn't drop. She was sure he would wake up and had no idea what she would say.

Once she was free of the couch, Will rolled onto the space she had vacated and pulled the blanket up. She watched him for a moment to make sure he was still asleep then tip-toed quickly up the stairs.

When he heard Maura's bedroom door close, Will opened his eyes for a moment and smiled.

Will drifted into the kitchen the following morning with a chattering Lizzie in tow. Maura was stirring batter for pancakes and felt her cheeks turn pink. She glanced around then had to laugh. He was rumpled and barefoot; his hair stuck up in places and a dark stubble covered his cheeks and chin. He smiled ruefully as Lizzie told Maura that Mr. Giant had slept on the couch all night.

"I don't know how much sleep I got once Jelly Bean discovered me. Not content with giving himself a wash while sprawled on my stomach, he kept butting my face with his head. I had no idea he likes me so much."

"He wanted you to feed him."

"What a letdown. And Princess Lizzie was kind enough to wake me up this morning with a detailed description of the picnic Miss Gracie has planned for today."

Will poured himself a mug of coffee then sauntered to the stove where Maura was pouring pancake batter onto a hot griddle in neat circles. He stood a little closer to her than she thought was warranted, bringing back some of the confusion from last night. She dribbled a little batter on the counter.

"Sorry about the couch last night," he said casually. "You were hogging it and the blanket, and I didn't want to wake you up."

She laughed self-consciously and apologized for taking over his stakeout. "I didn't mean to fall asleep. That couch is so comfortable! At the risk of sounding like Vic Stokes, I wonder if your aunt would consider selling it to me for my apartment? It wouldn't leave room for any other furniture but it would be worth it."

Will promised to ask her and left to get a towel and clean clothes. The plumbing in the carriage house was finished but he loved the outdoor shower. Before long she could hear the water running and cheerful whistling. Maura exhaled slowly. She had worried that things would be awkward between them, but his off-hand reference to their shared night on the couch made her relax a little.

After breakfast, Will packed his blueprints and other gear in a pillowcase, his knapsack currently being used to hold buried treasure. He had promised he would deliver the blueprints to his office today.

"I expect to be back tonight, although I'm not sure I'll make the ferry. If you get nervous, call Randy."

"We'll be fine. Give my best to Junie."

There was the briefest pause.

"Right. Yes, I will." He rode off on his bicycle.

Maura doubted Junie would let Will return that night, since he was spending virtually all his time on the island. As she walked slowly back into the house, she realized she had some doubts that Junie was even still in the picture. Why would any woman let her fiancé more-or-less move in with another woman, or be satisfied with short, infrequent visits before her wedding? She stopped in the middle of the parlor and her gaze was caught by the couch. She remembered how it felt to have him snuggled up against her for those brief moments before she panicked, for it definitely felt like a snuggle. Most likely he was unaware. She remembered the damp patch his breath made on her skin, and the scent of the soap he used. She had grown comfortable with Will, initially thinking of him as a casual friend from high school. He was safe, engaged to another woman. She knew he was honest and couldn't imagine him cheating on Junie. Now that image was flickering in and out, replaced by a Will with his shirt unbuttoned on the night of the mob, gripping her arms and laughing at her audacity; Will standing disheveled and barefoot in the kitchen after a night on the couch with her, looking at her with the faintest enigmatic smile. She remembered how he stood just a little closer to her than usual when she was making pancakes. Or had he? Maybe she was just more aware of him. She sighed; the summer was becoming more complicated.

Mothers were graciously invited to Miss Gracie's picnic. "You can watch your own kids for a change," explained Gracie. Dottie poured gin and tonics in paper cups and handed them around. The children complained about sand in their bologna sandwiches while their mothers enjoyed a little gossip. As with most island gatherings over the last two weeks, there was speculation regarding the whereabouts of the baker. Maybe, suggested the mother of one of the boys, he and Violet Wilson were lovers.

When Violet died, the baker couldn't stand being on the island without her and left.

"She was doing a lot of fanny-wiggling at other men for somebody who had a lover." Dottie drained the last of her gin and tonic from her cup. "I hear somebody is organizing search parties for the baker. But here's the funny thing: nobody knows what he looks like! I don't know how he would have met Violet if he was always hiding in the coffee shop."

"They could have known each other before they came to the island." The first mother was holding on to her theory that the baker and Violet had been lovers. "Something she once said made me think she was from New Jersey. One of the ladies at the ice cream social in June was bragging about living on a lake when they're not here. Violet chirped up that she had grown up on the edge of a beautiful canal but then it was turned into a highway about ten years ago. Well, my cousin lives in Bloomfield and was complaining about the Morris Canal being replaced with the new Garden State Parkway just about then. Does anybody know where the baker is from?" Nobody did.

Maura notice Gracie's frown and the set line of her lips. Knowing how nervous her friend had become about living alone and the mysteries taking place on the island, she changed the subject. The sky was becoming overcast and a wind was blowing up, so the mothers packed up the lunch remains and took their children home. Maura asked Gracie if she would like to come stay at the Watts house that night and play board games. After a moment's hesitation she declined, saying that she had promised Opal she would have a dress ready for her first volunteer event at the library bake sale tomorrow. Lillian's sister had lost a lot of weight and donated some expensive clothes to the Opal renovation project. Gracie was altering them for her.

Thoughts of Will's warm body pressed against hers kept sliding into Maura's mind that day, to be resolutely pushed aside. What did he mean by it? Her inability to stop this cycle of thoughts made her irritable. As the afternoon wore on and she and Lizzie straightened the house and played games, Maura began to feel annoyed at herself for making a big deal out of nothing. The rest of her summer would be ruined if she fell for Will; it would only make things extremely awkward. Her annoyance shifted to Will. If he wanted a comfortable place to sleep last night, he should have woken her up and sent her to bed. By now she was sure Will had meant nothing by creeping in next to her. He came from a warm and loving family where personal boundaries weren't important, but he should have known her loveless upbringing and marriage would make her uncomfortable with casual physical contact.

The three people she had assigned jobs to at the tavern, Randy, Bea and Barry, appeared on the doorstep after lunch.

"We came to report in, like you told us," said Barry. Maura invited them in, feeling a twinge of guilt at the wild goose chases she had set for them. As they sat around the kitchen table with coffee, each gave an account of their activities over the last few days. Barry spread out a map of the island and explained that there were three search teams looking for the baker. The territory for each was outlined in a different color. Each team had started at the coastline for their section and was working their way in toward the center of the island. Sections already searched were neatly marked.

"We should be able to cover the whole island by Sunday. It would be sooner, but all the young guys are out working." Maura was impressed and said so.

Bea and several friends had interviewed the heads of the island's committees and clubs to discover which Violet belonged to. They planned to attend their next meetings to see what information they could get. The head librarian, one of Violet's closest cronies, told Bea that her friend had been dropping coy hints that she was seeing someone.

Maura was surprised to learn that Randy had gone to the Boston library yesterday to see if he could find an obituary for Violet. She hadn't expected him to take his assignment seriously since he knew her purpose was to divert attention away from Opal.

"I didn't get anywhere because I didn't know where to look. I checked the Boston area papers and didn't find an obituary for Mrs. Wilson, but we don't know if she's from around here." Maura didn't mention the possible connection to New Jersey, as she didn't want him to waste more work time on what was likely a fruitless search. She thanked them and asked them to let her know if they found anything.

Fat raindrops began to fall by mid-afternoon. Maura went around and shut the windows, which made the house stuffy. Looking out to the street, she saw steam rise where the rain hit the warm pavement.

"Take your shoes off!" she directed a startled Lizzie. Maura then grabbed her hand and pulled her outside into the rain. They ran into the deserted street and began splashing in the puddles that were forming, the water warm on their bare feet. The scent of hot tar mixed with that of rich earth and growing things. Rain streamed through their hair and plastered their sundresses to them. Lizzie laughed with delight. Maura sang "It's Raining, It's Pouring" as loud as she could while they danced in the street.

A window in the Georgian slid up and Lillian's face appeared.

"What's all the racket?" she smiled.

"Come out and play with us!"

"No. My makeup will run and I just had my hair done. But I kind of wish I could!" Lillian closed the window.

Maura and Lizzie ran onto the green and chased each other in a game of tag. When thunder rumbled they hurried to the back door and stood dripping in the kitchen, trying to dry off with tea towels.

After changing into dry clothes and hanging the wet dresses on the shower rod, Maura made a pan of warm cocoa. The thunder was getting louder and the power flickered on and off several times. She made chicken croquettes and green beans for an early dinner, worried that they might not have power later. Jelly Bean hid under the couch in the family nook.

Maura looked at the clock. Ten minutes past seven. If Will had caught the ferry he should have been here by now. Unless he was holed up in the tavern or somewhere else in the harbor, waiting for the rain to stop. If Will went to see Junie, of course, he would likely stay to take her out for dinner and come back tomorrow. Or would he come back? What if Junie convinced him to stay in Boston, going back to the old weekends-only arrangement? And, she wondered again, was there still a Junie?

The sky was growing dark early because of the rain clouds, and remembering the window that Stokes must have unlocked, Maura felt a prickle of unease. What if he, or one of his cohorts, decided to break in tonight? She went around the downstairs and locked all the windows she had previously shut.

Will later explained his part in what happened that night:

It was close to midnight when he rolled his bicycle onto the pier in the Islay harbor. He had arrived at the marina in Gloucester much later than planned and spent half an hour in a phone booth, going down a list of charter boats in the phone book. Either no one answered his call, or he was firmly turned down. No one wanted to go out this late and in this weather for the long trip to Islay and back. He finally had success when someone picked up the phone and Will shouted, "I'll pay you double your normal fee!"

Standing now, with rain running down the neck of his windbreaker and flashes of lightening becoming more frequent, he struggled with indecision. The tavern was closed, it being Wednesday night, but he could wait under its overhang until the storm passed. Rain and scattered thunderstorms had been rolling over Boston all afternoon, but a significant storm seemed to follow the boat from the mainland and Will thought the worst was yet to come. He imagined Maura and Lizzie alone in the house while lightening crackled and thunder boomed, the sound of a window breaking or a lock being jimmied masked in the confusion. He resolutely set off on his bicycle.

By the time Will arrived at the house he was thoroughly soaked. He saw that Maura had left a lamp burning downstairs;

a wise precaution, he thought. He pulled his bicycle around the back of the house and stowed it under the tarp that Maura had put over her bicycle and cart, weighted down with rocks.

He looked for kitchen tea towels to dry off with but there were none in the drawer, Maura and Lizzie having used them earlier in the day for the same purpose. There was a note on the table in Maura's handwriting. *There is a plate of sandwiches in the refrigerator for you, and a blueberry pie on the back counter. Don't expect to find any berries left on your aunt's bushes.*

Will made quick work of the plate of sandwiches and cut himself a slab of pie. He rinsed the plates, then made the rounds of the lower story, checking the windows and front door. All were closed and locked.

"Maura, it's me," he called up the stairs, hoping that if she was still up he was loud enough for her to hear, but if she was sleeping he wouldn't wake her. There was no answer, so he crept up the stairs, his shoes squelching and leaving puddles on the treads. He changed into dry clothes, feeling uncharacteristically uneasy as the worst of the storm drew closer. Maura's door had been open when he passed and he couldn't help but peek in. She was sound asleep with Lizzie curled up next to her. Jelly Bean lay at the foot of the bed and opened an eye as Will tiptoed by.

He had planned to spend another night on the couch, but had had a long, tiring day and didn't look forward to sharing the sofa with Jelly Bean. He was a light sleeper and thought that if he kept his door open, he would hear any attempted break in. It didn't seem likely that any marauders would pay a visit in weather like this. Storms this far out in the ocean could be fierce and tonight's seemed to be shaping up that way.

Ten minutes after turning out the light, Will was finally drifting off to sleep when his ear caught the faint tinkle of breaking glass. It came between two rumbles of thunder and if it was a second or two later he wouldn't have heard it. He picked up the wooden baseball bat he had put next to the bed and crept into the hallway in his bare feet. The sound of a window sash being carefully raised reached him at the top of the stairs. He waited for a few moments for the intruder to get inside, then rushed down the stairs. Jelly Bean thought that Will might be going to the kitchen to feed him and started down the stairs at the same time. Will tripped over the cat in the dark and might have righted himself if he hadn't put a foot down in a puddle he had left earlier. The baseball bat flew from his hand and went crashing down the stairs. He grabbed at the railing but missed and went down the steps on his back.

This woke Maura and she appeared at the top of the stairs, yelling his name. She rushed down and slid in the water, but the railing kept her from falling. As she got to the bottom of the steps she heard someone struggling with the locks to open the back door in the kitchen. She bent over Will and after quickly ascertaining that he wasn't mortally injured, ran through the house into the kitchen. Before she arrived she saw a figure wrench the door open and flee into the storm. Without thinking, she ran through the door in pursuit but was brought up short by Will's booming voice shouting her name. Lizzie's cry immediately followed.

Will had limped to the back door and was looking at Maura with so much anger that she was taken aback. She mumbled something and ran past him and up the stairs to reassure Lizzie. It took some time to convince her that everything was fine and to get her back to sleep. When Jelly Bean jumped on Maura's bed and curled up next to Lizzie, she finally drifted off to sleep. Maura softly closed the door and stood in the hallway for a moment, preparing herself for a confrontation with Will.

When she reached the bottom of the staircase, Will had his back to her. He was sweeping up glass from the broken window. She glanced into the now-lit kitchen and saw that the door had been shut and locked.

Will slowly turned and gave her a furious look.

"What the hell did you think you were doing?"

Fourteen years of marriage where she had been trained to believe everything was her fault and nothing she did was right, with confrontations like this one, suddenly rushed back at her.

She didn't know what madness had seized her to run after an intruder into a wild storm, with no weapon. What if he had rounded on her and struck? How would Lizzie have managed without her?

Will saw the stricken look on her face and pulled her into his arms.

"Don't look like that. I'm sorry. You just scared the hell out of me." He stroked her hair. "What did you think you were going to do if you caught him, you madwoman?"

She pushed him away. "I don't know. I guess I just wanted to get a good look at him. I'm sick of other people trying to ruin my lovely summer." She turned her back on him.

"I want pie," Maura said suddenly and went into the kitchen. Will limped after her and watched as she cut two slices. Coffee dripped while they sat at the table and ate in silence. The storm seemed to be moving away.

"Did you get a glimpse of him?" Will finally asked. "It was dark in the parlor and I was lying upside down on the stairs. I could see the shape of a man but didn't have the right perspective to judge how tall he was."

"Yes, there was a bright lightning flash when I was passing through the kitchen. He was wearing a cap and jacket. The back door was wide open and I saw him run past the picnic table, which gave me something to measure him against. Will, I'm sure he was taller than Vic Stokes. Vic is squat, where this person was taller and leaner."

Will rubbed his chin and stared. "Interesting. I assumed it was him. Did you see where he went? Did he go around either corner of the house?"

"No. With the next lightening flash I saw he was about halfway to the woods out back."

Will said he was sure that Stokes had unlocked the parlor window. Starting from there, they ran through their island acquaintances as they sipped their coffee, wondering which might have a relationship to the police captain and a reason to break into the house. There was something in the house that someone wanted. Had Patrick told anyone about the coin? Or did Vic hire someone to steal an antique that he had recognized as valuable?

"Couldn't it have been Dunn himself?"

"I don't know," Maura said slowly. "His superstition is quite strong. He already thinks he's cursed from botching his boat renaming and is afraid that the island witch will put the evil eye on him if he steps on her land. If the incentive was strong enough he might brave it, like if he suspected we had a bathtub full of valuable antique coins. He once told me that it's safe for him to stand on the green because either the witch didn't consider that spot her land or there is no witch's curse. Maybe he would take his chances."

Will got up and took their plates and cups to the sink. Maura watched him run water in the sink.

"I didn't think you were coming back tonight."

Will paused in the act of scrubbing a plate with a sponge.

"It was a close call. One of the senior partners saw me and invited me to dinner. It was a rare offer I couldn't refuse if I wanted to keep working there. He told me that I had somehow gotten a good reputation in the firm and he wanted to discuss my future. It was a long dinner, and I headed north as soon as I got to my car. Thankfully I had a cache of coins for tolls in the glove compartment; I went through all of them trying to find someone who would take me to the island." He described his bike ride through the pouring rain and how he came to be lying upside down on the stairs.

There was no mention of Junie. Maura remembered how gently he had held her tonight and stroked her hair, and how he had shared the couch with her.

"Will...are you and Junie still together?" The question popped out without forethought.

He shook the water out of a mug and put it in the dish drainer, keeping his back to her.

"No."

She didn't say anything. He sighed.

"For her, it was over when she went to a party at a lake house that I refused to go to. The man she was seeing before we met was there and they picked up where they had left off. He's part of her social set and has quite a lot of money. Not that she broke off our engagement for that, but he can give her the lifestyle she's used to." He turned around and faced her. "Maura, she deserved better than me. I was in hell because I realized I didn't love her, but she's a sweet kid and I couldn't think how to end things without hurting her. When she told me there was someone else, I felt like a jerk for being so relieved."

His eyes looked into Maura's.

"For me, it ended the night the mob came with torches. I couldn't imagine her fighting them off with a garden hose." He watched her expression change from surprise to confusion to panic as she realized what he was saying. She stood and opened her mouth, then turned and fled through the parlor and up the stairs.

Will sighed.

"And how do I overcome that?" he whispered to himself.

There was a note on the kitchen table when Maura came down the next morning. It informed her that Will had sat up for most of the night in case the intruder returned, and that he was now getting some sleep in the carriage house. Maura, feeling a cowardly sense of reprieve, helped Lizzie dress for day camp and made her breakfast.

The path through the woods that led them to the bungalows was steamy after yesterday's rain. Maura, on the alert for signs that someone had passed that way in a hurry last night, saw the impression of a man's shoe in the soft dirt. It was long and rather narrow, with a toe that was rounder than was the current trend with men's shoes. She remembered that the rain had stopped shortly after the intrusion, which would account for it not being washed away. About twenty yards in, broken branches on several bushes suggested something large had crashed through them, heading toward the road that ran from the neighborhood around the green to the beach. She held Lizzie's hand a little tighter, suddenly feeling the loneliness of this stretch of woods.

Gracie seemed preoccupied when they arrived at the bungalow. Maura invited her to come back to the house with her after camp and have lunch. She intended to ask permission from Joe and Wally to let Gracie in on the whereabouts of the missing baker because she knew it was worrying her. She was honest with herself and knew that she was also hoping to avoid any resumption of last night's conversation with Will. Maura was relieved when Gracie accepted the invitation. She had been planning to deliver two dresses to Opal anyway.

With all the excitement of last night's break-in, Maura had forgotten her promise to meet Patrick that morning. The phone rang soon after she arrived back at the house. Patrick asked her to meet him on the road that ran from the town to the east end of the island where the inn was. There was a low stone wall just outside of town where they could sit comfortably without much chance of being overheard. He had to do a few things first but would meet her in an hour.

Maura really wasn't in the mood for a conversation with Patrick, but she felt even less inclined to be in the house alone with Will, so she agreed. She wondered again whether Patrick was involved in the break-in somehow. He didn't seem to believe her when she said there was only the one coin. He was a treasure hunter and a history buff; if the coins were as valuable as he implied, the possibility of getting his hands on them might be enough for him to overcome his fear of the witch's curse. She glanced at the clock then ran next door to Opal's house. After a little hesitation, Joe agreed to letting Gracie in on his whereabouts.

"If you trust her, I do. And I'm sick of running upstairs and hiding every time she comes over."

"Bring her here for lunch," directed Opal.

Patrick wasn't in sight when Maura rolled up to the short stretch of stone wall that had originally surrounded a homestead built by a contemporary of Josiah Watts. The house had burned down more than a century ago and much of the wall had crumbled, but the remaining piece offered a flat resting spot for anyone taking a stroll out of town. There was a small cluster of homes a little farther on, after which the road dwindled to the track that ran past the old settlement.

Patrick coasted to a stop and laid his battered bicycle in the grass. He sat down beside her and surprised her by cupping her cheek with his hand and giving her a quick kiss on the lips.

"Well, you're in a good mood!" She felt her face flush. She and Patrick had an odd relationship. While she felt a certain attraction to him, she really didn't have any romantic interest in him. His life style, his superstition and his disinclination to connect with Lizzie in any real way made any serious relationship out of the question. And she didn't quite trust him. There was the possibility that he had instigated the mob to go after Opal, and maybe even broken into the Watts house. On the other hand, there was no denying that she enjoyed his company. He had taken a gratifying interest in her book, providing helpful criticism and suggestions as he read the chapters. He had an amazing store of knowledge, from folklore to history to current events and seemed to know which bits she would find interesting. For her, they had drifted into an odd friendship; she wasn't sure how he regarded her.

Patrick grinned, obviously full of news.

"We found a new wreck. You have to promise not to tell anyone!"

He barely waited for her assurances, so much did he trust her by now. "It's southeast of where we've been looking this summer; it's a little deeper which means scuba gear. Currents could have shifted it there if it went down closer to Islay. There's nothing we've seen so far that isn't consistent with the period."

"Which period?" Maura guessed what he would say but gave him the opening for a dramatic delivery.

"The pirate Simon Herridge's time. It may be the *Starling*, still loaded with the treasure he had taken with him from England!"

Chapter 22

Maura was genuinely fascinated by the find of an old wreck, whether *Starling* or not, and Patrick ran on excitedly about how they had discovered it and what they had unearthed so far.

"The visibility is poor but we were able to measure the length and get the position of at least three masts. It could definitely be a bark of the *Starling* size. We're hoping we'll find artifacts that will date the ship." He went on to list the finds whose provenance could be helpful in identifying the ship.

"The last time we met you said there was something you wanted to tell me today," Maura interjected when there was finally a pause. "I'll have to leave soon to pick up Lizzie."

"Oh! Right. Sorry, this business has put everything else out of my head." He put his hand inside his jacket pocket and removed a small sheaf of papers, folded in half. After a moment's hesitation, he handed them to Maura.

"I haven't told you about these before because, frankly, I stole them. When Violet Wilson lent me the diary, I found them inside a slit in the leather cover. It didn't look like they had ever been removed. I was going to put them back but the diary disappeared when Violet died." He put his hand on her arm. "I'm giving them to you because you keep going on about how strong the witch was and making her sound like a heroine. It will give you something to think about."

Patrick picked up his bike then turned back to her.

"I'm going away for a day or two to make some arrangements and pick up equipment. I'll give you a call when I'm back." He pushed off.

Maura unfolded the packet of papers and saw that the words were closely written in an old-fashioned hand, filling all the space on both sides of each page. She regretfully put the sheets in her pocket until she had uninterrupted time to puzzle them out.

Joe was sitting on Opal's couch reading the paper when they arrived for lunch. Lizzie had gone home with Midge and Dottie for the afternoon. Gracie listened open-mouthed to the baker's recital of events that led him to hide out in the Uncle Irvin house.

"Yes, I'm glad you're not lying dead in a ditch but it's not exactly comforting that someone on this island wants to kill or kidnap you. And of course I won't tell anyone."

Maura had hoped that Gracie's fears would be alleviated once she knew the baker was safe, but her friend remained troubled. She decided not to mention last night's break-in; she was sure the intent of that was the theft of antiques, whether the coins or something that caught Stokes' eye. When they later walked to Midge's house to retrieve Lizzie, Maura tried to talk Gracie into moving in with them for the rest of the summer. She seemed to consider it, then shook her head.

"Nah, but thanks. You're a good friend, Maura. I have to have the camp down by the beach and it would be hard to run back and forth all the time." She gave her a mischievous smile. "And you already have a house guest." Maura rolled her eyes.

Will came down from the attic late in the afternoon and they sat on the patio with drinks. He seemed no different than usual, trading jokes with Gracie. Maura tried to join in but her emotions were too jumbled to add much to the conversation.

She watched the easy camaraderie between the other two and wondered if they would make a good couple. She already knew that Gracie thought Will was attractive. She was also lonely and ready to be in love again, as evinced by her disappointment with Steve. She would make Will a much better wife than Junie would have. She wasn't sure how Will felt about Gracie, other than obviously enjoying her company. Maura was dismayed by sudden little twinges of jealousy and thought longingly of past evenings with only Will, Lizzie and herself, pleasant and uncomplicated.

They had an early dinner, and the sun was still well above the horizon when Gracie stood to leave. Maura wasn't as nervous as her friend about walking alone and had planned to escort her to the bungalows with Lizzie. She hoped that Will would return to the attic so she could make the offer in his absence; she was afraid he would want to accompany them and she dreaded the walk home with him. She wondered if he had guessed her thoughts because after watching her for a moment he stood.

"You're looking tired, Maura. Princess Lizzie, would you like to walk Miss Gracie home with me while Mommy writes her stories?"

As she was leaving, Gracie turned back. All liveliness had dropped from her expression. She took a deep breath.

"Maura," she began, then stopped. Her eyes searched her friend's face. Maura hoped no sign of the absurd jealousy she had just experienced showed. Gracie and Will were now two of her closest friends and she wanted whatever was best for them.

Whatever Gracie had been about to say, she seemed to change her mind.

"You've been a good friend, Maura. I'll miss you after the summer." Her smile was a little crooked.

What was this about? It was unlikely that Gracie was unaware that she was out of sorts tonight. What construction had she put on it? Her friendship with Gracie was important to her so she gave her a reassuring smile.

"We have weeks to go, you nut. And we'll only be a short drive and a ferry ride away."

Gracie laughed a little and said goodnight. She joined Will and Lizzie on the sidewalk where they were in an animated conversation regarding how high the beanstalks had to be before they could climb them.

Maura watched, frowning, as the trio set off for the bungalows. What had Gracie wanted to say? She wondered if it had to do with Will.

She remembered the slips of paper that Patrick had passed her on the stone wall that morning. She put her hand in her pocket and drew them out, then settled on the comfortable couch in the parlor. After a few moments she frowned and scooted closer to the lamp on the side table. The ink wasn't as faded as she would have expected on a document from the early 1700s. Then she remembered that they had been folded and tucked inside the leather cover of the journal for two centuries. The handwriting was spidery and the formation of some letters unfamiliar. As Maura had noted that morning, the words were small and written close together. She worked out the first line:

This is the Confession of Isaac Belfour, First Officer of the Merchant Navy Ship Temperance.

Randy and his wife, Sandra, were in the tavern, having drinks with another couple. Sandra wasn't a natural drinker like her husband but after coming to the conclusion that she couldn't change him, followed his lead. No one was as surprised as Sandra when Randy stopped drinking, but when he switched to ginger ale she did as well.

He was eating French fries off a platter of fish and chips he was sharing with his wife when Patrick walked in. Randy frowned. He had just been wishing he had a stiff bourbon on the rocks and wondering what possessed him to come to the tavern. He was in a sour mood and the sight of the treasure hunter set up his hackles. It wasn't just because he had made a pass at Sandra one night; she knew how to deal with that. There was something all wrong about him but Randy couldn't quite put his finger on it. He suspected that Dunn was putting one over on Maura and it bothered him that she seemed to trust him.

Suddenly the bar was too smokey and crowded. He leaned over to his wife.

"I'm going out for some air, San. I'll come back to take you home." She lifted a brow but smiled a little and turned back to the other couple.

The *Lorelei* was tied up at the end of the pier where they had found Violet Wilson. Two young women strolled down from the crescent of houses around the harbor and disappeared inside the tavern. As soon as they were out of sight, Randy ran lightly down the pier and hopped onboard the *Lorelei*. He didn't know what he was looking for, but if there was anything that would incriminate Dunn in some unsavory activity it would be well concealed. He started with the cabin, removing items from the shelves and shaking out the sleeping bags. He went through the rows of books and found a cavity in a large hardcover with a broken spine. Inside the cavity was a thick notebook with a worn leather cover. The writing was faint and old fashioned, and impossible to read in the dim light. He put it back and continued his search. Randy was mentally timing Patrick's dinner, from ordering to consuming, and thought he could safely inspect the storage chests before the treasure hunter returned to his boat. He neatly stowed away everything he had pulled out in the cabin.

The chests were positioned to be easily accessible. Randy thought they would likely hold gear the treasure hunters used regularly and wouldn't be his first choice if he had something to hide. As he was about to open the first chest, his eye was caught by the outline of a hatch under coils of rope and a box of fishing tackle in the stern. He carefully slid these to the side so they could be replaced as he found them. A small padlock bound the hatch door to a ring on the deck. He took out his Swiss Army knife and easily popped the lock open. He was handy with tools of any kind and the lock wasn't anything sophisticated. Randy heard a boat chug up to a pier on the other side of the harbor and a man call out his thanks. Somewhere a woman laughed. Squatted down on the deck as he was, he knew he wasn't visible.

Randy lifted the hatch cover and peered inside. The cavity was crammed with items. There was a rolled-up rain jacket, stacks of old magazines, waist-high rubber waders folded into a neat square, a canteen, and a variety of miscellaneous smaller items. Something that felt like a hard ball with an attached stick was in thick wrappings. Randy carefully removed the contents and set them on the deck, keeping them in much the same arrangement as they had been in the cavity. He surveyed them with a frown; why stow useful items like a rain jacket and waders where they would have to be dug out from under ropes and tackle? It might make sense to hide old magazines if they were embarrassing, but these were mainstream periodicals that could be found in any library. Remembering the cavity in the detective novel, he flipped through the pages of a March 1953 edition of *Life*, then did the same with the other magazines. He picked up the folded waders and began to feel them over.

"Can you tell me what you think you're doing?" Randy's head shot up. The other treasure hunter, the blonde one, stared down at him with a frown. A duffle bag was slung over one shoulder, and Randy belatedly remembered the boat that had dropped off a passenger. He quickly ran possible responses through his mind, including pretending to be drunk, but nothing made sense except the truth. He stood up, still holding the waders.

"Your buddy is up to something fishy and I'm trying to find out what it is."

"What makes you think he's up to something fishy?" Steve's voice was sharp and his look intent.

"I heard him inciting the mob that attacked Mrs. Gertz's neighbor, for one."

"Why would he do that?"

Randy shrugged. "I heard him do it right after Mrs. Wilson died, and after Bob Welch disappeared. OK, maybe 'incite' isn't the right word, but he comes into the tavern and starts talking about the island curse. He mentions the old island witch story and that Mrs. Hansen's house sits on her land. He brought it up again after the baker disappeared."

"Not much of a reason to trespass on a man's boat and break into his locker. Dunn has an enormous interest in island history. If that's all you've got you can get the hell off the *Lorelei.*"

Without breaking eye contact with Steve, Randy upended the waders and shook them. The book he had felt inside fell to the deck.

Steve stooped and picked it up. He pulled a small flashlight out of his duffle bag and scanned the first few pages of a school composition book. After a moment he sat on the deck to be out of sight and Randy sat down next to him. Steve shone the light on the pages as he turned them. The first few were an innocuous log of gas purchases and maintenance repairs for the *Lorelei*. The latest date for a gas fill-up was last Tuesday. Why put an expense log in such an inaccessible place? The expense entries were followed by fifteen blank pages, then they came to a list of names.

"These are all people who live on the island," whispered Randy. "At least, I recognize most of them." He pointed to his own name, which had been crossed off. A good portion of the names had been crossed off and a few had question marks after them. Some had question marks but had then been crossed off.

Steve ran his finger down the list and found Violet Wilson's name. There was a checkmark next to it. They looked for Bob Welch but didn't locate his name. Maura Gertz was on the list as well as Gracie Fletcher, both with question marks. Opal Hansen and Wally Bye had lines through their names. Joe Fabiola had a question mark that had been crossed out and a checkmark added in a different ink.

The pages that followed were each devoted to one person on the list who had had a question mark or check next to his or her name. There were neatly hand-printed notes regarding age, residence when not on the island and other details. In a few there were newspaper articles cut out and inserted between the leaves of the composition book.

"G'night, Captain Kidd!" called a cheerfully drunk voice.

"Good night, Bill" Patrick's voice returned.

Steve leapt to his feet.

"Stow this all away carefully. I'll contact you in the next few days – don't do anything in the meantime."

Steve tossed his flashlight in his duffle and put the bag into the cabin.

"Hey Patrick!" he called as he jumped from the *Lorelei* to the pier. "I just got in. Come have a beer with me before we head out."

Maura was still curled up at the end of the couch when Will and a sleepy Lizzie returned. She gave them an odd, vacant stare then seemed to return from a faraway place. Will, as though aware that he had pushed things too far in the last few days, said quietly,

"I have to do some office work tonight so will spend the night in the carriage house. Thanks for keeping me company, Miss Lizzie."

Maura nodded absently. "Can you wait until I come back down? I have something I want to run by you. Come on, Lizzie Lou. Bath time!"

Will was at the kitchen table reading a document from his office, glasses perched on his nose, when Maura returned from putting Lizzie to bed. He looked up questioningly.

She sat down across from him and began without preamble.

"I found out what the island witch and the first mate were up to. And the settlers. This beautiful island was founded by a bunch of cut-throats and assassins."

Will smiled slightly. "Let's hear it."

She kept the pages that Patrick had taken from the diary in her pocket.

"The story goes that the shipwreck victims loved the island so much that they decided to stay here. Well, apparently they weren't planning to stay forever."

Isaac Belfour's confession described a colony that was focused only on survival for the first few years. The island was promising for growing crops, but it took a great deal of time and labor to clear and till the land, plant the crops and grow enough to feed the settlement. In the meantime they subsisted on fish, squirrels and, for a short time, ship stores they were able to recover from the *Temperance.* The ship had foundered close enough to shore that the surviving seamen were able to make several trips to it on homemade rafts before it completely broke apart.

As time went on, the younger men became restless. There weren't enough women for wives, and there was little beyond hard work to occupy them. About a year after they were marooned, another ship capsized off the coast of Islay. The survivors only numbered four women and two men. The women recovered from their ordeal but the two men died within days. In his confession, Isaac Belfour claimed that the men had been quietly murdered and buried to avoid further competition for the island's women. Prudence Payne accused the colonists and was summarily ejected and forbidden to return to the settlement.

The next ship to founder sailed into shallow, rock-strewn waters in an attempt to evade a naval ship that was after it. The captain and his small crew were able to escape in boats.

Isaac Belfour cleverly surmised the name the captain gave the settlers was fictitious because it changed regularly, as did the reported name of his ship and the names of the crew. They seemed to be entertaining themselves in this way, to the intense annoyance of the original colonists. The newcomers consumed precious supplies without assisting with their production. Added to their sins was the efforts of several of the seamen to attach the few single women on the island. When the settlers complained to the captain, he merely stared at them with an odd smile and idly twirled his walking stick. This accessory had a gold ball on one end and was brandished more than once as a weapon. His crew had brought four chests with them from the ship, which they never left unguarded. The colonists were sure they must contain things of great value. When the captain and his crew were caught late one moonlit night making for the boats they had arrived in, not only with their secret chests but with several of the women, there was a skirmish. Caught by surprise, the captain and several of his crew were killed. Three were taken prisoner and the rest escaped in one of the boats. The colonists discovered that two of the remaining boats held the chests that had been so carefully guarded; they were broken into and found to contain coins and jewelry, as the settlers had anticipated.

A celebration was planned for the following night and a trial for the prisoners the next day. Why precisely they were celebrating, or what the crimes of the prisoners were beyond stealing some of the stores wasn't explained. The general feeling appeared to be that they had put one over on the captain and his crew and were rejoicing because they didn't like them.

The first mate was present at the planning for these events, and he ran to Prudence Payne to tell her all. Prudence was afraid that they would execute the prisoners on a flimsy excuse and keep the treasure for themselves. She urged the first mate to think of a way to stop them. He came up with nothing, so she proposed putting something in their whiskey at the celebration to make them sleep. While they were out, she and the first mate would release the prisoners and let them escape in one of the boats, with enough food to last them a few days.

Prudence went over her home remedies and her plants and herbs. She hesitated, then put together a concoction that she thought would do the trick. They both knew she wasn't very good at the healer business and she directed Isaac to only put a small amount in each whiskey cask. He was appalled at the suspected plans to execute the prisoners, and thinking this was no time for excessive caution, tipped an extra-large dose into each cask. For good measure, he then added a splash from a concoction he had made from Prudence's other distillations when she wasn't looking. Maura had difficulty untangling the threads of self-justification in this section, but thought it boiled down to his ignoring Prudence's advice and thinking he knew better.

The colonists celebrated the following night and as had become their custom, toasted each other with whiskey. Everyone was either dead or dying the next day. Isaac and Prudence were horrified. They discovered that the prisoners had already been hung without a trial. In the middle of berating each other they heard a baby crying and took it back to Prudence's house.

Isaac blamed Prudence for making deadly medicine. Prudence blamed Isaac for not following her directions. They became obsessed with the possibility that the seamen who escaped would come back for the treasure and find out what had happened to their shipmates. They buried the executed prisoners and hid the treasure, hoping it would appear that they had left in one of the boats and taken the coins and jewels with them. They left the poisoned settlers where they had fallen. Not only was the thought burying a lot of people they had accidentally murdered daunting, but they reasoned that if anyone returned for the treasure chests the bodies might lead them to assume they were attacked by some outside group and the chests stolen.

The thought that their adopted daughter deserved better than the island was more and more frequently expressed by Isaac. What would happen to her when they were both dead? There was one remaining boat left from the ship belonging to the captain with the gold-headed cane. There had been two, but they had cast one off to maintain their story that the prisoners had left in it. Isaac and Prudence made plans to pack the remaining boat with supplies and set out to sea, taking their chances. They didn't know how far they were from land or what difficulties they would encounter. They waffled for several months until a storm swept the last boat out to sea.

Guilt for the murders haunted the two. They finally decided they couldn't live with it, so they planned to jump off the cliff with the baby. Prudence stood on the cliff edge and decided she couldn't be the cause of the baby's death on top of everything else. Issac gave her a big speech about how they were doing the right thing. She nodded and handed him the baby. She still had trouble jumping so he gave her a helpful push. She died on the rocks below. Now it was his turn but he lost his nerve. He convinced himself it wasn't fair to make the baby die for a sin she didn't commit, and someone should raise her. He argued to himself that the witch had paid for their crimes, and it was her fault anyway.

Isaac raised the girl and soothed his conscience by writing a confession and hiding it in the diary. His plan was that if they were ever rescued, he would hand over the diary with his hidden confession. And that's what he did. When a ship eventually landed, he gave a crew member his diary then jumped off the cliff – the first brave thing he did since he arrived on the island.

Will leaned back and let out a whistle.

"And how do you know all this?"

"Let's just say someone found missing pages from his diary. But Will, that's not the point! Isaac Belfour and Prudence Payne hid the treasure chests. And we found one of them under the carriage house. Why wouldn't the rest of the treasure be there?"

He stared at her.

"Let me get my flashlight!" Will jumped up and disappeared out the back door. Maura, knowing whose lot crawling under the house would fall to because of her size, pulled an old raincoat that must have belonged to Uncle Charlie from a coat closet. She ran upstairs, looked in on Lizzie, and changed her shorts for her gardening dungarees.

The roses behind the carriage house stood out in the darkness from the glow of Will's flashlight. He looked up when she joined him and took in the huge raincoat. He started to laugh, then caught himself.

"What are we doing, Maura? We must be crazy. Were you really willing to crawl into that yawning black hole this late at night?"

Maura looked down into the ditch that Will had dig out before Leo and Rebecca had come. He had opened the metal door, revealing an unappealing square of darkness. She had some misgivings about the bugs that were probably living in the crawl space, but she wasn't worried about anything of a supernatural nature. She was dying to know if the other treasure cases were down there. She looked up and nodded.

Will grinned.

"If those chests are down there, they've lasted a few centuries with nobody bothering them. They can last one more night."

"What if the bad guy is hiding in the woods, waiting to strike again tonight, and saw you uncover the hole?" Maura argued.

"I've been thinking about that. It's pretty well known I'm living on the premises. It was taking a big risk to break in with two adults here. Maybe he saw me leave – on my bike, in the harbor or on the ferry – and decided to take his chance while I was away. Throw in the storm and he might have thought he wouldn't get a better chance. Once the summer is over, the house will be emptied out and put up for sale."

Maura stared at the hole.

"If we wait until morning, the neighbors may be up and the men are coming to help you put up the drywall. No, I'm going in. Can you stand by the back door every few minutes and listen for Lizzie?"

Will reluctantly agreed and handed her the flashlight. She lowered herself into the hole, then squeezed through the square doorway into the space beneath the carriage house. The air here was cool but dank, smelling of the pile of rotting lumber to her left and of damp stone. She made a sweep with her flashlight. Other than the old lumber, the crawl space was empty.

Right away, Maura knew the raincoat was a mistake. The ceiling wasn't high enough to allow her to walk even bent over, but she could crawl or do a sort of crab-walk. The raincoat bunched under her and impeded her progress. She quickly discarded it. Her crawl to the rubble trench was awkward, with a flashlight in one hand and the unpleasant feel of very old dirt between her fingers. The flashlight beam caught what looked like mouse droppings and she wished she had thought to wear gloves.

"How's it going in there?" Will's deep voice, so close, was reassuring.

"It's a little creepy and kind of disgusting but I'm OK."

The rubble trench was a deep ditch, filled with stone as Leo had described. Maura slowly followed the trench around and saw several places where there was a gap between the tightly packed stone and the earth. One spot bore signs of having been recently disturbed; the edges of the earth fill were broken and something had been dragged a little way. That would have been Leo. It didn't take Maura long to inspect the whole perimeter of the trench; the area was smaller than the kitchen in the Watts house. There were no other signs of recent disturbances that she could detect near the other spots that had gaps.

Maura asked Will to bring her bathrobe and a towel down for her; she wanted to wash away every trace of the crawl space before going in the house. She stepped into the outdoor shower and lathered herself from head to toe with soap and shampoo. The steamy water felt wonderful in the cooling evening air. A towel, her bathrobe and her nightgown appeared over the side of the shower wall and she called an awkward thanks.

Cups of tea were steeping on the kitchen table when she went inside and Will was buttering thick slices of toast. Maura sat at the table, realizing how unaccustomed she was to anyone waiting on her.

Maura had only told Will that she hadn't found any more chests before she made a beeline for the shower. She now told him about the gaps next to the packed rocks.

"There were four, and one is almost certainly where Leo pulled out the chest of coins. The gaps may have been from anything – the ground settling, or maybe there had been posts at one point – but there were all on the same side and not far from each other. And they were pretty evenly spaced."

Will rubbed his chin.

"So the witch and the first mate – OK, Prudence and Isaac – steal the chests and want to hide them where they can keep an eye on them. Her house would have most certainly had a dirt floor. They dig holes just big enough for the cases up against the foundation, inside her hut. They bury them and maybe put her bed and other things over them. At some point someone finds three of the four and absconds with the loot. Any guess as to when? Did it look like anyone was digging in there recently?"

"No, as far as I could tell by flashlight, it didn't look like anyone had been disturbing the other holes."

They speculated fruitlessly on where the rest of the treasure might be while they finished their tea, then Will said he would sleep on the couch one more night.

The next day Gracie disappeared.

—·—

Chapter 23

There was a small group of mothers huddled together near Gracie's door when Maura and Lizzie arrived for camp the next morning. Lizzie ran to join Midge and another girl in the tiny backyard.

"Maura." Dottie waved her over.

"What's going on?"

One of the mothers handed her a piece of note paper.

"This was taped to the door."

The note read in block letters:

SICK – DO NOT DISTURB

The words seemed to have been written hastily. It occurred to Maura that she didn't know Gracie's handwriting.

"Has anyone seen Gracie's handwriting?" The mothers looked at each other and shook their heads.

"The door is unlocked," said Dottie, "and one of the windows looks like it was forced open. We were debating whether to go in when you showed up."

Maura turned the knob and slowly pushed the door open.

"Gracie?" There was no answer. Cold prickles ran down her arms. "Gracie, It's Maura. You OK?" Silence.

She began to feel rather sick. The other mothers crowded behind her as she began to search the bungalow.

"Someone watch the kids, OK?" Maura's voice was tight.

All the rooms - kitchen, living room, bedroom and bathroom were empty. There was no sign of a struggle, but the bed was unmade. This was a troubling sign, as Gracie kept her little home extremely neat. One of the windows was open and the cool morning sea breeze spilled through.

"Maybe she walked up to town to get tissues or a can of soup or something," a mother volunteered.

"Maybe..."

Maura opened Gracie's closet. It was full of clothes, hats and shoes, all neatly arranged. She couldn't tell if anything was missing. The only thing that stood out in the bungalow was a stack of used clothing that belonged to Lillian's sister. A few dresses, skirts and jackets were piled on the kitchen table next to a sewing machine. No preparations for day camp had been made – no muffins baked, no craft ready – which showed that Gracie either hadn't planned to have the children there that day or something had occurred before she could get ready.

The mothers took Maura outside to look at the window that was open.

"They used a prybar of some kind to jimmy it," Dottie said confidently. She realized the other mothers were staring at her. "What? We own a hardware store. With this kind of window, you push the bottom sash to separate it from the top one. You put your hand here to keep the pieces from engaging and keep lifting the bottom sash. They may have tried some combination of that and forcing it up with the prybar."

The mothers looked at each other with growing alarm. Maura's legs were trembling and she sat down at the picnic table. The children were now complaining that they were bored, so the decision was made for Maura to wait for a while and see if Gracie returned. The other mothers would return home and begin passing the word that Gracie might be missing and ask if anyone had seen her. Dottie took Lizzie home with her to swim in the pool and play with Midge for the afternoon. She said she would send her husband to report the possible disappearance to the police.

Maura waited an hour. Before she left, she scrawled a note and left it on the kitchen table. It asked Gracie to call her or any of the other mothers right away because they were all worried sick about her. She took the street home, rather than cutting through the woods to the Watts house's backyard. She knew Gracie had been afraid of the woods lately and was more likely to use the street if she had gone to town.

Will, a contractor and Randy were cutting drywall when Maura burst into the attic with the news of Gracie's disappearance. No one interrupted her while the words came tumbling out. She was breathing heavily from hurrying home from the bungalow. Will and Randy frowned with concern and the contractor looked confused. When he realized there was yet another mysterious disappearance, he agreed to drive Randy back to the harbor where he could spread the news and get a group together to ask if anyone had seen her.

Before Randy left, he pulled Maura aside.

"Mrs. Gertz," he began.

"Maura."

"Uh, Maura. Something happened last night that you need to know about. It could have something to do with Mrs. Fletcher missing. Can you meet me at the harbor in about an hour? I'm going to look for Barry and get him to organize his search parties." They were standing on the stoop and Randy cut his eyes to the contractor, who was putting his tools in the truck. He obviously didn't want his boss for today to be part of the conversation. "And can you check the coffee shop to see if the blonde treasure hunter is there and ask him to come too. He's probably out on their boat, but sometimes he comes in for lunch."

Maura and Will got on their bicycles and rode into town. Their first stop was the police station, but neither officer was there. It was likely Dottie's husband had reported the disappearance and Stokes and Krol were investigating. At least, Maura hoped they were. As far as she could tell, the island police took a half-hearted approach to looking into the island's mysterious occurrences. Her plan was to broadcast Gracie's disappearance to everyone she met. There was enough concern about Bob Welch, Violet Wilson and the baker that some of the residents might be inspired to search. If Gracie was shopping, or at the library she would be justifiably annoyed at all the fuss, but Maura felt that no time should be lost in the search.

A lunch crowd was growing at the coffee shop. Will pointed out Steve in a back booth with some young men, talking animatedly and making notes on a sheet of paper. She wondered if he was trying to enlist local divers to explore their new find.

Steve stood and smiled as she and Will approached their booth.

"Gracie is missing," Maura said baldly.

Under his tan, Steve's face drained of color.

"What? What do you mean?"

"Everyone!" Maura raised her voice. "Grace Fletcher, who runs Camp Boogie-Woogie from one of the bungalows, is missing. Has anyone seen her? She's about five foot four, dark wavy hair, very stylish. About thirty-two years old."

Wally had come out from the kitchen and stood with his mouth agape.

There were exclamations and a number of questions. Maura told them all she knew. A few people said they had seen her in town this week, but no one had seen her yesterday or today. Everyone agreed to pass the word and report any news to Wally.

Steve grabbed her arm painfully.

"Maura! Can we talk about this outside?"

They hurried out the door, followed by Will and Wally.

Out on the sidewalk, Steve cut his eyes to Wally.

"It's OK," she assured him, "Wally's a good guy." She was sure he was going to mention whatever had happened last night, so she forestalled him.

"Randy wants us to meet him at the harbor. I think you ran into him last night. He said to bring you if we found you in town." Steve nodded. They mounted their bicycles and Will and Steve pedaled off. As Maura was about to follow, Wally grabbed her sleeve.

"Maura." His voice was tight with anxiety. "Opal! Some of the crazy people may think she's responsible and come after her."

She thought rapidly, fully appreciating Opal's danger despite their stunt at the tavern.

"Can she and Joe move into your apartment until we know what's going on? I know it will be crowded but she should be safe."

He nodded. "We'll manage."

They found Randy outside the tavern, surrounded by a group of aging men. As Maura, Will and Steve coasted to a stop he said something to the men and raised his hand in thanks. They moved away, talking animatedly.

"They're spreading out to go door to door, asking if anyone has seen Mrs. Fletcher. Most people are at work right now, but I'll be waiting here when the fishing boats come in later and people get off work. I'll look to see who gets on the afternoon ferry and ask the ferry crew if they saw her." He looked at Steve with narrowed eyes, not fully trusting him.

"Where's your buddy?"

"Out on the *Lorelei*. He sent me into town to recruit local divers. Where can we talk?"

Randy and his wife rented one side of a duplex in the crescent around the harbor. Sandra had regular work cleaning houses for the wealthier summer residents and was away from the house.

They sat at a scarred wooden table in the outdated but neat kitchen. Randy flipped the caps off bottles of ginger ale and passed them around. He opened his mouth to tell them what happened last night, but Steve beat him to it. The urgency of the situation made him speak quickly and to the point. He described the contents of the composition book in detail, with Randy nodding in agreement and adding a point here and there.

Steve looked at each of them. "I'm very familiar with Patrick's handwriting and recognized it immediately. The book was hidden in a compartment I never remember him using and was covered by a mound of ropes and other items. The composition book itself was hidden inside a pair of waders. There's only one possible conclusion, I think."

"Dunn researched island residents, looking for eligible targets," Will said. "He was looking for a criminal association."

Steve nodded.

"I don't know what benefit he's getting out of their disappearances or deaths. But I think he's dangerous. And Mrs. Fletcher, and you, Mrs. Gertz, are both on his list with question marks."

Will stood suddenly.

"I'm going to the county sheriff's office on the mainland. The local office doesn't seem to take any of this seriously."

"I'm coming with you," said Maura, coming to a decision. "Randy, you'll manage the search parties?" He nodded.

"I'll get someone to run me out to *The Lorelei*." Steve was already headed for the door. "I'll search every inch of the boat in case he...has her onboard in one of the bigger compartments. And I'm going to ask him point blank what he's done with her."

Randy made some calls, looking for any local boat owners who could take Will and Maura on the two-hour ride to the mainland. They could catch the afternoon ferry back.

The trip to the mainland seemed endless to Maura. She was glad that Will didn't try to distract her from her anxiety about Gracie. He calmly led her through all the scenarios they could think of that might account for her absence, from the benign to the extreme. Maura was afraid the truth was one of the worst scenarios, but it helped to have them spoken out loud.

Will had left his car in the ferry parking lot on the mainland. He got a map out of his glove compartment and had Maura locate the address for the sheriff's office he had just gotten from a phone book.

Maura and Will met with a very polite lieutenant, who listened carefully and took notes. He agreed that the there was a lot happening for a quiet little island like Islay. After Violet Wilson's death, the island police had called them in. When the officers arrived Mrs. Wilson's body had already been claimed by her family and removed from the island. Captain Stokes said he had seen nothing suspicious in her death so, without a body, they decided not to pursue further inquiries. The lieutenant remembered Bob Welch's disappearance and that they had sent a search team to the island. They found no sign of him and eventually had to call off the search. Since there was no evidence of foul play, and nothing to prove that he didn't voluntarily leave the island, they abandoned the attempts to locate him.

"Your friend, Mrs. Fletcher, hasn't been gone long enough to be considered a missing person. We'll radio the Islay police tomorrow and if she still hasn't turned up, we'll send some officers over to look into it."

They headed back to the ferry terminal in silence. Will eventually broke it.

"We have some time until the ferry leaves. We missed lunch so I wouldn't mind getting something to eat. Is there anything you want to do before we head back?"

Maura looked a little bleak.

"Yes, I'd like to make some phone calls." They went to a bank where she exchanged bills for assorted coins for a pay phone.

The first call was to her in-laws. Norma picked up the phone.

"Oh, hello." Norma used the colorless tone she reserved for Maura.

"Is Cleve in?" Norma said vaguely that she thought he was out. Maura said she would call back another time. Annoyed, the older woman said she would just check and see if her husband was home.

"Hello? Maura? Is everything OK?"

"Hi Cleve. Yes. Listen, I've been thinking about your trip to Montreal…"

They were in a diner a mile away from the ferry landing.

"You're sending Lizzie away?"

Maura turned and looked out the window, but she knew Will caught the tears welling up in her eyes.

"I don't feel like Islay is safe anymore, but I can't take Lizzie away without knowing what happened to Gracie. And I can't look after Lizzie and hunt for her." A tear spilled over and she wiped it away. She turned and smiled a little shakily.

"Lizzie will be fine. She loves her grandparents, God knows why. Cleve at least is sensible and I gave him so many directions and threats that I'm surprised they still want to take her. I just... this has been the best summer and now it's all crashing down around us. I love your Aunt May for letting us stay in the house. And you... we both know the house was in great shape a few weeks ago and could have gone on the market. I suspect you've been fixing up the attic just to keep an eye on everything. I'm surprised your company hasn't fired you yet."

Will stretched out a hand and took hers. Just then the waitress put cups on the table and filled them with steaming coffee. Maura pulled her hand back and picked up her cup.

"My second call was to Rebecca. She's always offering to put her millions at my disposal and I always turn her down. I thought if there's anything she can do, it would be for Gracie, not me."

"That was a long call," Will smiled.

"Sorry! I called her collect at her office. She said she'll reimburse Rushing River. She asked me a ton of questions and is going to get her crazy group of friends together tonight to talk it over. She's going to ask her personal business manager for advice too – see about private investigators and that kind of thing." She put her hands over her face and laughed a little. "I feel like I've put a freight train in motion. If we get back to Islay and find Gracie camped on our doorstep, mad as hell, I'll be so happy. But it will take some work to pull back the troops. If only Islay was hooked up to the mainland by telephone!"

Gracie disappeared on Friday. Two days later there was still no sign of her. Maura and the other mothers did their best to keep any concerns from their children. Maura had Midge to play on Saturday, and on Sunday one of the families had a pool party for the campers.

The Watts house had become the unofficial command center. After Lizzie's bedtime there would be quiet knocks on the door. Wally reported that no one had come to the coffee shop with any useful information. Steve appeared the first night and said he hadn't found anything on the *Lorelei*. He had asked Patrick what he knew about Gracie's disappearance, but his partner just stared back at him and disavowed any knowledge. Patrick was annoyed that Steve planned to take some time away from the salvaging operation to look for Gracie.

"But he knows how I feel about her, so he can't be surprised. All he can talk about is this new wreck we found, and how urgent it is that we find something of value to raise some money to fund the operation."

On Sunday, a fat envelope was brought by courier. It contained a five-page letter from Rebecca and two cardboard sheets taped together at the sides. Maura immediately sat down and read the letter, then read it a second time. She sat there thinking until Will came in through the back door. She raised her eyebrows in question.

"Nothing. Between about six of us we've spoken with every boat owner who takes passengers for hire. No one remembers seeing a woman of Gracie's description Thursday night or Friday morning. That includes the ferry crew."

Maura felt another wave of anxiety, her heart beating irregularly and black thoughts drifting into her mind.

"Here," she said, handing Rebecca's letter to Will. "Read this."

Will read it through then went back and re-read parts.

"No one would ever look at her and guess that she was crazy."

"You don't think it would work?" Maura leaned forward.

"You know the guy. Do you think so? It's a pretty harebrained scheme."

Maura thought about Patrick.

"I don't know. It could work, or it could massively backfire. He's about equal parts ambition, greed and superstition. I think those can cloud his intelligence and judgement. He would have to be caught off guard."

"You sound like you want to give it a try."

"If there's a chance it brings Gracie back then yes, I'm willing to try it. Rebecca's Rushing River friends are all excited about playing their parts. David's parents are meeting me at the mainland ferry landing tomorrow where I'll hand off Lizzie, then she'll be away and safe for Tuesday night."

Will was silent for a moment.

"Does she know yet?" His voice was gentle.

Maura's bottom lip quivered for a moment before she brought it under control.

"Yes, I told her this morning. She's thrilled, but of course she doesn't understand what it will mean to be away from all of this – me, Jelly Bean, the house, Midge, you – for eight days. Then of course we'll be leaving soon after that." She hesitated, then burst out, "They won't be able to call me so I can hear her voice." Tears began to drift down her cheeks and she wiped them on her sleeve. Will moved to the couch and put an arm around her. She leaned against him and took some deep breaths.

"Lizzie and I will be all right. There's no other way we can do this."

Will shifted her slightly and raised her chin. He leaned down and kissed her lightly.

Maura's normal instinct for flight failed to kick in on this occasion. Will's lips were firm and his kiss gentle and comforting. His breath smelled like peppermint. She returned his kiss and was lifting her arm to place it around his neck when there was knocking on the door. She sprang up and ran to a window. Will cursed under his breath.

Steve and Randy stood on the front step. When the door opened, they took in Will's flushed face and Maura's scarlet cheeks and shuffled awkwardly, shooting each other glances.

"Any news?" Maura ushered them inside.

"No, but some of the boys have gone to the other side to question shops, taxies and nearby house owners." None of them had much hope that this would turn up anything. If Gracie was in any shape to go shopping, or to have lunch or stroll down the street, surely she would have contacted her friends. But at least it was some action.

"Vic Stokes and that idiot deputy of his organized a few searches." Frustration was strong in Steve's voice. "Our search parties have been over most of the island, but if she's hidden in a house or something none of us will find her."

"Listen," Maura said. "We have a plan."

Chapter 24

It was odd to see Patrick standing on the stoop instead of cowering on the green. He looked decidedly nervous, which was understandable for someone expecting to be struck dead at any moment. Maura was nervous too, but for different reasons. She had never been able to act, or lie, and she was expected to put on a convincing performance.

She smiled and held the door open. A flippant observation on his surviving the crossing of her threshold passed through her mind, but she kept it to herself. It had been a monumental effort to convince him to agree to come for dinner at the house. It wasn't until she hinted that she had something to show him and told him Prudence had come to her in a dream to say she wanted him to see it, that he reluctantly agreed. If she had to, she would show him the crawl space and the rubble trench. Will had taken the coins to Boston with him when he received an urgent telegram from his boss yesterday. There was a client he had to meet with if he wanted to keep the major new account he had been awarded. He knew there wouldn't be another opportunity if he didn't take this, so tried unavailingly to get Maura to cancel or reschedule the scheme. She said it was impossible; too much was already in motion and the Rushing River people were on their way. He finally promised to get back as early as possible and to avoid wrecking everything.

"For you." Patrick held out a small bouquet of roses, then leaned in and kissed her cheek. The house was literally covered in roses and rose bushes marched the length of the property line with Lillian's, but she thanked him and dutifully sniffed the bouquet.

"Let me put these in water and check on dinner." Maura turned on the kitchen light and took a vase down from Aunt May's old-fashioned sideboard. Her hands shook as she filled it from the kitchen faucet and mechanically snipped the ends off the roses. They were a deep blood red, very different from the confectionary pink and white roses that ran riot on the island. She leaned against the counter for a moment to get her breathing under control. She wasn't afraid for her physical safety; Joe the baker and Rebecca's husband, Dan, were in her bedroom with the door open, silently playing cards. She was experiencing stage fright, and annoyed that everyone seemed to think she could pull this off.

Maura opened the oven door to check on the Chicken Divan. The casserole dish of chicken, broccoli and mushrooms in a cream sauce was one of her favorites, but the thought of eating anything made her stomach churn. The mixture was bubbling a little but hadn't started to brown yet. She set the kitchen timer to ten minutes, then flipped off the kitchen light. She hoped that Randy had caught the signal: kitchen light on then off meant Patrick had arrived but they hadn't started eating.

Patrick was standing where she had left him and seemed relieved when she returned. She put the vase of roses on the mantel where the blooms glowed against the creamy wall. Maura returned to the kitchen and placed a platter of cheese and crackers on a tray with a frosted pitcher of Martinis and two glasses. She suspected he wasn't much of a drinker, but he accepted the glass she offered and took a sip.

"I see you drove here," she remarked.

"Yes, I have to be somewhere later tonight so one of the men from the tavern lent me his Jeep. I can get back to the *Lorelei* faster."

Conversation stalled. Patrick's eyes darted here and there, whether looking for treasure or witches she wasn't sure. Her mouth felt dry so she took several sips of her Martini. It was extremely cold, a necessity for a good Martini, Dan told her as he mixed them a little earlier. She took another sip.

Maura felt herself relax a little. The rehearsals for this evening had gone badly. There were too many people watching and offering criticism and advice. They were enjoying themselves; she was not. When the Rushing River contingent left to take up their positions, she felt some relief. Having survived a murderous assault before Lizzie was born, they seemed to consider this an exciting adventure. They had taken their own pitcher of Martinis with them to while away the time while they waited. Even though she had supported the plan, now that it was in action she couldn't see how it could be anything except a flop.

She hadn't taken into consideration the depth of Patrick's superstition or the effects of the gin. When the timer went off, Maura switched on the kitchen light and removed the Chicken Divan from the oven. She spooned the mixture onto two plates and put a bowl of parsley potatoes and a dish of asparagus on the kitchen table. She lit three candles and turned off the kitchen light. (Signal: candlelight meant they were now eating.) Patrick watched her for a moment, then came up behind her as she stood at the stove, pouring extra sauce into a gravy boat. He slid his arms around her waist and she tried not to tense. He briefly leaned his cheek against hers then stepped away. She turned and smiled a little, flustered for reasons he didn't suspect. He gave her a slightly seductive smile and pulled out her chair.

"We used to have a dining room but it was never used," she said a little breathlessly, "so the space is now a powder room and a pantry. We eat all of our meals in here."

"You sound like you think of this as your house."

She stared for a moment.

"I suppose I do. This has been a wonderful summer and I've never had my own place before, for just Lizzie and me. I'm going to be sad to leave it." She suddenly saw how she might make use of this conversation and added, "Somehow, I feel like I've always lived here. I have a recurring dream where I look out the window and the green isn't there, only forest. Nobody lives here except me, and I keep thinking something will come out of the woods." She had actually had the dream once, so was able to tell him this without stumbling.

Patrick looked at her intently. He leaned forward.

"Don't you think it's possible she's communicating with you?" Maura felt prickles on her arms. It's one thing to tell ghost stories; it's another thing altogether for someone to believe you're channeling the spirit of a long-dead witch.

"Ask her if there are more coins!" Patrick's voice was urgent. Maura's mouth opened but she decided it was too early to take the cue. She let her eyes go vacant for a moment and she took several deep, stertorous breaths. Patrick watched her with excitement. She coughed suddenly to break the spell.

"I don't think I want any witch communicating with me!" she gave a nervous laugh, which came naturally under the circumstances. Patrick sat back, disappointed. Maura changed the subject and asked him where he was going that night. He smiled but merely said he had to deliver something he had found. She made a few attempts to discover what it was but he only laughed. The sickening thought that the item to be delivered was Gracie grabbed her attention and she had to ask Patrick to repeat his last sentence.

"I said, if it turns out to have any value, I'll take you to New York for dinner and a show. I'll be gone a few days but will call you when I'm back. What was it you wanted to show me?" The last sentence was said a little sharply and Maura jumped.

"After dinner..." He narrowed his eyes and didn't return her smile.

Maura filled their Martini glasses again. She knew wine would be more appropriate with dinner, but the gang had decided it wasn't strong enough. She only took an occasional sip; she was relaxed enough now that she thought she just might be able to get through her part. She made coffee and they took it out onto the patio, the screen door banging behind them. The night sky was spangled with stars and a light, spicy breeze stirred a curl on her cheek.

Patrick told her that he had found more artifacts on the wreck that were consistent with it being the Starling.

"Historians think Herridge still had the best of his spoils on board."

"Under the salted cod," murmured Maura. Patrick frowned. Not far away, a motorcycle engine revved and the sound faded as it drove off.

"There could be a fortune in gold and jewels there. Steve and I don't want to bring in another salvage outfit. If we could just hire some divers who can keep their mouths shut... but it will all take money. If only I knew where those damn silver coins are!"

That was Maura's cue. Before she could begin, Patrick gasped.

"Look at the cat!" His voice had risen. Jelly Bean, returning from a carouse, had wandered back to the patio. He sat in front of Patrick, staring at him with his huge, ludicrous eyes as though horror-struck. "It senses something!" Maura, who was about to go into a trance, had to breath strongly through her nose to keep from laughing. Patrick glanced at her face and saw her eyes go blank. She moved them slowly until she was looking into his.

"The coins you seek are buried under a stone slab in the settlement, in the third foundation from the sea." Her voice came out as a raspy whisper. In rehearsals they had her try an English accent which was quickly abandoned. "The evil ones go to steal them tonight. You must get there first and take them for this woman!" They had had a hard time coming up with a reason why Prudence would want Patrick to find the coins for himself, since by his own account she was more likely to put a curse on him. Opal finally suggested that the witch might want him to steal the coins for Maura since she was supposedly trying to possess her.

The short speech sounded ridiculous to Maura's own ears, but Patrick's mouth was open and he was pushing his chair back to get away from her. She casually asked whether Steve's family might consider investing in the operation, just as though she was unaware that she had been in a trance. The fleeting thought ran through her mind that she was enjoying herself a little.

Patrick grabbed her arm roughly and pulled her to her feet.

"Come on! We have to move fast. Do you have a shovel? And a flashlight."

She stared at him. The expectation was that he would run off and leave her there, heading for the old settlement. She nodded and got a small shovel from the gardening tools closet. The flashlight she had used to inspect the rubble trench was still on the counter. As Patrick pulled her through the house and out the front door, she asked where they were going in a raised voice. She didn't expect him to answer, but she wanted Dan and Joe to know she was with Patrick.

He pulled the car door open and gave her a little push to get in. Maura didn't feel like she was being kidnapped, more that he thought she would want to be included, or that she could provide some assistance. He stepped on the gas and the car shot forward. He gave her an excited grin as he shifted into third.

"If we find the coins, I'll give you a cut. I mean, I'll need most of them for the *Starling* operation, but you deserve something. After all, *she* wanted you to have some of them." 'Prudence', of course, hadn't said anything about sharing with Patrick.

She thought he would take the road through town and continue on the dirt track that ran to the settlement. Instead, he was heading to the harbor, undoubtedly planning to take the *Lorelei*. Randy, on the motorcycle they had heard pull away, would have had plenty of time to get to the settlement and warn everyone they would soon be coming.

Maura remembered that having been in a trance, she wouldn't know what Prudence had said.

"Patrick, where are we going and who is *she*?" The Martinis were wearing off and so was her ability to lie well. Patrick gave her an uncertain glance.

"The witch. She said the coins are buried in the old settlement. The evil ones are coming tonight so we have to beat them to it. I wonder who the evil ones are," he murmured to himself, chewing on his lip. He seemed to be considering his various acquaintances.

"Why are we taking the boat? Why not just drive?"

He looked at her again then turned back to the road.

"Remember I have to be somewhere tonight – I have to deliver something. We can just head out on the *Lorelei* after we get the coins and you can come with me for a couple of days. Your daughter's not home; it will be fun. You can help me with the salvage arrangements."

Maura took some deep breaths. This was not at all part of the plan. What if the delivery was Gracie? She must be on the boat in that case. Steve had searched it a few days ago, but Patrick could have stashed her somewhere else. Would he really take Maura on a boat trip with her friend hidden in one of the compartments? He might if Gracie wasn't able to struggle or call out. Maura's breath caught and she turned it into a cough. Of course she wouldn't go away with Patrick on his trip, but she would wait until after this evening's scheme to tell him so.

The *Lorelei* was tied up at the end of the pier. Maura was glad to see the rowboat bobbing behind the stern. She had envisioned swimming across the cove in her white dinner dress and petticoat, then navigating the trail in a heavy, sodden mass of fabric.

Patrick helped her onboard and quickly untied the *Lorelei*. He jumped in and pushed away from the pier. They were soon going full speed out of the harbor. The night breeze blew Maura's hair out of it's carefully arranged style. Seeing that Patrick's focus was ahead, she drifted to the first storage chest that contained the salvage gear and knocked lightly on it. It occurred to her that Gracie wouldn't know it was her friend knocking so she sang out loudly.

"It's a beautiful night! The stars are spectacular."

Patrick looked back over his shoulder and smiled, then turned forward again. She knocked on the storage chest once more, and when there was no answer, drifted to the second one. She wished she could open them but couldn't think of a reason to do so.

There was no answer to her knock on that chest either. From Randy's description, she thought the cavity in the deck where Patrick had hidden his composition book would be too small for anyone to be stashed in.

They came to the inlet too quickly and Patrick motored inside. He cut the engine and dropped the anchor, then pulled the rowboat around to the side of the *Lorelei*.

"I'll get in first then help you in." She handed him the shovel, her flashlight and Patrick's old-fashioned electric lantern and he stowed them under the seats.

It was awkward climbing into the boat wearing her full-skirted dress and heels, but she made it without mishap.

The oars made little sound as they moved through the water, ending each arc through the night air with a muffled splash. Patrick stepped into the shallow water and pulled the boat up on the shore. Maura climbed out and wobbled a little as her heels sank into wet sand. His hand steadied her.

Patrick reached into the boat for the shovel, flashlight and lantern then they started down the path to the settlement. His febrile excitement suddenly seemed to dim. His need for the money must be critical for him to brave the clearing which terrified him, Maura thought.

"She wanted us to come here," he said as though reassuring himself. "We'll be OK."

The woods were dense and their flashlight and torch didn't penetrate far. The mosquitos were out in force. Maura sent a silent apology to those waiting in the trees. With the distortion caused by the dark and their lights, they had some trouble finding the entrance to the clearing. When they did spot it, Patrick stopped for a moment and held up his lantern. The ruins of the stone foundations stood out in the greenish light.

"She said it's under a stone slab in the third foundation from the sea. Since the closest access to the ocean is in that direction, it must be that one. As he pointed, Maura knocked the lantern out of his other hand and kicked it off the path. She tossed her flashlight after it.

"What are you doing?" Patrick's voice was shrill.

"They don't like light," Maura said in the raspy whisper she had used earlier as Prudence. "Look!"

Four shapes, a woman and three men, were rising above the foundations, shimmering phosphorescently in the darkness. Patrick gasped. Maura felt that he was about to run so she moved behind him to block his way and said in her own voice,

"They're holding chests. Patrick, who are they?" He shook his head and stared at the figures.

The woman who had glided from behind the third foundation held up her wooden chest.

"These are yours in exchange for Grace Fletcher." This was spoken on a mournful sigh.

Patrick's eyes flitted to the chests the apparitions held. He was still half-turned, ready to flee. He remained silent so Maura spoke up.

"Why do you want Gracie?"

"She is our daughter, in spirit. The witch and her lover murdered us and stole our child. We want her back. Give us Grace Fletcher and all these coins and jewels are yours."

"But I don't know where she is!" Patrick's voice was querulous. Maura shot him a look. Could that be true? Was this ridiculous act all a waste of time? Then she remembered what a good liar Patrick was and she was unsure.

The figures began slowly advancing toward him, holding the chests high.

"Bring us Grace Fletcher," said the woman, "or tell us where she is." The others joined in. "Bring us Grace Fletcher."

"OK, OK! I'll get her and bring her back. Come on!" The latter was said in a forceful whisper to Maura.

She didn't want to go with him but couldn't think of a reason to stay. Either he really didn't have Gracie or he had some alternate plan, like coming back in the daylight with Steve to dig under stone slabs. She just knew he wasn't planning to bring Gracie to the clearing that night. Patrick was pulling on her arm. In the midst of her rising fear inspiration struck.

"How many miles to Barley Bright?" she said softly.

Her smile was every bit as creepy as she hoped it was. Patrick threw her arm from him and backed up.

"What?"

"Bring us Grace Fletcher! Bring us Grace Fletcher!" the others intoned.

Maura continued in her spooky voice.

"How many miles to Barley Bright?
Eight, eight and another eight!
Will we get there and back tonight?
Look out! The witches will get you!"

"Bring us Grace Fletcher! Bring us Grace Fletcher!" Three torches suddenly flared up among the trees. Maura screamed.

"They're coming for me!" It was hard for Maura to cry out in the voice she used for Prudence.

It was too much for Patrick. He turned and ran off into the dark, heading for the *Lorelei*.

Maura blew out a big breath, thankful that he had been too afraid of her to try to take her with him. The others stood uncertainly in the clearing. What next? If she was wrong and he was going to get Gracie, how long would they have to wait? They hadn't thought this all through. Someone laughed.

Maura opened her mouth to say, "Well, I hope you kids enjoyed yourselves!" but before she could utter a word her arm was grabbed and she was yanked almost off her feet.

"Come on!" Patrick shouted. "I couldn't leave you here."

Maura had to run on her toes in long strides to keep up with Patrick. He still held tightly to her arm and if she slowed, he yanked with both hands. The Rushing River ghosts, suddenly realizing that Patrick had absconded with Maura, streamed after him. They were unfamiliar with the trail and were hampered by having no flashlights. Randy and two other torch bearers, friends of his, caught up and pushed them forward. Patrick, looking back and seeing a wave of phosphorescence and torchlight following them, swung Maura around onto the narrow path to the inlet and sprinted for the rowboat.

None of the pursuers had ever taken the inlet path so ran past it, not realizing their mistake until the sound of the *Lorelei's* motor starting reached them. Maura, standing at the side with heaving chest while Patrick opened the throttle, saw her friends lined up along the shore, yelling. Enough of this. She went into the cabin.

"Stop the boat. They're my friends!" Better for him to know that she and the rest of them had all duped him, taking advantage of his superstition, then being forced to go along with whatever crazy scheme he had in mind.

Patrick stared at her incredulously.

"They're not your friends! You heard her – they called you and your lover murderers and said you stole their child."

It was Maura's turn to stare. It occurred to her that she was largely responsible for his delusion about the settlers. She had encouraged him by her interest in his stories and his research about the island. She had written that silly novel about the shipwreck survivors from the witch's point of view, and he had come to believe the witch was communicating with her. She hadn't denied it; and had in fact written a good portion of this evening's script to exploit it. He had trusted her, and in turn she had used her knowledge of his character and weaknesses against him. It was exactly what David would have done, and it sickened her.

"Patrick," she said gently, laying her hand on his arm. He flinched and shot her a sideways look.

He was afraid of her. The realization jolted her and she suddenly wondered why he had been so insistent that she return to the boat with him. Patrick believed that she was, at least in part, the witch of Islay. That witch was locally renowned for her predilection in putting curses on men; add in the curse that Patrick already believed lay on the *Lorelei* from the botched renaming business and he was running an enormous risk. Why? She had told Will that Patrick was driven by superstition, greed and ambition. There must be something that was stronger than his very real fear. They had been heading back toward the harbor, but Patrick suddenly turned the wheel and they made a wide arc and were heading out to open sea.

Maura left the cabin abruptly and strode to the first storage chest. She pulled it open and in the starlight saw that it was packed with the type of gear she remembered seeing on her first trip on the boat.

"Here, what are you doing?" Patrick shouted. Before he could reach her she had flung up the lid of the second chest. There, tied tightly with ropes and gagged, was a body. Patrick grabbed her and whipped her around, but not before she had put a finger on its neck. Cold.

"Who said you could look in there?" A vein stood out in Patrick's neck.

Maura was so shocked she couldn't speak. He shook her but still she stared, her face white in the starlight. He abruptly dropped the outrage from his tone.

"Come on, Maura! He doesn't matter. He was a low-life, mixed up with the mob. He used to kill people for money, then he testified against his boss. What kind of a person does that?"

"Basker Beeks." It was all she could manage.

"Yes, yes. Not his real name, of course. If he had picked a normal name, I might not have been so suspicious. Really, Maura. He's not worth worrying about. He was a low-level thug."

"What are you going to do with him?" Her lips were stiff.

"Well... I turn him in to the man he double-crossed, and I get a finder's fee. Simple! I didn't have a chance to kill him. He must have had a heart attack or something after he went in the chest. It doesn't matter. The world has one less criminal, and we get enough money to start the salvage operations on the *Starling*. There's a lot more down there, you know! Herridge had a lot more treasure than what could have been held in the four chests we saw tonight. I'll go back for them in daylight, maybe later next week. I'll bring Steve."

"And Violet Wilson?"

He hesitated. But something had put him in the mood to confess tonight, and to justify himself. It didn't bode well for Maura.

"She was a nice lady. Very interesting and smart. We dated for a while... did you know that? She wanted to keep it secret, so sometimes when Steve was in Rhode Island she would spend a few days on the boat with me. She was older, and not beautiful, but there was something about her. She understood me. But then I saw her picture in the Newark paper. She was secretary to a congressman who was in the pocket of the local mob. She testified against him to avoid being pulled into the net. I was very disappointed in her."

"So you shot her in the face."

"You were the one who found her, weren't you? The island police never mentioned the bullet hole to anyone. They must be in league with the DA who's been sending people here, taking the riffraff and finding them places to hide out. They wouldn't want it to get about that Violet was murdered; there would be an investigation that might put a spotlight on things they wanted hidden. It was really pure luck that I stumbled on the scheme to hide mob witnesses on Islay. I was researching something in the paper and saw an article about a mob killing. There was a picture of Bob Welch, who had testified."

"Why did you leave Violet in the water, right next to the pier?" Everything Maura said was in a monotone, her eyes fixed blankly on a life preserver.

"I didn't mean to! After Bob Welch, who struggled all the way to Jersey and almost managed to jump over the side of the boat, I decided that taking them in alive was too risky. The mob bosses usually don't care; they just want payback and to send a warning. Beeks' guy was different; he wanted him alive and was willing to pay more for it. I won't get as much now, but there's nothing that can be done. I called Violet and asked her to meet me at 2 am on the pier. By then the tavern is closed and the place is quiet. We'd done it before when she was going to spend time on the boat; she didn't want people to see her getting on it with me. It all worked smoothly. She stood on the pier smiling at me. I walked up to her and quickly shot her so she wouldn't be afraid or anything, and she dropped into the water. It's pretty shallow there, as you know because you found her. My plan was that she would fall in, any blood would wash off, then I could tie a rope around her foot and drag her over to the *Lorelei*. In the middle of the night and using the pier that's away from the busy area, there wasn't much risk. My gun has a silencer. It all went perfectly except two teenagers chose the moment after Violet went into the water to come down to the edge and cuddle under a blanket. What were their parents thinking of to let them out?"

"I don't know what the world is coming to," Maura whispered.

"Exactly. They didn't once look my way. They were so wrapped up in each other that they didn't even look up when I moved the boat away from the pier and around that stand of trees that juts out into the water. I waited there for hours but they didn't leave until the fishermen were starting their day. It was pretty obvious what they were doing under that blanket." Patrick's tone was disapproving. A little part of Maura's brain wanted to laugh. The rest recognized her ex-husband's approach: if anything went wrong it was always someone else's fault. She took a deep breath.

"Patrick, where is Gracie?"

He went to the side and looked out at the dark water.

"Why does everyone keep asking me that? She's your friend. Why would I take her?"

"Violet was *your* friend."

He turned and looked at her, and for a moment his expression was bleak. Then he scowled.

"I don't have her."

He went back into the cabin and started the boat moving, still heading away from where she thought the island was. There was no sign of it now, in the dark. No little phosphorescent people jumping up and down in alarm.

Maura followed Patrick into the cabin. He shifted a little when she stood too close.

"Let's head home now. If the tavern's still open, I could use a drink." She tried to make her voice relaxed and natural, but it still had that odd, flat tone.

He looked at her and seemed about to say something, then changed his mind. After a few minutes of silence Maura went back out onto the deck. She was almost certain that Patrick meant to dispose of her somewhere out here. He wouldn't have confessed details of his crime to a woman he was afraid of and expect her to go home and forget about it. Fear was rising and stifling her ability to think. She took several slow, deliberate breaths. At any moment he could stop the boat and come after her. What if she just jumped into the water? She knew it would be cold, despite it being August. Too cold to survive for hours or days? She could swim or float for a while if her sodden dress didn't pull her down, but what was the likelihood any planes or boats would find her way out here? Maybe that was what Patrick was planning – to just push her overboard. Would he try to run her over with the *Lorelei* or would he leave her to drown? She suddenly remembered the huge fish that swam under the boat on their first outing, and Sally's remark about white sharks. Panic was rising again. If she couldn't escape, she would have to disable Patrick somehow. She slid out of her pumps, hoping she could maneuver better in her bare feet. Maybe there was a crowbar or something in the chest that didn't hold a dead body. She could sneak up behind Patrick and...

The motor cut suddenly and idled. Patrick was standing in the doorway of the cabin, his right hand behind his back. He started walking toward her slowly, as though he was approaching a frightened cat.

"It's OK, Maura. This is all the way it should be."

"What the hell are you talking about, Patrick?"

"It's kind of like a full circle. The settlers killed Captain Herridge. Then you killed the settlers. Do you know where we are right now? We're over the wreck of the *Starling*. By giving you to the *Starling*, they should all be satisfied."

"That makes no sense!"

"Nothing has gone right for me since the renaming," he continued as though she hadn't spoken. "This will be a *real* sacrifice to Poseidon, not like the stupid bottle of champagne that everyone else does. He should accept that and maybe even help Steve and me with the salvage operation. And it won't be bad at all; I'll just give you a hard rap on the head with this and you won't know anything about the rest of it. I'd use the gun but I can't risk blood on the deck." The hand that came out from behind his back held a heavy wrench.

He was completely crazy, Maura realized. Nothing she could say would make a difference to Patrick. For the first time she faced the probability that she would die out here.

"Patrick, I'm a mother! What would happen to Lizzie?"

"She'll be fine. You said she's with her grandparents, right? They can just keep her. She's young; she'll get over it."

The prospect of Norma and Cleve raising Lizzie shocked her out of her terror. Cleve, much as he loved Lizzie, would tire of having a child around the house. He would spend more and more time away from home, leaving the rearing to his wife. Norma would spoil Lizzie atrociously, as she did her son.

Patrick saw her face and frowned.

"Stop looking like that. You know it's really your own fault, Maura. You didn't have to come to the island. Just because the house was offered rent free you didn't have to jump at it. It was a little greedy of you; money isn't everything. And then you let yourself be susceptible to the witch. She couldn't have possessed you if you didn't leave yourself open. I'm sorry about this, Maura. We could have had something, you and I, but you didn't handle this well. Can you answer one question for me, though. Were you involved in any mob activity when you were in Jersey? I couldn't find anything in my research, but I might have missed something."

While Patrick was talking, he had been advancing on Maura and she had been taking steps backwards. She now stopped and stared at him incredulously.

"You're going to murder me, but first you would like to know if you can make some money handing my body over to a crime boss?" Her voice rose, and she looked like a woman who would drive away a mob with a garden hose. Patrick, who had never seen Maura angry, took an involuntary step backwards.

"You kill people to get a little extra cash. And this is *my* fault?" Her voice got louder and suddenly had a distinct Jersey accent. She took two more steps toward Patrick and he took two steps back. "If Violet hadn't accepted a job working for a guy who turned out to be connected to the mob, you wouldn't have murdered her, right? She should have had more sense? How was Basker Beeks responsible for his own death?" Her hands balled into fists. "You're just like my ex-husband! Not one stupid, asinine decision he made, not one affair he had with a teenage girl, not one job he lost was his fault. Somehow, it was all *my* fault! Or anybody else's fault except his. He was a self-centered, narcissistic, delusional jerk. Just like you, Patrick!" There was a tidal wave flowing through Maura. She heard the words coming out of her mouth with surprise but made no effort to stem them. Despite her desperation, this was a torrent that had been held back for years and she couldn't check if she wanted to. She saw Patrick's fear and it broke down the dam completely, giving her a sense of power she had never before experienced.

"Your failures are totally your own. *You* are responsible." Images of David's peevish face and her mother's accusing one jostled for attention in her mind's eye. "It wasn't my fault Dad left us; *you* drove him out with your tantrums and your possessiveness. It wasn't my fault you had an affair with a student while I was pregnant with your child. *You* did it. *You* were weak and self-absorbed and didn't care who you hurt. People *laugh* at you!" She felt some spit fly from her mouth. Who is the crazy one now, Maura? Patrick's eyes were bulging and he was scrabbling away from her. Without thinking, she raised her arms above her head and ran at him, hissing. He whirled away and stepped on one of her pumps that she had left on the deck. The shoe slid and his foot went out from under him. When he lost his balance and started to go over the side he grabbed for the railing, but Maura was too quick for him. She lifted his legs and tipped him over.

Maura stood gaping. All the exhilaration left her in a whoosh. When Patrick called her name and she heard him thrashing in the water, she ran to the cabin to start the boat. Then she ran back and tossed the life preserver, emblazoned with the name *Lorelei*, the siren who led men to destruction, into the water.

Thank God Patrick had showed her how to drive the boat on their first outing, but even still it coughed and almost stalled when she opened the throttle too quickly. In an effort to get away from Patrick she just drove straight in the direction the boat was already heading. But was she escaping him, or had he managed to grab ahold of the boat? Was he sneaking up behind her with the wrench? She whirled around in terror but she was alone in the cabin. It didn't mean she was alone on the boat, however. Should she go out and look? There was no way to know if Patrick was crouching outside, waiting for her. Her heart pounded in her chest and she felt slightly dizzy. She looked around for a weapon but found nothing more menacing than a coffee mug.

Where was she going? She hadn't the slightest idea what direction the boat was pointed in when Patrick idled it. Since they had driven away from the island to reach the site of the shipwreck, she hoped the boat was still pointing out to sea. She turned it in a wide arc, praying that she was now pointing back at the island. Because she kept looking over her shoulder for a wrench-wielding murderer, her perception of how far she turned was confused.

The *Lorelei* chugged on for almost two hours before it ran out of gas. While Maura had no idea how long it had taken them to get to the location where Patrick went overboard, she knew she was going in the wrong direction long before the engine stalled. There had been no visible lights since they left Islay. Twice she had changed direction hoping that if she didn't find the island she would come to a town on the mainland or another populated island.

Maura wasn't really surprised when the engine died. Maybe it was better to float here, waiting to be spotted when daylight came. She still couldn't shake the thought that Patrick was crouching on the deck or hanging onto the boat ladder. She desperately wanted to look but was just as desperately afraid to leave the cabin. Finally realizing the structure offered her no protection, and indeed made it easy for Patrick to easily corner her, she picked up the coffee mug and moved silently outside.

Chapter 25

Almost every boat on Islay, including the fishing boats, had been enlisted in the search for the *Lorelei*. Vic Stokes radioed the mainland for assistance and a plane would be sent out at the first signs of daylight. He said he didn't understand the concern about the boat's owner going off with a woman he had been seen to be on friendly terms with but was pressured into making the call. The search plane was thanks to a lieutenant in the sheriff's office who had been uneasy since his interview with Maura and Will.

Will had missed the late ferry due to a traffic snarl. He arrived by hired boat to find a small crowd congregated under a lamppost at the harbor docks. People were gathered around what appeared to be a group of zombie extras from a low budget movie. He recognized Rebecca in a tattered old-fashioned dress, her face caked in white makeup and her eyes rimmed in black and red. With her was the group that had come down from Rushing River as well as Steve and Randy. The harbor master and a number of boat owners and their crews were listening to instructions from Steve.

When Rebecca saw Will she ran over to him, her face taut with anxiety.

"Will, he took Maura."

Will's blood went cold.

"What do you mean?"

"It didn't go according to plan – probably because it was a terrible plan. He took her to the clearing. The scaring part went fine and he swallowed the whole you-give-us-Grace-Fletcher-and-we-give-you-treasure bit. He even said he would go get her. I think we scared him too much, though, and Maura clearly didn't want to go with him. She did a creepy recital of *Barley Bright* to scare him away and he went running off into the woods. We thought it was over but all of a sudden he was back. He grabbed Maura and dragged her with him. No, don't assume the worst yet. He said something like 'I couldn't leave you here', which sounds like he thought he was rescuing her. We hoped we would find her here, or back at the house, but they haven't shown up."

Will's expression was grim.

"Rebecca, the guy is actually insane. This was a very bad idea. What's being done to find them?"

"I know it was a crazy idea although... it seemed to be working. The police captain – Stokes? – called the sheriff's office back on the mainland and they'll send a search plane out as soon as it's light enough. Maura's friend Dottie is back at your house. If Maura shows up or if anyone calls with news, she'll call Ruth Grady, the harbormaster's wife. They have a ham radio set and she'll contact the boats that are heading out if there's any direction for them, or if Maura comes home."

Will saw Steve striding toward one of the larger fishing boats, in animated conversation with a man Will took to be the boat's owner.

"Hey!" he called in his booming voice. "I'm coming with you!"

Rebecca ran up behind them with her husband in pursuit.

The sun was well above the horizon before Maura heard a plane. She stood at the side of the *Lorelei*, wrapped in one of the sleeping bags and eating a package of stale cookies she had found in the cabin. The plane was far off, not worth waving at. It disappeared, then sometime later it appeared again, but closer. This time she waved and was thrilled to see the plane fly directly for her. It went overhead and she waved both arms, the last cookie falling from the package into the water. The plane wobbled a little, then flew off. From books she assumed that meant 'we see you'.

Close to two hours passed before a boat appeared on the horizon. She had become terribly thirsty and was unable to find anything to drink except a warm bottle of beer in one of the cubby holes. She drank it down, but it still left her craving a cold glass of water.

Maura almost cried when the big fishing boat was close enough for her to read the name. The *Queen of Islay*. Her friends stood at the rail, waving and calling to her. Two fishermen came alongside the *Lorelei* in an inflatable dinghy. She climbed in and was taken to the *Queen of Islay*. As soon as she was on the deck, Rebecca and Will enveloped her in a tight hug. Relieved tears ran down Rebecca's cheeks. Her ghost make-up had partially fallen off but much of it still remained in scaley patches. The black and red that had been lavishly applied around her eyes had been rubbed and now ran down her cheeks with her happy tears. The morning sun lit up the mess and her husband grinned appreciatively.

Maura broke free from her friends' embrace and told the group standing around that there was a body in one of the storage chests. Two of the crew took the dinghy back to the *Lorelei* and after opening both chests, looked back at their captain and nodded.

"Maura....Gracie?" Steve's face was white.

"No! No! It's Baskar Beeks." Steve steadied himself and nodded.

"Did Patrick say where she is?"

"No. And here's the odd thing. He freely admitted to the other murders, but he said he didn't have Gracie."

Steve looked hopeful for a moment, then his face fell.

"He's an accomplished liar, as you well know. Where is Patrick?"

"I... he went overboard. I threw him a life ring."

The captain overheard this and grinned.

"They found him floating in the life preserver."

"They found Patrick?" Maura wasn't surprised by the relief that washed over her. She, unlike Patrick, wasn't a murderer and causing anyone's death would have been hard to deal with.

"Yes. He's accusing you of trying to kill him."

"Oh! Well..."

"He says you put a curse on him and made him fall overboard."

Everyone standing nearby laughed. The captain moved away to radio the island police that the treasure hunter had a body on his boat. Rebecca, looking speculatively at Will's firm hold on Maura's arm, took Steve a little way off and began telling about the firm of private detectives her business manager was hiring to look for Gracie. His look lightened a little.

"Maura, what happened out there?" Will's voice raspy with relief and stress from the long night's search.

"Oh, Will. It was awful. I watched someone I thought I knew turn into a monster before my eyes. He really is insane. It's not only Joe Fabiola and Bob Welch who were hidden here after testifying in criminal cases. Violet and Basker Beeks were too. To get money to fund his salvaging business, he's been kidnapping them and turning them over to the mobs for a bounty. He's talked himself into believing they deserved it for making bad decisions and he's helping rid the world of criminals."

"Why did he admit to this and where was he taking you?"

The *Lorelei* had been given enough gas to get home and two of the fishing boat's crew would take her back to Islay. As the boats separated, the slower *Lorelei* was looking smaller as she fell behind.

"He fell for the whole witch thing last night. We thought if we dangled four chests of pirate treasure in front of him *and* scared him into thinking the ghosts would get him if he didn't produce Gracie, we would get results. The problem was that we scared him too much. I think when he ran back to the clearing to get me, it was because he didn't want to abandon me to the ghosts. But it occurred to him afterwards that the witch was now sharing my body and if he wanted to get rid of her, he'd have to get rid of both of us. He..." she paused and took a breath. "He wanted to hit me in the head with a wrench and throw me overboard. We were idling over the site of the wreck he and Steve found. It nicely tied up lose ends, he said. I would be a sacrifice to Poseidon to finally close out that renaming fiasco, and somehow the murdered settlers would be appeased by my death."

Will breathed heavily through his nose, his mouth in a thin line.

"Hell, Maura... Then what happened?"

"He began justifying all his evil deeds. The bad things that happened to his victims were their fault. It sounded so much like David that for a moment I started thinking maybe my predicament was my fault. He said Lizzie would be fine without me, that David's parents would raise her. Something inside me snapped at that. Up until that point he had been coming toward me with the wrench. I went after him, shouting like I was the insane one. I yelled at my mother and at David and I think foam was coming out of my mouth. Patrick was more afraid of me at that moment than he had been of the ghosts and backed away. Then..." she stopped and began to laugh with rising hysteria. She laughed so hard no sound came out. "Then...", she choked out, "then I raised my arms and ran at him, hissing!" Tears were running down her face.

Will stared at her for a moment. The anxiety of the preceding twelve hours had been hard to bear, but he joined her laughter despite himself.

"Just like the island witch, running at her attackers!"

Maura loved his ability to appreciate absurdity in even a situation such as this. He put steadying hands on her shoulders, and after a few deep breaths she was able to get ahold of herself.

"Exactly," she finally replied. "When I saw how scared he was of me it gave me a feeling of power, and that part of her story popped into my head. Then he tripped on one of my shoes that I'd left on the deck and started to fall overboard. When he tried to grab the side of the boat, I lifted his legs and tipped him over. Just like he accused me of."

Will looked around to make sure no one was within earshot. "Let's keep that part to ourselves. Nobody's believing him." His smile faltered and he pulled Maura against him as though he could belatedly protect her. After a moment she pushed back and looked up at him with a tremulous smile. She had experienced a monumental release at the moment she had driven Patrick overboard and her emotions were tumultuous in the aftermath. Will put his hands on either side of her face and kissed her. He whispered her name and kissed her again.

Rebecca, standing nearby, looked on in satisfaction.

"If you expect me to kiss you, you haven't looked in a mirror," said her fond husband. She gave him a sunny smile, her black, red and chalky white makeup even more of a travesty in the bright sunlight. He laughed.

"OK, I'll kiss you!" he said, making good on his word.

Details of Maura's ordeal and rescue had been radioed back to Islay and the mainland and Patrick was now in custody. Phone calls had relayed the news among residents. When the *Queen of Islay* chugged into the harbor a small crowd stood on the pier, cheering. The perpetrator of the strange happenings on the island had been captured, and Maura, his latest kidnap victim, was returning safe and sound. Life could get back to normal.

Maura scanned the crowd for Gracie but didn't find her. Anxiety for her friend had been briefly overshadowed by the night's desperate adventures but now returned in full force.

Chapter 26

The Rushing River contingent piled into Rebecca's Sixty Special and left on the afternoon ferry. Rebecca had given her friend a convulsive hug and demanded she write daily, cursing the lack of phone service to the mainland.

Maura showered and collapsed on her bed, sleeping for a few hours. When she awoke her first thoughts were of Gracie. Patrick's admitting to the other murders while disavowing any knowledge of her whereabouts gave her hope. She thought about the night before Gracie disappeared, and how she seemed about to tell Maura something before changing her mind. Had she been planning this? If only Gracie would contact her. At least the islanders no longer suspected Opal of the murders and disappearances; everyone assumed Patrick was also responsible for Gracie and the baker vanishing and waited for the police to get the truth from him. Opal could move back into her house.

She went down to the kitchen and Will was at the table with a cardboard packet in front of him. He looked up and gave her a slow smile that did something odd to her insides.

"Feeling better?"

She nodded a little shyly.

"I'm hungry though."

"There was a lot of Chicken Divan left. Can you stand to eat it after that business last night? Joe wrapped it all up and put it away."

"Yes!" She would never again give anyone the power to take away her joys in life, and that included Chicken Divan. She started to walk to the stove, but Will told her to sit.

He turned on the oven and it wasn't long before the kitchen started to fill with mouth-watering scents. Joe had brought a fresh-baked loaf of bread over while Maura was sleeping. He walked openly from the coffee shop, where he was again living with Wally and now Opal. No one had recognized him on the way because no one knew what he looked like. Will got out a plate and carefully cut and buttered some bread slices. She watched him put ice cubes in two glasses and pour lemonade over them. It was all done competently, without fanfare. No expectation of being admired or applauded for making a simple dinner. David once made dinner when she was sick with the flu. He spent the entire meal explaining every step of the process and was offended when she was too sick to enjoy the meal. But Will was not David. Will could never be David.

He put the lemonade pitcher back in the refrigerator and caught Maura's smile as she watched him. He stared at her for a moment then smiled back. After filling their plates and setting them on the table, he sat down across from her.

"Randy also stopped by while you were sleeping. Officers from the county sheriff's office went over Dunn's boat. Randy told them where to find his notebook. They also found a small gun and silencer that he probably used to kill Violet Wilson. And an old diary hidden in a cut-out in a book, which was probably Isaac Belfour's, stolen from the historical society. They took Dunn away, of course, and he was more concerned about being separated from his new salvage project than about being arrested for murder. They also took Steve in for questioning since he was Dunn's partner. No, don't worry. I think it's more to get information about Dunn. Randy explained how much help Steve has been."

Will washed the dinner dishes and handed them to Maura to dry. They talked about Lizzie, where she and the Gertzes would be right now and how many more days until she would be back on Islay. With the danger past, Lizzie couldn't be home fast enough. Her absence caused an ache in Maura's heart. They had come so far this summer in building their mother and daughter relationship. How much of it was being undone in the company of her ex-in-laws?

"Maura." Will turned off the water and held a dripping plate. She looked at him questioningly.

"Maura," he began again. He seemed to be unable to go any further.

She took the dripping plate from his hand and set it on the counter. Pulling his head down, she kissed him gently. He blinked in surprise then returned her kiss with interest. She slid her arms around his waist and hugged him closely.

"You're not just toying with me, are you?" he breathed into her hair.

She gave a shaky laugh and shook her head.

"I wish you had asked me to your prom," she whispered.

After a bit, Will took her hand and led her through the parlor to the stairs.

If there are ghosts in this perfect house, Maura thought, *some of them are smiling now. OK, the rest of them are probably a little shocked!*

The next morning Maura took a cup of coffee out onto the patio. Jelly Bean wound around her ankles then went off on his morning inspection of the gardens. A family of chipmunks had taken up residence there.

At the sound of the screen door closing behind her a few minutes later, she turned and stepped into Will's arms. His hastily donned shirt was fully unbuttoned and she enjoyed the feel of his warm chest with its silken hair against her cheek. Will looked over her shoulder and saw Lillian standing in the rose portal between the houses, holding a cup of coffee with her mouth in an O. She had heard the screen door bang behind Maura and had come out for their customary coffee chat. She wanted to hear all the details about the arrest of the treasure hunter. When Will smiled over Maura's head and put his fingers to his lips, she grinned and gave him a conspiratorial wink, then tiptoed away.

"Have I mentioned how much I like Lillian?" he murmured. Maura looked up at him quizzically.

Will was in the attic sanding woodwork when Maura took the bicycle and cart out. They were low on food and she was heading to the store. Since Lizzie had left with her grandparents, the cart had only been used to carry groceries. The towel she kept spread in the bottom of the cart in case any groceries leaked was sprinkled with bits of leaves and rose petals. She picked it up with the intention of shaking it out and stared at the white envelope that had lain underneath. It had no writing on it but it was sealed.

With shaking hands, Maura tore open the envelope. She read it through once, then ran into the house.

"Will! Will!" She pounded up the stairs and she could hear him running down the attic steps to meet her.

"What's the matter?" he asked in some alarm.

"A letter from Gracie! It's been in my bicycle cart all along, under the towel. Listen!"

They went into the boys' dormitory and sat on one of the beds.

Dear Maura,

After you read this, set fire to it in your big fireplace, stir up the ashes and bury them in your garden. I'm in a hurry but I can't leave without telling you a few things. I'll hide the note somewhere at your house and hope you find it quickly. And that nobody else does.

When Will and Lizzie walked me home last night, he told me about the break-in at your place. I've been up for hours worrying, and finally made up my mind: I have to go. I've been thinking about it for a while, and now I'm afraid I'm next. You may have figured out that I'm like Joe the baker. I'm not a criminal, but my husband worked for a company that was into some pretty bad stuff. He thought they were legitimate until he'd been there for a while and got a good look at their books. He was an accountant. There was a briefcase with ten thousand dollars in it that was supposed to be used to buy off a senator. Ernest (that's not really his name – our name isn't Fletcher either) was told to deliver it to the guy in person at a restaurant. They didn't tell him anything – what was in the briefcase or what it was for. Ernest was a sweet guy but kind of naïve. That's probably why they used him. He thought the delivery must be OK since it was a well-known politician and the meeting was at a nice restaurant. Well, the senator never showed up. Ernest took the briefcase back to his office and saw lines of police cars with flashing lights out front. He turned right around; by now he knew the company was up to no good and it looked like the police had caught up with them. He figured the senator got wind of what was going to happen and that's why he didn't show. Ernest told me all about it when he got home. He had opened the briefcase in the car and saw it was stuffed with money. He couldn't take it into the office because the police would assume he was in on all of it. He told me everything, then. All that wacky stuff he had been seeing, the cooked books and who was probably in on it. I had met most of them and their wives at dinner parties. Ernest was frantic about the money, so he hid it somewhere until things quieted down and maybe he could bring it back. He wouldn't tell me where it was, said it was safer if I didn't know. Well, he was wrong about that. The police arrested him as being part of the whole operation and he went to prison. The mob boss and some of his top people were arrested too. Some of their guys came to our apartment after Ernest was taken away and demanded the briefcase. I kept telling them I didn't know where it was. Thankfully, before they could do any damage to me the police showed up and took me away for questioning.

This is turning into my autobiography and I have to get out of here, so I'll just say that they offered a deal to Ernest. The police didn't have anything on me because there wasn't anything to be had, but the mob was after me for the money. In exchange for my safety, he told them where he had hidden the briefcase and agreed to testify. Either somebody else had found the briefcase first or the cops kept it, but they said it wasn't there. They had been keeping me hidden in a hotel room but the bad guys were still looking for me. To make sure they had Ernest's cooperation, they moved me to Islay before the trial.

The DA is Vic Stokes' uncle. The developer who built the bungalows was having a hard time selling them, so the DA and Stokes hatched this plan to put witnesses in them. You'll remember that Joe, Bob Welch and I all at least started in the bungalows. The deal was you got the first six months rent free, then you had to start paying yourself. They would arrange for money to transfer from our savings accounts to their contact in the mid-west, who forwarded it on to us. We would exchange letters with our families the same way. If anyone was checking their mail, they wouldn't see anything coming from Islay. I started the camp so I wouldn't have to pay everything out of our savings, but that dried up off season.

My sister wrote to tell me that Ernest was killed in prison, right after testifying. There were other people who testified so I don't know why they had to kill Ernest. I guess to make a point. The mob boss' brother took over the business and tried to make it look like he had cleaned it up, but there were still people asking about me and thinking I had the briefcase.

So that's my sordid story. I'm telling you the truth when I say I had no idea what was going on until the whole briefcase thing. I was a Sunday school teacher!

Islay felt safe until recently. Now I know that someone's caught onto the fact that witnesses have been stashed here. I wouldn't put it past Vic Stokes to brag about his brilliant idea.

I hate to leave here, especially since you and Lizzie came. I know you're only here for the summer but you wouldn't have been far away during the rest of the year and you could have come to visit me. It can get pretty lonely.

I told you all this so you won't worry. I jimmied my own window to make it look like someone broke in. I'm kind of hoping the bad guy will think someone else beat him to kidnapping me and maybe confuse him enough so he doesn't know where to look for me.

I'm also telling you this because you became my best friend over the summer and it bothered me that I kept things from you. I wanted to tell you last night that I was leaving, but I could see you were having a bad day and I couldn't bring myself to talk about it. I know I would have cried and that would have upset little Lizzie.

If anybody, OK Steve, thinks about looking for me, tell him not to waste his time. I don't look like me now and I'll use a different name. I've gotten good at hiding. Steve is a nice person and I think he cares about me a little, but I was too much Gracie for him to handle. You can tell him and Will about this, but nobody else please. Maybe just tell the others you got a postcard and I'm OK – had to leave for a family illness or something.

Give Lizzie a big hug from Miss Gracie and tell her I love her. I hope that someday I can look you up and we can be friends again. Until then, I'm on the lam!

Your friend,

Gracie

PS: My real name isn't Gracie. But it isn't all that far off.

Maura didn't read the second postscript out loud:

PPS: Don't be an idiot about Will. He's crazy about you.

"We have to find her, Will! She needs to know that Patrick has been arrested and Islay is safe!"

He rubbed his chin.

"Do you think she would come back? Or even should. This business will undoubtedly make the news, what with a treasure hunter, the murders, witches and curses. The story could easily make it as far as New Jersey, and the connection with the DA may come to light. The mob is still looking for Gracie, or more particularly, the ten thousand dollars."

Maura put her face in her hands.

"Poor Gracie," she whispered.

CHAPTER 26   283

A small group of middle-aged women who had occupied all the rooms at the Bayberry Inn for the last four days gathered in front of a booth to buy their ferry tickets. They chattered and dug through purses for the right change, tied their scarves more tightly over their hair and argued where they would have lunch when they reached the mainland. The last of their set, a dowdy woman who had come up behind them when they climbed out of the island taxi, silently put her money down. She wore an ill-fitting skirt and an outdated coat. A hat was anchored to her head with a beige scarf that tied under her chin. She wore no makeup or jewelry and her hair was in a severe bun. The young woman in the booth handed her a ticket but never really looked at her. Afterwards she couldn't describe any of the group, or even how many women there were.

Maura found Gracie's letter on Thursday, August 12. On Friday she was weeding the little flower bed at the front of the house when the island taxi pulled up. Before the doors opened, she could hear cries of "Mommy! Mommy!" coming from inside.

She dropped her trowel and whispered, "Lizzie!" The Gertzes had returned four days early.

Maura dropped to her knees and Lizzie catapulted herself into her arms. She held her daughter in a tight embrace and stroked her hair, murmuring how much she had missed her.

"I missed you, Mommy! And Jelly Bean and my crayons and my beans and Mr. Giant!"

Maura looked up at the Gertzes, who watched from the sidewalk. Cleve smiled but Norma looked disgruntled.

"You're back early," Maura said. "How did it go?"

Cleve shrugged his shoulders with a wry smile.

"She was fine the first day. She loved the boat ride. It wasn't until bedtime that she got homesick and that never let up. And all day long it was 'These aren't like Mommy's pancakes!' and 'Mommy wouldn't like the way you do may hair, Granny.' I guess she was a little too young to be taken away from her mama." Norma sniffed.

Maura spent much of her time after Patrick's arrest at the police station, being interviewed by the county sheriff's department. She told them everything she could think of, apart from Joe Fabiola's whereabouts and the contents of Gracie's letter. She thought Vic Stokes watched her a little anxiously. When Sergent Krol was caught red-handed lifting a wallet from an unattended beach bag, he did his best to drag Stokes down with him. He accused his boss of hiring him to steal an antique ceramic box from the old Watts house. When the mainland police asked her about it, she opened her eyes wide and said there hadn't been any break-ins.

'I hope you don't mind," she said to Will when she got home from the police station. "But I feel like we've had enough crime for the summer. I'm sure Stokes was imagining Krol lifting the unlocked window, daintily swiping the box and sneaking off with it. Not breaking in and crashing through the house. Stokes looked like he was going to cry when I said I didn't know anything about it."

"I'll ask Aunt May to give him first dibs on buying the box."

"I met Clay Grady, the harbormaster, coming out of the station. The sheriff's people were interviewing everyone connected with Violet's death, now that we know it was murder. I asked him why he hadn't admitted to seeing the bullet hole in her forehead. He said Stokes had told him it would be bad for island tourism if it got around and the mainland police would take care of it. So he kept quiet. We know the mainland police never saw Violet; Stokes must have called his uncle, the DA, who probably had the body whisked away as quickly as possible."

When Maura opened a cabinet to pull out a mixing bowl before dinner, she noticed a cardboard packet on top of a stack of mail. She remembered that it had been in the envelope with Rebecca's scheme for scaring Gracie's location out of Patrick. That, and the prospect of Lizzie going off with the Gertzes, had put the packet out of mind. She had a vague memory of Will having it when she went into the kitchen last night.

"What's this?" she asked, inspecting the packet. "I saw it in front of you last night and I didn't get a chance to ask."

Will was washing his hands in the kitchen sink.

"Open it!" He smiled and watched her.

Maura removed the top layer of cardboard. Inside were three sketches. No, not really sketches. They were beautiful, detailed drawings of a little girl with long curly hair, a cat with goggle eyes and an immensely tall giant that looked very much like Will. She stared at them, dumbfounded.

"Carlos illustrated the Lizzie and the Giant stories!" She looked at each drawing, tears welling up in her eyes.

"Who's Carlos?"

"He was one of the Zombies from Rushing River. He's married to Lucia, who made Lizzie's doll's ballgown, and is a successful portrait painter. He's had his work in Boston galleries. Oh, Will, these are lovely. When he was here the other night, he must have wondered why I didn't even mention them!"

Rebecca had included a note with the drawings. Maura read it out loud.

I had nothing to do with this, Mo. I swear! You'll remember I took your stories with the intention of having somebody at MacKenzie type them up professionally and put a cover on them. I brought them to the gallery and showed Lucia. She asked if she could take them home and try them out on her boys. They loved them! Well, the older two did. The youngest one slept through them. She showed them to Carlos, who is between commissions right now. He never illustrated a book before and wanted to give this one a try. He said to tell you that if you like them he'll do more illustrations. My secretary retyped your stories and fixed a few typos and spelling things. What you and Carlos do with the book is up to you, but all of us up here think you should see about getting it published. Not MacKenzie, of course, since we don't do that kind of thing. If you're interested, send the sketches back and I'll let Carlos know to do the rest. You will notice that I am NOT interfering!

"She took pictures of all of us when she was here last, which explains why these look so much like you and Lizzie. What do you think, Will? They're your stories."

"They're just as much yours – and Lizzie's. She told me what stories she wanted, and you made them make sense." He came up to her and took her hands.

"*Lizzie, the Giant and a Cat Named Jelly Bean,* by Lizzie, Maura and Will Howe. How does that sound?"

"It sounds wonderful!" she whispered. She cleared her throat. "Will, when I flipped Patrick overboard a big chunk of my mental flotsam went with him. He was manipulative and narcissistic like my mother and David, but so crazy that I finally and truly saw how they all used me. I felt like I threw all three of them into the ocean and it was cathartic. The thing is… I'm not sure how much flotsam is left."

Will smiled and pulled her against him.

"I'll take my chances," he murmured.

After a moment she said,

"But if we have any children, they're all getting Watts for a middle name!"

CHAPTER 27

Will's boss told him it was time he was back at work, so he reluctantly returned to Boston, coming back on weekends to help pack. The house was everything that an investment of hard work, money and love could make it. There was nothing lavish about it, just a restoration of its original beauty with the benefit of modern conveniences. A real estate agent came out and took a lot of pictures, exclaiming over the quality of the renovation work.

"There's a good market for quality summer homes right now."

Aunt May had asked them to pack up any personal items belonging to their family. She and her children would go through the boxes and see if there was anything they wanted to keep.

Within a week of the real estate agent's visit, a letter arrived from Will, informing her that the house was sold. His aunt was surprised but very happy that it all worked out so well. The new owner bought it furnished, which simplified packing quite a bit.

Lizzie followed Maura around the house, bemoaning every item belonging to Will's family that went into a box. She said the house would miss them. This commentary echoed Maura's thoughts exactly.

The summer was quickly winding down and she tried to make the most of their last precious days, rambling around the island, meeting the other families from Camp Boogie Woogie at the beach and having lunch at the coffee shop. She anxiously checked the mail every day, hoping for a letter or postcard from Gracie.

With Patrick identified as his attacker and safely out of the way, Joe resumed baking in the coffee shop kitchen. Word spread that the baker was back. There was no explanation offered for his absence, but that mystery took a back seat to the unfolding drama of the treasure hunter and his murders.

Wally and Opal resumed their relationship from where they had left it before their estrangement. They were getting married in a week and Wally would move into the Uncle Irvin house. Maura thought about their wasted years, each caring about the other but too hurt to do anything about it. Every night Opal would go up to her attic in time to watch Wally put the trash out. He in turn would look across the green to the decrepit house surrounded by a high wall, worrying about Opal. When rumors about Opal being the island witch began to go around, Wally often did a stealthy late night patrol of the green. He had been standing behind a bush when Gracie rode by one night on her bicycle. Worried about a lone woman out late when something wasn't right on the island, he stepped forward to offer to escort her home but only succeeded in scaring her.

What a difference this one summer made in the lives of a soon-to-be schoolteacher and her daughter, thought Maura. Lizzie was telling everyone that a giant was going to be her daddy. They had taken a day trip to the mainland and toured towns within easy driving distances to Maura's new school. They found a pretty lot in a partially-built neighborhood that had a brook running through the back of the property. Will would be able to catch a train to Boston every morning from a nearby station after they moved in. He was drawing up the plans for their house.

The doorbell rang the morning before Maura and Lizzie were leaving. She sighed. They had had visitors every day since Patrick was arrested, whether from officials connected with the case, or reporters or neighbors wanting to gossip.

"I'll get it!" she called to Will, who was in the kitchen, cleaning out the broom closet. They were going to the inn that evening for their last dinner on the island.

Maura opened the door to find a courier, who handed her a packet. Will came out of the kitchen and gave him a tip.

"It must be from Bec," said Maura, turning over the packet. "She's the only person I know who throws money around on special couriers." She opened the envelope and pulled out two sheets of note paper and a greeting card in an envelope. She began reading the note out loud.

"'I so wanted to come to Islay before you left to explain this in person and to celebrate your engagement. Which, by the way, makes me so happy I cry whenever I think about it! Unfortunately, we have an important town council meeting that I have to attend. After you read this, you can decide whether you want to give the card – '"

The next words were 'to Lizzie' but Maura shot a look at her daughter and saw she was listening. She read the rest of the note to herself and started to laugh. With the laugh came tears, and she groped for a box of tissues.

"Maura, what's wrong?" Will asked in some alarm.

"Mommy?" Lizzie looked dismayed.

"Nothing's wrong. Really! Lizzie, Auntie Bec has sent you a present." She took the greeting card out of its envelope and handed it to her. Lizzie smiled when she saw the drawing of a tall man, a woman and a little girl with long curly hair. They were standing in front of a house all holding hands and a black and white cat sat next to the little girl. Maura recognized Rebecca's limited artistic skills.

"What does it say?" Lizzie handed the card back.

"It says, 'Dear Lizzie. I know your birthday isn't until December, but I wanted to give you your present now. It's actually for you and any brothers or sisters you may have some day. And can you guess what it is? You're probably standing in it now! I know how much you love the house so now you can come back to it every summer, whenever you want. With lots of love, Auntie Bec.'"

Lizzie's mouth had hung open while Maura read.

"It's mine? The house is mine? The swing and the...the...beanstalks and my room and..."

"Yes, all of it!" Maura blew her nose and looked at Will. He was as amazed as Lizzie was. She laughed at his expression.

"Lizzie, go find Jelly Bean and tell him the good news!" She pulled Will down onto the couch next to her.

"Bec says she knew right away that she wanted to buy the house. She considered just offering your aunt the asking price and letting me live in it over the summer. Afterwards she would fix it up and sell it for a profit, like her other properties. The problem was that if she bought it outright, there would be no reason for you to come here. Despite the fact that you were engaged, she was sure that you and I were perfect for each other. So she cooked up the scheme where she would go in as an investor and take a percentage of the profit. That deal never really made sense to me, but it was your aunt's business. When Bec visited us and saw how happy Lizzie and I were here, she was determined to give us the house. And now that we're engaged, she's thrilled that the house will stay with Josiah Watts' descendants. Or at least for our generation, if you and I don't have children.

"Bec has been in agonies about how to give it to us, knowing that I get mad when she spends any money on me. She's always known why; not being able to support myself left me helpless and vulnerable. I would have left David early in our marriage if I had the means. Getting a degree and a paying job is really important to me, which is why I want to teach after we're married. At least until I can make some money writing."

"I know," Will said, putting his arms around her.

"But for some reason I can accept this house, which is probably the most ridiculously extravagant present given in the history of the universe."

They strolled out to the backyard, their arms around each other's waists. Maura looked at the kitchen as they passed through with new eyes. They weren't leaving forever tomorrow. They could come back any weekend they chose, and next summer she would be here again, making meals for the three of them.

Lizzie, not having a basin of warm water available, had washed her doll with undiluted dish soap and now turned the hose on it to rinse it off. The doll shot half-way across the yard.

Will grinned.

"We Howes do love our garden hose!"

The silver Pine Tree shillings were being examined by experts. There was some question about who they belonged to, but things were shaping up for May's family to get an unexpected windfall. They were in agreement that it would be shared with Will and Maura as well as Leo Conti, who had discovered the coins in the first place.

They occasionally speculated on what might have happened to the other three treasure chests.

"And what happened to Isaac and Prudence's adopted daughter after the rescuers took her away?" Maura wondered. "The journal didn't say how old she was, but Isaac was described as an old man when they were found. In those days that could have meant he was in his forties or fifties, and the girl may have been at least in her teens. Old enough to know where the chests were buried. Maybe she took them with her or went back for them. Patrick probably assumed that too until I showed him the Pine Tree shilling. No wonder he agreed to come to the house that night."

The first clue to the mystery was found in the Islay historical society, an office Maura hadn't bothered with because Patrick had been her source of information. An old article about the island's history, pasted in a scrapbook, described the rescue of fifteen-year-old Repentance Belfour from a deserted island and her subsequent marriage to the ship's boatswain. The first mate had never referred to her by name in his confession, only as 'the girl'.

The mystery wasn't solved until sometime later when Maura attended a seminar at a North Shore women's college. She happened to notice the inscription on the front of a building: Repentance Chadwick Library. Her interest was caught by the coincidence of the name, and with thirty minutes to spare, she went inside. The reference librarian was happy to share the story of Repentance Belfour Chadwick. She had been an orphan who married a seaman at a young age. They struggled for several years until they came into money unexpectedly. The couple opened a mercantile store which flourished, then opened several more. Through diversification and hard work, they became one of the first families in the area. Mrs. Chadwick was a strong supporter of various foundations and this college until she died at the age of eighty-five. Maura felt much satisfaction in knowing that Repentance, who may have been the island's first native-born resident, had absconded with the treasure of Islay and made a good life for herself.

Rebecca and Leo made an offer to buy the Uncle Irvin house from Opal. It would be a business partnership, with the bulk of the investment coming from Rebecca and Leo managing the substantial renovations. The deal Opal accepted was that she and Wally would retain a suite of rooms for themselves, free of rent. Opal was now helping out at the coffee shop, sharing the cooking with Joe.

"We're going to call it The Island Witch," said Rebecca. "You're sure you don't mind having an inn next door? When the rest of the neighborhood saw the drawings showing how we'll fix it up they were relieved, but you'll have it right next to you."

"It's fine! Once the restaurant is going it will be great to be able to step next door for an evening out."

"I was in a second-hand shop and found an old painting of a man who reminds me of your Uncle Irvin. If you look closely there's a definite a leer. I'm going to find a frame and hang it in the lobby."

"Let's put a tasteful plaque on it that says Uncle Irvin. People will ask who he was, but it will forever be one of the mysteries of Islay."

"I'm going to take Opal up on her suggestion to have some copies of your book printed up. We'll sell it in the gift shop."

"You mean *The Witch of Islay,* which was soundly rejected by publishers and agents as being too far-fetched? That was generally accompanied by an encouraging note that with more experience I might produce something worth reading?"

"Yes, that one. It will be a great souvenir for guests since it almost has the same name as the inn. Because, of course, we stole the idea from you. What other book might I be referring to? The *Lizzie and the Giant* book is already coming out in May."

Maura smiled smugly.

"An agent is interested in the stories I wrote about the island and the people here before I got sidetracked by *The Witch of Islay.* I have to change the names, of course. She said they're charming and they make her want to hop on the ferry and come over. I'll have to write more of them to make a book."

"Oh, Mo! That's wonderful. And maybe it will get us some business!"

A well-dressed businessman and his associate were ushered to a table in their favorite restaurant. The businessman's suit was cut by an expensive tailor, and gold cufflinks flashed in the overhead light. As soon as the men were seated, a third man approached the table and pulled out a chair. The associate started to rise and put his hand inside his jacket.

"No need," said the intruder. "I'm here on business that will make you happy." He put his business card on the table. "Skip Mackay, MacKenzie Enterprises. May I?" He sat without waiting for an answer and placed the briefcase he was carrying under the table.

The businessman picked up the card and held it gingerly between two fingers as though wary of germs. He looked at his uninvited guest and wasn't impressed. His suit was crumpled and there was a ketchup stain on his sleeve. It didn't appear as though he had combed his hair that morning and his tie was crooked. He was about to have his companion escort him out of the restaurant, then noticed the very expensive gold watch he was wearing. He was interested. "What is your business with me, Mr. Mackay?"

"I represent Rebecca Savard, owner of MacKenzie Publishing and the other concerns under MacKenzie Enterprises. She understands that your firm was inconvenienced a few years ago by the disappearance of a certain briefcase that belonged to your brother."

The businessman looked confused for a moment.

"It contained ten thousand dollars. Edward Mason was thought to have had it in his possession when he was arrested." The businessman looked around a little nervously and saw there were no occupied tables within earshot.

"Ah, yes. The infamous briefcase. What about it?"

"The widow of Mr. Mason, Gina Mason, was thought by some to know the whereabouts of the briefcase. Her life was made extremely unpleasant and she had to leave the area. She would like to be able to return to normal life."

"That should be easy. Tell her to bring back the money."

"She never had it."

The businessman spread his hands and shrugged his shoulders.

"Now, Mrs. Mason has become a friend of Mrs. Savard," Skip continued. "My boss would like to help her. The briefcase under the table contains ten thousand dollars, plus another four thousand for any inconvenience your company has experienced. And you'll notice that's a pretty nice briefcase to boot. In exchange, no one ever bothers Mrs. Mason again."

"If the briefcase really contains fourteen thousand dollars, Mrs. Mason's issue is closed as far as I'm concerned. If somebody else still thinks she has the original, there's nothing I can do about it."

"Don't sell yourself short!" Skip smiled encouragingly. "I'm sure you have a lot of influence in the area. I hear you've really turned your company around since you took over from your brother. It's doing well and getting good press."

The businessman tipped his head to one side and smirked a little, his hooded eyes watching Skip.

"There's an envelope in the safe at MacKenzie that contains a copy of this. There's another copy at the top-notch detective agency we hired. I'm reaching in my pocket for an envelope." He placed it in front of the businessman, who hesitated before picking it up. When he finished reading the document inside, his face was red and his mouth set in an angry line.

"It's all lies!"

"We don't think so, but don't worry. Unless something unpleasant happens to Mrs. Mason, or even Mrs. Savard or myself, the envelopes will stay where they are, undisturbed, for fifteen years. At that time, they'll be returned to you by special courier with a little extra bonus. All you need to do is let it be known that the money was returned and offer a penalty to anyone who annoys Mrs. Mason."

Skip left the restaurant, whistling. He walked five blocks before choosing a phone booth.

The phone only rang once before it was picked up.

"All set!" he said.

A November fog skimmed along the ground and created halos around the electric lanterns on either side of the heavy door.

A nondescript young woman, recently deposited by a taxi at the entrance to the long, pitted driveway, was glad for once to be wearing sensible shoes. The woods on either side of the drive were dark and deep, and bare branches dripped on the carpet of fallen leaves. It was a dreary aspect, but the young woman's pulse quickened. The job advertisement had claimed this was one of the oldest inns in the country in continuous operation. It backed up to an estuary, and it was the familiar scent of the sea that set her blood racing. The ad offered room and board, with a modest salary, to help with assorted duties at the inn. She was well-aware that 'modest salary' meant peanuts, but anything would be an improvement over the one-room apartment over the smoke shop in Pittsburgh. For more than a year she had yearned for the ocean, for color, for friends and for happier days.

The woman adjusted the beige scarf that covered her hair. Everything about her was colorless, from her face to her clothes to her old-fashioned handbag. She rehearsed her opening line as she heard footsteps coming in response to her knock.

Hello, I'm Nancy Adams. I called about the job. I believe you're expecting me.

The door was opened on a chain and a face peered out into the night.

"Hello. I'm Gracie Adams. Oh, nuts!"

What's Next?

If you enjoyed *The Treasure of Islay* and you haven't yet read *The Three Minute Bride,* you can find it on Amazon in eBook, print and Kindle Unlimited. It takes place in 1949 and tells Rebecca's story – see the description below. It's a stand-alone novel in the New England Seashore series.

The *Note in the Chimney* is a novella that takes place in Rushing River in 1945, before *The Three Minute Bride* and *The Treasure of Islay*. This book is free but only available to my newsletter subscribers. If you would like a copy, you can get it here: https://BookHip.com/MMNHZPC Existing subscribers can get it here: https://BookHip.com/TGSWGWD .

The Three Minute Bride
(available on Amazon)

When Rebecca MacKenzie's new husband falls to his death on their wedding day, she inherits a run-down, century-old house on a cliff overlooking the sea – in addition to his large publishing fortune. At loose ends, Rebecca heads to Maine to finish the renovation project Henry had started. She soon falls in love with the odd little seaside town and is befriended by a group of artists, an eighty-two-year-old ex-showgirl and a homeless dog.

When murder strikes close to home and an attempt is made on the life of the veterinarian living in the old lighthouse up the road, Rebecca can't shake the feeling that she is somehow at the center of it all. Will murder, nighttime intruders and a dark-eyed challenger to her memories of Henry let her find the peace and healing she had come to Maine for? Set in the post-war days of 1949, this novel is full of lovable, quirky characters, mystery, romance, humor and surprises.

The Note in the Chimney – a novella
Mysterious notes, a war orphan and an unspoken romance...

1945

Marriage to a naval officer seemed to offer Rose Evans everything she wanted: adventure, romance and the chance to have a family of her own. When Julian ships out for the Pacific in the last years of WWII, Rose moves to the old family farmhouse in the little coastal town of Rushing River, Maine to wait out the war.

A telegram arrives from the war office and informs Rose that she is now a widow, dashing every dream she had. She cocoons herself in her farmhouse, unwilling to let life hurt her any further. Her solitude is broken when Amelie, a war orphan in the class she teaches, is abandoned by the family she was living with. Rose finds herself the temporary guardian of an eleven-year-old girl who is forcing her out of her seclusion.

Notes apparently left by Julian before he shipped out begin appearing in unexpected places around the old farmhouse. At first, she is charmed by the sentiments in these short messages. They soon take on a sinister aspect and have Rose reassessing her marriage with Julian and whether she ever really knew him.

As the notes turn up one by one, town residents report seeing the ghost of a murderer who escaped from an asylum for the criminally insane over a hundred years ago. According to legend, he appears out of the swirling fog that frequently blankets the town. As the notes continue to pop up in the old farmhouse and more people encounter the prisoner, Rose begins to wonder...

is Julian really dead? Or has he returned to play his own secret game?

Visit me on Facebook or www.sarawadeauthor.com

facebook.com/sarawadeauthor

Acknowledgments

Thanks to Rachel MacNeill, founder of the Islay Whisky Academy, for the information and photos she shared. The academy is located on the real Islay, an island located on the west Scotland 'whisky coast'. She answered my questions regarding the storage of whiskey, how it might have been transported to America in the early 1700s and how whiskey casks would have fared in a shipwreck. If you are a whiskey (or Scotland) fan you may want to check out the academy's "Courting the Dram" course. (In this book I use the 'whiskey' spelling when I write as an American but use the Scottish 'whisky' spelling where appropriate.)

Thank you to Ron Miller for answering my questions regarding boats in the 1950s, which was very helpful for me in constructing the *Lorelei*. Chris Knowlton provided information on tools available for hunting for shipwrecks in the 1950s.

A huge thank you to my editor, Jessica Barber of BH Writing Services. I learned a lot from her direct and insightful feedback. Thanks also to my beta readers, Natalie Wright, Carol Plourde and Allison Potter, who each gave her own helpful perspective on my manuscript.

Made in United States
Troutdale, OR
01/04/2024

16660796R10192